Erotica Omnibus Five

D0434043

Also Available from X Libris

Eritica Omnibus One
Erotica Omnibus Two
Erotica Omnibus Three
Erotica Omnibus Four

Erotica Omnibus Five

Rough Trade
Emma Allan

Inspiration
Stephanie Ash

Velvet Touch
Zara Devereux

LIBRIS

An *X Libris* Book

This omnibus edition first published by X Libris in 2003

Copyright © Emma Allan, Stephanie Ash,
Zara Devereux, 2003

Rough Trade copyright © Emma Allan 1997
Inspiration copyright © Stephanie Ash 1995
Velvet Touch copyright © Zara Devereux 1996

The moral right of the authors has been asserted.

A CIP catalogue record for this book
is available from the British Library.

ISBN 0 7515 2703 3

Typeset by
Derek Doyle & Associates, Liverpool
Printed and bound in Great Britain by
Clays Ltd, St Ives plc

X Libris
A Division of
Little, Brown and Company (UK)
Brettenham House
Lancaster Place
London WC2E 7EN

Rough Trade

Emma Allan

Prologue

IT WAS HER birthday. It was June. It was hot. Very hot. Hot and humid. The sun was high and there wasn't a single cloud in the sky.

A party had been planned for that night. All her friends would be there. But her *best* friend, Andrea Hamilton, had asked her to go for a bike ride in the afternoon, down to the small lake they had found, their secret place. The water was fed from some underground aquifer and was always cold. It would be delicious to swim on such a day.

The ride made them hot and sweaty. Abandoning their bikes under a huge horse-chestnut tree, its shade extending out over the water's edge, they pulled off their T–shirts and shorts, kicked off their socks and trainers and dived, naked, into the water.

They swam for hours, or so it seemed, then lay on the grass under the broad-leafed tree, shaded from the sun. And that's when it happened. She could never remember how exactly, whose hand had stroked the other's body, or whose lips had brushed the other's mouth, as though it were the most natural thing in the world to do. Nor who

1

had been the first to cup one of their burgeoning breasts, tease a nipple to stiffness and pinch it with a playfulness that soon turned to deadly earnest. She did remember, as vividly as she remembered anything else that had happened in her life, that it was Andrea who had snaked her hand down over her belly and whose finger had probed into her labia, experimentally at first, then stroked between them.

From that moment on, however, the hesitant fumblings became more assured. As pleasure turned to passion, as the nascent feelings developed into strong sensations, she was shocked at the power her arousal could generate.

Andrea led the way. She was tall and slender and knowing. Her long blonde hair swept her friend's body as she came up on to her knees and began kissing her breasts, her hands running down her legs, caressing the incredibly soft, silky flesh of her inner thighs. She pulled them gently apart to expose the scarlet furrow of her sex. She dipped her head and kissed it as though it were another mouth, her lips squirming against it, her tongue darting out to lap at the sweet, copious nectar with which it was already flooded.

But despite the onslaught of pleasure this produced, where Andrea led she wanted to follow. She twisted around and wriggled her head between Andrea's thighs, so her sex, covered in a bush of hair so light and fluffy it looked like down, was poised above her.

Then they were joined. A wave of feeling engulfed them both as Andrea lowered her sex on to her friend's mouth, an invisible connection made between them, a circuit completed. What Andrea did to her, she mimicked; unimagined things, but exciting, almost too exciting. They licked and sucked and stroked each other's sexes with their tongues, using the same tempo. But as the feeling mounted in their bodies, the rhythmic tremors of instincts yet to be fully shaped soon demanded more. Only Andrea knew what to do, only she knew to move her tongue to the little almond sized promontory at the top of her friend's labia. Soon they were locked together, moaning, squirming, dancing with passion, every lingering sensation, every new nuance of feeling increasing their need, building to a crescendo.

She was not naive. She had experienced fumbled sexual longing before with boys; fevered embraces and guilty touches. But nothing like this, nothing as serious, as meaningful, as affecting. This took over her whole body with a pounding rhythm that got faster and more furious, bringing her to the edge of an abyss then plunging her over it. She clung to Andrea for support, the feeling of the blonde's own climax fuelling her own.

When it was finally over, when they had rolled off each other and lay on the long grass gazing up at the shafts of sunlight trying to filter through the filigreed canopy of leaves, she had no regrets. Andrea was still her best friend. But though she could still taste the sweet juices of the blonde's sex and her own body still ached with the aftermath of passion, she knew she would never do what they had just done again.

Chapter One

EVERY DAY FOR a week. The same routine. First thing in the morning after she'd dressed and made-up. She felt ashamed of herself. She felt like a guilty schoolgirl, hiding behind the lace curtains of her bedroom window so she could see but not be seen. She couldn't help herself. It was hot and after only a few minutes of digging he would strip off his shirt. His legs were already exposed, by jeans cut off at the top of his thighs.

Clare Markham had never seen a body like it, which is why it fascinated her. His chest was broad, his abdomen flat and delineated by hard, stringy muscles, his biceps bulging as he worked. He was tall with long legs which were contoured by thick, well-defined muscles, his whole body like some relief map of musculature. His buttocks were small and tight and hard, like two cantaloupes wrapped in denim.

But it wasn't only his physique that proved so magnetic. He was handsome too. He had short, blond, curly hair and very blue eyes, under a rugged brow. He had a small, straight nose, sharp, high cheekbones and a square jaw. She noticed he had small, very delicate ears.

He had arrived with the other builders on the first day that work had begun.

Clare had decided to have her house extended. She wanted a new kitchen to replace the small, poky room she used at the moment, and a new bathroom that would be en suite with her bedroom. The one could be conveniently constructed above the other. Two months ago she had been promoted to Managing Director of KissCo UK and the alterations were a sort of present to herself. The firm of builders she was using had been recommended by a friend who had been more than satisfied with similar work they had carried out for her.

Reluctantly Clare tore herself away from the bedroom window. The foundations were nearly in place and once they started knocking into the back wall to which the extension was being attached, she would not have such a good vantage point. For one thing she'd have to move into the front bedroom. Her daily routine would have to change.

Checking her appearance one last time in the mirror, she adjusted her short black hair with a single sweep of her fingers and marched downstairs.

'Morning, Mrs Markham,' George Wickes said politely, although he continued to insist that Clare was married, no matter how many times she told him she was not. 'Just making sure everything's going well. Sorry about the mess. Inevitable I'm afraid.' George Wickes was the head of the firm of builders and had arrived every morning to inspect the work. He was a large, avuncular man with heavy jowls and a ruddy complexion, the veins on his face very close to the surface. He had eyes like a basset-hound and, like Stan Laurel, seemed to take an extraordinarily long time to blink, as if the effort of raising his eyelids was too much for him. Even in the hot weather he wore a tweed sports coat with leather patches on the elbows.

'Going to be worse when they knock through,' Clare said.

'Yes, but we'll do that at the last possible minute. Less disruption that way.'

The whole of the ground floor, including the sitting room and dining room, had been stripped of furniture and sheeted with plastic. The carpets had been taken up and scaffolding boards laid on the floor as a path for the wheelbarrow loads of rubble dug out of the back garden, and the hard core that had to replace it.

'Morning, Mrs Markham.' The blond was coming towards them from the back, wheeling a barrow piled high with soil.

'Morning, Gary,' Clare said, her eyes inevitably dropping to the contours of his chest. Perspiration had run down his collar bone, carving a trail in the dirt and dust that caked his skin. The trail ended at the waistband of the sawn off jeans, the denim darker there where it had soaked up the sweat. Clare tore her eyes away, not wanting to be caught staring at his crotch. His muscles rippled as he manoeuvred the heavy load past her.

Leaving George Wickes to get on with his inspection she took her car keys out of her bag and followed Gary outside. He wheeled the barrow up a plank to the top of a large skip parked outside her house, and dumped the contents.

'Nice car,' he said as he headed back down and

saw Clare unlocking her 5 series BMW. He wiped the sweat off his brow with his forearm. He was looking at her, not the silver-coloured car. Clare was not tall, no more than five foot two in her bare feet, and Gary seemed to tower over her.

'Goes with the job,' she said, wishing she had the courage to say what was really on her mind and knowing she never would.

'Nice job, then,' he said. He had a strong South London accent.

Their eyes met. He smiled at her. It was a wistful smile. She wondered if he had ever entertained thoughts about her as graphic as the ones she'd had about him in the last few days.

'Are you working late tonight?' Gary was always the first to arrive and the last to leave.

'Yeah.'

'See you later, then,' she said cheerily, getting into the car. She started the engine but could not resist staring at those taut buttocks, each one a neat handful, as he wheeled the barrow back into her house.

For some reason traffic was light and it took Clare no more than fifteen minutes to drive from her house in Kensington to Grosvenor Square. She parked her car in the underground car park of KissCo's offices, one of only three employees allowed to do so, and took the lift up to her office. It overlooked a corner of the square and the hot weather had already brought people out on to the grass, men stripping off their shirts, women furtively hitching up their skirts to expose the maximum amount of leg to the sun's rays. None of the half a dozen men she could see stretched out on the grass had a physique to rival Gary's.

The phone on her desk rang before she'd had a

chance to sit down.

'Call from Houston,' Janice, Clare's secretary, said with the appropriate foreboding in her voice. Houston was the company headquarters and calls or correspondence from there often resulted in a great deal of extra work for Clare and her team.

'It's a bit early.' Clare sat down at her high-backed, leather swivel chair and looked at her watch. It was five to ten, which meant it was five to four in the morning in Houston.

'The early bird,' Janice joked.

'Put it through.'

The line clicked. 'Ms Markham. I have Bridget Goldsmith on the line for you.'

The line clicked again. 'Clare, good morning.'

'Ms Goldsmith, you're up early.'

Bridget Goldsmith was the President and Chief Operating Executive of KissCo worldwide. Clare was not at all surprised to get a call from her at such an early hour. The rumour in the company was that Bridget never slept.

'I've decided to come to London, Clare,' she said, getting right to the point.

'Oh?'

'The European launch is set for when?'

'First of September.'

'That's just over three months. I think I should come and have a look see before then. I'm going to schedule a trip to Paris too.'

'To see Claude,' Clare said coolly.

'Should be swinging by in, say, two weeks. I'll fax you the actual schedule when it's confirmed. Meantime can you work up a presentation for me. The ad agency, the marketing people. I want to review everything.'

'We're already in the process of combining a

presentation.'

'Good.'

'Is there a problem?' The European launch was to be KissCo's biggest marketing operation outside America. A whole new range of cosmetics was to be targeted at every major European country at the same time, with an integrated advertising campaign.

'No, no problem. I just want to have a look. My thinking on this is that it might be better to co-ordinate the launch from Paris.'

'I see.' Clare saw exactly. Claude Duhamel, the managing director of the French subsidiary, had recently returned from a visit to Houston. He had obviously not missed the chance to cast doubt on Clare's competence to handle such a large and expensive operation.

Clare's promotion had been sudden and unexpected. Usually all senior staff up for such important positions were shipped to Houston for extensive evaluations. But KissCo's UK managing director had been poached by a rival company and there had been no time. Clare, as the second most senior person, had been the only possible replacement. Claude had no doubt made capital out of the fact that she had not been properly vetted.

'Don't worry about hotels. We'll do it all from here.'

'Anything else you want?'

'I'll call you if I think of anything. Bye for now.' Having dropped the bombshell Bridget sounded cheery.

Clare put down the phone and began making notes. Janice peered in through the door. She was a plump, short woman who wore knitted twinsets whatever the weather. In combination with her tightly permed, rather thin, brown hair, they made her look at least ten years older than she actually was.

'Can I help?' she asked.

'Yes. Come in.'

They spent the next hour setting up meetings with all the departmental heads to advise them of Bridget's visit and instruct them what would be needed for it. The presentation they were working on would have to be a great deal more detailed if it was going to be made to Bridget in person rather than sent out to Houston by courier.

It was about an hour later when the phone on Clare's desk rang again. This time it was her private line.

'Clare Markham,' she said answering it herself.

'Clare, it's David. How are you?'

'Could be better,' she said, rather abruptly.

'We're still on for tonight, aren't we?' She heard the worry in his voice that something might have come up which she would use as an excuse not to see him.

'Yes, of course.' Actually seeing David Allston tonight was the last thing she really wanted to do, but she didn't have the heart to disappoint him. David's attitude to their relationship was like that of a small child with a new toy. She couldn't bare to snatch it away from him, however much she would have preferred to have an early night and curl up with a good book.

'Great. Do you want to have dinner?'

'I can't cook. My kitchen's been ripped out, remember?'

'Shall I book a table at The Ivy?'

11

'No, no. Nothing like that. I'm not in the mood to get dressed up. The local Italian will do.' Bearing in mind what David would inevitably demand from her after they'd eaten, going to the Italian restaurant she frequented just off Kensington High Street seemed to involve the least effort after what was undoubtedly going to be an exhausting day.

'OK. Eight, then? Is that all right?' She could hear the excitement in his voice. The child had been given his toy again: now, she knew, he would spend the rest of the day planning what games to play with it.

It had been a long day. Every time Clare had arrived home since the building work had begun Gary had still been busying himself in the back, usually on his own, his two other workmates long gone. But tonight Clare was late and he too had gone. The house felt empty. She missed the banter they usually shared.

It was already seven thirty. She went upstairs to the bathroom at the front of the house, stripping off her black suit as she went. In the new bathroom she would have a separate shower cubicle with a powerful shower, but at the moment she had to make do with the shower attached to the mixer taps of the bath and a glass screen at the side of it to prevent the water splashing over the floor. She adjusted the temperature to lukewarm, pulled off the rest of her clothes and stood in the rather sluggish stream, allowing the water to wash over her.

As she closed her eyes and turned her face into the water she thought of Gary, his hard body covered with sweat. She wondered what it would feel like against her. She had had a variety of men in her life and some had been moderately fit, but she'd never had anyone like him, someone whose muscles looked as though they had been shaped in stone by a sculptor. She imagined wrapping her arms around him, hugging him, feeling his strength. The thought made her shudder.

She washed herself quickly, dried herself on a large white towel and cleaned her teeth. In her bedroom she chose a cream and pink patterned cotton dress with a V-neck and cool short sleeves. Though it had a full skirt it was split to well above the knee and showed a lot of her slender, shapely legs. Just as she finished her make-up the doorbell rang.

'You're very punctual,' she told David as she opened the front door. David was always very punctual. Punctiliously punctual. She couldn't help wishing he wasn't.

'Sorry,' he said, kissing her on both cheeks and looking shamefaced.

'I've just got to get my bag,' she said.

'Place looks like a bomb's hit it.'

'Worse to come yet.'

She grabbed her handbag, took out her keys, set the alarm and double-locked the front door. David's burgundy-coloured Bentley was parked behind the builder's skip. He opened the passenger door for her then got behind the wheel.

'Sure you don't want to change your mind about the venue?'

'No,' she said emphatically.

They dined without fuss, ordering only one course and a single bottle of red wine. Clare had the impression that her lack of appetite suited David perfectly. He was impatient for the meal to end.

13

She had met David Allston at one of KissCo's parties held to launch some new product or other, but she had never discovered why he'd been invited. She guessed, since he was the sort of person constantly pictured in the gossip columns of *Queen*, *Tatler*, and even *Vogue*, KissCo's public relations department had thought his presence might attract a photo opportunity in some such magazine, although on this occasion, at least, they had been disappointed.

David Allston was, in fact, Viscount Bonmouth, the eighth Viscount in a succession dating back to 1781. He looked the part. He was slim – even thin – with a beautifully tailored suit from the firm in Saville Row that had catered to his family for one hundred and fifty years, serving his father and his father's father. His white cotton shirt was from a shirtmaker's in Jermyn Street, who'd also served three generations of Allstons, and his hand-lasted shoes were from Loebbs. He had neatly cut brown hair and a fine, delicately boned face, with a narrow straight nose, and hollow, almost feminine cheekbones. His eyes were light green and oddly nondescript, shallow set and small though he did have the longest eyelashes Clare had ever seen.

His manner suggested his pedigree too. There was a poise about him and an innate elegance that meant no matter how he was sitting or standing he seemed to be perfectly in equilibrium. A little too perfectly sometimes, as his grace could be seen to border on the effeminate. His attitude was not haughty, however. He was not the sort of aristocrat who had seen everything and done everything and was bored with life. He was more like a clever and enquiring child, ready to take on new experiences. And, like a child, he could be very determined to get his own way.

'So when does the big boss arrive?' David asked, as Clare told him of Bridget Goldsmith's decision.

'Two weeks.'

'I'm sure it'll all be fine,' he said. He had never shown much interest in her work or work in general. As far as Clare knew he didn't do much more than see that the family 'pile' in Hertfordshire was kept in good order. He certainly hadn't ever worked for a living and she imagined that it was hard for him to understand the exigencies of the daily grind.

'Do you want coffee?' he asked in a manner that suggested he hoped she would say no. He would have loved merely to have told her to get ready to leave but years of breeding had dictated that in social situations his own needs and desires should never be allowed to take precedence over those of anyone else, particularly those of a woman. From an early age, David had been indoctrinated that, according to the scheme of things, women existed to be cherished and adored, though, of course, they were not necessarily to be taken very seriously.

'Not really,' she said.

'Me neither,' he said, as if they were sharing a secret.

He summoned the waiter and paid the bill with alacrity, hustling her out of the restaurant and into the car as quickly as he dared. The drive to his house was accomplished largely in silence, Clare finding she was in no mood for small talk.

The Allston family's London residence was in a Nash terrace in Regent's Park; it was a corner house with large rectangular windows, curved side walls and a grandiose, stucco-fronted façade with a portico. In square-sided wooden planters, pollarded, ball-shaped bay trees stood on each side of the black, panelled front door.

'Would you like a drink?' David asked, as they walked through the large vestibule, where a huge crystal chandelier hung from a domed ceiling above a black-and-white chequered marble floor.

'Yes. A brandy would be nice.' She needed a brandy to fortify herself, the moment of truth approaching rapidly.

He led the way into the sitting room, where large oatmeal–coloured sofas were arranged around a large fireplace, its grate currently occupied by an arrangement of dried flowers. Normally, she knew, drinks would be provided by the butler, who divided his time between the London and country houses, but on this occasion David went to a large, walnut cocktail cabinet and poured the brandy himself, not wanting to summon the butler from the Stygian depths of the house.

He handed her the drink. She was standing by the window, looking out at Regent's Park.

'Cheers,' he said.

'Nothing for you?'

'No. Not in the mood.'

An air of expectancy hung between them like autumn fog. He was watching her every movement, like a dog waiting for its master to get up and take it for a walk. She knew exactly what he wanted her to do to initiate the complicated ritual that had developed between them. Some nights she would tease him, delay the inevitable, make him wait. But tonight she was too tired for that. She swigged down half the brandy, which she discovered she didn't really want, and put the glass down on a French, Hepplewhite-design, mahogany card table.

'Would you excuse me for a few minutes, darling,' she said, trying to keep the weariness out of her voice.

The look of relief on his face was obvious. 'Of course.'

'I won't be long.'

As she turned to walk towards the door he caught her hand and pressed it to his cheek. 'You're very special,' he said, kissing her fingers.

As she walked up the grand, sweeping staircase and along the corridor to his bedroom, she wondered if it were true. Was she special? How many other women had agreed to participate in David's demands for stylised, ritualistic sex? Perhaps countesses, baronesses and duchesses were used to such things. Or perhaps not. It was entirely possible that she was the first woman who had indulged David's fantasies in this way.

She pushed open the bedroom door, knowing exactly what she would find. There, on the large double bed, the counterpane and bedding already removed, were two beautifully wrapped boxes, one large and rectangular, the other small and square, one on top of the other. Both were wrapped in bright gold foil with gold ribbon.

Clare closed the bedroom door firmly. It had to be closed. She walked over to the bed. Tossing the smaller box aside she sat on the white linen undersheet and ripped the ribbons off the large box. She delved into the layers of white tissue paper. Her hands lighted on something soft and

17

silky. She held it up, the tissue paper falling away. It was a pink body, beautifully and expensively made in the finest silk, with lace insets over the bosom and at the hips. There was a matching pink suspender belt in the box too, and a pair of very sheer, white stockings. There was also a white lace garter. And the letter of course, right at the bottom of the box.

She got to her feet and stripped off her dress, panties and bra, then clipped the suspender belt around her waist. She slipped into the body. The silk was so soft and sensual she felt a flush of sexual pleasure. Her nipples puckered instantly. She glanced into the mirror on the opposite wall. It was a perfect fit. David had a list of all her measurements. The pink suited her dark colouring and the tightness of the garment showed off her figure. She had a good figure, her breasts firm and round and high, her waist narrow, her hips generous but not flabby. The lace over her breasts was transparent and she could see her quite large, rose-red nipples under it. The legs of the body were cut high and its crotch was thin, not quite covering the whole curved plane between her legs but leaving the flesh on either side of her labia clearly visible. Her pubic hair was black and, though not particularly thick, formed a definite dark shadow under the pink silk.

Sitting on the bed she took the stockings out of their cellophane packet and rolled them, one by one, up her slender legs. The suspenders were too long and each had to be adjusted until they held the stockings taut. She spread the elasticated garter between her fingers and inserted her left foot into it, drawing it up her legs until it banded her thigh just below the white welt of the stocking.

At least, she thought, this was underwear she would be able to wear outside the bedroom. So often the boxes David had left on the foot of the bed had contained more outrageous items – cupless bras and crotchless panties, tiny, incredibly tight, red-satin waspies with long ruched suspenders, or patent leather high-heels that had forced her foot up almost vertically. They were all the stuff of his highly developed fantasies, leaving her body decked out like that of some cheap whore.

Smoothing the sheer, white stockings up over her legs, satisfying herself that they were wrinkle free, Clare picked the letter out of the box. As usual it was a single sheet of heavy cream vellum, with deckle-edges, folded in half. She spread the paper out. It was covered in neat, italic script. There were no mistakes, no deletions, no insertions. She knew that David had worked on it for a couple of days, before copying it out like some ancient illuminator of biblical texts. It was a script – her script – the distilled essence of his latest sexual imaginings. He would never have dared to ask her, face to face, to do the things the letter contained; she was sure of that. This was the way he had evolved of giving his fantasies full reign.

She read the page twice. Half of her – or was it more than half? – wished he would simply charge into the bedroom, throw her on the bed and take her without ceremony. The other half enjoyed the ritual dressing and preparation, and the peculiar sense of anticipation it gave her. She was not quite sure what inspired her excitement. Perhaps it was merely the fact that all this was so outré? Or was it the power, the element of control, the fact that David had cast her in the dominant role, master of his sexual pleasure? She had never played these sorts of games before and would certainly never have imagined that they would excite her. But, to her surprise, if she were honest with herself, she found they did. Which is why, she supposed, she had not only gone on seeing David Allston but had allowed the games to become increasingly more elaborate.

She heard David's footsteps climbing the stairs. The ten minutes were up. She knew he would have been counting the seconds. Quickly she swept the wrapping paper on to the floor and dimmed the lights to a pleasant glow. She placed the smaller, still unwrapped, box on the bedside table, then sat down on the edge of the bed again. As always she was quite surprised to find her pulse was racing.

He knocked on the door three times.

'Come,' she said.

The door opened. He was naked. His clothes would be neatly stacked on one of the sofas downstairs, his shoes lined up side by side, his shirt folded as though for a suitcase, even his socks rolled into coiled balls.

'Sh . . .' she murmured. 'Don't make a sound.' He closed the door behind him with infinite care, then turned towards her, his penis already beginning to stiffen. 'We have to be very quiet. No one must catch you in here with me. You know that, don't you?' It was the first line of the script. It invariably started in the same way.

'Yes,' he whispered. He stood with his back to the door, his eyes roaming her body.

'No one must ever find out about this. No one.' The second line was the same too.

'I know.'

'Come over here, then.'

He took a step forward then stopped, anticipating, like a bad actor, what the next line of the script would be.

'Stop. You know better than that, don't you?'

He looked shamefaced. His cock hardened further, growing to its full stature. 'Yes,' he said. He dropped to his knees on the long–pile cream carpet.

'That's better.'

Slowly he shuffled forward on his knees until he was right in front of her.

She raised her left foot and wriggled her nylon covered big toe against his left nipple. It made his cock quiver.

'You know what to do?' she said. Again this part of the script was always the same.

'Yes,' he whispered. Even if she hadn't been able to see the excited state of his cock, his expression would have betrayed how he felt. Sexual arousal blazed in his eyes, its tension etched in every line of his face. He took hold of her left foot with both hands and brought it up to his lips, kissing it lightly, little nibbling kisses all over the white nylon-covered flesh. He sucked gently on her toes, crowding them all into his mouth at the same time. A tear of fluid forced its way out of his glans.

'Now the other one,' she demanded, snatching her foot away and making him pick the other off the floor. He followed the same procedure.

Clare could not suppress a shudder of delight. She felt her excitement mounting. It was a physical thing, a direct connection between the nerves in her toes and those in her sex. There was a certain thrill attached to having a man kneeling at her feet, prepared to do her bidding. But, of course, it wasn't really *her* bidding; it only appeared to be. What she was going to ask him to do was all the product of *his* imagination.

'All right, that's enough,' she said.

'It was lovely,' he whispered.

'You know what I want you to do now?' She stood up. Taking the back of his head in his hand, she pushed his face into her flat, pink silk-sheathed belly. She felt his hot breath against her flesh. Her sex throbbed. 'Do you know?'

'Yes,' he moaned, the word gagged by her body.

She released him. Very slowly he raised his hands to the white garter on her thigh and drew it down her leg. When he reached her ankle she raised her foot so he could pull it free. He immediately held the garter to his mouth, kissing the lace and inhaling the scent of her body. This was always the same too, an established part of the ritual.

'Get on with it,' she ordered.

David looped the garter around his wrist then crawled over to a large, bow-fronted chest of drawers with brass handles. He opened the bottom drawer and pulled out a pair of white satin French knickers with lace-trimmed legs. There were other things in the bottom drawer too, other props for his little dramas, but none would be used tonight.

'Don't make me,' he said pathetically, though it was clear it was what he wanted more desperately than anything else.

22

'You know it's what I want.' Another line from the script.

He got to his feet, stepped into the satin knickers and pulled them up over his legs. He had very slim, snake-like hips but even so the knickers were too tight. They stretched tautly over his navel, his phallus trapped inside them, every inch of it outlined under the satin. The tear of fluid it had produced immediately soaked into the material, darkening the white.

'Don't you look pretty?' Oddly enough it was true. There was something feminine about David's body. His skin was soft and very white and, although he had no muscle tone, he was not fat either. His only obvious display of masculinity pressed against the white satin.

'Please.'

'Come back here, now.'

He got back on to his knees. As he crawled back towards her she picked the small gold box from the bedside table and tore off the wrapping paper. Inside, as she'd guessed, was a black silk sleeping mask.

'If I screamed the whole house would come running.' That wasn't exactly what he'd written but it was close enough.

'Yes,' he said breathily, as he knelt with his hands on his knees in front of her once more.

'They'd see you like this.'

'Please don't scream.' He said it with conviction, completely engrossed in the imaginary situation.

'I won't. But only if you do exactly what I tell you to do.' Sometimes Clare wondered if the scenarios they acted out were based on fact. There had been many variations but the basic tenets were always the same: a man at the mercy of a woman. Had he smuggled himself into one of the maid's rooms at the country estate, in his adolescence perhaps, and been punished for his trouble in exactly this way? Would that explain his obsession, his burgeoning sexuality becoming fixated on a particularly strong experience?

The patch of wet on the front of the French knickers was getting larger and making the material transparent. She could actually see his glans and the eye of his penis from which the sticky fluid leaked.

'Well?' she said with all the imperiousness she could muster.

'Please, I'll do anything you say.'

'Put this on.' She threw the sleeping mask on to the floor in front of him. 'You don't think I'm going to let you see me naked, do you?'

'No.' He picked the mask up and slipped it over his eyes, adjusting the elasticated straps so that it fitted snugly.

Clare paused. She was very excited now. She found she had become wrapped up in his fantasy too. The sex she had had before meeting David had always been spontaneous, never knowing what would happen next. This was the other side of the coin, sex planned down to the last detail. She knew exactly what David was going to do to her next and she found that knowledge arousing.

She saw David's head moving very slightly, trying to pick up a sound as a clue to what she was doing. She found she was in the mood to tease him now, and kept perfectly still. Then, as quietly as she could, she extended her foot and pressed her toes against his cock. He started. That wasn't in the script.

'Is that nice?' She rubbed her foot up and down.

He didn't reply. He didn't say anything that he hadn't rehearsed.

'All right.' She reverted to her role. 'If you do as I say, no one will know you've been here. Is that understood?'

'Yes.'

'Good.' You know what you have to do now.' She stood up and held the back of his head again but this time maintained a distance from his face. His hands groped up between her legs, over the stocking tops to the top of her thighs. Pressing into the soft, hot flesh of her labia he struggled to locate the three poppers that held the gusset of the pink silk body in place.

His fingers fumbled around ineffectively, enjoying the liberty they had been allowed.

'Concentrate,' she scolded.

He pulled two of the poppers free but couldn't find the third. She stepped back, tutting loudly. 'Not very good.'

The third popper made a loud metallic click as she freed it. The two halves of the gusset parted, hanging down front and back. 'I hope you can do better than that.' The longer the game went on the easier she found it to play her role. What was more, the easier it came to her the more wrapped up in it she became. It *was* exciting. She could feel the impression his fingers had made on her sex.

Clare sat on the bed. She put her foot up on to his chest for the second time. 'Kiss it,' she said almost in a whisper. she wondered if, years ago, David *had* tried to take advantage of one of the maids and she, seeing an opportunity to blackmail the young master, threatening to go to his father, had used him as shamelessly as this. If she were an actress she'd certainly use that scenario to provide her motivation.

David brought her foot up to his mouth and kissed it again. This time he kissed the inside of her ankle and immediately began to work his mouth up her calf. When he got to her knee she ordered him to stop. Resting her heel on his shoulder she raised her other foot, this time pushing her toes against his lips. 'Now the other one,' she said.

He repeated the process, kissing and nibbling his way up along the white nylon. She rested this heel against his other shoulder, spreading her knees apart and allowing his mouth to venture up to her thigh. She flicked the gusset of the body up. Had he not been blindfold he would have had a perfect view of her sex.

His tongue licked at her stocking top. As he leant forward she rocked back until she was laying on the bed. She hooked her legs around his neck and crossed her ankles, splaying her thighs further apart, her sex open for him.

She could feel her body pulsing rhythmically, playing its own sensual music. Her hips were undulating almost unconsciously, as David's mouth worked its way over the nylon welt and on to the creamy soft flesh above it. She was naturally olive skinned and the contrast between the very white welt of the stocking and her skin was marked. After the coarseness of the nylon against his tongue and lips it would also seem impossibly soft.

He licked his way right up to her labia, moaning with pleasure as his mouth made its first contact with her sex.

'You naughty boy.' There wasn't much left of the script now. 'You are very naughty, aren't you?'

'Oh yes.' He formed the word without taking his mouth away from her. She could feel his lips moving.

'I shouldn't allow you to do this, should I?'

She found herself imagining she was in some dingy below-stairs room in the Allstons' country estate, forcing the young master to give her pleasure. The maid would have been a first-class bitch requiring his attentions night after night, constantly reminding him that refusal would mean reporting him to his tyrannical father.

Clare could feel her sex was wet. With her labia spread open by the position of her legs, her clitoris was exposed and she could feel it throbbing.

'No, no, you shouldn't,' he said.

'But I'm going to.'

As she said this his tongue pressed against her clitoris. He was good at this. Very good. No man had ever been better in her experience. His mouth seemed able to mould itself to her sex. He had a way of stretching her labia with his lips, pulling her clitoris taut while, at the same time, his tongue worked on it with the most perfect of touches, alternating between stroking it up and down, pushing it back against the pubic bone, or tapping it at its most sensitive spot.

It all made her writhe with pleasure. She dug her heels into his back, levering her sex still harder against his mouth, and snapping her head over to one side as this produced a new jolt of intense feeling. His chin was jutting against the opening of her vagina. The wetness of her sex was seeping all over it.

She knew what he would do next. For her, at

27

least, the fantasy was slipping away, as waves of physical pleasure unleashed their hold on her. The way his tongue seemed to be able to create piercing shards of intense pleasure astonished her. Now she didn't need anything else; mind games were simply surplus to requirements. The only thing she needed was what he was already supplying, altering the position of his mouth slightly, angling it up to make the opening of her vagina accessible so he could slip one, then two, then three fingers into it. He did not penetrate her with them. He held them there, waiting for the right moment, the blindfold concentrating all his attention on his sense of touch. He would feel when she was ready, when the provocation of his tongue on her clitoris took her right to the edge.

She was rigid now, the muscles of her legs looped around his neck corded and hard, her fingers clutching at the sheet as if for extra support. 'Yes,' she moaned.

At that second she came. The flood of her orgasm drowned her in sensation, but not before he'd driven his fingers up into her sex, as deep as they would possibly go, the impact of one chasing the impact of the other. Feeling was layered upon feeling. The wave of orgasm was extended, deepened, honed to a new intensity. Clare gasped, still able to feel, in the middle of this maelstrom of sensation, the relentless movement of his tongue against her clitoris, each tiny stroke magnified and amplified into a whole new panoply of pleasure.

It must have eventually ended. He sensed her crisis pass and pulled his fingers gently out of her body, moving back on his haunches as she raised her legs from his shoulders.

It always ended the same way, at least it had since she'd agreed to co-operate with the ritual. He remained where he was kneeling in front of her, still blindfolded, his back straight, his hands at his sides. She would roll off the bed and walk over to the bedside table, her stockings rasping against each other as she moved. There was a bottle of perfume in the top drawer of the bedside table – cheap, flowery perfume. She'd take it out of the drawer and carry it back to where he knelt. Sitting on the bed again, she'd take the stopper out of the bottle and rub it under his nose. He would inhale deeply and moan.

Lifting her foot, she'd rub her sole against his distended phallus. Instantly she'd feel it jerk. Equally quickly the white satin would darken and the already wet patch enlarge to cover most of the front of the knickers, his body shuddering profoundly as it did so, like a ship holed below the waterline. He'd drop forward, his head against her knee, clutching her leg in his arms.

It was always the same. It was almost five months since Clare had had penetrative sex.

Chapter Two

HAD SHE KNOWN Bridget Goldsmith planned to descend on London, Clare would never have allowed work to start on the extension. What with all the necessary planning and work the visit entailed, the last thing she needed was to come home at night to a house that looked as though it were in the process of being demolished.

She could have moved out. She could have gone to stay with her friend Angela. Instead, once the builders had breached the back wall, she had moved her clothes and make-up into the front bedroom, next to the bathroom, and she had made do, eating out, since her kitchen had disappeared, and taking comfort from the fact that George Wickes assured her the building work would definitely be finished in two weeks' time.

There were, however, two compensations. The first was that she could see the work in progress and check it was all going to plan. It only took two days to knock out the wall to which the extension would be fitted and after that every day brought new additions, the new walls rising, floors and ceilings gradually fitted in place. She began to be able to imagine what it would look like when it was finished.

The other compensation was more venal: Gary. Clare had asked him what his surname was. Newby, Gary Newby. He maintained his pattern of being the first to arrive and the last to leave. He frequently worked stripped to his shorts. Although she was not able to observe him as closely as she had from the back bedroom, she still caught glimpses of that magnificent body.

Exactly one week before Bridget's arrival Clare had taken a call from Angela, her oldest friend, just as she'd arrived home from work.

'Hi, darling, how's tricks?' Angela always sounded chipper.

'Don't ask. I'm up to my eyes in building rubble.'

'That's what I thought. Do you fancy a bite to eat and . . .'

'And?'

'A little diversion.' Angela Barker was a journalist for a glossy magazine, a sinewy blonde whose long hair seemed to attract men like moths to a flame. Like moths too, many had got themselves badly burned. Angela was forthright and down-to-earth and not one to suffer fools, even handsome or rich fools, gladly. Her attitude to men was entirely pragmatic. If they gave her what she wanted at the time they were tolerated. If not they were abandoned.

'OK. How long?'

'Ten minutes.' Angela lived in a mansion-block just around the corner.

'Fifteen. I've got to change.'

'Done.'

Replacing the phone under the dust-sheet that

covered the table in the sitting room, Clare rushed upstairs. It was always the same with Angela. Everything was arranged at the last minute. Nothing was ever planned.

She managed to shower and change into a summer frock in ten minutes, seeing Angela's Ford Escort Cabriolet draw up outside as she applied her make-up.

The doorbell rang, but, before she could get downstairs, Gary, who was clearing up after the day's work and taking two bucket-fulls of rubbish to the skip, had answered it for her.

'Hi,' Angela said, none too subtly eyeing the bulging muscles of Gary's naked chest. 'God, Clare you really should stop taking the HRT,' she added, laughing.

'I'm Gary,' the builder said self-consciously. 'Just got to drop these in the skip.'

'You can drop me in the skip anytime,' Angela retorted, as Clare rushed downstairs.

'Excuse my friend, Gary; she's a wolf in wolf's clothing.'

'Yeah,' he smiled, heading out to the skip.

'He's gorgeous,' Angela said. The women kissed on both cheeks.

'Got time to see what used to be my house?'

Clare led the way to the back of the house, where a gaping hole was supported by a new RSJ.

'Oh, it's lovely,' Angela joked. 'Did you do this?'

Gary had come back in, carrying the empty buckets. 'Some of it.'

'How much longer?' Angela asked.

'Not long now.'

'Two weeks? Looks like it's going to take months.'

'Naw,' Gary said seriously. 'The basic structure's in.'

'Gary Newby, this is Angela Barker.' Clare introduced them.

'Pleased to meet you,' he said. 'Won't shake hands. They're filthy.'

'You are a big boy, aren't you?' Angela commented, unabashed.

'Angela, behave!'

'Such big strong muscles. I like a bit of rough trade.'

'That's enough, Angela. Come on, let's go. You have to excuse my friend, she has a mission to be outrageous.'

'That's all right with me,' Gary said. Angela was wearing a tight one-piece suit in cream, its low-cut neckline showing a great deal of her ample cleavage and the material clung tightly to her long legs. In the roving eye department Gary and Angela were evenly matched.

'Can you lock up, Gary?'

'No problem. Have a good time.'

Clare pulled Angela into the hall. She opened the front door and bundled her out, but not before Angela had said, in her loudest voice, 'What a hunk!'

She repeated it as they climbed into the car. 'Now I know why you wouldn't move in with me,' she added.

'I hardly noticed him,' Clare lied airily.

'And?' Angela started the engine and drove away, seemingly at a hundred miles an hour.

'And what?'

'Do I have to spell it out?'

Clare rapidly did up her safety-belt as they cornered with a screech of tyres.

'Oh, come on, Angela – he's a builder.'

'You're not a snob, are you?'

'I don't mean that. I can hardly seduce him though, can I? What am I supposed to do, drift down to the concrete mixer in my black negligée? Anyway, he's probably married with four children.'

'Still . . .' Angela let the word linger in the air. 'So talking of sex, how's David?'

'The same as ever. Just the same.'

'What does that mean?'

Clare had not shared the secret of David's complex sex-life. 'Oh, I suppose I should end it really. It's not going anywhere.'

'Why? I thought you liked him.'

'I do. But "like" isn't "love".'

'Oh, keep him on the hook until you get a better offer. That's what I'd do. Don't burn your boats.'

'Oh, it's difficult.'

'Is he good in bed?' Angela always got to the point.

'So-so.'

'Ah.' Angela sounded as though she had just discovered the meaning of life. 'Drop him then.'

'A few seconds ago you told me to keep him until someone better comes along.'

'Yes, but if he's no good in the sack there's no point.'

'I've got to do something.'

'There's always Gary.' Angela grinned. She had a large, sensual mouth and a set of very white teeth.

'And what about your sex-life?' Clare asked, glad to change the subject.

Since Angela's propensity to consume men at

34

an alarming rate was an inexhaustible topic, her tales of her latest adventures took them through the rest of the journey.

They fetched up in Streatham. Angela parked the car and headed for an old-fashioned-looking pub on a busy corner of a main road.

'I thought we were going to eat,' Clare complained, quite hungry now.

'I've got to just do this first. Come on, it starts in five minutes.'

The poster outside the pub was life-sized. It featured an incredibly muscular black man, with a deep barrel chest, and large prominent veins on all his bulging muscles. His head was shaved and his body oiled, the leather pouch that covered his genitals almost grotesquely distended. Mr Macho, according to the poster, was performing tonight, at seven, nine and ten thirty.

'Oh no,' Clare said, when she realised what Mr Macho was likely to be doing. 'I'm not going in there.'

'Why not?'

'He's a male stripper, right?'

'I've got to write about it for the magazine.'

'It'll be obscene.'

'Oh come on, don't be so po-faced.'

Angela pushed through the panelled glass doors, their brass handles and fingerplates brightly polished. Inside, the ground floor was packed with people, mostly women. Angela produced two free passes and flashed them at the large bouncer who guarded the stairs to the upstairs room where the performance would take place. He grunted and allowed them to push past the hordes of other women who were buying tickets at the table to his left, which had been hastily arranged to act as an impromptu box office. The women all chatted and giggled and nudged each other with nervous excitement.

Angela led the way upstairs. They found themselves in a large rectangular room with a circular rostrum at one end. The room was already packed exclusively with women. They ferried drinks from a long bar on one wall to the tables, tin trays laden with gin and tonics and pint glasses of lager, most of the tables exhibiting an array of examples of what had been previously consumed.

The nervous excitement of the women was more pronounced up here; the heat, the alcohol and the level of noise increasing the women's volubility, which, in turn, was an indication that a certain amount of bravado was necessary to get them through the evening.

Clare looked around. She guessed that few of the women had ever been to such an event before. Some, despite the drink and eager comments, looked distinctly uncomfortable. Or perhaps that was just her, reading her own feelings into their blank faces. She most certainly didn't want to be there, and would have turned round and left but for the fact she knew that for the next ten years Angela would have ragged her for her lack of daring.

Clare searched for a place to hide and pulled her friend over to the far end of the bar, the furthest point from the rostrum.

'Do you want a drink?' Angela shouted over the noise.

'Not really.'

There were four large Bose speakers suspended from the ceiling in each corner of the room. Suddenly they produced a loud tapping noise, followed by the ear-splitting wail of feedback, as a woman in a man's black dinner jacket and bow-tie dragged a microphone on its stand into the centre of the rostrum. The spotlights suspended on a bar above the stage were faded up, lighting the whole area in a rose-tinted hue.

'Ladies . . .' the announcer said, as soon as the whine in the sound system was sorted out. 'Ladies, this is what you've all been waiting for.' There were cries of 'Yes, yes, yes,' from the audience. 'The Freeman's Arms,' the woman continued, 'is proud to present for your entertainment tonight, the one and only, the exciting, the dynamic, Mr Macho!'

The scream of approval was deafening. High-heel shoes stomped on the wooden floor as the lights in the room dimmed.

A silver lurex curtain had been hung on the wall at the back of the rostrum. The curtain twitched. It twitched again; then, obscenely, tented outwards, something poking it from the other side just below waist level. The women roared at the size of the protrusion.

'Oh, god,' Clare muttered, glaring at Angela.

'Not exactly subtle,' she conceded. She had taken a spiral bound notebook from her handbag and was writing notes in shorthand.

The curtain was thrown aside and a tall black man stalked on to the stage. He was wearing chiffon harem pantaloons over tight, red, satin briefs. His chest was hairless and just as muscular as the photograph outside had suggested. As he stepped forward the loudspeakers began to play an instrumental version of 'Goldfinger'. In his hand Mr Macho held a black rod, a larger version of a magician's wand.

'Did you think that was me?' he yelled into the microphone. He addressed the question to the women sitting nearest to the rostrum.

'Yes,' the audience screamed as one.

'Naughty girls! I'm *much* bigger than that.'

He tossed the wand to the woman in the dinner suit, who had retired to the side of the curtain, then began gyrating his hips in time to the music.

'Look at those muscles,' Angela shouted into Clare's ear. 'Reminds me of your Gary.'

They reminded Clare of Gary too, and, despite herself, she felt a pang of desire.

The stripper began to pull the chiffon pantaloons down over his hips, turning his back to the audience and bending over so they were peeled over his very tight buttocks. When he got them to his knees he jumped around to face the audience again. He sat on the floor, jack-knifed his legs out in front of him and pulled the pantaloons off over his ankles.

'Now it gets interesting,' he promised as he sprang to his feet.

'I really don't want to see any more,' Clare murmured.

'Don't you, love?' asked the woman standing next to her at the bar. 'I do. I want to see the whole bloody thing.'

Very slowly, constantly grinding his hips in time to the music, the black man hooked his thumbs into the waistband of the satin briefs and pulled them down an inch or two, then coyly pulled them up again to cries of 'More!' from the crowd. After repeating this teasing three or four times he finally stripped the satin to where it was just covering his genitals. He turned around again and quickly pulled the briefs to the floor, his tight buttocks dimpled at the side.

The women screamed out obscene remarks as to what they wanted him to do next. He smiled at them over his shoulder and tutted into the microphone. Then he spun round a complete 360 degrees, so fast none of the women glimpsed a thing. He did this twice more, before turning slowly so he faced the audience. His genitals were covered in a black leather pouch, held in place by a draw-string. It looked as though he was partially erect under the leather.

'Now I need a volunteer,' he said. Immediately he leapt off the rostrum into the crowd. A follow-spot had been switched on and tracked him as he sat squarely on the lap of a large, very overweight woman in a bright orange dress, his hand groping one of her massive breasts. The woman blushed a deep red but put her arms around the man and hugged him tightly. He had a struggle to escape from her clutches.

When he finally managed it, he ran amongst the tables up to the bar, where a young brunette in a very short black mini-dress was standing with a drink in her hand. He took the drink from her, tasted it and grimaced. 'Her horse has got diabetes,' he joked. 'Do you want to help me out?' he asked her, taking her hand.

'No way,' she responded, snatching her hand away.

He bound over to a pretty blonde in a black halter top, white hot pants and black tights. She backed away but her friends pushed her towards him.

'We have a volunteer,' he announced, taking the girl by the arm and leading her to the rostrum, her resistance only nominal.

As they climbed on to the stage there was wild applause and cries of 'Get it off'. The music had changed to a slow version of 'Man with the Golden Gun'.

'On your knees,' the stripper ordered the girl, grinding his hips to the music again.

The blonde giggled, looked to her friends for encouragement and then, egged on by them, got down on one knee.

'Right, here we go, ladies!' He pulled the girl's hand up to the draw-string at the front of the pouch. She did not hesitate. She pulled the bow that held it in place and tore the black leather pouch away, holding it aloft like a hunter's trophy to an enormous cheer from the audience.

'Can we go now?' Clare wondered. Angela ignored her, straining to see the black man's cock.

The stripper dropped to his knees. He pushed the blonde back on the rostrum and climbed on top of her. He bucked his hips up and down as if he were having sex with her, while she, in turn, folded her black, nylon-sheathed legs over his back. The women in the audience began to chant in time to the man's thrusts. 'In!' they screamed, followed by, 'Out!'

For the first time, and very much to her surprise, the spectacle affected Clare. She felt a throb of excitement. She could not tear her eyes away from the big, powerful muscles of the man's buttocks and thighs, which rippled as he powered forward. Her excitement flowed from unbidden thoughts about what it would feel like to have that broad, hard body on top of her, thrusting an equally broad and hard cock into the depths of her meltingly soft sex. The surge of feeling made her realise what she'd been missing all these months.

40

The black man peeled the girl's legs from around his back and sprung to his feet, his cock slapping against his thigh.

'Who's next?' he bellowed, leaping into the audience again. He picked up a tumbler containing a gin and tonic, dipped his cock into it and stirred it around. 'Cocktails, anyone?' he teased.

'Let's go,' Clare said. This time she wasn't going to take no for an answer. She took Angela by the arm and began pushing her way through the crowd.

Unfortunately the stripper spotted the movement. He leapt through the tables and planted himself squarely in front of her, his muscular frame glistening under the light from the follow-spot. 'Not leaving already?' he said. 'Can I mix you a drink?' He indicated his cock.

'No, thank you,' Clare replied. Even through the baying cries of the women he must have been able to tell from the tone of her voice that she was serious. Or perhaps it was the expression on her face. In any event his experience told him she was not the right woman to use in his act. But he was getting an entirely different reaction from Angela, who was at Clare's shoulder.

Dancing up to her, he grabbed Angela's hand. She squealed with delight and surprise as he pulled her towards him and began wriggling his body against her like a snake.

It was only a matter of seconds before he'd transferred his attention to another woman, sitting at the nearest table. He pulled her chair out to face him and straddled her knees, without sitting on them, so his cock was right in front of her face.

Clare didn't wait to see any more. She wrestled

her way to the exit and down the stairs, Angela following in her wake. Pushing through the double doors she stood on the busy street outside.

'Well, that was fun,' Angela said as she joined her. 'What a mover!'

'You didn't really enjoy it?'

'Come on, let's go and eat. I'm starving.' They walked back to the car. 'All right, I admit it wasn't sexy. But it was interesting. And that guy had a beautiful body. Have you ever had a guy like that?'

'No.'

'Don't you wonder what it would be like?'

Clare had wondered what it would be like with Gary. 'No.'

'I think it would be great.'

'Is that a fantasy of yours? Some hunk?'

'Yes, a nice bit of rough trade,' Angela said, unlocking the car. 'Isn't that what we'd all like, really?'

Clare didn't answer that question.

'You're sure you don't mind?'

'Why should I mind? If it gets the job done more quickly it's good, isn't it? The sooner I get out of this mess the better.'

'I don't want to mess up your evening.'

'What evening? I'm only going to watch telly.'

'All right then. I'll only be another hour.'

Gary, as usual, had been the only man left working when she got back from work. He'd asked Clare if she'd mind him working late, to finish the last section of plaster on the new interior walls.

'Do you want a beer?' she enquired.

'Can I have it when I'm done?'

'Of course.'

Clare wandered up to the front bedroom. As that

and the bathroom were the only places not affected by dust and rubble she'd put her telly at the foot of the bed. She switched it on and lay on the bed watching it without being conscious of what was actually on. She had had another hard day preparing for Bridget's visit, due in three days' time. Most of the presentation was ready but Clare had found mistakes in some of the statistics and had ordered last-minute changes to the marketing strategy. Although each country was going to be given the same packaging and artwork, Clare wanted it made clear by the advertising agency that the individual ads should be tailor-made for each national campaign. Results of product-launches in which an American commercial had merely been re-voiced and run without any other change had been extremely disappointing, though she knew that that was the approach Bridget Goldsmith favoured. She wanted the presentation to contain the evidence that supported her own point of view.

The sun had been out all day and as the house faced south – another reason Clare slept in the back – the front bedroom was hot. The sultry heat made her drowsy but the loud thuds and bangs as Gary worked away prevented her from dozing off.

Instead she daydreamed. Gary was stripped to his shorts again. Inevitably she compared his physique to that of the black stripper. Perhaps the black man's muscles were slightly better defined, the result, no doubt, of pumping iron in a gym. Gary's muscles were formed by hard physical labour.

Like most women, she thought, Clare had always believed a man's mind was more important than his body, but she could not deny that she had been acutely aroused by watching the black man performing simulated intercourse. Equally Gary's body was affecting her. Over the last weeks she had been intensely aware of it.

She wondered what Gary would do if she wandered downstairs in something light and flimsy. The collection of lingerie donated by David Allston was quite extensive. She could put on the pink silk body. Or there was a short, black, lace slip with spaghetti straps, the lace making it almost totally transparent. What would he do if she wafted into the rubble of the back room wearing that?

Clare was not naive about sex. She had pursued everything in her life with tenacity, determination and thirst for knowledge. This attitude had served her well in business. She had risen rapidly through the ranks of KissCo and was the youngest managing director of any equivalent company in the UK. It had served her well in her sex life too. She had pursued her sexual aims with quite as much ambition as her career. She had selected lovers on the basis of merit, quickly discarding men who proved unsatisfactory lovers. Some might have thought her ruthless but Clare liked sex and saw no point wasting time in a relationship where, at the end of the day, it was going to leave her unfulfilled.

Her thirst for knowledge had made her a formidable competitor in business. She knew more about almost everything in the cosmetics industry than any of her rivals. She knew more about how business worked too, about financing, sales promotion and advertising, and the psychology of management. There wasn't a single aspect of KissCo's operation she did not understand better than the departmental head who ran it.

She had applied the same zeal to her private life. She had become interested in art deco and had researched it to such an extent that she was regarded by some auction houses as an expert on the period. Her enjoyment of sex had motivated her to approach that subject with similar application. She had bought books, watched porno movies, and talked to all her friends about their experiences. She had been astonished, but not shocked, by the diversity of sexual behaviour. Over the years she had read about every sort of sexual perversion. They fascinated her. Not because she had the slightest desire to be tied to a mediaeval rack and whipped, or dress from head to toe in black rubber, or any of the hundred-and-one other activities the books graphically described, but because it never ceased to amaze her that such things could be sexually arousing at all.

But quest for knowledge had revealed more practical information. She had, for instance, become an expert on masturbation. In school the basic sex lessons had barely touched on more egocentric goals, but her extra-curricular reading, at that time confined to various how-to-do-what books, had explained in great detail the advantages and techniques involved. She had quickly learned to explore her own body with the same thoroughness she employed on everything else. Later, having successfully invented a series of procedures to stimulate herself to very vivid orgasms, a friend had told her about dildos. Their introduction into her masturbation routine had been nothing short of explosive, the combination of a hard cylindrical object buried in her vagina and the artful cajoling of her clitoris producing enviable results.

Her knowledge of the byways of sexual experience had been good preparation for David Allston. She found him attentive and charming and, what was more important, the way he manipulated her body, the way he used his fingers and mouth on her, had given her intense pleasure, even if when it came to full sexual intercourse things had been less than satisfactory. Had he not been so good at foreplay, he would have become a victim of her ruthless selection policy, the survival of the fittest. But he was good: foreplay had become the main event.

When after their first few weeks together he'd brought her a gift-wrapped, black lace teddy and a pair of black hold-up stockings, with lace tops, and a little card suggesting that she might like to go and change into them while he waited downstairs, she'd found the idea exciting. There was something about getting dressed up for sex that appealed to her. Her response had clearly encouraged David. The gifts had become more elaborate, the cards extended into letters, his brief attempts at intercourse abandoned in favour of more exotic gratification.

Since the rituals had always resulted in a wonderfully satisfying orgasm for Clare, she had raised no objections. There was no one else in her life at that moment. But recently the rituals had become ritualised. She began to yearn for spontaneity. As her reaction to the black stripper had clearly demonstrated, she yearned for penetration too.

Clare felt a strong and powerful pulse emanating from her sex. It caused her nipples to pucker. They felt cold, little chips of marble nestling in her bra.

Getting up off the bed, she switched off the television. She usually had a bath or shower when she got home but had decided to wait until Gary had finished. She supposed she felt faintly embarrassed about being naked while he was in the house, however silly that seemed.

Clare thought of herself as liberated and independently minded. She wasn't too concerned with social niceties or the quibbles and taboos of conventional morality. That did not mean, unfortunately, she thought, that she had escaped the conventions of the sexual role that she had been nurtured in from an earlier age. In the mood she was in she would have loved to be able to go downstairs, not fancifully dressed in flimsy lingerie like something from a scene in a porno film, but dressed as she was now, and ask Gary if he would like to go to bed with her. As simple as that. But it was just not possible. She couldn't do it. Man *had* to proposition woman. Those were the rules. As yet female liberation had not changed much in that direction. At least, not for her. She'd seen Angela Barker take the initiative in a way she would never have had the courage to do.

'Mrs Markham?' Gary's voice interrupted her reverie.

'Yes?' She stepped out of her bedroom. He was standing at the bottom of the stairs.

'All done. It didn't take as long as I thought.' He was pulling a check shirt on over his chest.

'Do you want that beer now?' she asked, walking downstairs. He was looking up at her, with a

47

serious expression on his face.

'Thanks,' he said.

She went to the fridge. The old kitchen had been demolished and the fridge stood on a wall in the dining room, covered in a film of dust. She took a beer. The glasses had been packed away but Gary usually drank straight from the bottle. She managed to find a bottle opener and peeled off the metal top. Still feeling coquettish she wondered if she was actually going to do anything other than give him a beer.

'Aren't you going to have one?' he wondered, walking back into the dining room and taking the bottle from her.

'I'm fine,' she said.

'See.' He indicated the new wall which now formed the back of the house. 'Plastered all that up.' Pink plaster covered the whole of the area where the new kitchen would be. 'I'm not in tomorrow. Got to let the chippies in to lay the floors and put in the skirting boards.'

'Mr Wickes said you'd be finished next week.'

'Yeah, definite.'

'It was quick.' He was handsome. She loved the way his lips curled up at the edges as he talked. She loved his rugged, tanned hands, and the way his blue eyes seemed to sparkle. He had the air of a man who had discovered the meaning of life and found it permanently amusing.

'Got to keep the customer happy.'

'Don't you want to sit down?' Three of her oldest straight-backed chairs had been ranged against the dining-room wall and covered with dust sheets for the use of the workmen. 'You've been on your feet all day.'

'Must be going,' he said.

48

'Not another beer?' The first had been consumed rapidly.

'Yeah. OK. One more. Thanks.'

He sat on one of the chairs as she took another beer from the fridge and opened it. She wondered what she thought she was doing. Why on earth hadn't she just let him leave?

'Cheers,' he said.

'Have you worked for Mr Wickes long?' She sat down on the chair at the end of the row, leaving one between them.

'Five years. He's a good man. Looks after his men.'

'Is that what you always wanted to be, a builder?'

'Me? No. I wanted to be an astronaut. I wanted to be the first man to walk on the far side of the moon. I'd have liked to stand there looking out into space and not be able to see the earth.'

Clare saw the idea create a spark in his eyes. For some reason that made her heart go out to him. 'Why didn't you?' She leant forward, resting her elbows on her knees.

'What, with a CSE in woodwork? No chance.'

Clare felt confused and uncomfortable and hot. She wasn't seriously going to try and seduce him, was she? That was just an idle daydream. She thought of Angela's reference to 'rough trade'. She wondered what her friend would do in this situation.

'Are you married?' The question came out all wrong. It sounded too blunt and obvious. 'I'm sorry, none of my business.' That made it worse. She felt herself blushing.

'No, never have been either,' he said, appearing not to notice her embarrassment.

'Involved?' She could hardly believe she'd said that.

'No. Look, I'd better go.'

'There's no hurry, is there?' She smiled, a tiny rather nervous smile, and leant back in her chair trying to imagine she was Angela, cool, determined and fearless.

'Look, Mrs Markham . . .'

'Ms. I'm not married. Like you, I never have been.'

'I think I should tell you something.'

'And that is?'

He looked directly into her eyes for the first time. She felt her heart pumping faster. 'I've been hanging around here a lot.'

'Have you?'

'You know I have. It's because you're a fantastic-looking bird.'

With blinding clarity, like the sun coming out from behind heavy cloud, Clare suddenly knew what she was going to do. 'Does this happen a lot, then?' she asked.

'What?'

'Women you're working for, throwing themselves at you.'

He laughed. It was a lovely open sound. 'And here was me thinking I was doing the throwing . . . And, yeah, as it happens, it does. Practically every house I'm in some bird is all over me like a rash. It's a wonder I get any work done.' He said it with self-depreciating humour that Clare found irresistible.

'You *are* a very attractive man.'

'I'm glad you think so.'

'Are you?'

'If you want the truth, Ms Markham, I've really

been lusting after you.'

Clare smiled. Ten minutes ago she would have been alarmed if he had said such a thing. Now it pleased her. 'Lusting isn't really the right word, is it?' She was conscious that her cultivated received pronunciation sounded artificial against his earthy, South London vowels.

'Why not?'

'Because lusting implies urgency and force.'

He laughed that gorgeous laugh again. 'I could have been arrested for doing what I've been thinking.'

'And now?' Clare asked. She couldn't remember ever having been so bold.

'Is this a wind-up? Are you serious?'

She didn't need to think about her answer. Being so daring was turning her on. He was turning her on. 'Perfectly,' she said in her precise, clipped accent.

He put the bottle down on the floor with studied concentration, then slowly got to his feet. He stood directly in front of her, looking down into her eyes, his expression quizzical. Then he stooped, put one arm around her shoulders and one under her knees and, with no apparent effort, lifted her up, cradling her like a baby. He brought his lips to hers and kissed her hard, his tongue plunging into her mouth, hot and phallus-like.

Clare felt a pulse of desire so strong it made her whole body shudder. Suspended in his arms she felt almost weightless, and for some reason that gave her a sense of vulnerability. But the vulnerability was exciting. She couldn't ever remember a man picking her up physically before, nor any with the strength to do so. She kissed Gary back hard, wrapping her arms

51

around his neck and grinding her mouth against his, enjoying the huge sense of exhilaration that shot through her. It wiped away any doubts she had about what she was doing.

'I need a shower,' he said, finally breaking the kiss.

'Upstairs,' she said breathlessly. He smelt of sweat. At any other time she might have found the smell unpleasant. At this moment it was intoxicating.

Without putting her down, he walked out into the hall and climbed the stairs. He knew where the bathroom was and pushed the door open with his foot.

'Don't put me down yet,' she said, as she felt him stoop to release her.

'Why not?'

'I like it. You're so strong.'

'I have to be,' he said, grinning. 'And you're so soft. You smell like flowers.' He kissed her again, lightly this time, using his tongue to trace the outline of her lips. He kissed her cheeks and her forehead and her nose. He kissed her eyelids, then her mouth again, but this time as forcefully as he had downstairs.

Clare was melting with passion. Her body seemed to have turned liquid, as liquid as the juices she knew were oozing out of her sex. She had never had sex with a man she had known for such a short period of time. She had never had sex without carefully vetting the man first and considering all the consequences and repercussions. The fact that fifteen minutes ago Gary Newby was someone with whom she'd exchanged no more than casual small talk made her feel almost light-headed with arousal. Hadn't she longed for spontaneity?

'Let me shower,' he insisted, putting her down. 'I'm dirty. Plaster-dust all over.' A large bulge pushed out the fly of his sawn-off jeans. He stripped off his shirt.

'You're a very sexy man, aren't you?' Clare purred. Though her feet were back on the floor she felt as if she were floating.

She ran her hand over the denim and unzipped his flies. 'God, I feel so naughty.' As if to demonstrate, she fished inside the jeans. He was wearing white boxer shorts. She fought her way inside them until her fingers closed on his hot, hard penis. 'That's what I want,' she said, pulling it out.

His cock was large, long, thick and circumcised, the diameter of the glans slightly bigger than the shaft that supported it. The ridge at the bottom of the glans was also very pronounced like a miniature ski-jump.

Gary unbuckled his belt and pulled his jeans down with the boxer shorts. His cock was still caught in the fly of the shorts and was dragged down with them, until it suddenly sprung free, quivering and vibrant, a proud totem to his masculinity. 'Let me shower,' he repeated, pulling off his heavy steel-capped boots and his socks so he could strip his jeans and shorts over his ankles.

What Clare actually wanted was for him to take her there and then. She wanted to be screwed. She wanted to be fucked. The words excited her. She was trying to think of a single reason why she couldn't have what she wanted.

Gary reached for the mixer taps and turned the water on. He climbed into the bath and let the water flow over him. He reached for the soap and lathered his body, then allowed the water to wash the lather away. The water ran pink with the plaster dust. It took a matter of seconds but to Clare it seemed like hours.

'No,' she said as he reached for a towel, not prepared to wait any longer. 'I want you like this.'

Without waiting for him to respond she grabbed the edge of the bath with both hands, bent over, straightened her back and wriggled her bottom from side to side, hoping he would take the hint.

He did. With water still dripping from his body, he climbed out of the bath and stood behind her. 'You can't wait, can you,' he said, stating the obvious.

'No, I can't. I've had to wait too long already. For heaven's sake, Gary . . .' She looked up at him, letting him see the need in her eyes, '. . . can't you see what you've done to me?' As if to illustrate the point she pulled the light cotton shirt-waister she was wearing up over her hips. With a total lack of modesty she had never exhibited before, she drew the gusset of her silky white panties to one side and thrust her buttocks up towards him. She knew he would be able to see her sex. It would be glistening with wetness.

'Look at that,' he breathed, momentarily hypnotised by the spectacle.

'Gary,' she whined. Voyeurism was not the point of this exercise.

'Yeah. Right,' he said. Gary thought of himself as experienced with women, but this woman was something new. Her cut-glass accent and the air of confidence and sophistication she exuded had attracted him to her from the start. But she wasn't like any of the girls he dated, and he'd never imagined he'd even get to first base. Women like her, rungs above him on the social ladder, simply didn't get involved with brickies, even brickies who did plastering too, even brickies with blonde hair and blue, come-to-bed eyes. Even the single women whose houses he'd worked on, if they were educated and posh like Clare Markham, had never displayed anything but cursory politeness. Oh, he wasn't naive enough to believe they didn't stare at his body and wonder. But looking wasn't doing. Until now.

He moved up behind Clare, gripped the top of her hips, and forced his erection into the cleft of her buttocks. He found her blatancy exciting.

'*Yes,*' she hissed. She hadn't had a man inside her for five months. She hadn't realised how much tension that had caused until it was about to be released.

He bucked his hips and guided his cock into the crease of her labia. He could feel her heat and wetness.

'Yes,' she repeated. 'I need it.' She squirmed her buttocks from side to side, feeling his glans knocking against them. She felt his cock nestling into the opening of her vagina which seemed to purse around it, welcoming it with a kiss.

He waited, his fingers gripping like a vice. She tried to push back at him but his hold was too tight. He was teasing her, making her wait. It only increased her arousal. At that moment she could have sworn she had never wanted a man more in her life, that she had never been so totally and absolutely consumed by lust. Nothing else mattered but the moment he chose to plunge inside her. She could feel the length of her vagina contracting, like a mouth desperate for air. The seconds stretched into hours. She actually believed she would come like this, come over the crown of his cock without further penetration, if he didn't do something soon.

But that proposition was not put to the test. Without any warning Gary bucked his hips and lunged his cock forward. It drove up into her, parting the soft, silky wet walls of her vagina, stretching her, filling her more completely than she had ever been filled before. He did not withdraw it again. Instead, while his hands pulled her back on him, using his considerable strength to flatten her buttocks against his iron hard navel, he pushed even deeper. It was only a matter of a fraction of an inch but it felt like he had broken through some barrier in her body, some secret barrier she had not known about, another hymen buried so deep only his size had managed to breach it.

And that was enough. Enough to produce a surge of feeling that blossomed instantly into an orgasm, an orgasm that consumed her like the flames of a fire consumed oxygen. It affected every part of her, made her tremble uncontrollably, made every muscle contract, every sinew stretch, her body completely embroiled in it. She thought she could hear herself screaming the word 'god' over and over again but whether she had actually pronounced it or whether it was just echoing in her mind she could not tell.

Eventually her body turned from total rigidity into quivering jelly. So much so that if Gary's hands hadn't held her she would have collapsed on to the floor. But they did. His steel fingers supported her weight. He had let her orgasm run its course, but now he was beginning to move,

56

stroking his cock in and out almost imperceptibly at first. Then the movement became more marked. He pulled out of her further, until his glans was almost at the opening of her vagina, then thrust all the way back in, slowly but powerfully.

'Oh god, Gary, you feel so good.' The aftermath of orgasm drained away sufficiently for her to be able to register individual feelings again. The outward stroke of his cock created a great void in her, the inner a wonderful sense of fulfilment. He filled her like no other man had. She knew what she wanted now to make her fulfilment complete. She wanted his spunk. She needed it. What made this realisation even more exhilarating was that she could feel, with every millimetre of her sex, that she was going to get precisely what she wanted and very soon.

As he slid into her, the slick of her juices making the penetration frictionless, she used all the muscles of her sex to squeeze his phallus. She felt it react immediately, jerking against his silken grip. She waited until he was right up in her again, up beyond the secret barrier, up where she had never been touched before, then squeezed for a second time. It produced another convulsion in his cock, matched, to her surprise, by an equal shock of pleasure in her.

She had never had sex like this. Even before the complex rituals indulged in by David, sex had been studied and artful, an exercise in self-knowledge and self-discipline, in getting men to do to her what she had discovered she liked most, then planning how to please them in return. She insisted on foreplay, on having her nipples stroked and her clitoris caressed. This was entirely different. He hadn't touched her nipples. She hadn't even taken off her bra. Her clitoris, though throbbing and more alive than she'd ever known it, remained neglected. It didn't appear to matter. As surely as day follows night she was going to come again the moment he ejaculated, because she knew she would be able to feel it happen as graphically as she'd ever felt anything.

He was hammering into her now, his own need asserting itself. Each inward thrust was so powerful it almost took her breath away, each threatening to make her lose control again. But she hung on by her metaphorical fingernails, clinging to the cliff face of consciousness, determined to feel him come.

Suddenly he stopped, jamming his erection into the depths of her body, pulling her back on him. He looked down at her bottom, the silky white panties stretched out all askew across her buttocks, the gusset bunched up at one side of her sex, its elastic biting into the softness of her flesh. His cock twitched, kicking against the tight, wet tube that surrounded it so sensually. It twitched again and a huge spurt of semen jetted out of him, spattering into her body, followed by another and another and another.

This time Clare was sure that she screamed. Though she had been prepared for it, though she'd felt his cock convulsing inside her, the heat and strength of his spending took her by surprise. His spunk was hot, burning inside her. She could feel every drop of it, every spot where it splattered out instantly transformed into a seething mass of raw nerves. She came as she knew she would, her second orgasm just as deep and affecting as the first, her body shuddering. She clung to the edge of the bath for support.

'Didn't even take my dress off,' she said, wanting to say something and not capable of thinking of anything else. She felt totally confused. As he pulled out of her she suffered a renewed tremor of sensation, like an orgasm in miniature. It added to her sense of bewilderment. Now that their passion was spent, its suddennness and intensity burnt out, there was a gaping emotional vacuum. She had gone so far away from anything that passed as normal behaviour for her, that it was difficult to get back into character, to re-establish the essential bearings of her life again. She sat on the edge of the bath, facing him.

'Sorry,' she said, 'I'm feeling a little shaky.'

She was looking at his body. He did remind her of the stripper. She suddenly had a vision of that tight black bottom bucking up and down on the pretty blonde. She shuddered.

'I'll take that as a compliment,' he said. He picked up a towel and began to dry his body, still wet from the shower.

'It is one,' she said.

'Another satisfied customer. I'll have to put in for more overtime from Wickesy.'

It took a moment for her to realise he was joking. 'Worth every penny,' she said weakly.

'What now?'

She needed to shower. Her body felt sticky. But she was suddenly shy. He had taken her more profoundly than any man she could remember and yet she felt inhibited about taking her dress off in front of him. She scolded herself for being silly and unbuttoned the dress quickly.

'Turn the water on,' she said, as she unclipped her white bra, trying not to feel self-conscious.

59

'You look great,' he observed.

The panties were still pulled to one side. She skimmed them down her legs and stepped into the bath as he turned the water on. The lukewarm water felt good.

'Do you want me to go?' He was watching the water flow over her firm, round breasts.

'No.'

'Do you want to go and get something to eat?'

The water refreshed her. She thought she could feel wetness – hers or his? – leaking on to her thigh. She washed it away with the soap. 'Yes, that's a good idea.' But there was a better one, as far as she was concerned, a much better one, though whether he'd be able to oblige again she did not know.

She got out of the bath and towelled herself dry, then took his hand and led him through to the bedroom.

'I can't go anywhere posh,' he said. 'Not in that clobber.'

'I could order take-away,' she suggested.

'There's something I'd like to fucking take away,' he said fiercely. He grabbed her hand and pulled her into his arms with such force it nearly knocked the breath out of her. His lips mashed against hers as he squirmed against her nakedness, his chest squashing her breasts. This was a new experience. She wrapped her arms around him and hugged him to her. His body felt wonderful, every inch as hard as steel. What was more surprising was that his cock was unfurling rapidly against her belly. By the time he broke the kiss it was as erect as it had been before.

'God, you're enthusiastic,' she said. She was having trouble believing he could recover so quickly, but there was the evidence right in front of her eyes. Not that she was complaining.

'That's your fault,' he said, glancing at his cock.

'You certainly make a woman feel desired.'

She dropped to her knees. Unsubtly, with no preliminaries, she sucked his cock into her mouth. A few minutes ago she had felt befuddled and disorientated. But she had recovered as quickly as he so evidently had. He moaned as she took him deep in her throat, cramming as much of him into her as she could.

'Great,' he mumbled.

She sucked again, feeling his cock react with a jerk. His hardness and his size made her sex throb. She began bobbing her head up and down on him, wondering if she could make him come, enamoured of the idea of feeling him come in her mouth.

'No . . .' he gasped after a moment or two. 'That's not what I want.'

He stooped and plucked her off the floor, gathering her in his arms, taking her bodily, and literally throwing her on the bed, the impression of where she had lain earlier still held in the quilt. Before she could register anything else, he had fallen on her, forced her legs apart, and stabbed his erection into her. There was no resistance. Her sex was wet. Soaking wet. No doubt part of her liquidity was his previous spending but she knew this frantic assault was arousing her strongly. Being wanted like this, being desired so ardently, must be the most powerful aphrodisiac in the world.

His right hand squeezed between their bodies to grasp her breast. He pinched her nipple. This time his tactics were entirely different. He didn't tease her. He didn't thrust into her and hold himself there. He simply hammered into her, using all his athleticism to pound his large cock into her sex, stroking it back and forth with a speed and power that she found hard to believe anyone could sustain for long. But he did. He went on and on.

Clare's orgasm, she supposed, was instantaneous, the urgency of his first thrust provoking an enormous release of feelings. But, though he must have felt her sex contracting around him and her body trembling, and heard the little mewing noises she made, he did not pause. He just hammered on, as hard and as efficiently as before, each inward stroke filling her completely, taking his cock deeper into her sex, opening her, until it felt almost as if it were splitting her. He hammered her into another orgasm that made the first pale into insignificance, then on, through that into a third, at which point she lost the last vestige of control. She wasn't really sure what happened after that, whether she just kept coming, whether she had orgasm after orgasm, or whether her body was just so prone, so helplessly vulnerable and exposed that the sensations she was experiencing, the acute pleasures, were in fact one superabundant climax.

In the middle of it all – or was it at the end, she could not tell – she felt him come too. But she was too far gone to respond. Where before she had felt every jet of his ejaculation, now it was reduced to a vague awareness of his cock bucking inside her, and a new flood of wetness seeping into her sex. She could not cope with anything else. Her body had raised its defences, saturation point reached. It was something she'd never felt before.

How long it was before he stopped, before his

pistoning buttocks came to rest, and he rolled off her, finally sated, she did not know. But almost as soon as he had, exhausted and overwhelmed physically and emotionally, Clare fell asleep. When she awoke he had gone.

Chapter Three

'MORNING, MRS MARKHAM.' George Wickes smiled courteously.

'Morning, Mr Wickes.' Clare was on her way out of the front door.

'Everything all right? Just come to check up, as usual.'

'Everything's fine. Really taking shape now.' The carpenters had fitted the floor of the new kitchen and bathroom and were busy installing the new kitchen units.

'Should be finished tomorrow. Then you can start to get back to normal.'

Gary Newby had not turned up at the house since their night together on Tuesday. She remembered him saying he wasn't coming in the next day, but it was Friday and there was still no sign of him. She didn't have his number or address.

'That'll be wonderful. Ah, while you're here – I just wondered . . .' She didn't know how to put it.

'Yes?' He looked worried, as though there was going to be a problem with the work.

'Gary. I just wondered if Gary would be coming in again.'

'Should be. He's on another job at the moment. He'll be here to finish up tomorrow, though.'

'Oh.' Tomorrow was no good. She had accepted an invitation to David Allston's country seat for the weekend. She would have done anything to get out of it, but couldn't think of a good enough excuse. Besides, she was going to take the opportunity to tell him that, as far as she was concerned, their affair had to end. Even without the incredible sexual experience with Gary she had decided David had to go; *with* it any last doubts about the rightness of her decision had been brushed aside. She hadn't the slightest idea if she was going to have a relationship with Gary but that wasn't the point. The point was that he had shown her that she needed something entirely different when it came to sex, and it was something she very definitely was not getting from Viscount Bonmouth, and would never get.

'Nothing wrong, I hope?'

'No. It's just that I . . . I promised to lend him a book and I won't be here tomorrow, I'm going away for the weekend.'

'That's all right. Give it to me. I'll see he gets it.'

'No. I mean . . . it's all right. I'll leave it out for him.'

'Yes, that's it. Leave it on one of the new units in the kitchen.'

Damn him, she thought. She could hardly ask Wickes for Gary's telephone number.

'He'll definitely be here tomorrow?'

'Definitely. Got to get all the rubbish out and in that skip and have the skip taken away. Then the decorator can start on Monday.'

'I'd better rush.' She looked at her watch. She couldn't afford to be late today of all days. Bridget Goldsmith had flown in last night and had arranged to meet her first thing this morning.

'Don't worry about a thing. You won't recognise the place on Monday morning.'

'Thank you.'

'And don't forget that book.'

She looked puzzled for a moment, having forgotten her own lie. 'Book?'

'For Gary.'

'Oh. Right. I won't. I won't . . .' She dived through the front door and out to her car.

'She's waiting in your office,' Janice said. 'Apparently she's been in since eight thirty.'

'Jet lag.' Clare looked at the clock on the office wall. It was two minutes to nine. At lease *she* wasn't late.

'Here goes, then.'

She opened her office door. Bridget Goldsmith was sitting on the grey sofa that lined the wall opposite Clare's desk. She was reading one of the briefing files on the European launch.

'Clare, how punctual,' she said, getting to her feet. She extended her hand. Her fingers were long and bony and each one was beringed. Two gold bracelets clinked against each other as she shook Clare's hand.

'Nice to see you again, Bridget; you're looking well.'

They had only met once before, at the KissCo conference in New York. Though they had barely exchanged a word on that occasion, Bridget's personality had made a strong impression on Clare. She had worked her way up through

66

KissCo and had expanded the company's worth by fifty per cent since she took over two years ago. She was a woman who knew what she wanted and was used to getting it.

'Thank you. So do you. The air at the top obviously suits you.'

Bridget was on the thin side of slender. She had a huge mane of chestnut-coloured hair and very dark green eyes, set in a rather small, slightly pinched face. Her skin was tanned. She had never been seen wearing anything but white, with white accessories and hundredweights of gold jewellery, necklaces, bracelets, brooches and rings. Today she was wearing a white safari suit, white high-heeled shoes with a gold motif set on the toes, and a large gold medallion dangling down between her rather small breasts.

'This is good work,' she said, sitting down again and tapping the file. 'Very good work.'

'Thank you. Would you like some coffee?'

'Just hot water with a slice of lemon. Never use coffee.'

'Of course.' Clare sat behind her desk and ordered the beverages from Janice. 'So where do you want to begin?'

'Before we get down to the nitty-gritty . . .'

'Yes?' Clare said, having no idea what was coming next.

'As this is my first time in London I thought you might be able to arrange a few outings for me.'

'Of course. What sort of outings?'

'I'm just mad about history. It's the one thing America doesn't have.'

'History?'

'I don't mean buildings or museums or anything like that. What I'd really like to do is meet some genuine relics.' She laughed at her own joke. Laughter was not something that came easily to her and the sound she made was more like a horse braying. As Clare was still looking puzzled, she added, 'You know, royalty. Like Lady Di.'

'You want to meet Princess Diana?'

'Is that possible?'

'I doubt it. Not at such short notice. In fact, I think she's abroad.'

'Charles, then.'

'Ah, same problem. They're booked up months in advance.'

'Oh dear. What about a duke, then? I'd really like to meet a real live aristo. Someone with pedigree. I never have. Never even met a knight.'

Clare's secretary knocked on the door. She put the drinks down on Clare's desk and retreated without a word.

'I thought my office had made all this clear.' The tone of Bridget's voice became accusatory. If Bridget's wishes were not fulfilled it would be Clare who would be blamed.

'I suppose . . .' Clare was thinking aloud. She had planned to use this weekend to tell David Allston that there was no future in their relationship. For that reason she hesitated. It would be no problem to ask David to entertain Bridget. He was definitely a 'real live aristo' and could explain his family history in great detail to her. He might even be persuaded to introduce her to one or two of his aristocratic friends. The trouble was that if she did that, Clare would be obligated to him and could hardly tell him the bad news.

'Suppose what?' Bridget promoted.

Clare didn't have any choice. If this week went badly, if Bridget wanted to be bloody minded, she could go back to Houston and give the European launch to the Paris office and Claude Duhamel. In a matter of months the English operation could be run from France and Clare would end up being the managing director of a warehouse and distribution operation.

'Would a viscount do?'

'Duke, earl, viscount, baron, lord. That's it, isn't it? Gee, a viscount would be just fine.'

She'd missed out marquesses, but Clare didn't correct her. 'Viscount Bonmouth. Created 1781.'

'Five years after the start of the War of Independence,' Bridget said in an awed tone.

'Yes. He's a friend of mine. He's got a house in London and a country estate in Hertfordshire. I'm sure I could wangle an invitation to dinner.'

'Gee, I'd be real honoured.'

Clare appeared to have scored a gold star, several gold stars. 'I'm seeing him tonight. I'll ask.' She was trapped. There was no going back now. She'd just have to delay the inevitable. She felt bad about that, but not that bad.

It had been another long day. Bridget had not left her for a second, reviewing every aspect of KissCo's UK operation as well as the details of the European launch, though the formal presentation was not until Monday. Her reputation for thoroughness was well-founded. She'd gone through every detail. They hadn't stopped for lunch but had sandwiches sent in, and it was well after seven before Bridget announced she was going back to her hotel.

As Clare drove her BMW along the A40 she experienced a wave of exhaustion. She turned the air-conditioning on to full blast to refresh her, and looked at the dashboard clock. It was eight fifteen. It would be at least an hour before she reached Althorp House. She punched David's number into the car phone.

'Is David there?' she asked.

'Hold on, ma'am.' The butler had answered the phone and recognised her voice.

'Clare?'

'David. I'm running late.'

'No problem,' he said. 'How long?'

'An hour.'

'So shall I get them to hold dinner?'

'Just a snack would be fine.' The thought of eating an elaborate meal served in the baronial dining room by David's obsequious servants was not appealing. The idea of the whole weekend was becoming truly unattractive. She knew David would have spent the week planning one of his elaborate sexual charades, and then there would be dinner for the county set on Saturday night. But now she could do nothing but grin and bear it.

An hour and a half later she was sitting in front of a grand Gothic fireplace in the dining room of the House. The dining table could seat sixty, but only one end was set with places for two and a selection of cold cuts, smoked salmon, salads and bread which Clare consumed eagerly, discovering that she was hungrier than she'd thought.

David sat opposite her, picking more desultorily at the food. His body language, coiled and nervous, suggested a child on Christmas Eve, his eyes sparkling with anticipation while he tried to remain ostensibly calm. Clare didn't need to guess why he was in such a state.

'Look, perhaps you're too tired,' he said, aware of her languor. He said it in the tone of a man who was prepared to cut his own throat but hoped it would not be necessary.

'No, I'm fine,' Clare replied lamely. 'I'm feeling better now I've had something to eat.'

'Oh good.' David looked relieved. He had spent a great deal of time creating tonight's scenario and most of the week anticipating it. But he was a gentleman first and foremost, and if Clare had said she was too tired he would have had to delay his gratification with as much good grace as he could muster. 'Take your time, take your time,' he said. 'More wine?'

She nodded. He poured the white wine into her crystal glass.

'So who is this Bridget?' he asked.

Clare had broached the subject at the beginning of the meal. 'My boss. Boss of bosses. *Le grand fromage*.' She sipped the wine. Oddly, she found herself thinking about Gary, perhaps because she was becoming increasingly aware of what awaited her upstairs. The contrast between the spontaneous, cataclysmic sex she had enjoyed with him and David's calculated, scripted games was marked. She wondered where he was now. Was he giving some other woman the benefit of his considerable prowess? She shuddered at the thought.

'You're not cold, are you?'

'No. Just someone running over my grave,' she countered, trying to chase Gary's phantom away.

'It's been so warm.'

'I'm not cold really. This is delicious.' She stabbed another piece of smoked salmon and dragged it on to her plate.

'So this woman wants to meet an aristocrat?'

'Yes. Would you mind?'

'Of course not. Does she want to come here or

71

the London house?'

'Doesn't matter.'

'I'll organise something. Actually, next Friday I was going to have a little gathering in London. I was going to ask you to come. I suppose she could come too. The Duke of Tidmouth's going to be there. That might impress her.'

'Perfect. That's very kind of you.' She touched his arm.

'There's puddings,' he said with reluctance, obviously hoping she wouldn't want any, anxious to get on with the main business of the evening.

'No. Nothing else. Well, a coffee perhaps.'

'Absolutely.'

The butler was summoned and a maid cleared away. Coffee arrived in a Georgian silver pot on a Georgian silver tray with white, bone-china cups. The butler poured Clare a cup, knowing her preference for black coffee with no sugar.

'Thank you,' she said.

'Ma'am,' he replied curtly, leaving them alone once more.

Clare sipped the coffee and looked across at David. Now that they were only minutes away from realising his plans his excitement was visible.

Her feelings were more ambiguous. Gary's impact on her life had been more affecting than she would have imagined. She had tried to shunt aside her thoughts about him and what he had done to her, to catalogue it as casual sex that, while satisfying, did not touch the main stream of her life. But it was not as easy as that. Over the last three days she had found herself daydreaming about him in graphic detail, every moment, every second of their encounter vividly replayed.

She could see it, feel it, even taste what it had been like. She could remember exactly how he had felt as he plunged into her vagina, precisely how he had held her effortlessly in his arms. It was like she had been given a wonderful present, which she could take out and examine with huge delight whenever she felt the urge.

The urge had become urgent. Twice since Tuesday night Clare had masturbated and on both occasions had come ferociously as she relived the experience with the builder. She had deliberately recreated the conditions, masturbating in the bathroom, bent over the side of the bath. She masturbated on the bed. Both the places he had taken her. Usually she could extend her masturbation rites for a long time, luxuriating in the feelings she created, but the thoughts of Gary had provoked her too powerfully, and her orgasms had been achieved in no time at all.

She sipped her coffee, wondering what David had dreamed up for tonight. If Bridget had not intervened she might well have decided to use this moment to tell him their relationship was over, get in her car and drive back to London, ready for Gary's arrival first thing in the morning. But now that was impossible. If she could tip the scales against Paris by introducing Bridget to a real viscount then she had no qualms about doing it. She hoped the French Revolution had effectively reduced the chances of Claude being able to compete in this area.

It meant she felt obliged to go through with David's plans for tonight. Actually she supposed she could have used the time-honoured excuse of a headache. But there were two reasons she couldn't do that. One was the way he was looking

73

at her, like a puppy-dog waiting to be told it could jump onto its master's lap. The other was her own need. She needed sex. She needed it badly. She would much rather have had Gary. She would much rather have him carry her upstairs and throw her on to the bed and proceed to ravish her as totally as he had on Tuesday night. But Gary wasn't on offer. David was. And needs must when the devil drives . . .

'Do you want more coffee?' David asked.

'No.' She looked into his eyes, brushing the tip of her forefinger across her bottom lip.

'Or a brandy?' He didn't want to be the one to suggest it was time for bed.

'No, David. I think it's time we went upstairs now, don't you?'

'I'd like that,' he said. 'I just . . .' He hesitated.

'Just what?'

'If it's . . . I mean . . .' A cloud had passed over his face. 'If it's too much . . .'

Clare looked at him intently. 'If *what's* too much?'

'I don't want you to do anything you're not comfortable with.'

'I won't,' she said, getting to her feet. 'Give me twenty minutes.' She needed more time tonight. She wanted to shower first.

'Right,' he agreed, looking at his watch.

She walked up to the bedroom she had been allotted, a vast room on the first floor, over-looking the carriage driveway at the front of the house. It was appropriately called the blue room, although the name came from the colour scheme of the walls, carpet and upholstery rather than any sexual connotation.

Clare shut the door behind her. One of the

maids had unpacked the few items she had hurriedly grabbed from her house after work, and hung them in a vast walnut wardrobe. There was an equally imposing four-poster bed, the posts elaborately carved, its drapes a heavy and rather dull brocade. As she had expected, there were the usual gift-wrapped parcels on the bed, but this time there were three of them which David had sneaked away during dinner to deliver.

Judging from what David had said downstairs, the script for tonight's interlude was a little more complicated than anything he had suggested before. Clare was intrigued despite herself.

Clare stripped off her clothes. She walked into the cavernous and old-fashioned bathroom, the cast-iron and self-standing bath, the toilet with an overhead cistern and a chain. Incongruously, a modern shower cubicle had been installed in one corner. Showering quickly, Clare towelled herself dry on a large, fluffy white bath towel and went back into the bedroom.

She took the small square box and placed it on the bedside table, then tore the gold wrappings from the larger rectangular box. Inside were the usual layers of white tissue paper. Searching among them Clare pulled out a white lace unitard – a nylon leotard and tights combined into one garment. A neatly hemmed hole had been cut out where the crotch should be. The box also contained a pair of white, patent-leather high-heels.

The letter was at the bottom of the box. She unfolded the single sheet of paper and read the italic script. All was revealed. David's fantasies had always followed a pattern. They featured two themes, which Clare recognised from her own extensive reading on the subject of sexual behaviour. The first was what the books liked to call submission. He wanted her to dominate him. The second was an element of transvestism. David liked to wear women's clothes, more precisely, their underwear. Whether this was a separate strand of his sexuality or part of his desire to be submissive, Clare did not know or care. But it was there. She had often wondered if he dressed as a woman on his own, not just in silky knickers but in full drag, with tights, shoes, sock-filled bras, a dress and a wig. It was perfectly possible, she thought.

Each letter, each of the rituals they'd played out, developed these two themes, extending them, getting closer, Clare suspected, to the re-enactment of the event that had begun this strange sexual obsession. Tonight he had suggested another step towards it, though she was sure, from what he'd said, he considered it a giant leap. It explained why the third gold-wrapped box was long and thin.

Clare picked up the white lace and climbed into it. She pulled it up, smoothing it out over her legs. The upper half had full sleeves and a deep V-neckline, the tight material flattening her breasts slightly. The fact that the garment left her entire sex exposed, from the top of her labia at the front to the little crater of her anus at the back, made her feel quite aroused. The arousal was welcome. She wasn't sure she would have been able to cope with what David wanted her to do without it.

She slotted her feet into the shoes. The four-inch spiky heels tipped her feet into a sharp angle. She took her make-up out of her bag and quickly darkened her eye-shadow and refreshed her mascara and lipstick. She was not sure how she felt about doing what David had suggested. A good part of her, a part she would have to hold at bay, was not at all sure she wanted to go through with it. The rest of her could be persuaded, if reluctantly, that it might be exciting.

The tentative tap on the door came at exactly the appointed time. She wondered if he'd been standing outside counting the seconds.

'Come.'

He'd expected her to be sitting on the edge of the bed but she stood by the cheval-glass in one corner of the room. He could see the semi-transparent lace stretched over her slender, curvaceous body from the front, and in the mirror he could see the back too, the contours of her tight, round buttocks firmed by the high heels.

'Well,' she said. 'You know what to do.'

David hastily got to his knees. He was wearing a short, white, cotton robe.

'Good.' she went over to the edge of the bed and sat down. 'Now come here.'

He shuffled towards her on his knees as he had done so many times before. She saw his cock begin to protrude from the front of the white cotton.

'Faster,' she urged impatiently.

He arrived within a foot of her.

'Take your robe off.'

Immediately he tore the robe off his shoulders. His body seemed effeminate but then, she knew, she was comparing it to the rugged muscles of Gary's powerful physique. David's phallus was not as large either, though it was now fully erect.

She raised her legs and pressed the little horseshoe-shaped steel heel of the shoe into his right nipple. He gasped.

Clare's mood was changing rapidly. She began to feel a certain anger at the way she was being used. She tried to fight it back, using the sexual need she felt so strongly to keep it at bay.

'What do you want, David?' she asked.

'You know what I want,' he said in a whisper. this wasn't in the script.

'Yes, I think I do. You see that.' She pointed at her clothes. She had folded them neatly over a small boudoir chair. 'I want you to get my knickers.'

He looked puzzled and even a little alarmed. She had never varied the game to this extent. The underwear he was supposed to put on was in the drawer of the bedside table. But he decided against saying anything and crawled over to the chair. Clare had been wearing small bikini pants in black satin. He picked them up. They still carried a vestige of her body heat.

'You know what to do.'

'You want me to put them on?' The surprise in his voice was streaked with excitement.

'Yes.'

He got to his feet. His hands were trembling. He pulled the black satin up over his legs and hips. The panties were too narrow to completely cover his erection, so the upper half stuck out over the top. As he smoothed the material out he made a low breathy sound, the result of extreme excitement. He'd never imagined she would allow him to do this.

'Do they feel nice?'

'Oh yes,' he said passionately. 'So soft, so silky.'

'Come back here.'

When he was kneeling in front of her again she

tossed the long rectangular box on the floor.
'Open it,' she ordered.

He ripped off the gold foil and opened the box.
It contained a long, thin riding crop with a
braided leather handle. At the tip of the whip was
a thick loop of leather.

'Give it to me!' she demanded, holding out her
hand. He handed her the whip.

'Right, now get the blindfold.'

He did as he was told, taking the box from the
bedside table, unwrapping it and extracting the
black, silk sleeping-mask. She pointed to the spot
in front of her and he crawled back to it. The
elasticated waist of her panties was cutting across
his erection, digging into the flesh.

Clare held the whip in her hand. She had read
about men – and women for that matter – who
had a penchant for receiving corporal punishment and others who were equally turned on
by administrating it. She had never had any
desire to experience either. But the anger she had
felt earlier seemed to be able to flow out of her
through the whip. If this is what David wanted
she could use her anger to satisfy his needs.

'Put the blindfold on, David,' she ordered. She
wasn't following the script at all, but judging from
the state of his erection he didn't mind in the
least. He slipped the silk over his eyes.

Clare lifted her foot to his nipple, using the
pointed toe to prod it this time. Tentatively, as if
he expected a rebuke at any moment, he raised
his hand to her foot, gently bringing it up to his
lips, then kissing and licking at the white leather.
Resting her foot on his shoulder, as she had done
before, she held up her other foot for the same
treatment.

'You'd better do a good job,' she said. There was a line like that in his script. He wanted to be punished for failing to please her. Was that what the maid, who Clare suspected had been at the bottom of his obsessions, had done to him all those years ago? Had it been her sadism that had started all this? Or was the maid just a figment of Clare's imagination?

David's mouth was working up along her thigh. She crossed her ankles around the back of his neck, spreading her legs apart, her labia opening. 'Do it,' she said, not wanting to wait while he inched his way up her leg. He'd given her the power to command, so why shouldn't she use it?

Instantly his mouth plunged on to her sex, his tonguing darting up to her clitoris. She felt a surge of pleasure. God, he was good at this. Unbelievably good. He seemed to have an unerring ability to find the spot that produced the most intense sexual feelings, and manipulate it with just the right pressure and the perfect rhythm. It was wonderful. Wonderful. It was what she needed badly. She allowed herself to wallow in it, an orgasm swelling in her like the overture of an opera, sensual and gentle, not sharp and intense.

'Stop that,' she commanded, the moment it was over.

He stopped immediately.

'Not very good, is it?' she lied. That corresponded to his script.

'No. I'm sorry.'

'You're going to be.' The script again. 'Get on all fours.' She got to her feet. She imagined the young maid exercising her power over the young master, realising he was becoming increasingly involved in her games. Without thinking about it too much she raised the crop and slashed it down across the black satin that was stretched tightly across his buttocks.

'Oh my .god,' he moaned. His whole body quivered.

'Again?'

'Yes, yes . . .'.

She stroked the whip down again. It hit harder this time. He groaned loudly. Without asking she applied a third cut. This time his groan was squeezed out between clenched teeth. She saw his whole body go rigid and shake convulsively. There was little doubt that he had come.

How long was it, she wondered, since he'd dared to ask a woman to do this to him? Had he ever dared ask? Clare realised that she didn't care.

Quietly she walked around to the side of the bed and lay down. The ambiguity she had felt earlier had not gone away. Had it not been for a raging sexual need, she would have walked out on him whatever the consequences. But she was determined to have her own needs satisfied. She felt dirty. She hoped an explosive orgasm would wash her clean.

'Give me the blindfold,' she said, her voice level and unemotional. She held out her hand without looking up at him and felt the silk folding into her fingers. Quickly she fitted the sleeping-mask over her own eyes. The blackness was a wonderful relief, offering her anonymity. She spread her legs apart, wishing she had taken the time to strip off the ridiculous bodystocking.

David didn't have to be told what to do. She felt his weight shifting on the bed. He knelt between her legs, kissing her inner thigh until he reached her labia. His mouth sucked at her sex, making her moan. He dipped his tongue into her vagina, pressing it surprisingly deeply and wriggling it around. Then he moved up to her clitoris, finding the magic spot, stroking it with that perfectly measured rhythm, tonguing the little nub of flesh from side to side.

The waves of sensation David had always created in her began to change her mood, excitement reasserting itself over her disgust.

'Oh god,' she moaned, snapping her head to one side. And then, unbidden, he walked across the screen in her mind. 'Yes,' she said aloud. It was Gary. Naked. Tall. Erect. A smile flicked around his mouth, as he looked at her, a knowing smile, knowing her need.

Her body reacted with a huge surge of feeling as David's artful tongue worked on her clitoris. She knew she was going to come. She could feel Gary's body in her arms as hard as steel, pressing down on her, squeezing her breasts as that big cock nudged at the entrance to her sex. 'Yes, yes,' she encouraged.

She tossed her head from side to side wildly, lifting her buttocks off the bed, angling her sex up to him, wanting him more than any man. The phantom timed it perfectly. As the frequency of the waves of feeling got shorter, the time between the crests of pleasure reducing rapidly, and the explosion of orgasm crashed through her body, Gary surged into her, filling her, stretching her, making her whole again. Her body locked, her thighs clamped around David's head.

'Darling, darling, darling,' she cried, her body trembling helplessly.

Chapter Four

'GARY?'

'Who is this?'

'Clare.'

'Clare?'

'Clare Markham. You're standing in my house, remember?'

In the middle of a very disturbed night's sleep Clare had suddenly realised how she could contact Gary. He would be working in her house on Saturday morning and might answer the phone. She'd dialled her own number at nine o'clock in the morning.

'Oh right, Ms Markham.' He sounded distant and unfriendly.

'Clare,' she corrected. 'I didn't have your number,' she explained.

'My number.' He sounded puzzled now.

'Yes, so I could ring you.'

'Why would you want to ring me?'

That was not the reaction she'd been expecting. 'After Tuesday night I thought that might be obvious.'

'Oh.'

'Gary, you *do* remember?' she asked with alarm.

'Yeah sure,' he said noncommittally.

'Well?'

'Well what?'

'I'd like to see you again.'

His tone changed. 'Really?' he said brightly.

'Of course,' she replied. 'Did you think I wouldn't?'

'Yeah.'

'After what happened between us?'

'I just thought . . .'

'What?'

'You know . . . it was just, like, a one off.'

'God, Gary, it was wonderful. Wonderful. Didn't you think so?'

'Yeah. It was great. But you're a posh lady. I thought when you woke up in the morning. Well you know. I'm only a bricky. That's why I left.'

'We established every woman you've ever worked with has thrown themselves at you, right?'

He laughed that lovely laugh. 'Yeah, right.'

'Well I'm throwing myself again. Will you have dinner with me tonight?'

'Is that what you want?'

'Very much.'

'Where are you now?'

'I had to go to a girlfriend's last night.'

'Right. By the way, it's nearly finished. Another couple of hours. They're putting the carpets back right now. It looks great. What time will you be home?'

'Afternoon.'

'I've got to get home and change.'

'Good, so come around seven.'

'Great.'

'See you.'

'See you.'

He was right, Clare thought – it was great.

'Can't be helped. I'm really sorry.'

'That's all right. When did she call?'

'She called me on my mobile. There's nothing I can do about it, David.'

They were sitting on the terrace overlooking the sweeping lawns of gardens rumoured to have been created by Capability Brown. A large table had been set with a white linen cloth and a lavish breakfast.

'That's perfectly all right. You'll stay to lunch.' He was being remarkably understanding about it.

'Of course, I'd love to. As long as I'm back in town by three. She wants to go over our whole campaign strategy.'

'Well, ask her if she'll come to dinner with us all next Friday, will you?'

'That's very kind of you, David.' His kindness was making her feel guilty about lying. Not guilty enough to want to change her mind, however.

'And mention Philip.'

'Philip?'

'The Duke of Tidmouth. That should get you extra brownie points.'

'He really is a duke?'

'Yes. Created 1654. That'll impress her.'

'I'm sure it will.'

Clare was treading a delicate line. On the one hand she wanted to tell David the truth and drive back to London as fast as she could. From the way she had treated him last night, Clare was surprised David hadn't already guessed the truth. The truth was that she had crossed an invisible line when it came to her idea of what was and what was not acceptable. The disgust she had felt was not pleasant and not something she wanted to repeat. She was determined never to play any of David's games again. Never.

On the other hand, since David appeared not to realise how she felt, it suited her interests not to charge in with both feet and spell out her indignation. To be fair to him, he had tried to warn her that what he had planned might be one step too far. If she had not been so wrapped up in her own need for sexual gratification, she could have simply said no. She liked David. He was a gentleman. But his sexual obsessions were becoming more pronounced. If there had been a maid, or some other woman in the household, who had entertained him illicitly for her own pleasure, she had certainly left an indelible mark on him.

'So what do you want to do before lunch?' he asked. 'The pool's a lovely temperature. Or we could go for a ride?'

They had done a really good job. Not only had George Wickes kept his promise of being finished on time, but his men had cleared up the dust sheets, replaced the furniture and carpets, and cleaned the house. In fact, the house was so clean, from top to bottom, Clare wondered if he'd employed a specialist firm to scrub it out.

There was still the decoration to be done, of course. The new kitchen and bathroom had to be tiled, and her bedroom and the dining room where the walls had been knocked through had to be repainted. But that would be completed in a few days and would cause little mess. In short, her house belonged to her again.

It was four by the time she got home. Lots of time to get ready for Gary. She decided to start by taking a bath. As the new walls around the new bath were untiled she thought it would be wiser to use the old bathroom.

In the bath she lay quietly trying to sort out her thoughts and emotions. Such a lot had happened in a short space of time. There was Bridget and the presentation. They had not, as yet, discussed Clare's ideas on the advertising campaign for the launch, which she knew were diametrically opposed to the American's. That was a battle yet to be fought. Although taking her to meet David and a 'real live' duke would be a considerable coup, Clare was not naive enough to believe that Bridget's reputation for being a hard-nosed business woman would allow such incidentals actually to sway her final decision.

Whatever else happened on Friday night, however, Clare was determined she wasn't going to get into another situation where she was expected to perform with and for David. Somehow she would have to finesse her way out of that. And, at a later date, tell him what she had intended to tell him this weekend, that enough was very definitely enough.

She wondered if Gary had affected her feelings. Had sex with Gary not been so extraordinary would she have felt such disgust at David's demands? She had seen David through Gary's eyes, his sexual foibles forming part of the decadence of the aristocracy as against the dignity and simplicity of the working class. Clare smiled. She was even introducing British class distinctions into her sex life.

The thought of Gary made her heart leap. It

was ridiculous. She was behaving like a love-sick schoolgirl, like she had in the fifth form at school over Andrew Jenkins. She'd developed such a crush on the one-year-older sixth former that every time she saw him across the playground it would send her into hopeless paroxysms of joy, fear, embarrassment and sexual excitement, a cocktail of emotions that left her drained and weak.

But, unlike with Gary, she had never managed to have her wicked way with Andrew Jenkins, despite a few attempts to lure him into the copse at the side of the school playing-fields. Her passion for Gary was based on altogether more solid ground. The thought of what he had done to her created a deep pulse in her sex, right up in the centre of it, a pulse she felt she could put her finger on if she pressed hard enough just under her belly button. It reminded her of that odd feeling she had experienced as he powered into her, the way he had seemed to break through to a part of her sex that had never been encroached on before. That was where the pulse emanated from, that was where he had left his mark on her.

She sat up, the water washing off her breasts. Almost unconsciously she had been grinding her thighs together and her clitoris, trapped between her labia, was beginning to respond. She looked down at her nipples and saw they had knitted themselves into little, hard, puckered buds of corrugated flesh.

'Damn,' she said aloud. She stood up and soaped her body vigorously, trying to ignore its demands. But the slick of lather she created only made matters worse. Everything she touched seemed to have suddenly become invested with the ability to deliver a shock of sensual pleasure. She slid down into the water, to wash all the soap away, then stood up and got out of the bath.

It attracted her like a magnet. She took a towel and dried herself off as she walked back into her old bedroom at the back of the house. She went straight to the bedside table and opened the drawer. As much as she told herself this was absurd when she expected Gary in three hours, the impulse was too strong to resist. She took out her thick, cream, plastic vibrator. It was a straight cylindrical tube, ribbed for two-thirds of its length and had a smooth, torpedo-shaped top.

In a spirit of annoyance with herself for conjuring up the spectre of Gary, Clare threw the towel aside and lay on the bed. Callously she jammed the tip of the dildo against her clitoris and turned the gnarled ring at its base to set the vibrations to maximum, in no mood for subtlety. She gasped as her clitoris erupted with sensation, the hard pulsing frequency burrowing into it.

Clare held the dildo firmly, crushing the little nut of nerves back against her pubic bone. The sensations increased. She used her other hand to gather up her left breast. Squeezing the pliant flesh she pinched her nipple between her fingers. Again, not content with temperance, she used her fingernails to create more bite. She moaned as the stab of pain shot through her body, translated instantly by her arousal to acute pleasure.

Unceremoniously, her orgasm already beginning to build up in her body, she caught hold of her other breast and repeated the process. Again the pain provoked by the cutting edge of her nails was turned in to hot, throbbing pleasure, taking her closer to her climax. Thinking of Gary, as she had last night, she moved the head of the dildo to the maw of her vagina. She held it there for a second, just as Gary had held his erection there the first time he'd taken her; then, not able to resist her need any longer, she plunged the dildo up into her sex. There was no resistance. It slid all the way up on a flood of juices.

The dildo was a poor substitute for the real thing but she writhed down on it, as she used her other hand to manipulate her clit.

'Gary, oh god, Gary,' she screamed aloud. She arched her buttocks off the bed, offered herself to him, to the phantom who she seemed to be unable to drive from her mind.

But even as the orgasm was unleashed, even as the shocks of feeling coursed through her body creating delicious, intoxicating pleasure, even as she jammed the dildo right up her vagina, her fingers pushing it so deep the stub-end disappeared inside her, she was aware that it had not touched that secret place, the new special place Gary had discovered in the upper reaches of her sex.

She saw his red Toyota pick-up park a little way down the street. She had been waiting, guiltily, in the front bedroom watching for it, the love-sick schoolgirl unable to do anything else.

She managed to resist the temptation to run downstairs and fling open the front door before he'd walked up the garden path. Instead she waited at the top of the stairs and walked down sedately once he'd rung the bell.

'Hi,' she said.

'Hi.'

He was wearing a crisp, white shirt and very pale, spotlessly clean jeans with a pair of dark-blue dockside shoes. He was smiling.

Clare felt her pulse race. After a few days the details of his face had faded, but if anything, he was more handsome than she remembered. In fact he was gorgeous. His blond hair was freshly washed and his chin newly shaved. He smelt of a subtle, musky aftershave. His eyes were looking at her steadily, their expression a mixture of amusement and unease.

'Come in,' she said. Clare felt a momentary embarrassment, not sure whether she should kiss him or not. He was much taller than she remembered and she would have to stretch up on tip-toe to reach, so instead she touched his arm and led him through into the sitting room. 'Would you like a drink? Glass of wine?' She realised that, despite asking him for dinner, she'd prepared no food. Food was the last thing on her mind. They'd have to eat out, hopefully much later.

'I'd prefer beer,' he said. He seemed to be a little tentative too, shifting his weight from one foot to the other.

'Sit down then. I'll go and get it.'

'What do you think of the job?' he shouted through to her as she took the beer from her new fridge. She poured a glass of red wine for herself.

'It's great. I can't believe it's all so clean.'

'That was me,' he said. He had sat in the corner of one of the two matching sofas. She handed him the bottle of beer.

'What do you mean?'

'I stayed late. It really was a mess. Didn't want you coming home to that.'

'That was very nice of you.' She sat down next to him and touched his arm. 'I thought Mr Wickes had hired a professional cleaner.' She nodded at the bottle. 'Would you rather have a glass?'

'This is fine.'

Clare realised she couldn't think of a single thing to say to him outside the subject of the work on her house. They didn't know each other well enough for silence to be comfortable, so she scratched around desperately for something to say.

'What's your next job?' she asked, finally coming up with a topic.

'Fulham. House conversion into two flats.'

'That's interesting.' It wasn't. She didn't know anything about building. 'Is it going to be difficult?' Not as difficult as this conversation she guessed.

'Not really. Except there's an architect. They're always farting around, getting in the way.'

'Really?'

'Yeah. They charge the client a fortune for what a good builder would do anyway. It's a total waste of money. I mean, look at your job here. As long as you know what you want, who needs it?'

'Right,' she said.

The silence fell again, heavy and increasingly oppressive. Clare cast around for some subject to get them out of the mire. The truth seemed to present the best approach. 'Gary,' she said. His name sounded strange. She had said it so many times in her head over the last few days but out loud it assumed a different character. 'It's not easy, is it?'

'No,' he agreed. 'I very nearly didn't come.'

'I'm glad you did. Really glad. It's just that what

happened between us . . . well, I guess our bodies sort of went on to automatic. Our minds need time to catch up.'

'Is that what it is?'

'I'm sorry.'

'What are you sorry for?'

'You don't look very comfortable about all this.'

'I'm not. You're not the sort of woman I normally . . .' He stopped. She had the feeling he was going to say 'fuck'. 'Go out with.'

'Does that matter?'

'I don't know. It feels like it matters. We ain't got much in common. I mean I can't even talk like you. You sound so posh.'

'That doesn't matter either. It doesn't mean we can't be friends, does it?'

'Is that what you want?'

'I want to get to know you, Gary. If you feel the same about me that's the basis for something, isn't it?'

'You're very good at words. I'm not. They trip me up. I don't know what you want. I thought Tuesday was, well, you know, just a one-night stand.'

'Is that what you'd like it to be? I don't want you to feel obligated.'

'No. See. That's not what I meant.'

'What then?'

It was though he was having a debate with himself, trying to work out what to say and what to do, his brow furrowed and his eyes unfocussed.

'I'm not good at this,' he said, almost to himself.

'I don't see . . .'

Before she could finish the sentence Gary caught her by the arm, twisted her round to face him and kissed her full on the mouth, his other hand clamping around her cheeks. He pressed his lips down on hers and plunged his tongue into the warm wetness beyond them. She was taken by surprise, but recovered quickly, sucking on his tongue as she wrapped her arms around his back, feeling the same electric sensations she had experienced on Tuesday night, the awkwardness between them evaporating in the heat of passion.

'Oh Gary, Gary,' she muttered without taking her mouth away from his, her lips moving against his, the words almost gagged on his tongue.

She was wearing a light-red shift. In anticipation of what she hoped would happen between them she had not worn tights, panties or a bra. As Gary's left hand slid around to the back of her neck, pressing her forward on to his mouth, his right hand travelled up between her thighs. A grunt of pure pleasure followed his discovery of her wantonness, his fingers sinking into her thinly haired labia.

Without breaking the kiss Clare twisted around slightly so she could part her legs. Immediately she felt his forefinger moving up to the fourchette of her labia, delving under the little hood of flesh to find her clitoris. The search was short. Her clitoris was hard and swollen, pulsating as though to draw attention to itself. She moaned involuntarily as his finger nudged against it.

'Please, please . . .' she tried to say, not at all sure what she was begging for. He smothered the words with his mouth, sucking on her lips hungrily.

His finger felt rough and calloused. He pressed her clitoris as though it were the button to some strange machine. She found that it was, a machine that generated such a kick of sensation that it ignited the first stirrings of orgasm. He was not at all gentle. He was not at all subtle. He merely pressed her clitoris back with the tip of his finger, then rotated it as if tracing a tiny circle. At the same time she felt the fingers of his other hand parting her labia lower down. She was wet. Embarrassingly wet. If he had any doubts about how much she wanted him they would surely be wiped away. Two fingers moved together to probe the opening of her vagina. They worked themselves against it, but did not penetrate, scissoring apart to stretch it and create a new sensation of pleasure. Her vagina felt as though it were alive, reacting to this provocation with a massive contraction.

'You're so hot,' he said as he moved his mouth down to her neck. The feeling of his lips and hot tongue lapping at her flesh made her throw her head back, the sinews of her throat corded like rope. That made it easier for him to fasten his mouth on them, sucking the skin in.

He took his hand away from her vagina momentarily and fumbled at the top of her dress, trying to pull it off her shoulders. After a minute he lost patience, grabbing the material and jerking it so roughly the strap tore away. He cleared the dress from her breasts and dropped his head on to them, taking each in turn, sucking as much of the flesh into his mouth as he could manage, then concentrating on the nipple, sawing it from side to side, against the edge of his teeth.

Clare was coming. Her whole body was quivering. Exactly as before, his assault this time had been so sudden and unexpected, even though she had hoped it would happen, that it took her completely by surprise. She wanted that wonderful cock inside her again, but just the idea of it, in conjunction with the physical ravishment he was subjecting her to, was sending her over the edge. As his teeth created a delicious torture on her nipples – pain and pleasure so co-mingled she could not separate the two – her sex seemed to catch fire, the pleasure consuming her. His hands had gone back to her sex and she forced herself down on them as best she could, wriggling her vagina against one hand and her clitoris against the other.

'So good, so good,' she told him, when she was able to form words again.

'I know.'

He had no intention of leaving it at that. Even before she had recovered, with the tentacles of orgasm still wrapped around her body, Gary slipped down on to the floor at her feet. His rough hands seized the calves and pulled her legs apart, hooking her feet over his shoulders. She was pulled forward, her buttocks hanging over the seat of the sofa. He dipped his head and pressed his mouth on her sex.

It was what David had done to her so many times and yet it could not have felt more different. She gasped. His mouth was hot, and his tongue licked her like a flame, the lightest touch a shock. He swept it all the way up between her labia in long, wide strokes, using the full breadth of his tongue. She was so sensitive, all her emotions so fevered, she thought she could feel the nodules of his tastebuds acting like sandpaper against her tender flesh. It was not unpleasant. At the moment she doubted anything he did to her could be that. It was just another new sensation to add to the catalogue of them, each sending thrills of pleasure to every nerve.

She would have liked to have time to analyse it all, as she was in the habit of doing with everything in her life. But there was no time for that and no room for it either. There was no time or space for anything but the pounding arousal that was mounting in her again. She didn't have the ability to step back from it all, and try to work out why and what he was doing to her had the effect it did.

His tongue changed position, centring on her clitoris. He pressed it back just as his finger had done. But his tongue was hot and sticky and there seemed to be a pulse in it, blood coursing through it rhythmically, the tempo of it somehow matched to the frequency of the pleasure that was throbbing in Clare's body. He didn't move it at all, as though he knew what she could feel. And that was enough. A second orgasm broke free. She gasped, her fingers gripping his blond hair, holding his head firm, the feeling he was giving her so perfect, so precise, so wonderful she couldn't have borne it if he had moved even a fraction of an inch.

It was a long time before she came down from her high. At least it felt like a long time. Time was relative in this situation, prone to the gravitational pull of unremitting passion.

'Oh Gary, what are you doing to me?' Her fingers were still twisted in his hair. She let it go, then wiped his wet mouth with one hand.

He smiled and got to his feet. He kicked off his shoes, peeled off his white socks, unbuttoned his shirt and stripped it off.

'Let me,' Clare said eagerly, the large bulge that distended the fly of his jeans right in front of her. She leant forward, unbuckled his brown leather belt and unzipped the pale denim, his erection making it difficult. She pulled his white boxer shorts and jeans down to his knees.

The sight of his cock sent a new thrill of pleasure through her. It seemed to revive all the waves of pleasure she'd already experienced, like a tuning-fork setting off all the resonances in the same key. For a moment she felt completely thrown by the tremor of feeling this created.

Then she slipped to her knees and took his erection into her mouth greedily, in no mood for delicacy, sucking and chewing on it, then forcing it deep into the back of her throat, so deep she had to control the reflex to gag. She would love to make him come like this, she realised. For all her desire to feel him ejaculate in the depths of her sex, she would love to be able to provoke him so much that he simply could not stop himself from coming in her mouth. The idea made her sex clench of its own accord.

Gary laced his fingers into her hair, just as she had done with his moments before. She strained to look up into his face without taking her mouth away, trying to tell him with her eyes what she wanted him to do. She pulled her lips back and ran her tongue around the very pronounced ridge at the base of his glans. That made his cock twitch. She did it again, then plunged her mouth down on him again, sucking so hard her cheeks were dimpled.

'You're good at that,' he said coolly.

'Love it,' she managed to say, the words gagged on his cock. She sucked on him hard again, then began to bob her head back and forth, turning her slick, wet mouth into a perfect imitation of her slick, wet sex.

Gary gasped, swaying back slightly. But she knew he was still in control. 'No,' he said quietly, but did not attempt to move away.

'Yes,' she said, pronouncing the word against his cock. She brought it almost all the way out, then slid it back in, her tongue licking the underside of the broad shaft, her hands clutching at his bare buttocks now, feeling their hard muscles. His cock pulsed, swelling in her mouth. She felt his body change subtly, his level of resistance lowering. She might still get her own way.

Clare established a rhythm, sawing her mouth to and fro with absolute regularity, making sure her lips brushed the ridge of his glans on the outward stroke and then sucked hard on the inner. Her fingers dug into his buttocks. Without breaking the tempo she moved one finger down to the cleft of his bottom and searched for the hole of his anus.

His cock was slicked with her saliva. She used her whole mouth, moulding it to him, sucking on him, wanting to make it an irresistible receptacle for his spunk. the idea of feeling him jetting over her tongue and down her throat was turning her on so much she could feel her clitoris throbbing against her labia. Unconsciously she wriggled her bottom from side to side.

Her finger found its target. She pressed it into the little crater, and felt the resistance of his sphincter. The resistance was only momentary. As her finger slipped into his anus he moaned loudly. She felt his cock jerk wildly too. She was going to get her way.

Without changing her rhythm she slid her finger deeper, screwing it into him. She could feel he had passed the point of no return, that this last intrusion was more than he could take. His cock was pulsating, his spunk pumping into it. She felt it swell even more, every vein and contour of it rigid, ready to spit out his seed.

'You're making me come,' he said, his voice low and breathy.

Her finger was completely buried in him now. she twisted it around. As his cock twitched violently she jammed it into the back of her throat. Instantly she felt it kick again and a stream of hot spunk shot out from it, splashing into her throat. Instinctively she found herself suckling on him, wanting to milk him of every last drop of semen, her own body reacting to his ejaculation with a surge of pure pleasure mixed with a feeling of triumph. His spunk tasted sweet. She tried to swallow it all but there was too much. Some dribbled out of her mouth and down her chin.

Gary pulled her head back, his cock slipping out from between her lips. He looked down into her eyes. She could not read his expression. It might have been anger. Or was it lust? Roughly, with undue force, he took her by the shoulders and spun her to one side, so she fell back on the floor, her finger snatched from his rear. In the same instant he fell on top of her, rolling her over on to her back, her dress riding up over her hips. His jeans still around his ankles, he forced her legs open with his thighs and plunged his cock, glistening with her saliva, into her vagina.

Immediately he began to pump it in and out. Once again Clare was taken by surprise. After his orgasm this was the last thing she'd expected him to do. Her surprise increased the impact of his assault. Her body and her mind seemed to close around him, everything narrowing to the compass of her sex, focussed entirely on the feelings it was generating.

He thrust up into her, but he was not as deep as he had been before. Clare could feel he was not as large and not as hard, his cock beginning to soften. He was not stretching her or filling her but that did not stop him hammering into her, the strong muscles of his buttocks powering him forward.

And then the most extraordinary thing happened, something Clare had never experienced before. There, inside her, inside the wetness of her velvety vagina, she felt his penis beginning to grow. As he pounded into her, as her silky wet sex clung to him, just as minutes before her mouth had done, his phallus began to swell. It was the most wonderful feeling, not just physically but because of what it represented. It was the most graphic presentation of desire she could imagine.

Gary stopped thrusting. Instead he jammed his cock as far into her as it would go and let her feel it grow. As it expanded it pushed against the neck of her womb, stretching the soft flesh that enclosed it so tightly.

Clare's body responded with a storm of sensation. She could still taste his spunk in her mouth, still feel the impression his cock had left in her throat, and yet he was inside her sex now, as hard and as big as ever. No man had ever done this, for her and to her. Every nerve was registering that fact. She was completely overwhelmed, emotionally and physically. She was accelerating to orgasm so fast, so furiously, that she hadn't the slightest control. Not that she wanted any. She didn't want anything to get between the waves of pleasure and the effect that they were producing. Her sex was on fire. It had never been so completely filled, so ripe, so replete.

Where before his cock had broken through the secret barrier of her vagina as though battering down a door, now the secret hymen gave way with infinite slowness, pushed back millimetre by millimetre. Ultimately, after what seemed like an eternity, it broke through, his glans surging into the new territory it had found. Or that's what it felt like to Clare. And that's what made her come, a crimson tide of passion simply engulfing her, pulling her down in its undertow.

But that wasn't the end. It was only the beginning. Gary felt her orgasm ringing through her body like the vibrations of a bell. He let it pass, waiting until the last tremor of feeling had taken its toll, then began thrusting forward, his cock as hard as steel, harder, in fact, than it had been before. Her sex, by contrast, was incredibly soft and wet. He dug his hands into her buttocks, using his strength to lift her up towards him, despite her weight and his own.

'Gary, Gary,' Clare moaned. 'What are you doing to me?'

'What you want,' he growled between gritted teeth.

After the climax she had just experienced, Clare could not believe she could take any more. But almost immediately, as the sword of hot flesh stabbed into her, she felt her sex clamping around it, and a new shaft of feeling told her that she was wrong. Her body seemed inexhaustible, insatiable, rapacious. She found her hands were clawing at his small, tight buttocks, urging him on, the feeling of his muscles rippling with effort giving her yet another thrill.

It had never been like this. She was good at sex. She loved sex. She had had good lovers. But it had never been like this. She could come so quickly, so effortlessly. She proved it now, a third orgasm breaking like an enormous tidal wave over his cock.

This time he paid no attention to it. He had his own needs now. He thrust on. On and on and on.

Chapter Five

'DARLING, HOW ARE you?'

'Overworked and underpaid.'

Clare kissed Angela Barker on both cheeks then pulled herself back up on to the bar stool she had been occupying. Angela wriggled on to one beside her, the fact that this made the short skirt she was wearing reveal even more of her slender, shapely thighs attracting the attention of several men.

'The usual?' Clare asked.

'Please.'

Clare caught the bartender's eye and made a signal to indicate that she wanted another glass identical to the one already sitting on the bar in front of her. Angela had rung her at lunchtime and they'd agreed to meet in their regular haunt, a club tucked away in Bruton Place which was equidistant from Angela's office and Clare's. Angela had said it was urgent.

'So?' Clare asked. 'What's the problem?'

'No problem. Just an opportunity.'

'So what's the opportunity?'

'You know that builder of yours? That hunk.'

Clare looked at Angela steadily, hoping her face gave nothing away. She hadn't told her friend anything about the developments with Gary Newby. 'I didn't realise you were so interested,' she said.

'Come on, he's gorgeous.'

'So?'

The champagne arrived. They both raised their glasses and clinked them together.

'We've got this new photographer. He wants to do a session with non-models. You know the theory, new faces make more of an impact. I think it's a feature on men's suits or something. Well, what's-his-name would be perfect, wouldn't he?'

'I suppose so.'

'Come on, he's got a really good face, and his body . . .'

'Mmm . . .'

There must have been something in her eyes that alerted her friend. 'Hold on a minute,' she said. 'Is there something you haven't told me?'

'Well . . .' Unfortunately Clare found herself blushing.

'You dirty dog – you've fucked him, haven't you?'

The word 'fucked' caused the man at the next bar stool to look around and examine both women carefully.

There was no point in denying it. 'Yes.'

'And?'

'And what?'

'And how was it? I've always fancied a bit of rough trade.'

'Angela!'

'Perhaps I should have my house extended. Come on, give. Let's have all the details.'

'If you want the truth, I don't think I've ever had sex like it.' Clare whispered so the man on the next stool couldn't hear.

'See! I'm definitely going to get my house done. Come on tell me more. Did he have a really wonderful weapon?'

'Angela! Stop it.'

'Only asking.'

'So what about these photographs?' Clare tried to change the subject.

'Do you think he'd do it?'

'I don't know. I'll ask him.'

'You're seeing him again, then?'

'Tomorrow.'

'Get him to give me a ring at the office. What did you say he was called?'

'Gary Newby. Is there any money in it?'

'Of course. I'll go over all that with him. Come on, you've got to tell me more. At least tell me how it happened.'

'I'm not sure.'

'When did it happen?'

'Last Tuesday.'

'And you didn't tell me till now! What happened?'

'He was working late. I offered him a beer. Next thing I know we're in bed together. It was extraordinary. I mean I was just completely swept away.'

'Sounds wonderful. So what else?'

'I'm not going to give you details.'

'And what did you talk about afterwards?' Angela said pointedly. 'You don't exactly have a lot in common, do you?'

'I'm not looking for a husband, Angie. He's a nice guy, I like him.'

'And he's got a big cock?'

Again the man at the next bar stool looked round.

'Stop it. He's taking me out tomorrow night.'

'What, down to the local for a jar and a game of darts?'

'Now who's being a snob?'

'You're not going to let it get serious?'

'It's probably just sex.'

'Probably?'

'OK. Definitely just sex. I know what I'm doing, Angie.'

Clare had been friends with Angela for a long time. They had talked each other through many relationships and, in Angela's case, through a disastrous marriage. However much she would have preferred not to talk about it, what Angela said made sense. It was only a reflection of the thoughts she had had herself. The gulf between her and Gary was enormous and probably unbridgeable if she were looking for a husband. But she wasn't and it didn't stop her having fun with him. Apart from a few one-night stands in her youth (mostly when she had been the worse for alcohol) Clare had always selected her partners on the basis of personality and compatibility. But Gary was different. She had sex with Gary on the basis of a single criterion: her almost overwhelming lust. She had not cared, and still didn't, what sort of man he was, whether he was intelligent, witty, well-read or sociable. All she cared about was getting him into bed. Anything else was a matter of little concern to her. The fact that she had never felt that way about any man before was irrelevant. For once in her life careful planning and deliberation were not going to get her anywhere. If it all ended in tears, as well it might, it would still have been worth it. Of that she was sure.

'And David?' Angela asked. 'Are you going to keep them both?'

'I went down there last weekend. I was going to tell him it was over. Not because of Gary. Just because.'

'And?'

Clare told her about Bridget and her penchant for 'aristos'.

'Well, you've got nothing to feel guilty about, have you? From what you told me he's used you. Now it's your turn to use him.'

Angela's pragmatic attitude to life was refreshing.

'Yes,' Clare said. 'I suppose you're right.'

'What time's your flight?'

'Ten in the morning.'

'And you're sure that's all right?'

'Clare, I'd fly back from New York if it meant meeting a viscount and a duke.'

Bridget was sitting in the boardroom which she had converted into her office for the duration of her stay. Huge blow-ups of all the KissCo display advertisements had been framed and hung around the walls, the eyes, eyebrows, cheeks and lips of various models shaded with KissCo cosmetics and photographs in tight close up.

Clare had learnt that Bridget had decided to fly out to Paris in the morning and was not scheduled to return to London until the following Tuesday. She thought she'd better tell her of David Allston's invitation, feeling sure she would want to change her plans.

'So I'll tell him yes?'

'You bet. Where is this going to be?'

'He's got a really beautiful house in Regent's Park.'

'Great. And this duke?'

'Created 1654 apparently.'

Bridged looked almost stunned at that news. 'Jesus,' she said. 'That's before they discovered America.'

'Not quite.'

'I really appreciate this, Clare. I really do. You and this Viscount Bonmouth, he's slipping you the torpedo, right?'

Clare could have told her to mind her own business. Instead she said, 'Not exactly.'

'Is he married, then?'

'No.'

'What, he's a faggot? A lot of aristos are, I know.'

'I don't think so.'

'So you are having an affair?'

'In a desultory way. Nothing serious.'

'Pity. Jesus, I can't imagine what it's going to be like having dinner with a duke and a viscount.' Bridget's normal steely-eyed intelligence seemed to fly out of the window when it came to contemplating 'aristos'.

'They're only people.'

'No, they're a part of history. Real history.'

Suddenly her tone changed. 'So let's talk about Storey and Willis.' Storey and Willis were the advertising agency who'd planned the campaign for the European launch.

'They're good. Very good. They handle a lot of big accounts.'

'Like who?'

Bridget fired off a list of questions. Apparently

109

the subject of her dinner engagement was closed.

'Hi!'

'Hi!'

He stood outside her front door. It was Wednesday night and he was exactly on time.

'You look great.'

Not sure where she was being taken, Clare had settled for the little black dress. It was silk with a box neckline and a knee-length skirt. She wore very sheer and shiny black tights.

'Thanks. So do you.' She had never seen him in a tie, let alone a suit. The grey suit fitted him perfectly. It made him look older, and no less attractive. Clare's initial response to seeing him again was just as extreme. Her heart was beating so fast it made her breathless. 'Do you want a drink?'

'No.' He said it quickly. Clare sensed he was tempted to come inside but knew if he did they would probably never go out again.

'Shall we take my car?' she asked.

'No, I brought mine. Not the pick-up. Don't worry.'

'I wasn't worried.'

She switched on the burglar alarm and double-locked her front door. He led her to a Ford Mondeo parked a little way up the street. He opened the passenger door for her and closed it after her. As he got behind the wheel he glanced down at her legs, sheathed in the glossy nylon.

'I get this funny feeling when I see you,' he said.

'Like what?'

'Like I want to rape you.'

'It wouldn't be rape, I can tell you that. I feel the

same. Do you want to go back to the house?' She half-wished he'd say yes.

'Yes.' But he put the key in the ignition and started the car.

'Where are we going?'

On Sunday morning, after a renewed bout of love-making as energetic as Saturday night, he'd asked her if he could take her out. She'd accepted eagerly, glad of another chance to be with him, but she hadn't questioned him about what they would do and she still had no idea.

'The Key Club. You ever been there?'

'No.' She'd heard of it, though. It was a night-club frequented by the glitterati. The choice surprised her.

'Friend of mine runs it.'

'Really?'

'We were at school together. Lewisham Comprehensive. He's a real high-flier.'

'Sounds like fun.' She wriggled a little uncomfortably in her seat, finding it hard to control an almost irresistible desire to throw herself at him. 'Do you remember my friend Angela?'

'The blonde with the long hair?'

'Yes.'

'She was a bit of all-right,' he said.

'Well she's a journalist. Works for one of those glossy magazines. They're doing a feature of men's fashion and they're looking for new non-professional models. She thought of you.'

'Me!' He laughed. 'What, poncing about on a catwalk?'

'No. Just having your picture taken in some nice clothes.'

'I get to keep the gear?'

'I shouldn't think so, but it pays well.'

111

'Pays money?'

'Absolutely. Are you interested?'

'Yeah. I've never done anything like that before. Beats laying bricks.'

'Here.' She took out a slip of paper from her small, black suede handbag. She'd written out Angela's name, the telephone number of her office and her extension. She tucked it into the breast pocket of his jacket. 'Just ring her up and she'll make all the arrangements.'

'Great.'

He drove quietly, not trying to be macho by speeding or over-taking unnecessarily. They were driving into Knightsbridge past Harvey Nichols.

'Where is this place?' Clare asked. The Key Club had featured in the gossip columns of the tabloids, recalcitrant film or pop stars 'caught' escorting the new man or woman in their life in or out of the premises, but she had no idea where it was.

'Swallow Street, off Piccadilly,' he told her.

They drove down the Hyde Park underpass and found a place to park in Jermyn Street. He ran around to open the passenger door for her. It was a warm evening and there were lots of people roaming the streets, gazing, often wistfully, into the windows of the expensive shops that littered the area.

Gary took her arm and they walked up to Piccadilly. It felt good. Part of the reason she was so sexually attracted to him, she thought, was that he gave off an air of power and physical indestructibility. That made her feel protected. He was tall and broad. Even though she wore her spiky high-heels he was more than a foot taller than her. Both these things made Clare feel especially feminine. In a world where she had broken down the barriers of male dominance, and had paid the price of frequently feeling unfeminine, it was nice to relax back into a more old-fashioned attitude.

There was a queue outside the triangular canvas awning that covered the entrance to the club. Apparently there was no dress code. Men wore anything from T-shirts and jeans to Armani suits; the women an equally diverse gamut of costume, from full-length slinky evening dresses with slingback heels, to satin hot-pants and tank tops with Doc Martens. All were held at bay behind a thick, red, corded rope by two bouncers who looked as though they were refugees from defensive positions in American Football.

Gary walked to the head of the line.

'Good evening, Mr Newby,' one of the bouncers said, smiling and revealing a set of teeth of which a fair proportion had been capped with gold.

'Hi, Harry,' Gary answered cheerily.

The bouncer unclipped the red cordon and allowed them through.

'Evening, Mr Newby.' Inside the swing-doors a pretty redhead sat at a bow-legged gilt table. she was wearing a tight-fitting gold leotard, a keyhole-shaped inset of plain lace cut into the front of the costume. It exposed a great deal of the girl's full cleavage and her flat navel.

'Hi, Betty.'

The girl's eyes examined Clare critically. It wasn't difficult to read her expression. How did anyone get so lucky as to go out with Gary Newby, it said in five-foot-high neon envy.

Gary signed a large leather-bound register, then turned to take Clare's hand.

'Have a nice evening,' Betty said.

This was definitely not what Clare had been expecting. She'd imagined him taking her to some little Italian restaurant in Fulham, not the premier night spot in London. She'd expected him to be hesitant and gauche, not obviously relaxed and at home, and clearly well-known to all the staff. Clare gave herself a metaphorical kick for indulging in unwarranted class distinctions.

They walked through another set of swing-doors. The bar of the Key Club was large and comfortable, and heavily air-conditioned. The arctic blast of chilled air that greeted them was not unwelcome, however, after the heat outside.

'Good evening, Gary.' The *maître d'* stood at a lectern to one side of the door. She was a tall and elegant brunette, wearing a high-cut leotard that was designed to mimic a man's evening dress with a black jacket, a white shirt and a black bow-tie. The woman's long legs were sheathed in black fishnet, the cut of the leotard so high that the crease of her pelvis could be seen under the tights. The garment also necessitated a very severe bikini-line depilation as its crotch was not much thicker than dental floss.

'Hi, Miriam,' Gary said. 'This is Clare Markham.'

'Nice to meet you, Ms Markham,' the woman said, shaking Clare's hand perfunctorily. 'Do you want to have a drink or go straight into dinner?'

'Drink first,' Gary decided.

Miriam turned on her heels and led them over to a corner table, a semi-circular, button-back, red-plush banquette wrapped around a circular table in the American style. There was a white candle floating in a glass bowl in the centre of the table, the water strewn with red rose petals.

114

'Thanks, Miriam,' Gary said, as they squeezed into the banquette. 'Is himself about?'

'He'll be in later,' she replied. She looked at Gary with a smile, and Clare caught, for the briefest of moments, an expression of lust on her face. Then her more professional demeanour returned and she walked back across the bar, her long legs attracting admiring glances from most of the men she passed.

Clare looked round. Beyond the bar was a large restaurant, bustling with waiters. It was decorated in shades of blue, with dark blue walls, a pale blue carpet and a huge display of cornflowers placed on a table in the centre of the room dramatically lit by an overhead spotlight. The rest of the restaurant was dimly lit, with candles flickering on every table, their light reflecting off the sparkling polished glasses and silver cutlery that was set on crisp, starched, white linen tablecloths.

'You like it?' he said.

'Beautifully done. So tell me about your friend?'

A girl in the club uniform of gold leotard with a keyhole-front arrived at the table with an ice bucket containing the stout bulbous bottle of Dom Perignon. She set it down with two tall flutes. 'Compliments of Mr Furness,' she said, expertly opening the champagne without allowing it to pop. She poured an inch of the wine into Gary's glass for him to taste but he dismissed the gesture with a wave of his hand and the girl carefully filled both glasses.

'Cheers,' he said, clinking his glass against Clare's. He looked straight into her eyes, and Clare felt an extraordinary surge of desire. It was a reaction to the longing she saw in his eyes. She wished they had been at home, in her bed, with his naked body . . . She shuddered and her nipples stiffened as surely as if they had been touched by a cube of ice. She pulled herself together.

'You said you were at school together?' she said, pursuing the subject of his friend.

'Yeah, that's it. He was always two steps ahead of the game, but we were mates. He used to run all the school dances, stuff like that. We both left school at sixteen and he got a job as roadie to some pop group and he was off. By the time he was twenty he was managing them. They had a couple of big hits. He used the money to buy a club 'cause that's what he always wanted. He sold that a couple of years ago at, like, a mega profit and bought this place. It was on its uppers then.'

'He turned it around?'

'Yeah. And some. He's rolling in it.'

'And you're still friends?'

'Yeah. We still go out for a bevvy. Go to the dogs in Waltham. And the races. And I've helped him re-build his houses.'

'Houses?'

'He's got one in Hampstead, one in Almeria, and a place up here.' He pointed to the ceiling. 'Lets me use them whenever I want. He reckons he's going to buy a place in New York next.'

'A club?'

'No. A flat. That'll be great. I fancy it over there.'

'Were you ever ambitious?' She sipped the champagne. She kept getting the feeling that this was all a waste of precious time. Why were they sitting here making polite small talk when they

116

could have been in bed together, that hard, big cock buried in her soft, melting sex?

'Nah. Not my style. As long as I get my wage packet at the end of the week I'm happy. I don't want any hassle. I'm too lazy. I could never do what Mal does. He works all hours.'

'Mal?'

'My friend. He never stops. I wouldn't want that, not for all the money. Constant worry. Constant stress. All I got to worry about is me mortar going off. Life's too short.'

'I suppose so.'

'And what about you? You've got a good job?'

'Yes.'

'Well then. You must know how Mal feels. Like a treadmill, ain't it?'

'Stop the world, I want to get off? Yes, I suppose it is. But if you don't try you don't get.'

'Right. Don't get me wrong. I like all this. But if I had to really knock myself out to get it, I'd probably not bother.' He smiled, his life laid out before her, its simplicity making her feel slightly envious.

A gold-leotarded waitress arrived with two huge menus, bound in antique leather. She was plumper than most of the other girls and the leotard cut deeply into the soft flesh under her arms and around her buttocks.

'Have anything you want,' Gary said, as if he thought she might be inhibited to order the most expensive things.

They looked over the menu for some minutes, then Miriam was summoned to take their order. 'Your table's ready whenever you are,' she told them, giving Gary yet another generous smile.

'Great,' he said, getting to his feet. 'I'm starving.'

They stood up. As a waitress arrived to take their

glasses and what remained of the champagne over to their table, Miriam escorted them through to the restaurant. Again they were seated at a corner table, where they could survey the rest of the room. Clare spotted a knighted actor having dinner with his wife, and a well-known playwright with a woman who was very definitely not his wife. In fact the scandal of their affair had been all over the papers. Clare knew the photographers would be waiting outside to catch more compromising snaps. Angela had told her how it worked. Waiters at places like this were given a financial incentive to tip off the picture desks of the tabloids whenever a likely couple made an appearance. The restaurants and clubs benefited from the publicity, the papers got their pictures, and the couple in question found themselves in the gossip columns again. Certainly, Clare thought cynically, they would be disappointed if they didn't. There were plenty of restaurants they could go where no one would disturb them.

The service by waiters dressed in black trousers, white shirts and the traditional French, long, linen *tabliers*, was quick and impeccable. They brought the Caesar salad both had ordered almost before the couple had sat down, preparing it on a trolley in front of the table.

'So tell me about you now?' Clare said.

'What you see is what you get.'

'You said you've never been married?'

'No.'

'Anything serious?'

'Yeah, a couple of times.'

'And?'

'I chickened out. What about you?'

'Same.'

Gary had the ability to tell her all she needed to know in remarkably few words. With other men she would have quizzed them endlessly about their relationships, wanting to know all the details, but 'I chickened out' seemed to sum up his attitude perfectly. Perhaps it was the fact that their relationship was based on lust and the necessity for anything else had been pared to the bone.

'You're some woman, Clare,' he said. She thought it was the first time he'd used her name. 'I mean you look great.'

'So do you,' she countered. 'You're a very attractive man.'

'Yeah, I've been told. But I'm not in your class.'

'What does that mean?'

'I'm just . . . what did your blonde friend call me? Rough trade?'

Clare thought she might be blushing. She was glad the lights were so low. 'She didn't mean that.'

'Yeah, she did. And it's true. Mind you, I'd prefer to call meself a rough diamond.' He grinned. 'Still don't explain why you're here.'

'Probably pure lust, if you want the truth. Given half the chance I'd tear your clothes off and take you right here in the middle of the restaurant. I'm not sure I've ever felt that way about a man before.'

'Funny,' he said, his grin getting broader. 'I feel exactly the same about you.'

'So you don't think I'm using you to get my hands on your body?'

'Yeah, I do. You ain't going to go out with me for my brain . . .'

They ate their dinner quickly, whether because

they were hungry or because of an unconscious desire to get home neither could say. But Clare, unusually for her, waved away the dessert trolley and settled for a large cappuccino and a small Armagnac.

'Do you want to dance?' he asked. 'There's a disco downstairs.'

'Not really. I want to save my energy.'

A tall, well-built but slightly over-weight man in a white tuxedo and black bow-tie strode across the restaurant towards them. He put his arm around Gary's shoulders and shook his hand vigorously. 'Well, look what the cat's dragged in.' His accent had the same south-London burr as Gary's.

'Clare Markham, this is Malcolm Furness,' Gary said.

'Charmed,' Malcolm said, his eyes giving Clare a none too casual inspection. He shook her hand, rather stiffly. 'Do you mind if I join you?' Without waiting for an answer he grabbed a chair from the adjoining empty table and pulled it up at theirs.

'Gary's told you all about me then, has he? It's all lies,' he said, looking at Clare. He had a podgy round face, with thick jowls and small green eyes. He was bald apart from a horseshoe of hair around his ears and the back of his head, the hair loss making him look a lot older than his friend. Although he was not as handsome physically as Gary there was no doubt that he was an attractive man. He exuded a sort of sexual magnetism Clare was sure a lot of women would respond to. 'Have they looked after you?'

'The food's very good,' Clare said, conscious of her precise vowel sounds in comparison to the two men.

'Well, you're a bit of class, ain't you? Cut above Gary's usual scrubbers. Where did you find her, mate?' He held his hand up to attract a waiter's attention. One scurried over immediately. 'Bring us a bottle of shampoo, Gordon, will you? D–P.'

The waiter hurried away.

'Well now, isn't this cosy.'

'Business good?' Gary asked.

'Excellent. I'm thinking of opening in Madrid. Some guy wants to put up the dosh. Might be fun. You'll have a glass of shampoo, yeah? Before you hit the disco.'

'Actually, we were going home,' Clare said.

'Love it, love it,' Malcolm said clapping his hands. 'I don't think Gary's ever been out with a bird who said "actually".' He was laughing. Oddly it was the same lovely open sound Gary made. Clare was being sent up but it was impossible for her to take offence. 'Well, if you're not going to dance, let me show you somethin' before you go.' Malcolm got to his feet as the waiter brought the champagne. 'Can it,' he told him curtly. 'Come on,' he said. 'Won't take a tick.'

'He wants to show off his pad,' Gary explained. 'Humour him.'

'I'd like to see it,' Clare said, hoping it would not take too long. She had never spent so much time with Gary without sexual contact and her body was beginning to make its frustration felt.

Malcolm led the way across the restaurant and out through a pair of heavy double-doors. In the long corridor beyond they could hear the distant but insistent beat of rock music. They walked down to another set of doors which led to a red, carpeted staircase. At the bottom of the stairs there was another door, heavily padded with quilted red leather.

'This is the main club,' Malcolm explained. 'The bar and restaurant are members only but the disco's open to all. Within reason.'

As he opened the door, the noise hit them like an express train. A cavernous hall was filled with writhing bodies dancing aggressively to loud rock music, shafts of multi-coloured light flickering on and off in time to the tempo of the bass. Around the sides of the room a balcony had been constructed and here the gold-leotarded waitresses swayed between the tables, carrying trays of exotic-looking cocktails.

Malcolm led them along the edge of the dance floor. At the side of the small stage where two DJs kept the music flowing continuously, he used a key to unlock a small, nondescript door, just behind a bank of speakers mounted on a metal gantry. It opened on to a small corridor, its walls lined with cases of beer and soft drinks. At the end were the stainless steel doors of a lift.

'My private escape route,' he explained, closing the outer door, shutting out at least some of the raucous sound. He pressed the call button of the lift and its door slid open. They crammed inside and Malcolm pressed the single button on the control panel. 'Only one stop,' he said.

They travelled up several floors and arrived at the top with a slight jolt. The doors opened on a small hallway with a single door at one end.

'Home, sweet home. Gary did most of the work by the way,' Malcolm said.

He unlocked the door and stood aside, gesturing for them to go in. Clare found herself in a vast open space, like a New York style 'loft', round steel pillars supporting the ceiling. Three of the walls were stripped brick but the third was made entirely from glass and afforded a panoramic view over London. She hadn't realised they were so far up. She gazed at the vista, the traffic of Piccadilly at the front, with Eros and Piccadilly Circus to the left and the Ritz and Green Park to the right. Beyond that Clare could see Buckingham Palace and the Mall and the tangle of roads that led into Trafalgar Square.

'What a view,' she said, walking over to the glass, mesmerised by the sparkling lights of the city.

'Now we'll have that shampoo,' Malcolm said.

He switched on the lights. Spotlights were carefully arranged on overhead tracks so they lit different areas of the loft separately, creating 'rooms' within the whole. The spotlights illuminated the kitchen, the far corner of the room and another area, in the middle, where four huge and identical sofas were grouped in a square around a large glass coffee table.

Malcolm walked over to the kitchen and took a bottle of Dom Perignon out of a stainless steel fridge the size of a small car. He selected champagne flutes from one of the kitchen cabinets, also fronted in stainless steel, and opened the bottle with a pop.

'I could look at this for hours,' Gary said. He had come to stand next to Clare.

'Can we go home soon?' she whispered.

'Mal's fun,' he said, as if that were a reply.

Malcolm put the glasses and the bottle on the coffee table and slumped on to one of the wild-silk upholstered sofas. He leant forward to pour the wine. 'This is where I come to escape that bleedin' noise.'

Clare turned away from the window. Though it was in the furthermost recesses of the room and not lit directly, she could see a large, very low double bed. In the dim light she thought she could make out a figure lying on the ruffled white sheet.

'Well, here's to your taste in women, pal,' Malcolm said, handing Gary and Clare their glasses.

The champagne was delicious, cool and refreshing. Clare sat down next to Gary.

'Honey, you awake?' Malcolm shouted loudly without looking round. 'It's showtime.'

The figure on the bed stirred. It stretched and yawned.

'She's always sleeping,' Malcolm said.

'Hi, honey.' The figure got up from the bed and walked into the light. She was young, probably no more than nineteen, and tall, with raven-black hair so long it hung down her back and brushed over her small but pert buttocks. Her face was long, with high cheek-bones, a large, sensual mouth and big, dark-brown eyes. She was naked apart from a pair of tiny black panties, no more than a triangle of shiny silk attached to thin black straps. Her breasts were small, like inverted saucers, but her nipples were as big as doorknobs and each was surrounded by wide, dark areolae.

'Say hello to everyone,' Malcolm said.

'Hi, guys,' she said. Her accent was American. She walked over to the sofas and curled herself up next to Malcolm.

'This is Liza,' he said.

'I'm Liza,' she agreed.

'I pick up a lot of strays in my job,' Malcolm said, looking at Clare. 'I saved this one from a white-slaver, didn't I, honey?'

'You sure did.'

'A what?' Clare said in astonishment.

'She was being shipped out to Africa.'

'Are you serious?' Clare asked.

'Yeah. Perfectly. In this business you see a lot of it. She was working downstairs. These guys promised to get her a job as a dancer – that's what she is, a dancer . . .'

'Dancer,' Liza agreed sleepily.

'They gave her a one-way ticket to Cairo. Well a couple of my girls went the same way. Never came back. Never seen again, so I knew these guys.'

'He saved me.' The girl sat up. She picked up a glass of champagne and drank half of it. 'My saviour,' she said, running her hand up Malcolm's thighs until it reached his crotch.

'You see how grateful she is?'

'You're such a jammy sod,' Gary said.

'I think we should go now.' Clare touched Gary's arm.

'No, don't go,' Liza said with feeling. 'I love to dance.' She jumped to her feet, her lethargy gone. There was a hi-fi stacked in a black metal frame over against one of the steel pillars. She ran over to it and turned it on, a haunting saxophone filled the air, as it played the melody of 'My Funny Valentine'.

Almost before Clare realised what was going to happen the American had cleared the coffee table of glasses and jumped on to it, her body swaying to the music. Sensually she ran her hands down the sides of her body, then back up again, over her navel and her petite breasts. She squeezed and kneaded the scant curves. Her long black hair swung across her back, as she swayed her head in time to the music.

Clare's reaction was unequivocal. If anyone had asked her ten minutes ago what she would feel about watching a semi-naked girl performing an exotic dance three feet in front of her eyes she would have replied that the idea had no appeal. But she couldn't have been more wrong about her reaction. The lithe body of the girl and the sinuous movements she was making with it were hypnotic. She couldn't tear her eyes away from her. What's more she felt her pulse racing.

'Lovely little mover,' Malcolm said. He was stripping off his jacket and bow-tie, and unbuttoning his shirt.

The American brought her hands over her cinched, narrow waist and hooked her thumbs into the thin black straps that held the triangle of her panties in place. Bringing her knees together she turned so her buttocks were facing Clare, then slowly inched the black silk over her hips and down her legs. Clare saw the long slit of her sex emerge. It was pursed between her thighs, the labia completely hairless. With the black silk at her knees, she raised herself off the glass and stripped the panties away.

Gary slid his hand on to Clare's thigh. She tore her eyes away from the girl to look at him. His eyes were seeking her assurance that she wanted to stay. He found it, Clare's excitement obviously written in her face. He smiled, then turned back to the spectacle on the glass table.

The girl, kneeling on all fours now, spread her thighs apart. Clare watched as her right arm was pushed through between her legs and began to caress her buttocks, her hips swaying from side to side in time to the music, her head hanging down so her long hair brushed the glass. She spread the cheeks of her buttocks apart so Clare had a clear view of her anus, a little wrinkled crater, and her smooth, rather thin labia. Gradually working lower the fingers parted the folds of her sex deliberately exposing the crimson mouth of her vagina. It was wet and glistened under the bright spotlights.

Still in the same position, Liza drove one finger deep into her sex. She gave a little mew of pleasure then withdrew it, added a second finger and plunged them both back in. Taking both out, she bunched together three fingers and pushed them into her sex, their combined breadth stretching her labia around them.

Clare felt each penetration as though it were in her own body, each producing a stab of sexual excitement. She tried to suppress a moan but wasn't sure she succeeded. Gary's hand had worked its way up under her skirt and was clutching at her thigh, and she saw Malcolm glancing, casually, at the flesh he had exposed, then he looked up into her face and their eyes met. He smiled and she wondered if he could see her arousal.

In a graceful, balletic movement, the American slowly removed her fingers from her vagina, then lay flat out on her stomach, twisting around so she faced Malcolm. She inched herself towards him, sinuously like a snake, her generously curved buttocks swaying from side to side.

Malcolm shifted to the edge of the sofa. Liza reached forward and took hold of his knees, using them to lever her face up between his thighs, her body forming a bridge between the table and the sofa. Clare saw Malcolm's hand disappear under her head and a moment later caught a glimpse of his erect penis, before Liza gobbled it into her mouth.

At exactly that moment Gary's finger pressed up between Clare's legs. With the unerring accuracy he had demonstrated before, he pressed the sheer nylon of her tights into her labia, and found her clitoris, rubbing it delicately up and down. Clare felt a surge of pleasure. Her whole body shuddered. She hadn't realised how much Liza's performance had affected her. But Gary's finger was tapping into a source of sexual energy that had already been created. She told herself women were not supposed to be aroused by voyeuristic pleasures, especially involving other women, but it appeared patently obvious that she had been.

Clare had never thought of herself as particularly moralistic or conventional, but a strong, puritanical streak was struggling to assert itself. It was telling her that she should get up and walk out. She had never been in the same room with a couple in the throes of sex. She had seen porno movies – though she found them of limited appeal – but had never, in real life, seen what Liza was doing to Malcolm or, for that matter, allowed anyone to see what Gary was doing to her. This was turning in to an orgy and the voice in her head was telling her that, like her last experience with David Allston, it was going too far. But with David she had felt disgust and distaste. Here, now, she felt no such thing. If she were honest with herself, at the deepest level, all she felt was an overwhelming sense of exhilaration. Buried deep in her sexual psyche, there was also another strand of arousal caused by all this, that gave a new edge to her feelings, but which, as yet, she could not properly identify.

Gary's finger was relentless as she watched the brunette pull her head back from Malcolm's cock, then plunge down on it again. Malcolm was looking straight at Clare, his eyes focussed on her legs.

With the agility of an acrobat Liza pulled her mouth off Malcolm's erection, rolled over on her back and jack-knifed her legs into the air. She seemed to somersault over the gap between the edge of the table and Malcolm's knees and land squarely in his lap facing outward, his erection sticking up from her loins, as if she had sprouted a penis.

Clare stared at his cock. It was wet from Liza's saliva, broad and gnarled with large, prominent veins, its foreskin still partially covering the glans. As she watched, Liza took it in her hand and jerked his foreskin back, circling the newly exposed glans with her thumb and forefinger. It throbbed visibly and Malcolm moaned. The American raised herself on her haunches and guided the cock into her thin labia. With no hair to obstruct the view, Clare could see it disappear as the girl sunk down again.

Gary got to his feet. He stripped off his jacket. there was a huge bulge tenting the front of his trousers. He kicked off his shoes and socks and pulled down his trousers and boxer shorts. His erection sprung free.

'Lovely,' Liza said.

'What do you want me to do?' Clare asked. She needed help. She had never been in a situation like this before. It all felt unbelievably wicked and more wanton than anything she had ever done before, but the element of the forbidden, of breaking taboos, the fact that she knew she shouldn't be doing this, only served to increase her excitement. It was too late to turn back now, much too late.

Without saying a word Gary took her by the shoulders, pushed her over on to her side then rolled her on to her stomach. Taking her by the hips his strong arms pulled her up to her knees, facing along the length of the couch. Climbing up on to the seat behind her, he pulled the skirt of the dress up roughly. She felt his cock nudging against her nylon-covered buttocks, then pull back as his hands grabbed the waistband of the tights and pulled them down until they banded her thighs.

Liza had begun to bounce up and down in Malcolm's lap. Clare could see his erection sliding in and out of her, slicked with her juices. He had wrapped his arm around her body and his fingers were pulling at her big, fat nipples. Each inward thrust of Malcolm's penis into the obviously wet depths of Liza's vagina made Clare's sex clench in sympathy. Malcolm's hands had cupped Liza's breasts, and continued to pluck at her nipples. That in turn, made Clare's nipples pulse. Nestling in her black lace bra, they were puckered and hard, their arousal so extreme they seemed to be pulling at the flesh of her breasts, stretching it as taut as a drumskin.

Gary's hands were circling her buttocks, pushing her dress up to her waist, then caressing the bare curves. She could feel the heat of his cock. He gripped her by the hips and pulled her backwards towards him, the top of his glans parting her labia as it nosed into her vagina.

Clare's body experienced another shock of pleasure. Gary had made no attempt to thrust up inside her, and yet the sensations his cock created was almost as great as if he had. There were theories, she knew, about chemical reactions between some men and women. That was the only way she could explain the effect he had on her. She had had good sex before. Very good sex. But never anything like this. Sexual exhilaration flowed through her body like an electric current.

Gary lent forward. She felt his hand slide around her body and into her lap, delving into the bunched-up tights until it found the apex of her thighs. Her labia were already stretched apart by the breadth of his erection, and her clitoris was exposed. It was so swollen he found it instantly, pressing it back against her pubic bone then pushing it up and down as he had been doing before. It was exactly what Clare wanted. But then Gary always seemed to know what she wanted.

Her clitoris reacted to this new onslaught with a pulsating burst of sensation. She felt her sex purse around his glans. Since she had known Gary she didn't think she had ever orgasmed so quickly or with such consummate ease. The ability to manipulate and control the feelings that lanced through her, which she had used so effectively in the past, had simply disappeared. There was nothing she could do but allow herself to be swept along by the flow. And that's what was happening now. As Gary's finger moved against her engorged clitoris, dragging it up and down, Clare's body lurched into gear, the sensations of pleasure coming in waves, an orgasm already in play.

'Please,' she said, wriggling her buttocks against him, trying to show him how much she needed deeper penetration.

'Pretty please,' he said. His other hand reached

131

forward to her neck, pulling her head back until it was almost at right angles to her spine, then caressing the taut sinews of her throat. With her head up Clare found herself staring at Liza's naked body and Malcolm's cock, thrusting rhythmically into it. The sight only accelerated her passion, rushing her towards orgasm.

Exactly at the right moment, as if he were so attuned to her feelings her body had given him some secret signal, Gary plunged his cock forward with all his strength. Clare couldn't tell whether she'd come the second before this invasion or the second after it. But whichever it was, the feeling of his cock filling her again so completely created a new intensity, pushing her to limits of pleasure that tested anything she'd felt before. Her body went rigid, every muscle clenched, every tendon stretched, her mind blank but for a curtain of crimson that oscillated in time to the frequency of her pleasure.

It took a long time for her to regain her senses. Her orgasm had been so sudden and so intense it had wiped out her memory, like a deep sleep sometimes could. For a moment she was not sure where she was or what she was doing. She shook her head, trying to clear it. Liza and Malcolm had stopped moving and were both looking at her. She registered their presence with a shock, then discovered it was a pleasant one.

Clare was strangely calm, almost detached. She knew exactly what she wanted. And she had every intention of getting it. Her orgasm had put her in touch with her feelings, with that hidden, secret strand of sexuality she had not been able to identify. She knew what it was now.

Slowly she rocked forward on her knees. Gary's

cock popped out of her, a disjunction that caused her to shudder. But it did not divert her from her aim. Getting to her feet she kicked off her shoes and stripped the tights the rest of the way down her legs. Gary looked puzzled, unable to read the expression on her face.

Clare unzipped the black silk dress, slipped it down over her shoulders and wriggled it over her hips. She stepped out of it then threw it on to one of the sofas. She was naked now but for her black lace bra. She saw Liza's eyes looking at her body, and Malcolm doing the same, his head peering around the brunette. Slowly she reached behind her back with both hands and unhooked the clip of the bra. Then, like an expert stripper, she used one hand to hold the cups against her breasts while the other slipped the thin shoulder straps over her arms.

She had never behaved like this before. She had never done anything so blatant but she knew precisely why she was doing it now. The look of lust in Malcolm's eyes, and the fact that she knew Gary behind her would be equally inflamed by the sight of her naked body, was tremendously exciting. But that was not what affected her most.

Liza was brunette whereas Andrea had been blonde but there was something about her, something that, unconsciously, Clare had obviously recognised from the moment she had climbed up on to the coffee table, something that had stirred memories of her childhood friend. Perhaps it was her long, lithe body. Perhaps it was her eyes, and the way she'd looked at Clare. Perhaps it was the way she moved so sensually. Or none of those things, just the fact that for only the second time in her life, she had found herself staring at the naked body of another woman, displayed overtly for her benefit.

Whatever it was, it had jolted a powerful source of sexual excitement. Clare had kept that memory hidden away, not shamefully, because she felt no shame. It was just a secret, her secret. A secret she had shared with no one else, the wonderful pleasure she'd experienced that June afternoon on her birthday, something she could not forget. Fortunately it hadn't got in the way of her relationships with men; in fact it only served to enhance them, teaching her how strongly her body could respond in the right circumstances.

Andrea had never tried to touch her again after that. They had remained good friends but the experience was never repeated. Since that time Clare had never had another lesbian encounter, nor had felt the slightest desire for one. Until now. Now those particular floodgates seemed to have opened and a tidal wave of lust was carrying her along. She didn't want to work out why – that would have been fruitless. She knew she would never have the faintest idea. She couldn't have worked out how she knew Liza was open to such an approach either, but knew it for a fact.

Clare let the bra fall away from her breasts. They quivered at their sudden freedom. She cupped them in her hands and squeezed them hard, so their nipples stuck out more prominently. Then she took a step forward, hooked her hand around Liza's neck and stooped to kiss her on the mouth. As she had known she would, Liza kissed back eagerly, her tongue dancing against Clare's.

The first impact was marked. Clare hadn't

kissed a woman for so long she had completely forgotten what it felt like. She was astonished at the difference from kissing a man. The mouth was softer, more pliant, melting against hers.

'Well, look at that,' Malcolm said, looking at Gary.

Clare took Liza's hand and pulled her to her feet, Malcolm's cock disengaging with a plop. As the American stood up Clare embraced her, crushing their bodies together and feeling a new wave of passion. She was sure the girl would not reject her advances, but if there had been any lingering doubt it disappeared as she felt the way the girl writhed in her arms, responding with clear enthusiasm. She could feel the hardness of her big nipples pressing in to her own breasts, and the girl's thigh levering up between her legs until it was rubbing against her wet labia.

They didn't say anything to each other. There was no need. Both were high, primed by the men. Both had the same desires, perfectly matched. As though with practised ease they slid on to the sofa next to Malcolm, laying out full length on it, while their tongues and mouths remained locked, their bodies undulating subtly, responding to a rhythm that was buried in each of them, the beginning of a circle that could have only one end.

As Clare had taken the initiative, she continued to make the pace. Breaking away from Liza's mouth she licked and nibbled her way down to the girl's long neck, over her chest to her nipples. Breathlessly, her heart thumping against her ribs, she sucked the left nipple into her mouth, pinching it between her teeth, making the girl gasp. She transferred her mouth to the right and produced an identical effect.

'Oh yes, yes, that's what I want,' Liza cried, stretching out on the sofa, her arms above her head, one foot slipping to the floor so her thighs were open and her sex exposed.

Clare's excitement was intense. She licked her way over the girl's belly, the thoughts of Andrea, of that hot birthday afternoon adding to her arousal. She was out of control, she knew, and it didn't matter. Nothing mattered to her but her desire. Her tongue explored the American's belly button, making her arch her buttocks off the sofa, then dipped down between her legs, her mouth crushed against the girl's hairless, thin labia. A surge of sensation seized both women simultaneously. They both moaned, though Clare's exclamation was gagged on Liza's sex.

'Together,' the American said urgently. 'Both of us.'

There was no need to explain what that meant. It was what Clare wanted too. Feeling that strange calm that had gripped her minutes before, she got to her feet. Liza's body lay supine stretched taut by her need.

For a long moment Clare stood there, knowing both men were watching her, acutely aware of their eyes on her naked body and waiting for her next move. Liza looked up at her too, those big brown eyes pleading with her to finish what she had so unexpectedly begun.

And that is what she did. With her pulse racing, she knelt on the sofa and swung her thigh over the girl's shoulders, so her sex was poised above her head. Then she leant forward and, for the second time, pressed her lips into the brunette's hairless sex, lowering herself on her haunches so the girl could do the same thing to her. She had known how it would thrill her. But the anticipation was a pale imitation of the actual event. As the circle closed, a charge of pure pleasure shot through them both, at the same time. A line had been thrown back into the past and, as Liza's tongue, hot and wet, delved into her labia to find her clitoris, the past was reeled in, the intervening years fading away, the memory sharpening until it was crystal clear, a direct connection made between then and now, the one feeding off the other.

Their bodies were joined, their mouths and sexes connected, completing a circuit, their feelings, like an electric current looping around a cooper coil, charged up to a higher voltage. Every sensation provoked an equal and opposite response, the feeling of Liza's tongue artfully circling Clare's clitoris, somehow expanded by the fact Clare was doing exactly the same thing to her. There were so many different sensations it was impossible to keep track of them all. But, over-riding everything, Clare's mind was caught up in a maelstrom of images, memories of Andrea's body inevitably intermingled with the reality of how Liza's felt. Clare had deliberately stopped herself from using the memory as an icon of sexual pleasure. But now it was out, now she had given in to it, the potency of its effect on her was marked, expanding her consciousness of everything she felt.

Clare was coming. Clare was sure she'd come the moment their sexes had been locked on to their mouths, but everything was so exaggerated now, and so extreme, that her earlier orgasm seemed like nothing in comparison to the one that accelerated through her now. Everything she did to Liza, and everything Liza did to her, every touch, every caress, every delicate movement of tongue and clitoris was amplified in their vortex of feelings. So it seemed were their orgasms, their bodies perfectly in tune, every wave of pleasure mirrored and matched in the other, their mutual climax approaching rapidly.

Who came first it was impossible to tell. By that time they were barely divisible, their two bodies united into one, a writhing mass of flesh, heaving, sweating, gasping for air with the same urgency and passion, clinging to each other for support, knowing exactly what the other felt.

Clare hadn't really recovered when she felt hands pulling at her shoulders. She was only vaguely aware of being peeled off Liza and carried, bodily, over to the other sofa. The first thing that shocked her out of her enervated state was the sudden intrusion of a large, hard, throbbing phallus, burying itself in her soaking-wet sex.

She opened her eyes. Gary was poised above her, looking down into her face. His eyes were alight, wild with lust. He began pounding his cock into her, thrusting it as deep as it would go, his balls banging against her labia like two battering rams. For a moment Clare felt her body swoon, literally overwhelmed by sensation, unable to cope. But that did not last for long. Sharp, almost painful feelings took hold of her. Suddenly she wanted more. In fact, she wanted more very much and more of what Gary was so comprehensively giving her.

She glanced over at Liza and saw Malcolm positioned above her too, her legs wrapped around his back, his buttocks pummelling up and down.

'This what you want,' Gary said between gritted

teeth. It was not a question. His cock was twitching violently. What he'd seen had fuelled his need. His cock was always hard and hot but she had never felt it like this before. Despite the massive spending she had already had, she knew she would come again just as powerfully. She watched with fascination as Malcolm pounded into Liza. It was a mirror image of what was happening to her, being able to see what Gary was doing to her from a different perspective as well as feel it. The image excited her but then everything excited her. She felt Gary's cock swell and knew he was going to come. She knew also with absolute certainty that his ejaculation would provoke her again, as it always had, her seeming indefatigable body already on the brink of a mind-racking, nerve-jangling orgasm.

Chapter Six

AT EIGHT THIRTY the next morning Clare's phone rang, waking her from a deep and apparently dreamless sleep. It was Bridget Goldsmith.

'Look Clare, I'm sorry to ask you to do this but I need you to come to Paris this morning. We've got to go over some problems with Claude.'

'Fine. It's an hour ahead, right? I suppose I can be there by midday.' Her mind had snapped into gear.

'Come straight to the office. We'll be waiting.'

'Fine.'

Clare rolled out of bed and into the bath. In fifteen minutes she was dressed in a smart, lightweight grey suit. She drove her car to the airport, left it in the short-term car park and bought a club-class ticket to Paris on the first available flight.

There was a thirty-minute wait. In the lounge she dialled her secretary's home number on her mobile phone and told her of the change of plans, asking her to call the French office and arrange for a car to meet her flight.

She called Gary's home. She hoped he'd be free tonight. She badly wanted to see him again, and tell him that what had happened last night had changed nothing as far as she was concerned. There was no reply. She tried his mobile. That, the operator told her, was switched off.

Fortunately the flight was on time. It landed in Paris at ten to eleven, which was ten to twelve French time. A large black Citroën was waiting for her. Thirty minutes later she was sitting in the offices of KissCo on the rue St Honoré.

Claude Duhamel was a chunky man, with wild, bushy eyebrows and thick, wiry hair. He did not like Clare. She did not like him. Both knew that, in all likelihood, after the European launch KissCo would rearrange their European operations and one of them would be left running a distribution organisation with no responsibility for marketing. That amounted to a serious demotion.

Claude had picked up on Clare's declared strategy for advertising. Perhaps seeing that Bridget approved of the idea of using the commercials already running in America, instead of making costly new ones for each country in the EC, he had strongly objected to Clare's plan.

After an hour's discussion, with Clare's research on previous campaigns where American commercials had been used and achieved a deeply negative impact faxed over from London, they adjourned for lunch at Lasserre. A small lift took them to the first-floor dining room where, as Paris was hotter than London, the electrically-operated roof had been retracted, the whole room beautifully cool and light. The gourmet food was all but ignored, the battle raging between the two points of view, with Bridget taking a far from impartial stand.

Nothing was resolved. They continued the discussion back at rue St Honoré.

'Well, I guess it's going to be up to me to decide,' Bridget said finally. As usual she was wearing white, a trouser suit with narrow, quite tight-fitting trousers, and a jacket that buttoned up to the collar-bone, under which she wore no blouse. Her chestnut hair was tied into a rather severe chignon that made her look distinctly older, despite the fact her face was remarkably unlined. A big gold brooch, shaped like an Egyptian scareb, was pinned over her left breast.

'In the end,' Claude said, wanting to have the last word, 'it comes down to money. Re-making the commercials would be a gigantic waste of money.'

'I couldn't agree less,' Clare said.

'You've made your views clear,' Bridget told her.

'They are not just views. They are backed up by reams of evidence.'

'The examples you are using are not for cosmetics,' Claude said. 'They are entirely different products. The analogy is false.'

The argument was going round in circles, getting nowhere.

'So, let's leave it there. It's my job to decide.' Bridget smiled. 'The buck stops here. If you don't mind, Clare, I'm going to fly back to London with you.'

'Of course,' Clare said, though she did not relish the idea. It had already been a long day after a late night and she was tired. Sitting next to

Bridget on the plane would not be restful. Shop talk would continue.

'I hope you will think very seriously about what I have said,' Claude interposed. 'Not just about the advertising.'

'Give me the weekend. Then I'll let you know.'

The black Citroën took them back to Charles de Gaulle and they walked straight on to the next flight back to London.

'I wanted to ask you about tomorrow night,' Bridget said as they refused the club-class stewardess's offer of a glass of champagne, and opted for orange juice instead.

For a moment Clare's mind went blank. 'Tomorrow night?'

'The dinner, Viscount Bonmouth . . .'

'Oh, right.' She'd forgotten all about David. Last night had wiped that slate clean.

'I was wondering what I should wear. Will it be very formal?'

'Formal?' Clare had an image of Bridget dressed to the nines in ermine and pearls, with long, white, lace gloves and a tiara.

'You know, evening dresses?'

'I shouldn't think so. Do you want me to ask?'

'Would you? I'd hate to turn up in a cocktail dress when everyone else is in ball gowns. Do aristos dress for dinner?'

'They don't in the country.'

'No. But this is in town and he did say there's going to be a duke there. How do I address a duke?'

'Your Grace, I think.'

'Jesus. Really? Your Grace?'

'I'll give David a ring.'

'Would you? I haven't got a long dress with me so I'd have to go get one.'

'I'll ring him now if you like.' There was an airphone built into the seat in front of them.

'Perfect. Just got to go to the powder-room.'

As Bridget made her way down the aisle Clare took out her address book and dialled David's number. There was no reply from the London house and the butler in the country told her that David would be out until seven. She left a message for him to call her, then dialled Gary's mobile phone.

'Hello?'

'Gary, it's Clare.'

'Hi.' The line was a little echoey, a slight delay in the time the signal took to bounce off the geo-stationary satellite.

'I had to fly to Paris, sorry.'

'Where are you now?'

'In the plane on the way back.'

'So how are you?'

'Busy.'

'I didn't mean that.'

'If you mean physically, I'm sore.' She lowered her voice. 'Deliciously sore.'

'Yeah, I bet. You shouldn't have been so greedy.'

'You make me greedy.'

'Where does it hurt, exactly?'

'You should know.'

'I tried to phone you earlier.'

'At the office?' She'd given him all her numbers.

'Yeah. I got your secretary. I thought you were a secretary.'

Clare wasn't sure whether he was joking. They

had never talked about her job. 'I'm a very important cog in a very unimportant wheel,' she said, a little defensively.

'What are you doing tonight?'

'Nothing. Can I see you?'

'You're not too tired?'

'Are you?'

'I'm fine.'

'Come around to my house when you've finished.'

'I'm knocking down a chimney. I'm covered in soot.'

'I can wash your back.' And your front, she thought to herself, her sex suddenly reminding her of its existence with a strong pulse of feeling.

'Yeah? I might like that.'

Bridget Goldsmith slid back into the seat beside her.

'So might I. I'll be back about seven.'

'It's a deal.'

They exchanged goodbyes. As she put the phone back in its housing Clare realised her hand was trembling.

'He was out,' she explained. 'I've left a message.'

'Call me at the hotel, would you? I might have to go shopping in the morning.'

She unlocked her front door at six forty-five. Wanting to stay alert after her late night, Clare had not had a drink all day. But now she needed one. She went into her new kitchen. The tilers had finished the walls and floor on Wednesday, and apart from a little painting scheduled for tomorrow the extension was finished. It looked good but, unless she had managed to convince

Bridget Goldsmith of the efficacy of her plans, it would be her last extravagance for some time. Bonus-related pay was not a feature of running a distribution depot.

Opening a bottle of champagne, she took it through to the sitting room and slumped on to one of the sofas. The wine was too cold but that was refreshing.

She was just thinking about going upstairs to shower when the phone rang. As it was exactly seven o'clock she knew it would be David.

'Clare? Hello, darling, I got your message. I had to come up to town. I was going to ring you anyway.'

'Really? You go first then.'

'I just wondered what you were doing tonight. I've been out on one of my little shopping expeditions.'

'Oh.' Clare's heart sank. She knew what that was code for. More gold-foil-wrapped parcels. Worse, it meant David had not picked up on her disgust at their last encounter. She supposed it was possible that he could have taken her departure from the script as an excess of excitement, that she had finally begun to express her own regime of fantasies. She cursed Bridget Goldsmith. If it wasn't for her she could have told him the truth.

'I thought perhaps you might like to write the letter this time. I have to tell you, darling, what you did, it was wonderful. I've been thinking about it. You know I'm very stuck in my ways. I was a bit miffed at first. But, well, the more I thought about what you did the more I thought it was just amazing.'

'The trouble is . . .' She tried to think of an excuse.

'It would be a nice prelude to tomorrow night. Tomorrow night's special too. I think you'll be surprised.'

'You haven't forgotten I've invited Bridget?'

'No, no, of course not. I know that's important to you. But after dinner. Well, let's just say after last Friday I think you'll be very pleasantly surprised.'

'Look, David, I can't make tonight. I've just got too much work to get through. I've been in Paris all day. You know what it's like with Bridget here.'

'Oh.' The disappointment in his voice was obvious. He had geared himself up for another erotic interlude, an outfit for Clare no doubt waiting to be gift-wrapped. What would it be this time? A cheap red suspender belt with ruched black suspenders, and fishnet stockings, or incredibly expensive couture creations in silk as soft as the nap of a peach? Clare didn't care. She didn't want any part of it.

'I tried to ring you last night,' he said. She could hear from his voice he was pouting like a child whose favourite toy had just been taken away.

'I was working late.'

'I tried the office. They said you'd gone home.'

'I told them to say that, David. I didn't want to be disturbed.'

'Oh, pity. There's nothing wrong, is there?'

'No,' she lied. 'Look, Bridget asked me to find out what she should wear. I think she's got the idea that ermine and tiaras are statutory with members of the British aristocracy.'

'It's black tie for the men. Something slinky and long would be nice.'

'I'll tell her.'

'What about you, what are you going to wear?'

'Any preferences?'

'Red. You know I love you in red.'

'I don't have a long red dress.'

'I wasn't talking about your dress.'

'David!' She mimed shock.

'You remember that tight, red body I bought you. The satin one with the lace insets and the suspenders. You could wear that. And if you're wearing a long skirt you could wear stockings too.' She could hear his voice getting more breathy. 'I love to think of you sitting at dinner all prim and proper when I know what you're wearing underneath. You're so gorgeous, Clare.'

She remembered the red body. It was a silky satin, woven with Lycra so it clung to her like a second skin. The lace insets were positioned so as to veil her breasts and her lower belly.

'I'll think about it,' she said.

'I don't see why I can't see you tonight,' he said moodily.

'Please, David.'

'You could make it up to me.'

'I have got work to do.'

'What are you wearing now?' That was another piece of code. They had played this game before. It always started with the same question.

Clare sighed. If today had shown her anything at all it was how tight Bridget's decision about the European launch was likely to be. Claude's arguments had been so close to Bridget's view that Clare needed any edge she could get, and David's dinner party was a very definite trump card. If it were cancelled things might look bleak.

'Where do you want me to start?' she asked wearily. She sipped her champagne to fortify herself.

'Shoes.'

'Black. Patent leather. Very shiny. Very high heels,' she said.

'Very shiny?'

'Yes.'

'Tights or stockings?' His voice was thin and reedy.

'Stockings, of course.'

'What sort?'

'Fifteen denier, Very sheer. Very glossy. Midnight blue, with thick tops, very thick and dark.'

'Skirt or dress?'

'Skirt. A short skirt. Too short really. Too short for stockings. One of those stretchy ones. Clings to my bum.' She heard a sharp intake of breath.

'Colour?'

'Red.'

'Blouse?'

'White. Too tight over my tits. Satin.'

'A white blouse?' He sounded puzzled, as though something were wrong.

'Yes.'

His voice stuttered as he said, 'Bra?'

'Black. I know I shouldn't wear black under white. It shows. Everyone can see it.' She knew for some reason that especially excited him.

'What sort of bra?' His voice was becoming increasingly strangulated.

'Underwired lace cup with a plunge front.' It didn't take much imagination to guess what he was doing. Descriptions of female clothes always seemed to excite him, the more tarty the outfit the better. She imagined him standing in his bedroom by the phone, his erection in his hand.

'What sort of material?'

'Lace.'

'Pushes your tits together.'

149

'Up and together. Quite a cleavage.'

'Such lovely tits. Are you wearing a suspender belt?'

'Yes. Black too. Very thin.'

'Satin?'

She could hear him panting slightly. 'Yes, with a lace frill.'

'And panties?'

'Yes.'

'Black?'

'Naturally.'

'What kind of panties?'

The conversation was coming to an end. Like a lot of David's rituals he liked it to end in the same way. She had to remember what was required of her. At least, she thought, this was better than spending the night with him.

'French knickers,' she replied on cue.

'Satin and lace?'

'Yes.'

'Black satin and lace.' He said it with a sort of reverence in his voice.

Her next line was always the same. 'Like the sort I like to see you wear, David.'

'No!' He cried in mock horror.

'Yes.'

'Got to go now,' he said.

'Mmm . . . so have I,' she added as suggestively as she could. The line went dead.

'I told you I was filthy.'

He stood in the hall. His hair was so caked in dust it stood on end and his face was encrusted with grime apart from white patches around his eyes where he'd obviously been wearing goggles. His T-shirt and jeans were so dirty they would have stood up on their own.

'Fortunately I have a brand new bathroom, with a brand new bath and newly-tiled surrounds,' she said, grinning and trying to resist the temptation to throw him to the floor and rip his trousers off. It wasn't easy.

'They've finished, then? Grouting dry?'

'They did it on Wednesday.'

'Should be all right, then.'

'You can christen the bath. I've only used the shower so far.'

'Great.'

There was always a slight uneasiness between them on first meeting, she thought, or perhaps it was just that her overwhelming desire for him made it difficult to concentrate on anything else.

'Go on up, you know the way. I've opened a bottle of champagne.'

'Can I have a beer first to wash the dust away?'

'You can have anything you want.'

He took her arm just as she was about to turn away and looked into her eyes fiercely. 'You, all right?'

'Fine,' she said with a sparkle, wanting him to see she bore no scars.

'Good,' he said, releasing her. He climbed the stairs, taking the steps two at a time.

As Clare opened his beer, pouring it into a glass this time, she heard the water running in the new bathroom overhead. She was glad it had been such a full day at work. It had given her no time to dwell on the events of last night, or her reaction to them. The truth was she felt not one iota of regret and she had no intention of developing it out of some false sense of morality. Certainly what had happened was beyond anything she'd experienced before.

Certainly she had no desire to make a habit of it. But in terms of pure hedonistic pleasure she could never remember having had such a good time.

Clare had always been careful. She had not exactly measured out her life in coffee spoons, but she had dealt with sex as methodically and intelligently as she had dealt with all the other aspects of her life. She had never allowed herself to act on impulse. Until Gary, that is.

Gary's sexual charisma affected Clare in two ways. It had affected her physically. The orgasms he had induced in her at the drop of a proverbial hat had been shattering. She had always considered herself a good lover, good for her partner and good for herself, adept and sexually aware of her own body's needs; but what Gary did to her was something quite other. It made her feel that her previous sexual experience had been too studied and controlled – controlled by her. With Gary she was completely out of control and had been from the very first time, bending over the bath in what she would call, from now on, the old bathroom. She had not been conscious of doing anything, of making calculations as to what was or was not the best thing to do. Her body had responded at the most primitive level. Even the thought of what they had done created a response she had never experienced before, her nipples hardening, her sex becoming moist and prickly as surely as if it were a conditioned reflex to a physical stimulus.

But her extraordinary receptiveness to Gary had spilled over into other areas. It seemed to have swept away all her inhibitions. Admittedly, David Allston's sex-games had tested the frontiers of what Clare had thought of as acceptable, but his elaborate fantasies had been as nothing compared to the situation she had found herself in last night. And it was her response to that situation that had surprised her. As little as a week ago she knew, without the slightest doubt, she would have walked – not to say run – out of Malcolm Furness's 'loft' the moment Liza began to slither her tiny black panties down her long slender thighs. Instead her reaction had been total fascination. Just as Gary's sexual prowess had overwhelmed her physically, it had affected her mentally too, allowing her to listen to the wilder side of her nature – to respond, she supposed it was fair to say, more honestly, without the circumspection she usually imposed on all her actions.

The same motivation accounted for her reaction to Liza. It had been an experiment but one she had undertaken due to the new responsiveness Gary had inspired, the ability to react at a purely instinctive level. Not only had the experiment been a success in terms of her physical pleasure; it had released, like a genie from a bottle, the spectre of Andrea, a spectre that had haunted her for years. However hard she had hidden the experience from herself, because she had no idea how to cope with it, she had never been able to forget what had happened and the ghost could not be laid to rest. The excitement she had felt in Liza's arms, the feelings the girl had given her and she had returned in equal measure, and the powerful orgasm they had shared, had made Clare realise quite simply that she had nothing to be afraid of from the memory of what had happened with Andrea. The pleasure had been unequivocal. It had also been, more importantly, under her control. She didn't imagine she would want to repeat the experience of being with a woman again, but if she did, if another moment arose, she would not fear it, as she had after Andrea. Before she had feared that lesbianism was like a sort of virus that she might catch and keep. Now she knew it was just another sexual experience, another means of arousal, with no implications or consequences for her future sexual orientation.

She collected her champagne glass from the front room and went upstairs. The bathroom door was closed.

'Can I come in?' she asked, feeling a little foolish.

'Yeah. Nothing you ain't seen already.'

She opened the door. Gary was lying up to his neck in bubbles in her new white bath. He grinned.

'This is great,' he said, as she handed him the beer and sat on the edge of the bath. She hadn't had time to change and still wore the skirt of her business suit and a white blouse. 'You gonna get in too?'

That sounded like a good idea. 'Mmm. I think I will.'

She stood up and undid her blouse, suddenly feeling a little self-conscious. Apart from last night, when circumstances were far from normal, she'd never really undressed for him. They had rarely made love naked, their passion being so great their clothes had to be merely torn aside. She was wearing a pink jacquard bra. She unzipped her skirt and stepped out of it. Inevitably, it seemed, her pulse quickened.

'You have an extraordinary effect on me,' she told him. She pulled her flesh coloured tights down. Her matching pink panties had high-cut legs trimmed with lace.

'Nice arse,' he said. The triangular back of the panties was stretched tightly over her buttocks. She could see it in the mirror that had been so recently fitted behind the length of the bath.

'Glad you think so,' she said, trying to be casual about unclipping and discarding her bra.

'Nice tits, too.'

'Thank you, kind sir,' she mocked, sliding her panties down her legs.'

'You're not very hairy down there,' he said, looking at her pubes.

'No. Never have been. Do you mind?'

She stepped into the opposite end of the bath and sunk down into the water, stretching her legs out on either side of his body, glad for the moment of the protection of the mountain of bubbles, and congratulating herself on deciding on such a large bath tub.

'No, I like it.' He raised his leg and pushed his foot up against her crotch, wriggling his toes. 'You were really in the mood last night, weren't you?'

'I surprised myself,' she said, trying not to blush. She raised her leg, swung it over his thigh, and planted her foot against his cock. Her display had evoked the right response. He was already erect, his phallus only just submerged under the surface of the water. She pushed the sole of her foot against it.

'See what you do to me,' he said.

'You're very responsive.'

'So what? You into women too? It was quite a show.'

'Let's just say it was a one-off.' She didn't want

to tell Gary about Andrea. She had never told anyone about that. 'And what about you? Was it a one-off for you? Or does Malcolm often invite you up there for a little party?'

Gary grinned. 'Malcolm's a bad boy. I often think the only reason he went into nightclubs was so he could have wall-to-wall tarts.'

'You didn't answer my question.' She pushed her foot against his cock even harder, pressing it back on to his navel. She felt it twitch.

'We've had a few nights up there. He can usually conjure up a couple of dollies to do the business.'

'Like last night?'

'Don't do any harm. You enjoyed yourself, didn't you?'

'I thought that was obvious.'

'I've never been out with a bird like you.'

'Fucked or dated?' Clare asked pointedly.

Gary laughed. 'See. Real smart. Dated, then. Some of Mal's birds were classy little pieces.'

'Is that what I am?'

'Yeah. Posh. Educated. Smart.'

'Does it make any difference?'

'Not to me. It does to you, though.'

'Does it?'

'It makes things a lot easier.'

'Easier?'

'Yeah. With me you get what you see. A bit of a laugh and a good fuck. No complications. No problems.'

'What sort of problems?'

He pushed his big toe between her labia. The water had washed away all the natural lubrication she knew she had been producing since he walked into her house, and her sex felt a bit dry.

'You know. If I was like you – I mean if I was some bloke with a degree and a plum in his mouth with his rabbit, and a good job behind some desk . . .'

'What?'

'Well then you'd immediately be thinking that was it. You know. Marriage. Kids and the like. With me you ain't got none of that.'

'Don't I?'

'Oh come on, love. No point pretending. This ain't ever going to go anywhere. A bit of a laugh and a good seeing-to. That's it. End of story.'

Clare looked at him. He was smiling, the corner of his eyes wrinkled up by his amusement. She thought he was probably the most beautiful man she'd ever seen in her life. Almost unconsciously she wriggled her bottom so her clitoris butted up against his toe. He was right, of course, completely right. There was no point pretending. Realistically, though she hadn't thought it through, there was no long-term future in their relationship. They had nothing in common apart from sex. That didn't mean, in the short term, they didn't have a very healthy mutual interest in each other. There was something very freeing about being involved with a man for such narrow reasons, no actions held to account at a later date, no worries about what might or might not go wrong.

'And what if I told you I was in love with you?' she asked coquettishly.

'You're not. And you won't be.'

'I'm in lust with you.'

'Yeah. Great, ain't it?' He moved his foot. Miraculously his big toe found the opening to her vagina. It had been sealed by the water, dry and

157

unyielding, but he pushed forward until the seal broke. Beyond, where the water had not penetrated, was a well of hot, sticky juices.

Clare moaned. 'So what's going to happen?'

'You'll get bored or I'll get bored.'

'As simple as that.'

'Life's too bleedin' complicated as it is without making it worse.'

It was Clare's turn to laugh. Gary's total lack of ambition, his contentment with his lot and his reluctance to allow emotional complications to disturb practical considerations were deeply rooted in his personality. His feet were planted firmly on the ground and no 'tart' was going to change that, certainly not one with a plum in her mouth and a good job.

'This is the first time we haven't just thrown ourselves at each other,' she said.

'I had my protection on. Dust and baked-on sweat.'

'But now you're all squeaky clean . . .' She rubbed the sole of her foot up and down his cock. 'I want to show you something,' she said, having an idea. She got to her feet, the water running from her body, his toe unplugged from her sex. Drying herself perfunctorily on one of the big fluffy bath towels that were draped over the new towel rail, she marched into the bedroom through the doorway Gary had built.

'So what's all this?' he asked, coming out of the bathroom with a towel in his hand, his erection sticking out in front of him.

'This,' she said. She stripped off the counterpane and lay on her back on the white undersheet. Twisting around to her bedside table she opened the drawer and extracted her vibrator.

'I want you to watch.'

Gary looked puzzled. He was standing at the foot of the bed. Clare stretched her left leg over to him and touched her foot against his knee, then spread both her legs wide apart. She pushed the tip of the dildo down between her labia, until it was resting against her clitoris, and then switched it on, the hum of its vibrations filling the air.

Gary's eyes locked on her sex. She used her spare hand to squeeze at her right breast. 'Mmm . . . feels good,' she said, undulating her hips.

'Do you do this a lot?' he asked. His erection seemed to be pointing directly at her.

'What, use the vibrator or let men see me doing it?'

'Both.'

'I use the vibrator a lot.' She raised her buttocks off the bed, slid the tip of the vibrator down her labia and then pushed it into her vagina. Very slowly she let him see it disappearing into her sex. The look in his eyes excited her. Her sex was thoroughly wet now. As she drew the vibrator out she knew it would be slicked with her juices. 'But I'm very particular about who I let watch,' she said.

'Christ, look at that,' he said as the dildo slid back up, her labia pursed around it.

The vibrations began to affect her. She groaned as the dildo filled her, the strong oscillations somehow matched to the frequency of pleasure already coursing through her body. The dildo was not a substitute for that big, thick cock she could see right in front of her, but she was excited by what she was doing and the way she had got Gary to stare at her so intently.

'I get hungry, you see,' she said, sawing the dildo in and out more rapidly.

159

Gary's fist circled his cock. He held it tightly, making the protruding glans swell.

Clare pulled the dildo right out of her vagina and centred it on her clitoris again. The sudden concentration of vibrations on the little nub of nerves produced a wave of pleasure that made her roll her eyes closed.

'You bitch,' he said, with no venom in his voice. 'You little bitch.'

She opened her eyes again. Gary wasn't looking at her sex now. He was staring into her face as if all this contained a meaning he was struggling to understand. After last night she couldn't believe he was shocked, but that would have been one way to read his expression. Then, almost as quickly as it had appeared, the shadow of doubt, or concern, or whatever it was, evaporated. He was not good at being passive. He was a doer, not a watcher.

Clare supposed, at least unconsciously, that what happened next was what she'd been trying to provoke. In one fluid movement Gary sprung forward, took hold of both Clare's wrists, stretched them out above her head, pinioning her by them, his lean, muscular body pressing down on top of her. His rock-hard erection slipped between her legs. Raising his hips he guided his glans into her labia, forcing them apart just as the dildo had done.

'Oh Gary.' The contrast with the dildo was marked. It had been cold and inanimate. His cock was hot and large and pulsing with life.

He stretched her arms out above her head until her sinews were taut. He opened his legs using his ankles to spread her legs further apart too, spread-eagling her flat across the bed, his cock at the centre of the X their bodies formed. He raised his hips so he was arched up over her, and only the tip of his cock was touching her clitoris. Then he jerked his cock, making it move against her. That was enough to make her shudder, her sex contracting like a fish gasping for air.

'Let me have it,' she begged.

'What do you want? Me or that thing?'

'You, of course.' She was confused. He couldn't possibly imagine she preferred the dildo to him.

He stayed as he was, his body rigid, poised above her, all his strength concentrated on spreading her limbs apart. His cock brushed her clitoris with an infuriating lightness of touch.

'*Please.*'

She had never wanted him so much. She could feel every inch of her empty vagina and every inch of it wanted to be filled by him. It was a void, an aching void, needing him to make it complete. She tried to raise her head, to struggle up but with no arms to use for leverage she made little impression on his iron grip. The feeling of his body, of his sinewy, corded muscle gave her need another cruel twist.

'Please!' she said, her tone angry not begging.

Suddenly, with almost brutal force, his body collapsed on top of her, his legs scissored together, his cock driving up into her so forcefully his pelvis hammered against her labia. As she had always felt with him, the meat of his cock filled her completely, causing a sensation of pure pleasure so strong she could do nothing but wallow in it. Her sex recovered quickly, wrapping itself around the intruder in a convulsive spasm, clinging tightly to every inch of the hard, unyielding flesh.

Clare thought she could wrestle herself back

161

under control after the initial impact, and she could have done, had Gary pulled out of her, even slightly. But he did not. Instead, his body as rigid as a board, he focussed his energy on forcing his phallus even deeper into her, his glans pressing up against the neck of her womb. His strength was such that as he arched his body like a bow, his arms straight and supporting his weight, he was actually dragging her off the bed too, her sex hooked on his cock.

She had never felt him so deep, nor his body so taut. She wrapped her arms around his back, and pushed herself down on him, wanting what he wanted, her senses reeling, her orgasm breaking like a wave over the hardness impaled inside her. She rolled her head from side to side, making a peculiar baying sound she had never heard herself make before, her orgasm radiating out from her sex. It did not fade. Like a thunderstorm caught in a valley, it came round again, each streak of lightning no more or less intense than the last, each clap of thunder making her whole body tremble and quake.

It went on forever. It was still rolling through her body when she felt him relax back on the bed, his grip on her limbs slackening, his buttocks starting to rise and fall, plunging his cock in and out like a piston rod. It didn't take long for this new strategy to affect her as much as the old. As he pumped into her, each forward thrust creating that strange illusion of breaking through that secret barrier in her sex, her nerves girded themselves for another onslaught.

Her hands raked his back. She dug her fingers into his buttocks, wanting to feel his pounding muscles. He turned his head and kissed her hard on the mouth, thrusting his tongue between her lips, its heat a match for the heat of his cock, an electrical connection established between the two, using her body as its helpless conduit. Again she was propelled into a heady orgasm, or was it just the same one, extended and intensified until it felt like something new? She didn't know or care.

'Oh Gary, Gary, what are you doing to me?'

He didn't stop. He hammered on. Perhaps he felt she was not finished, sensed that she could come again. Or perhaps it was his own need that drove him forward so relentlessly, all the way in and practically all the way out, the base of his shaft grinding against her clitoris on the inward stroke. Whatever the motivation she came yet again, a sharp, almost painful shock of pleasure emanating from her beleaguered clitoris, completely different from the last two orgasms and yet essentially the same.

Gary stopped. He pulled out of her and rolled to one side.

'Turn over,' he ordered.

'Can't,' she muttered. It was true. Her body wouldn't respond.

He took hold of her and turned her over on to her stomach. Kneeling behind her, he took hold of her hips and pulled her up to her knees, just as he had last night on Malcolm Furness's sofa. He looked around for the vibrator.

The feeling of his hot, sticky cock nestling itself into the cleft of her buttocks revived her.

'Aren't you going to come?'

'Yes,' he replied.

Every time Gary had come inside her before it had made her come again. But this time she was not so sure it would have the same effect. After last night and what he'd done to her already this evening, she felt as though she were satiated. She couldn't have been more wrong.

His hands held her buttocks. He was spreading them apart, looking down at her reddened labia, and the little, perfectly circular hole of her anus. A lot of Clare's juices had run down between her legs and the cleft of her buttocks were wet. Slowly he pressed his glans against the corrugated flesh.

Clare knew at once what he intended. 'No,' she said sharply.

'Yes,' he insisted.

'Gary, I can't.' She felt a shudder of fear. Men had tried to have anal sex with her before. She had always refused them. The trouble was she didn't want to refuse Gary. 'I've never done it,' she told him.

'I want it,' he said quietly.

The desire in his voice excited her. The single most exciting thing about Gary was probably the fact that he so self-evidently desired her so much. The fear Clare felt transmogrified into something more complex. Whatever else she was feeling, Clare's lethargy had disappeared.

'Be gentle,' she said.

He pressed forward. She felt the little ring of muscles resist. For an instant she had the desire to pull away, yet she held her nerve. She knew there was bound to be pain, but everything Gary had done to her before had brought her tremendous pleasure so she was prepared to believe that this would too. She tried to relax.

'Try,' he said.

She made a conscious effort. He felt her body give way. He pressed forward and watched as his glans sank into her.

Clare felt a shock of pain that took her breath away. Her body tensed again, all her nerves screaming in protest. But almost immediately the wave of pain was translated into a surge of pleasure, a sort of pleasure that, even bearing in mind the extremes she had experienced in the last few days, she had never felt before. It was a pleasure on the same wavelength as pain and of the same incredible intensity, one barely distinguishable from the other.

Clare braced herself again. Gary had hardly penetrated her at all and he was readying himself for a second thrust.

'Love it,' he said. His hands grasped her hips. The wetness of her juices had lubricated his cock. He thrust forward hard, the breadth of him stretching her, his excitement all the greater for knowing he was the first to do this to her. His cock slid deeper, then, with another push, as deep as it would go.

Clare gasped. Another wave of pain rushed through her but this time she knew what to expect. Just as instantly as before, the pain mutated to quite extraordinary pleasure, wave upon wave of it. And then, among all the feelings that invaded her, in the mass of new sensations that having a big hard cock buried in her rear for the first time, produced in her, she felt another burgeoning emotion: relief. Her fear had been unjustified. There was pain but it was far outweighed by swelling, orchestrated pleasure.

Tentatively she pushed back against him. His cock twitched inside her. She seemed to be able to feel every inch of it, the smoothness of his glans and the ridge underneath it, though she was sure that was just her imagination playing tricks in her over-heated mind. The pain was now no more than a tingle of discomfort, and that was overlaid with a flood of passion. It was good. She had never thought it would be but it was wonderfully sexy. She wriggled her bum from side to side and experienced a whole new range of thrills.

Gary leant forward. She felt his hand snake under her belly. Something hard pressed up into her labia. It found the opening of her vagina and was inside her before she realised what it was. He'd found the vibrator and used it to invade her sex. Her whole body heaved, the two phalluses buried inside her, divided only by the thin membranes of her body. So much of what Gary had done to her was like nothing she'd ever experienced before, in extent if not in fact. But this was both. Not only had she never had anal sex, she had never had two phalluses inside her at the same time. Her rear passage seemed to be able to deliver pleasure with as great an impact as her vagina. Gary's cock had filled her but this feeling doubled that sensation. Her body had never been so stretched, her nerves hardly able to cope with the intensity of it all. There was nothing else. The only reality was the two phalluses and the two passages of her body that clung to them, and her clitoris pulsating wildly.

Just as she thought she could feel no more, more came. Gary turned the control of the vibrator and its familiar vibrations began to pummel at her. As quickly as if someone had flicked a switch Clare felt herself coming, a huge current of sensation, a tidal wave of passion, about to break over her.

But there was more. The vibrator imparted its

oscillations to Gary's cock, as they were pressed so closely together. The two vibrated in harmony but Gary's cock also began to jerk forcefully against the tight confines that imprisoned it. Each tiny kick provided Clare with a rush of euphoria. She could feel it swelling too and knew he was going to come.

That realisation hit Clare at exactly the same moment as her orgasm. Milliseconds later, as the waves of thick, super-heated pleasure coursed through her she felt his cock swell for the last time. Pleasure turned to pain momentarily as it stretched her untrained rear to its limits. but the pain was twisted back into pleasure in time for her to feel his ejaculation. She would have sworn she could feel every spurt of it, as it splattered into her, where no man had come before. Each jet produced a spasm of gratification that made her whole body shake, the vibrations of the dildo elongating each until, by some alchemy, a new pleasure was wrought, like the effect of fire on metal, a white-hot passion that burnt everything it touched.

Both were exhausted. The dildo slipped from her body long before his cock softened and slid out too.

They lay side by side, alone and yet together, their bodies touching, but with no energy left to feel the contact.

Chapter Seven

HE STAYED FOR breakfast. He told her he liked to start the day with bacon and eggs so she ran to the corner shop and bought bacon because she had none in the house. She gave him orange juice and coffee and a mountain of wholemeal toast which he spread with strawberry jam, telling her he preferred marmalade.

He sat in her new kitchen, which was big enough for a kitchen table, in her white towelling robe, its arms too short for him, its shoulders barely containing his broad back.

'What are you doing tonight?' he asked as he finished off the last piece of toast.

'Dinner. Business dinner.' It was half true.

'Oh.'

She was delighted that he looked disappointed. Though they had quite sensibly agreed there was no future in their relationship and that their motives were purely carnal, she was glad he wanted to exercise his carnal desires at every opportunity.

'So what about Saturday?' she suggested.

'I was going to tell you about that.'

'Go on.'

'You know that photo-shoot you told me about.'

Photo-shoot. That sounded as if he'd been talking to Angela. 'Yes.'

'Well, it's tomorrow afternoon. Angie said it might go on most of the night. They want to do some night shots, apparently.'

'You got it, then. Why didn't you tell me before?'

'We got sort of busy.'

'What happened?'

'Angie sent this photographer guy round to the site. He took a couple of shots on Polaroid. Then Angie called me on my mobile to say I was on. Good, eh?'

'Very. How much are they paying you?'

'A thousand if they publish. Five hundred if not.'

'Not bad.'

'Money for old rope.'

'I could come and watch.'

'Can you do that?'

'I go to most of our campaign shoots.'

'What sort of campaigns?'

'Cosmetics. That's what KissCo does.'

'Right KissCo. That's what the girl said on the switchboard when I called your office. They do all those big billboards with the girl with hairy eyebrows and the huge mouth.'

'The bigger the mouth the more lipstick. Anyway, that's what I do.'

'What?'

'Run KissCo UK.'

'No wonder you've got a bleedin' BMW.'

'Company car. Look, I'll ring Angie. She can

give me all the details. Then we can have dinner afterwards.'

'If that's all right.'

'I'll arrange it. Angie won't mind.'

'Christ,' he said, looking at his watch. 'I've got to go.'

He finished his coffee and dashed upstairs. A few minutes later he was in her hall in the dirty jeans and T-shirt he'd arrived in last night. At the front door he gathered her into his big arms and kissed her hard on the mouth, squeezing her to him. She felt his cock stir against her belly and wished they could have kept the world at bay for a few more hours.

'Angie?'

'Clare, darling, how are you?'

'Fine. I gather you've got yourself a new model?' Clare had waited until she was at work to call her friend.

'Who told you that? Oh, of course, I forgot. Pillow talk.'

'So tell me all.'

'Jeff went around to see him. You know what Jeff's like, he gets the hots for anything that looks as though it's real. He went ape. Brought back some snaps. Margy said yes. The rest is history.'

'You're shooting tomorrow?'

'Afternoon and evening.'

'So I gather. Is a thousand the going-rate?'

'Now why should that interest you?'

'He's a friend, Angie.'

'A friend. Come on, Clare, it's me you're talking to.'

'I just want to make sure he gets the going-rate.'

'A thousand's fair. Take my word for it.'

'Good. So can I come along?'

'What?'

'Can I come and watch the shoot?'

'Ah . . . no.' Angela's voice was hesitant.

'No? Why not?'

'Clare, do I have to spell it out for you?'

'Yes.'

'We're going to feature Stickshift.'

'So?' Stickshift was the fastest growing competitor to KissCo, a Spanish company backed by German money that was pouring millions of pounds into a slick marketing campaign that suggested wearing their cosmetics would produce instant sexual gratification. The phallic connotations of the company's name, based on the American word for a manual gear lever, featured heavily to establish a sub-conscious psychological connection between their products and the results they could induce.

'Come on, Clare, you know it's not possible. You wouldn't have Conchita Martinez at one of your shoots.'

'No, but I thought this was about men's suits?'

'It is. Was. But Margy's done a deal with Stickshift to split the costs. Girls are going to be pouting their lips all over your lover-boy.'

'I could come in disguise.'

'Clare, I'd get shot.'

She knew Angie was right. If anyone from Stickshift was near one of KissCo's photographic sessions, Clare would blow a fuse.

'All right. Just take care of him, then.'

'I will. He's safe in my hands. Trust me.'

'I wouldn't trust you as far as I could throw you, which with your weight problem, isn't very far.'

'You're only jealous of my tits.'

'True. Have fun.'

Bridget had hired a chauffeur-driven Daimler for the duration of her stay and it had been decided that they should travel together in it to David Allston's house.

As usual Bridget was wearing white – a white chiffon top with full sleeves over a tight, strapless dress that clung to her body as though it had been painted on. The designer of the dress had layered a large chevron in a shade of off-white over the front of the dress, its apex reaching down to mid-thigh as if to draw attention to the fact that from this point the full-length skirt was split all the way up from the ankles. The split revealed a great deal of Bridget's long legs, sheathed in sheer, white nylon. Her white suede shoes were emblazoned with a gold crescent-moon.

Clare's outfit was less revealing. The last thing she wanted to do was tantalise David Allston. She had chosen a rather severe crêpe dress in burgundy, with long sleeves and a full skirt. Only the sweetheart neckline revealed a hint of flesh, but no more than a hint, the neckline not low enough to expose much of her cleavage.

The chauffeur double-parked the Daimler outside the Nash house and raced around to open the rear passenger door for them. A dark-green Rolls Royce was parked behind David's burgundy-coloured Bentley, its chauffeur already asleep behind the wheel, his cap pulled down over his face.

They walked up to the front door. Clare rang the bell. She was expecting the butler to answer but it was David Allston himself who opened the door.

'Hello there,' he said cheerily, stepping forward to kiss Clare on both cheeks.

'This is Bridget Goldsmith, David Allston,' she said.

'Or, if you prefer, the Viscount Bonmouth,' he added, seeing Clare had missed the opportunity and wanting to impress her boss.

'I'm so pleased to meet you, my Lord.' Bridget had looked the form of address up in the office copy of Debrett's. She curtsied and then shook his hand.

'Actually, I really do prefer "David". Come in. Come in.'

'This is some house,' Bridget said, as she stepped into the vestibule.

'Been in the family for two hundred years. Nash, of course. He designed the whole lay-out of Regent's Park and Regent Street. I don't know if you knew that. Wonderful man. Unusually for the eighteenth century he lived to see the whole scheme completed. Most of them popped off before they were fifty.'

'Is that so?' Bridget said, staring at David as though he were a godlike figure.

'Come through. Come through. You're interested in history, Clare tells me.'

'We have so little of it in the States.'

David led the way into the large sitting room. there were four other guests all standing by a large fireplace, the grate filled with a display of dried flowers.

'Let me try and introduce you,' David said. 'Not very good with names. This is Bridget . . .'

'Goldsmith,' Bridget prompted.

'Right. Bridget Goldsmith, a visitor from America, and my dear friend Clare Markham.'

The four guests nodded and smiled. 'This is Virginia Ansel,' he said, indicating a large divaesque woman in a voluminous blue velvet dress. 'Her friend Anna Holmes.' He gestured towards a waif-like girl with long but stringy blonde hair who wore a yellow satin and lace creation that did nothing to hide the fact she was painfully thin. 'And Philip and Celeste Richardson, the Duke and Duchess of Tidmouth.'

Bridget and Clare shook hands with the guests as they were introduced. When Bridget got to the Duke she curtsied and bowed her head sharply. 'Your Grace,' she said solemnly.

'Let me get you both a drink,' David said.

Clare was surprised that there were no servants. It appeared that the guests were helping themselves to champagne, several bottles of which had been dug into a pile of ice in a large round silver bowl standing on a mahogany side-table. David picked out one of the bottles and poured the wine into two long thin flutes.

Bridget's attention was riveted on the Duke. He was a small, slightly plump but comparatively young man with thick, lank black hair and very dark brown eyes that gave the impression of a certain beadiness, but which were examining every contour of Bridget's figure quite overtly, apparently oblivious to his wife who stood at his elbow. Celeste Richardson was tall, taller than her husband, and Clare guessed older, her dark auburn hair pinned up to her head, her rather long face etched with lines, her green eyes large and bright. she had an air of detachment about her, as though she were watching everything at one remove. Of all the women her dress was the most spectacular, a black-and-white print, boned, grosgrain corset-style with a full, pleated, chiffon, black skirt.

'Can I have a word?' David asked Bridget. He looked at his other guests. 'I think we're all agreed, aren't we?' he said to them. They in turn all nodded or mumbled 'yes'.

'What is all this?' Bridget wondered.

'I haven't the faintest idea,' Clare said. She hoped it wasn't one of David's little games. She'd thought she made it clear enough that her career was on the line with this woman.

'Please let me explain,' David said. He took her arm and led her over to the window that over-looked the park.

'David's told us so much about you,' Virginia Ansel said.

'We know all your secrets,' the Duke added.

Clare wasn't paying that much attention. She was trying to read the expression on Bridget's face. At the moment it looked like puzzlement.

'Have you known him long?' she asked Virginia.

'We joined two years ago.'

'Joined?' Clare thought that was an odd word to use.

'The Society of Oser,' Celeste said.

'What?'

'David's little jokes. You know what he's like,' the Duke said.

Oser was French for 'to dare'. A cold hand gripped Clare's heart but she saw the expression on Bridget's face change from puzzlement to what was quite obviously delight. David leant forward, his face only inches from her ear.

'It's only Anna's third time,' Virginia said.

'More's the pity. Didn't know what I was missing.'

175

'What is this Society?' Clare said.

'Oh.' The Duke said looking at his wife uneasily. 'He hasn't told you? We thought . . .'

'I'm sure David knows what he's doing, darling,' Celeste said quickly. 'Would you like some more champagne?'

'No, thank you.'

David led Bridget back to the little gaggle of guests. Whatever else was going on Clare was glad to see her boss was beaming with delight.

'So are you going to tell me all about your family, your Grace,' she said to the Duke. 'I'm really fascinated.'

As Philip launched into an explanation as to the origins of the dukedom, David took Clare's arm. 'I really appreciate you coming tonight, Clare, I want you to know that,' he said with such an intensity it was obvious he wasn't just talking about dinner.

'What is all this?' Clare asked. 'What's going on here? Where are the servants?'

'Their night off. Don't worry, there's a beautiful buffet. Everything's arranged.'

'And the Society of Oser?'

He took her by the arm and led her into a corner. 'Don't worry. I've explained it all to Bridget. She's a surprisingly sophisticated woman. We don't usually invite singles but I explained to the others and they all agreed once they'd seen her . . .'

'Explained what?' Clare was becoming increasingly confused and annoyed. What was there to explain about a dinner party?

'What happened between us, Clare, at the house last time,' he continued, ignoring her question. 'It was difficult for you, I know.'

'I have to talk to you about that.'

'I know. I know. It was all too sudden. But I

knew you'd understand. I knew I could trust you, Clare. You are such an amazing woman. What you did . . .'

'I couldn't help my reaction.'

'That's the point, isn't it? I knew then. I knew it would be all right. I know I've been very demanding. I know my sex-life is a bit of a maze.'

'To put it mildly.'

'Yes. As you say, to put it mildly.' He was looking straight into her eyes as if trying to see into her soul. 'I know what happened. That's what made it so exciting for me. It was the first time, the first time you got involved; the first time you thought about yourself and not just about me. God, it was wonderful, Clare. I haven't been able to stop thinking about it. That's why I had to phone you. The way you looked. The expression on your face. Your voice. So strong. So imperious. And what you made me do. Oh darling, I know that's just the beginning.'

Clare had been right. She guessed yesterday he had completely misconstrued her reactions to what had happened. He'd used the fact that she had not kept to his script as evidence for her excitement, not as an indication of her disgust.

'Look, David, we need to talk,' she said emphatically.

'Yes, yes, of course. I know what you are going to say. No more letters. No more scripts. We don't need that now. What you did on Friday was better than anything I could have made up. We are on the same wavelength now, I know.'

With Bridget ten feet away on the other side of the room this was not the time to tell him the truth, Clare decided.

'That's the point,' he said. 'That's why I wanted

you to come tonight. Then you'll see everything.'

'Everything?'

'It's a question of finding a way to express yourself. Finding a way to express what you need. That's the point, isn't it? I feel so foolish. I've been stifling your expression. You've been so unselfish, so giving, it never occurred to me to ask what you wanted. But here you can do whatever you please, you can take whatever you want to take. And I can show you what I really am, Clare. No more half truths.'

'David, I really don't think this is the place.'

'No. You're wrong. Everyone here is the same.'

'The same?'

'I'd never have dared ask you here before. But now. Now I know it's what you want too, even if you haven't properly realised it yet.'

None of this was making any sense to Clare. 'What have you got planned?' she said with a sinking heart.

'You'll see.'

'And you've invited Bridget to join in?'

'A remarkable woman.'

'What if she'd refused? Did you think about that? This was supposed to be a dinner party.' Whatever else was going on, dinner was clearly very low on the agenda.

'We would have had our buffet very sedately then wished her goodnight. But she said she knew the moment she walked into the room. The Americans are very instinctive, aren't they?'

'Knew what?'

'Something in the eyes, she said.' He turned around to the other guests and said, in a loud voice, 'Ladies and gentleman, as my butler would say, dinner is served.'

178

The guests all appeared to know where to go. They filed through a door at the back of the sitting room into a large dining room, its walls decorated with a collection of Chinese Imari plates. The vast mahogany dining table had been laid with what the Victorians called a cold collation. There was a whole salmon in aspic, a glass bowl full of crevettes – their tails hanging over its edge, several dozen oysters, plates of salami and cold meats, as well as potato, tomato, green and pasta salads. There were silver sauce boats filled with mayonnaise, cocktail sauce, and vinaigrette dressing, and baskets full of a variety of different breads. At the far end were a selection of desserts, glazed strawberry and raspberry tarts, a concoction of meringue and chocolate, and a huge mound of profiteroles as well as a crystal bowl of fresh fruit salad. Several bottles of red and white wine had been opened and stood next to sparkling solid silver cutlery, white crockery, crystal glasses and starched linen napkins on a separate table near the door.

The guests ploughed into the food unceremoniously. After her conversation with David, Clare was not feeling hungry but watched as Bridget sliced herself a piece of salmon and spooned tomato salad on to her plate.

'How's the Duke?' Clare asked her, walking over to her.

'He's a charming guy. Real cute. Never dream he was a duke if you saw him on the street.'

'David talked to you, right?'

'Sure. I knew as soon as I walked in the door. Did he tell you that?'

'Yes.' She wanted to ask what she knew but couldn't think of a way to put it without making

179

herself seem incredibly naive.

'Mind you, I'd never have guessed you'd be into it. Don't worry though, honey. I'm not prejudiced. It ain't going to affect your prospects. Well, that would be hypocritical, right? To tell you the truth, there's a little group in Houston I join when I'm in the mood.'

The conversation only succeeded in confusing Clare further. She hadn't the faintest idea what David or Bridget was talking about. She felt like Alice who had just stepped through the looking-glass into a world she did not understand. All that was important to her at the moment, however, was that Bridget seemed to have taken whatever was going on in her stride.

Bridget resumed her dialogue with the Duke as soon as he had collected his food. Clare took some salad and picked at it unenthusiastically, watching as David joined the conversation with her boss. For a while she stood alone, watching the guests devouring the food, their appetites keen, apart from the blonde, who went straight to the fruit salad and ate nothing else.

'Bridget's your boss, isn't she?' Celeste asked, coming to stand at her side.

'Yes.'

'She's an attractive woman.' The Duchess was staring at Bridget openly, her eyes roaming the American's body.

'I suppose so.'

'So are you, of course. Very. It's always fun, isn't it? Imagining.'

'Imagining?'

'Perhaps that's the wrong word. Anticipating would be better.'

'Anticipating what?'

The woman had a small mouth with very thin lips. Clare saw the tip of her tongue lick her upper lip.

'Anticipating what I would do with Bridget, for example. Or you. I'm not sure which prospect excites me most.'

'Ladies and gentleman.' David's voice interrupted her musings. 'I think it's time to get on with the proceedings. As you know, we have a guest amongst us tonight but she has agreed to participate. When you've all finished supper we will begin.'

There was a little smattering of applause as David walked out of the room, pausing only to smile, a little nervously, at Clare.

'What's going on now?' Clare asked, getting increasingly annoyed at all the obfuscation.

'David didn't tell you in the sitting room?'

'Not really.'

'How interesting. I wonder why that is. He must want to see your instinctive reaction. Are you easily shocked?'

'No.'

'Let's see.' Celeste stooped slightly, as she was taller than Clare, took her chin in her fingers and kissed her lightly on the lips, her tongue darting out into Clare's mouth in the briefest of intrusions.

Clare was so surprised she barely reacted at all. The woman took this to be a green light and kissed her a second time more forcefully, this time using her hand to squeeze Clare's left breast.

'Darling . . .' The Duke strolled over. 'You've started without me.' He put his plate down and stroked his wife's bottom. 'She's lovely, isn't she?'

'Apparently David still hasn't told the young lady why we're all here.'

The Duke laughed. 'He is naughty.' He looked at Clare, putting his hand on her upper arm and caressing it. 'We are here, how should I put it, because we have certain preferences which we like to indulge. Publicly. David got us all together. He's very clever when it's a matter of *oser*.'

Clare glanced across the room at Bridget. The American was talking to the blonde waif, though her companion had disappeared. As she watched Bridget touched the girl's mouth with her finger. The girl smiled. Presumably Bridget had been told what was going to happen and had no objection to the idea. Nor any, judging from the way she pulled the blonde into her arms and kissed her on the mouth, to lesbian relationships.

'And what is David's preference?' Clare said coolly, not at all sure which of the two emotions she was experiencing – horror and fascination – was going to predominate. She could still feel Celeste's tongue darting between her lips.

The Duke smiled. 'I'm sure you know that already. It's very much the same as mine. But he's going first tonight.'

'Going first?'

'Follow us,' Celeste said. She put down her plate, most of her desserts uneaten, and took Clare's hand, like the spider who had chosen to escort the fly personally into the web.

There was a small door at the far end of the dining room. Celeste opened it and led the way through. The corridor beyond was long, narrow and windowless, the only light coming from a single naked light bulb swinging from the ceiling. There was only one door off it at the far end.

Again Celeste opened the door, this time allowing Clare to go first. She found herself in a large room, the walls draped with long scarlet velvet curtains. Strewn across the red, carpeted floor were three or four rather old-fashioned sofas, upholstered in Dralon, and dotted with different-shaped cushions. There were two armchairs in the same material. All the seating faced the same wall, where a platform jutted out into the room, a miniature version of a stage in a theatre, complete with a bar of spotlights above it. On the 'stage' was a mattress and a prie-dieu consisting of a narrow rectangular box about three feet high, with a padded step at one side, for kneeling to pray. The top surface, where the elbows would rest, was padded too.

At the back of the room was a large walnut wardrobe. It had two doors and four large drawers. Beside it was a side-table laden with drinks, bottles of gin, brandy, whisky and vodka, red and white wine and a wine cooler containing champagne, as well as all the appropriate glasses. The room had a curious smell, a combination of woman's perfume and something Clare did not recognise, a musky heady scent.

'Make yourself at home,' the Duke said. He slumped on to one of the sofas while his wife poured herself a glass of wine.

The door had closed itself on a hydraulic spring. It was pushed open again by Anna, who led Bridget into the room.

'Very cosy,' the American said, glancing at Clare.

'She's not having you all to herself, is she?' Celeste asked.

'Not necessarily,' Bridget replied.

The Duchess sidled up to Bridget, then ran her hand down the American's body, digging her

183

fingers into her crotch. She leant forward and kissed her on the mouth. Immediately Bridget embraced her, kissing her back ferociously, turning her head and mashing their mouths together, her hand slipping on to Celeste's chiffon-covered buttocks.

'What about me?' Anna said, pushing herself into Bridget's back and embracing both women.

'Are you feeling left out?' the Duke said, looking from the triad of women to Clare.

Clare was not at all sure what she was feeling. At least everything David had said to her earlier made sense now. He had misread the fact that she had made him attend to her needs so forcefully, last Friday, as an indication that her sexual preferences were as complex as his own, imagining she had been too inhibited to tell him what she really wanted. It was a triumph of twisted desire over commonsense, his optimism flying in the face of reality. How long he had been holding his soirees of like-minded individuals she did not know, but he had obviously taken her behaviour as an opportunity to introduce her to his more arcane rituals.

Bridget's presence and acquiescence had added additional spice to the proceedings as far as David and his friends were concerned, but additional complications for Clare. She had never heard the slightest hint on the company grapevine that Bridget was gay, or bisexual, but clearly that is what she was. The evidence was right there in front of her eyes.

Clare needed a drink. She poured herself a brandy and sat on one of the two armchairs. Watching the three women, their arms linked around each other, their mouths kissing and licking each other's mouths and necks, hands exploring their softly fleshed bodies, revived no memories of Andrea, or Liza for that matter. She felt no flash of excitement.

At that moment the lights in the room dimmed. She saw Anna lead Bridget over to one of the sofas, while Celeste joined her husband. The bank of spotlights above the stage lit up, bathing the whole area in bright white light.

Virginia Ansel marched out from the wings, the velvet curtains concealing a small doorway. She was wearing a black leather corset – her large breasts only just contained in the cups of its bra, her waist cinched in by its strong laces and heavy boning – and long black stockings, their welts stretched over her meaty thighs, clipped into short leather suspenders. She wore black calf-length boots with stubby heels, but was without panties. Buried deep between her gargantuan thighs Clare could see tufts of pubic hair. In her left hand she held a riding crop. Clare recognised it immediately. It was exactly the same type David had given her a week earlier.

David followed the woman on. He was naked apart from a pair of white satin, lace-trimmed French knickers, a pair he had worn with Clare several times. They were too small and the material was stretched tautly over his slender, girlish hips.

'Stand still,' the woman barked. He stopped dead in his tracks. 'Dirty boy,' she said. 'Aren't you?'

'Yes.'

'Naughty, naughty boy.'

Clare saw the outline of his penis in the satin beginning to unfurl rapidly.

'Yes.'

'All the trouble I have to go to for you.'

'Yes.' David's face was twisted by his excitement. Clare had seen that expression so many times, a combination of shame at how he was behaving and acute arousal.

'Get down, then. You know what I'm going to have to do.'

'Yes.'

Viscount Bonmouth knelt on the prie-dieu. The big woman came around the other side of it so she was facing him. She took his hair in her hand and wrenched his head up so he was staring into her enormous bosom.

'Kiss it,' she demanded. She pulled the front of the bra-cups down and her big breasts spilt out like melting ice cream. David reached forward and began licking and kissing the flesh.

Clare heard a moan of delight. She looked to her left and saw that Anne had slipped on to the floor in front of Bridget, who had squirmed the split skirt up over her hips so the girl could bury her face between the American's thighs. The light from the stage provided enough illumination for Clare to see the girl's tongue burrowing into the nylon tights.

When she looked back at the stage, Virginia had turned round, her large flabby bottom perched on top of the prie-dieu. David was licking it enthusiastically, covering every inch of flesh with his tongue.

Celeste got to her feet. She went to the wardrobe at the back of the room and opened one of its doors. Clare's eyes followed her. She saw a selection of whips, tawses and wooden paddles hanging from hooks screwed on to the inside of the door. There were several school-type canes with curved hands and a riding crop identical to the one Virginia was using. It was this that Celeste selected.

'Not good enough,' Virginia announced. David redoubled his efforts. The big woman leant forward, angling her buttocks up and allowing him access to her sex, its labia covered with curly black hair.

Thwack. The sound echoed across the room. The Duke was bending over the arm of the sofa, his trousers and pants around his knees, Celeste towering above him.

Bridget stood up. She unzipped her dress and peeled it off her body. Her tights followed and her white thong-cut panties. She positioned the blonde, who still sat on the floor, so her back was against the sofa, then walked forward straddling her body until her pubes were pressed against the girl's face. Then, forcing the blonde's head back against the seat of the couch, she knelt on the edge of it, pressing her sex down on to the girl's mouth.

Clare looked at the stage. Virginia was standing behind David with the whip raised in her right hand. She stroked it down on to his satin-covered buttocks. David gasped.

Clare felt very little. The emotions she had experienced earlier, both the horror and the fascination, had been replaced by a curious sense of calm. She saw it all now, David's whole plan. He had brought her here to show her, more explicitly than words could do, what he expected from her. He'd assumed last Friday had been his first glimpse of the tip of an iceberg that she had never revealed to him before – that she had, for once, asserted her own needs. But nothing could be further from the truth. Her reaction had been caused by a mixture of anger and sexual need, not by some strange desire. In the past Clare had gone along with his games purely because she had liked him, and, if she were honest, she liked the things he did to her. But that was not what she wanted from a man. Gary's arrival on the scene had made that perfectly clear to her.

In his twisted way she realised this performance had been like a proposal of marriage, a statement of what he wanted and what he was, a first step on what he hoped would be a meeting of minds.

Clare finished her brandy in one gulp.

Thwack. The sharp sound of leather on satin-covered flesh made her flinch.

She got to her feet. To her right the Duke of Tidmouth was on his knees, carefully licking his wife's high-heeled shoes. To her left Bridget was staring into space, seeing nothing, her hands crushed back against her own breasts, her body trembling in the throes of orgasm – the first, Clare was sure, of many.

Without a word, Clare opened the door. She walked through into the narrow, dingy hallway. The door closed noisily on its spring, making her jump. In the dining room she walked past the abandoned food and out into the vestibule. She opened the front door and slammed it after her.

The Daimler was parked a little way up the street. The driver spotted her and got out of the car, opening the rear passenger door.

'It's all right, I'll walk,' she told him.

And walk is what she did.

Chapter Eight

THE PHONE RANG twice before she picked it up.

'Hello?'

'Clare?' It was Bridget's voice.

'Yes.'

'Are you busy?'

'No.'

'Have you eaten?'

'No. I thought you were going home today?'

'I stayed over. I'm scheduled on a flight on Sunday afternoon. Would you have dinner with me?'

Clare would have liked to say no. 'Of course.'

'Pick me up in half an hour.'

Having dinner with Bridget Goldsmith was not Clare's first choice for a Saturday evening. Her first, second and third choice would have been Gary Newby, especially after last night. What she had seen may not have excited her directly but it had left her with a desperate yearning for sex; not sex in general but sex in particular, sex with Gary. Going to bed with Gary, with all his energy and power, and his simple, uncomplicated sexual needs, would wipe away the slightly disorientated feeling she'd had all day. Like Alice, after inhabiting the world behind the looking glass, she found the real world distinctly odd.

After everything that had happened in the last week it was not a question of taking a moralistic stand. That didn't mean she hadn't been bruised by the experience. What made it worse was that she knew it was, at least in part, her fault. If she had refused, from the beginning, to join in with David's sex games they would not have escalated into the more serious ones, and he would have not imagined – for even a second – that Clare had sexual leanings similar to his own, and would never have invited her to attend a meeting of the Society of *Oser*.

Clare looked at her watch and went upstairs to change. She supposed spending the rest of the evening with Bridget was better than spending it on her own, endlessly dwelling on the events of last night and cursing Angela and Angela's magazine.

She had a quick shower in her new cubicle and tried Gary's mobile phone once more. She called it three times already in the irrational hope that he'd finish early. The operator told her his phone was switched off.

Quickly she put on make-up and selected a dress, a simple stone-coloured, jersey strap-dress that left her shoulders and arms bare and had a knee length skirt. By the time she found the matching high-heeled shoes, Bridget's Daimler was drawing up outside.

The doorbell rang.

'Good evening,' she said.

'Hi, Clare.'

'Would you like to come in for a drink first?'

'Sure. The night is young.'

Clare led the way into the sitting room. As usual Bridget wore white, a loose-fitting silk shift. Her tights were flesh-coloured and shiny and she was wearing little white sandals.

'Hey, this is real nice. Very classy.'

'I've just had some work done. Things are not quite back to normal.' I'm not quite back to normal either, she thought but did not say.

'Looks fine to me.'

'What would you like?'

'Vodka rocks.'

Clare walked into the kitchen, the ranks of ash-fronted cupboards perfectly matched to the large terracotta tiles on the floor.

'Nice little garden too,' Bridget said, following her through.

Clare got ice from the fridge and knocked it out of the tray over the sink. She poured herself a gin and tonic, and handed Bridget a tall glass of vodka.

'Cheers,' she said. The American sat at the kitchen table, so she joined her.

'Cheers.' Bridget took a sip. 'Listen, I came here for a reason. Two reasons. You know me. I don't like beating about the bush.'

'So I gather.' From the look on Bridget's face the news didn't look good.

'The first is that I was out of line last night, way out of line. I got carried away. No excuses. I was always into history. Always had this thing about it. I suppose what with David and the Duke . . . it was like getting high. I was out of control.'

'You don't have to explain to me.'

'I think I do. I assumed you were into it too. I didn't realise . . . well if I had . . . The point is I

191

wouldn't like it to be known in the company what went on. I like to keep my private life private. Strictly private.'

'I understand. No one will hear it from me.'

'I like women, always have. Don't get me wrong, I like men too. Kinda swing both ways. Variety is the spice of life; that's what they say, don't they?'

'It's none of my business.'

'OK. Well, now that's out of the way. Second reason. Business.' She was looking at Clare intently. 'You run a tight ship, Clare. I'm impressed. I like the way you motivate your staff. I like your sales figures. I like your attitude. On the other hand I did *not* like what I saw in Paris. I've decided that the European launch should be handled in London as planned.' She paused for that information to sink in. 'I also want you to initiate a study into whether it would be possible to run the whole European operation from London. Cut out the French office first, say, then the German, Spanish, etc. Do you think you could handle that sort of responsibility?'

'If it was thought out and carefully planned.'

'Of course we'd have to work out a new remuneration package, share options, a seat on the main board.'

'Of course.' Clare tried to sound calm despite the fact she was being handed the opportunity of the biggest advancement in her entire career to date.

'Good. That's what I thought you'd say.' Bridget was smiling, a thin, weak smile but a smile nevertheless, her dark green eyes crinkled at the corners. 'So, do you mind if I ask you about David? I won't be offended if you tell me to go to hell.'

Clare's mind was still spinning with the

implications of what Bridget had said. She tried to snap it back into gear. 'Actually, I'd rather like to talk about it.'

'I love that.'

'What?'

'The way you say "actually". So English.'

'I suppose it is.'

'So what? You've had it with the Viscount now?'

'Yes. It was all my fault. I mean my fault it went so far. He obviously has very . . .' she searched for the right word '. . . exotic sexual needs, that I can't satisfy.'

'Can't or won't?'

'Won't.'

'But you must have known before last night?'

'Oh, I did. David had these little games he liked to play.'

'Like what?' Bridget asked eagerly.

'Oh, he used to buy me all sorts of lingerie – like me to get dressed up for him. Then he started to want to wear some of it himself. I thought it was harmless. To tell you the truth, I was never that interested in him to care too much what he wanted.'

'But you didn't know about the Society?'

'Not until last night.'

'Must have been a shock.'

'It was.'

'Do you think all aristos like to be whipped? The Duke had a go with Virginia after you'd gone.'

'We have caning at our best schools. Perhaps they get a taste for it.'

'Sure was interesting.'

Clare sipped her gin and tonic. Whether it was

193

due to the alcohol or Bridget's news, she was feeling very much better. The thought of going out to dinner was suddenly very appealing.

'God, just talking about last night is making me horny,' Bridget said. It was completely out of character. Clare had never heard her make any reference to herself, let alone to her sex life.

'You had a good time, I gather,' she said cautiously, not wanting to explore too far down that road in case Bridget took offence.

Apparently the American was in the mood for revelations. 'Between you and me, I had a very good time. That little blonde was a slut! Virginia had got her well trained.'

'And you like that?'

Bridget smiled again, an odd, crooked smile this time. 'It can be lonely at the top. I suspect you and I are similar in some ways. We're both very controlled. Very self-disciplined. We have to be. It's a hard world out there. Every so often it's necessary to let the reins slip. Some people do drugs. Or booze. Sex is my preferred option. I find it very easy to give myself up to sensuality. And there's something wonderfully wicked about doing it with another woman. It has one drawback, however.'

Clare realised Bridget hadn't asked her if she'd ever been with a woman. She wasn't at all sure what she'd have said. 'What's that?' she asked innocently.

'It always makes me horny for a man.'

'Really?' Clare breathed a sigh of relief.

'And how.'

Clare knew that feeling. After Liza she had wanted Gary desperately. On the other hand she *always* wanted Gary desperately.

'I suppose that's the difference between an amateur and a real dyke. Pity there's not such a thing as a male brothel. I could really use one right now. Men get all the breaks when it comes to sex, don't they?'

'I suppose so.' The conversation was making Clare feel horny too. She ached to feel Gary inside her again – that big, broad cock filling every inch of her. The thought made her squirm uneasily on the chair. 'So where do you want to eat?'

'You choose. It's your town.'

'I wonder . . .' The thought of Gary and Liza had made her think of the Key Club. As they were finally departing his loft, Malcolm Furness had told her that she was welcome at the club at any time. She only had to ring. she decided to see if he was as good as his word. 'Won't be a minute.'

She walked into the sitting room and picked up the phone book. She looked up the number and punched it into the phone.

'The Key Club. How may I help you?'

'Mr Furness, please.'

'Hold the line.'

'Mr Furness's office.' The voice was female.

'Is he there?'

'I'm sorry, he's not in at the moment. May I ask who's calling?'

'Clare Markham.'

'Yes, Ms Markham. May I help you with anything?'

'It's just Malcolm suggested the other night, if I ever wanted to use the club . . .'

'Certainly, Ms Markham. He mentioned it to me. Do you want to dine or dance?'

'I was hoping for a table for two.'

'What time?'

Clare looked at her watch. It was eight fifteen. 'Nine.'

'Table for two at nine. Just mention your name to the man on the door. I'll make all the arrangements.'

'That's very kind of you.'

'Our pleasure. And I'll tell Malcolm you rang.'

'Would you? Thank you.'

'Not at all.'

Clare smiled as she put the phone down. Taking Bridget to the Key Club would be another feather in her cap, though from what had just transpired she hardly needed one. More over, it was always possible that after his long and arduous day posing for photographs Gary might decide to drop into his old friend's club for a drink.

'Clare Markham,' Clare told the burly bouncer with the gold teeth, who was holding back the queue that seemed to be a permanent feature outside the Key Club.

The doorman smiled. 'Yes, Ms Markham, right this way please.' He unhooked the red cordon and ushered them through. Bridget looked suitably impressed.

The girl in the tight, gold leotard behind the desk had also been briefed. 'Good evening, Ms Markham,' she said before Clare could announce herself. 'Please go straight through, no need to sign in. Mr Furness has taken care of everything.'

Clare led the way into the bar. The *maître d'*, in her pastiche of a man's evening dress, wished them good evening and showed them to the same corner table Clare had occupied with Gary. She told them that Mr Furness would like to offer them a bottle of champagne or anything else they would care for. They settled for champagne.

Over dinner they discussed business. Fortunately Clare had given a lot of thought to the integration of the whole European operation. It would represent considerable savings in costs and manpower, and she explained her ideas of how it could be achieved with the least disruption. Bridget listened carefully, making pertinent points with her usual bluntness while she demolished a large entrecôte steak, a plate of potatoes and a double portion of pear and almond tart with whipped cream – one appetite, perhaps, being used to slake another.

'It seems like you're already ahead of the game on this,' Bridget said, as the desserts were cleared away and the waiter brought *demi-tasse* cups of expresso coffee.

'It always seemed like a logical progression. I wasn't going to bring it up until after you'd made the decision on the launch. The idea could work equally well if it were based in Paris.'

'With Claude? I don't think so. I wasn't impressed with his arguments on the commercials.'

'He was on your side.'

'True. But you convinced me we were wrong. The greatest asset of management should be the ability to listen. Anyway, that's enough business. In the absence of a male brothel, what do you suggest we do now?'

For a moment Clare wondered if Bridget was going to proposition her. She dismissed the idea at once. If Bridget was concerned with anyone in the company being told about her sexual proclivities, she certainly wouldn't want to compromise herself by sleeping with one of the senior executives.

'It's a funny thing, isn't it? Women have caught up with men in a lot of ways. I mean we run companies, do deals. Pay for our own dinner. Have more heart attacks. But we still can't go out and rustle up a man like a man can go get a woman. I mean, if you go up to a guy in a bar and tell him you want to get into his pants they either think you're a serial killer with a vendetta against men, or a hooker.'

'It's changing a bit.' She thought of Gary. She had definitely taken the lead in that situation.

As the waiter poured the last of the half-bottle of dessert wine they'd ordered (with Bridget's chauffeur-driven Daimler outside they didn't have to worry about driving), Clare spotted a familiar face walking towards their table.

'Clare. Well, you look terrific.'

Malcolm Furness towered above them, his bulky body clad in a black evening suit, a yellow bow-tie and matching cummerbund. He took Clare's hand and stooped to kiss her on the cheek but his eyes were riveted on Bridget.

'Malcolm Furness, Bridget Goldsmith,' Clare said. 'This is Malcolm's club.'

'Pleased to meet you.' Bridget smiled, extending her hand.

'And you. May I join you?'

'Sure,' Bridget said.

A waiter was summoned to pull up another chair.

'Thanks for arranging all this,' Clare said. 'It was really nice of you.'

'No problem. I'm glad you came. Everything OK? If it wasn't, I'll have the person responsible taken out and shot.'

'It was just perfect,' Bridget said. 'Love it here.'

'Thank you. Sorry I wasn't in earlier. Had to go to dinner with one of my investors. Boring old fart. He thinks 'cause he's got money in the place he's got the first choice of all the girls who work here.'

'Some of the girls are very attractive,' Bridget said. 'Especially the *maître d'*.'

'You're very attractive,' Malcolm said bluntly.

'Thank you. I'm very glad you think so.'

'How about some more wine? Or some champagne?'

'That's a great idea,' Bridget said.

Malcolm signalled to a waiter who appeared to know what he wanted without being told.

Bridget was leaning forward, her elbows on the table, staring at Malcolm, her eyes wide open, her whole attitude subtly changed, her body language suggesting a receptiveness and softness that were not characteristic. The Chief Executive of KissCo had melted away to be replaced by a much less daunting animal. Perhaps, Clare thought, when it came to men that was a trick she should try to learn.

'You know, you've got a lovely mouth, Malcolm,' she said.

'My friends call me Mal.'

'Are we going to be friends? I do hope so.' She touched his arm and batted her eyelids.

'Yeah, right.'

The waiter arrived with a bottle of Dom Perignon. He opened the bottle noiselessly and poured the wine into three glasses before crushing the bottle back into a bucket full of ice.

'Well, cheers!' Malcolm said, picking up his

glass. 'I hope you'll come again.' He was still looking at Bridget.

'Bridget's off to Houston in the morning.'

'Really. Houston. I've never been there.'

'You'll have to come over. I'm sure we could show you a very good time.'

'I'm sure you could. As long as you gave it your personal attention. What time's your flight?'

'Don't worry, I don't have to get up early.' If she had made her interest in Malcolm any more obvious, Clare thought, she would have been sitting in his lap.

'Are all Houston women so up front?' he asked.

'Oh dear, am I scaring you? We were just talking about that, weren't we Clare? How women have to wait for a man to make the running. I mean, I can't say to you that I'd love you to take me to bed, can I? Wouldn't be ladylike.'

'I thought you just had,' Malcolm countered. He was grinning from ear to ear, but not smugly.

'Ask him to show you his loft,' Clare said. She decided she could get to like Bridget. She admired her directness.

'Your loft?'

'Yeah. Upstairs. You want to see it?'

'Only if it's got a large bed. Otherwise let's go to my hotel.' She squeezed his arm. 'I'm sorry, is this putting you off? I know a lot of men find assertive women a big problem. They can't get it up or off, whichever.'

'Both probably,' Clare said with a smile. Bridget's attempt to shed her executive role hadn't lasted long. Perhaps she'd sensed it was not a part she needed to play with Malcolm.

'You're quite a lady,' he said.

'What makes you think I'm a lady?'

'Let's go then. Have you seen Gary?' for once he turned to look at Clare.

'Gary?' Just the sound of his name sent a shock-wave down to her sex. Clare was clearly in the same state as Bridget.

'Yeah. He called me about ten. Said he was coming over.'

'Here?' Clare said in disbelief. She couldn't believe her luck.

'Yeah.'

'Who's Gary?' Bridget asked. Her fingers were drawing delicate patterns on the top of Malcolm's hand.

'A friend of mine,' Clare told her.

'Another viscount?'

Malcolm laughed. 'Gary's a prince among men but he ain't no lord. We're both from the other end of the social ladder. We went to school together.'

'Well, I haven't seen him,' Clare said.

'Perhaps he's upstairs.'

Clare looked puzzled.

'In the flat. He's got a key,' Malcolm explained. 'He can use it whenever he likes. Come on, let's go and see.'

They got up. Malcolm grabbed a passing waiter. 'Have the booze sent up, there's a good boy,' he said.

'Certainly, Mr Furness.' The waiter collected the bottle from the table.

'Shouldn't waste good champagne, should we?' He took Bridget's arm. 'I've got a dumb waiter from the kitchens right up to the flat. Handy if I ever fancy anything.'

They walked down to the disco. It was full, *Saturday-Night-Fever* full. A gyrating mass of

201

people danced to music so loud it was at the absolute limit of tolerance of the human ear; the heat extreme too, most of the dancers' clothes soaked with perspiration that was evaporating to give the room the air of a sauna.

They travelled up in the lift. Though the space was limited, it was no accident that Bridget's body was pressed against Malcolm's.

Malcolm took out his key and unlocked his front door.

'Be it ever so humble,' he said, throwing the door open and indicating that the women should go through.

The lights in the loft were already on. As before, the lighting was selective. The lights around the kitchen and the four sofas in the middle of the room were all off, but the halogen spotlights that illuminated the far side of the room, where the large double bed was, were burning brightly. And their bright white light revealed a startling and startled tableau. Kneeling on all fours on the bed was a long-haired, big-breasted blonde. She was naked, her breasts hanging down to brush the cream sheet that covered the mattress. At the back end of her long body a man was kneeling behind her, his navel butting against her buttocks, his penis quite obviously buried in her sex. He was a black man, his body delineated by groups of muscles, each one separate and distinct like an anatomical chart of the human form. At the other end of the blonde was a white man, almost equally well-endowed in terms of his physique. He was standing at the edge of the bed, his fingers laced into the blonde's hair, most of his cock firmly held in her mouth. The woman's long, straight and slender back formed a sort of bridge between the two men.

The tableau was frozen. For a moment no one moved.

Clare recognised them all. The blonde was Angela Barker. The black man was the male stripper from the pub. The white man was Gary. An intimate little threesome.

'Well, look at that,' Bridget said, almost under her breath. 'It's not only the aristos who know how to have a good time!'

Gary was the first to react. He pulled out of Angela's mouth. Under the bright lights his cock was shiny with Angela's saliva. As there were no lights on by the front door he was straining to see who had come in.

'Is that you, Mal?'

'Yes, and me,' Clare said. She walked over to the bed, her high-heels clacking on the wooden floor where it was not covered with rugs. '*Me*' she repeated, brazenly sitting on the bed by her friend. 'Hi, Angie, having fun? I didn't know this was the sort of shoot you had in mind.'

'Clare! Hell, where did you come from?' Angela said.

'I thought you might need some help. Don't let me interrupt, please,' she added, looking up at Gary.

'Hi,' he said weakly.

'What is all this?' the black man said, impatient, no doubt, to get on with what he'd already started.

Clare's emotions were complex. She felt angry with Angela. She also felt jealous. But her overriding emotion at that moment, seeing Gary standing there, with his magnificent weapon sticking out in front of him like the lever that operated a machine, was a quite inordinate lust. There would be time for anger later, but not with Gary. She did not own him. They had made no vows, plighted no troths. Her feelings about Angela were a different matter, but they would have to wait.

She looked up at the stripper. She remembered his hard body and the sheen of his very black, hairless flesh, like the nap of finest silk. It excited her. The contrast between the colour of his skin and Angela's made the blonde look deathly pale.

'He's been on the shoot with us,' Angela volunteered. 'I used them both.'

'So I see.'

Her anger flared momentarily, then died away. In another situation she might have seen Angela's actions as a betrayal. But Angela knew how she felt about Gary, that it was lust not love. And Angela had always been more prone to act on impulse. Presumably the same impulse had applied when it came to the black stripper.

Clare had a choice, at least in theory. She could turn and walk out of the door. She was getting good at righteous indignation. But this situation was completely different from last night. Last night her sexual excitement had been virtually non-existent. Her fascination had turned to disgust, well at least to total disinterest, very early on. Not for one moment had she wanted to snatch the whip out of Virginia's hand and set about David, or, for that matter, bid for the attentions of the waif-like blonde. Tonight, however, her sexual arousal had already been primed. In the few short minutes since she'd walked through the door it had increased exponentially, humming now with a power she

204

simply could not control. This was exactly what she'd wanted after all – well, almost exactly.

'Come here,' she said to Gary in a school ma'amish tone that David would have loved.

Gary stood in front of her, his erection inches from her face. 'Are you cross?' he asked sheepishly.

She leant forward, ran the tip of her tongue over his glans, then sucked his cock into her mouth until it was embedded in her throat, as a way of giving him an answer.

He moaned. He moaned again when Clare sucked hard, dimpling her cheeks with the effort and feeling his cock throb.

'You want me to go?' the stripper said.

'No,' Angela said quickly. 'You stay right where you are.'

The stripper grinned. He gripped Angela's fleshy hips and began moving in and out of her as he'd been doing before they were interrupted.

Clare decided she wanted that too. She wanted it very much. She pulled her mouth away from Gary's cock and stood up. The stone-coloured jersey dress slipped to the floor, both men watching her.

She suddenly remembered Bridget and looked around for her. The rest of the loft was dark and she couldn't see what had happened to Malcolm and Bridget. There was one thing she was sure of, however. After last night she knew Bridget was not likely to be easily shocked.

Gary came up behind her. He sunk his mouth into her neck, making her skin pimple. His hands slipped under the cups of her white satin bra, pushing it up over her breasts, then cupping them – pressing her nipples between the sides of his fingers. His erection was nestling into the nylon-covered curves of her buttocks.

'Sorry,' he whispered in her ear.

'Don't say you're sorry,' she said. 'Just fuck me, Gary. I need it.'

His hands slid down the sides of her body. He hooked his thumbs into the waistband of her tights and pulled them down over her thighs. Dropping to his knees behind her, he rolled the nylon down to her ankles then raised each of her feet in turn, pulling off her shoes and stripping the nylon away.

'Bend over,' he said quietly. She unclipped her bra and threw it aside before she did as she was told, then bent at the waist, her hands on the mattress, her legs straight. His mouth pressed into her buttocks. She wormed her feet apart, her thighs opening, allowing him deeper. His tongue explored the hole of her anus, then dipped into her vagina. It was her turn to moan. His tongue felt hot. It probed remarkably deeply.

Clare looked across to Angela. Their faces were not more than a foot apart. The ecstasy in the blonde's expression excited her. She looked up at the black man but he was not looking at her. Instead his eyes were locked on Angela's buttocks, watching his pummelling cock sliding in and out between her pursed labia.

Almost unconsciously Clare pushed her buttocks up, changing the angle of her sex, and making Gary's tongue flip from the mouth of her vagina up to her clitoris. It was swollen. He licked it enthusiastically, pushing it up and down with the tip of his tongue.

Clare felt her body shudder with sensation. It seemed to be so much more impressionable now, more susceptible to the slightest contact. After only a few seconds of this treatment she felt the first trills of orgasm running through her nerves.

'No,' she said. She didn't want that. She tore herself away. Clare climbed on to the bed and rolled over on to her back, opening her legs and bending them at the knee, holding her arms out for him.

The invitation was obvious. Gary did not need to be told what to do. He lay down on top of her, his big erection crushing into her labia. As she wrapped her arms around his back and thrust her legs up into the air, he raised his hips and plunged into her. Clare gasped. The unique sensation he inspired flowed through her again, her sex filled, satiated, complete.

'Oh god, Gary. That's wonderful,' she whispered in his ear.

'I know.'

Gary's cock buried inside her body was exactly what she wanted. It succeeded in wiping away everything else. The unpleasantness of last night was forgotten. David was forgotten. Clare closed her eyes. The feelings he generated were so strong, so tangible, they invaded every part of her. They were like a mud bath; she could wallow in them. But not for long. The thick, warm, fuzzy sensations turned, in seconds, to sharp, hot, luminescent need, creating and demanding a more acute form of satisfaction. As Gary pressed up into her, arching his body to concentrate his whole effort into penetrating her more deeply, Clare's body arched too, pushing against his weight as the intensity of orgasm shot through her.

She opened her eyes as she heard Angela gasp.

The stripper was imitating Gary, not pounding into the blonde but pulling her back on him while he used all his strength, his map of muscles rigid with the effort, to push his cock more deeply into her. Angela's eyes were open, but they saw nothing, glazed over and unfocused, her breasts quivering, her long blonde hair twisted and dishevelled.

The lights had been turned on in the middle of the room where the four sofas formed a square, and a movement caught Clare's eye. A foot came into view over the back of one of the sofas. It was still shod in a white sandal. As she watched she saw the crest of a man's buttocks appear then disappear again instantly. Clearly Bridget's newly discovered passion for Malcolm Furness had come to rapid fruition, so rapid they had not bothered to remove her tights, some other arrangement made to allow access.

Gary began to move inside her, his big cock sliding in and out of the slippery tube of her tight vagina. Every thrust was a symphony of pleasure, different tunes played in different chords but all with the same pounding tempo. Clare could feel his cock swelling and throbbing too, every inch of it thrilling her. He was going to come. Had she arrived a few minutes later it would have been Angela, not her, who would have been granted the pleasure of his ejaculation.

She wasn't sure whether everything that was going on around her was an added excitement or a distraction. Would she have rather been alone? She couldn't work that out. There was no doubt that watching Angela *in extremis* was exciting her. In all the time she had known Angela she had never made the connection before, but now, seeing her long blonde hair sweep across the bed, as her head swayed from side to side, she suddenly reminded her of Andrea. That thought needed to be worked on too. Would she like to push Gary aside and see how Angela would react if she tried to kiss her? The world, it seemed, was full of possibilities, endless permutations, implications and consequences.

In fact she soon realised there was only one thing she wanted to feel. She raked her fingernails down Gary's back. Her left hand worked down into his buttocks until she found the opening of his anus. Without hesitation she stuck her finger into it, twisting it around and pushing it in as deeply as she could. The intrusion caused a violent spasm in his cock. Clare found his ear with her mouth and stuck her tongue deep into the inner whorls. Another wild jerking. His cock reared deeper into the velvety glove of her sex.

'Give it to me, Gary, don't make me wait!' She sounded like the star of some cheap porno film, but she didn't care.

She twisted her finger again. Immediately his cock kicked twice in rapid succession and she felt his spunk, hot and sticky, jetting out into the depths of her sex. Her own body reacted as it always had, a tight ball of feeling locking every muscle and straining every sinew, pure concentrated pleasure arching through her, followed by another sensation almost as strong and certainly as sensual – the melting, delicious pleasure as her orgasm released its grip and she was left, seemingly floating in mid-air. Despite everything that was happening around her, for that moment she was only aware of herself and Gary, their bodies wrapped around each other tightly, his softening cock at the core of her, where a damp, warm wetness was already beginning to trickle out.

She was also aware, after that moment has passed, of another sensation, one that revived all her sexual energy, and exhilarated her like nothing else. Gary's cock was moving inside her again, subtly sawing up and down. As it did, she felt it swelling, hardening again, ready for more.

It was raining. The hot weather had broken with a thunderstorm. It had rolled around all afternoon, forked lightning streaking the sky, and sheets of rain bouncing up off the ground, guttering overflowing with water, unable to cope with the volume. In between the cloudbursts thunder rattled the windows, so loud it sometimes seemed to be right overhead.

Clare sat in her new kitchen, watching the rain run off the new windows. She was tired. She hadn't wanted to know what time it was when Bridget's Daimler had dropped her off at her house last night, but, to make matters worse, when she had finally got to bed she had been unable to sleep. Everything that had happened to her whirled around in her head, just like the thunderstorm was doing now.

It had been a roller-coaster ride. Having got on the train, it had travelled too fast to enable her to get off. It had looped and spiralled and plunged through unknown and dangerous territory under its own momentum. But last night it had ground to a halt and, a little unsteadily, Clare had finally staggered to her front door and, with a sense of relief, shut it against the world.

In the small hours, watching as the first tendrils of light found the gaps in the curtains at her bedroom window, she experienced a whole panoply of emotions. Anger. Disgust. Excitement. Regret.

She went from being angry with herself for not having turned and walked out of Malcolm's loft as soon as she'd seen what was going on, to being so sexually excited at the memories of what had happened that her whole body came alive, her nipples stiffened, her sex moist. She experienced disgust and revulsion at what she had seen – at what she'd allowed herself to participate in – followed instantly by regret that she had not done more, that she had not had the courage to take the black stripper or pursue the desire she had felt to see if the experiment with Liza could have been repeated with Angela. She regretted, more than anything, that she'd told Gary she was tired and wanted to go home alone.

It was all very confusing and lack of sleep didn't help. She couldn't work out whether she was angry with Gary or not. She supposed if there was anyone to blame it was Angela. She *was* angry with Angela. She'd lied to her, a lie of omission admittedly, but a lie nevertheless. She hadn't told her about the black stripper being used in the photo-shoot because that might have tipped her off to Angela's plans for extra-curricular activities after the shoot. Nor, she suspected, had Stickshift been involved. That was just a hastily concocted excuse to keep her away. Though it might have been Gary's idea to use the loft, Clare was sure Angela would have had another plan up her sleeve if they had not been going there.

All these musings were streaked with yet another consideration: Bridget's visit had been a success beyond her wildest dreams. Promotion to the main board was a coup and her career prospects had never looked better. However depressed she might be about her private life, that was a considerable consolation.

The phone startled her out of her reverie.

'Hello?' she said.

'Hi, Clare. It's B.' Bridget had never used that diminutive before. Did it indicate a new level of intimacy?

'Hello, how are you?'

'Ragged. What about you?'

'The same. Where are you calling from?' The line sounded a little hollow.

'The plane. I just wanted to thank you. You certainly know how to show a girl a good time! I'm going to have to return the compliment when you're over in Houston.'

Clare remembered what Bridget had said at David's house. She shuddered at the thought that she might be introduced to another Society of Oser. For the moment her orgy-quota had been filled.

'It wasn't planned,' she said quickly.

'Sure. Listen. That guy you were with, Mal's friend?'

'Gary.'

'Was that his name? What does he do?'

'He's a builder. He built my house extension.'

'Oh.' She sounded disappointed.

'Is there a problem?'

'I thought I heard the blonde mention something about a shoot. I thought he was a model.'

212

'First time. She works for a magazine. They picked him for an assignment on men's suits.'

'Great! Get some copies of the photographs, will you? Courier them to the States. Tomorrow if you can.'

'Why?'

'That new men's perfume we're doing. We need a new face. Don't you think he'd be perfect?'

The Zeal range of men's toiletries was a new product-line for KissCo, the first time they had ventured into the male domain. The fragrances had been developed and the packaging designed, but as yet the advertising agency had failed to come up with the right face to identify with the product. Naturally, as market research showed, men would only buy such products if they felt they would make them sexually irresistible so the man chosen had to be a hunk. Bridget was right. Gary was perfect. Better than perfect. Who was more sexually irresistible than him?

'You're right!' Clare said enthusiastically. 'He'd be sensational.'

'So you'll get on to it?'

'I'll get the pictures tomorrow morning. Meantime I'll get him into our people and do some shots we can e-mail on the computer.'

'Great. Have fun. See you in Houston.'

Clare didn't hang up. She punched in Gary's number. There was no reply.

She tried again after half an hour. Still no reply. She wondered if he might be with Angela. They had apparently gone their separate ways last night, but at the moment she wouldn't put anything past her friend. Perhaps she had both men in her bed and was giving them a repeat performance. She punched her number into the phone.

213

'Hello?'

'Angela.'

'Hi Clare.' Her voice sounded subdued, expecting trouble. 'Listen, I know what you're going to say.'

'I'm not going to say anything,' Clare said, surprised that the sound of her friend's voice had wiped away any animosity.

'It was just an impulse, that's all. You know me.'

'Forget it.' It was impossible to be cross with her.

'You know what a greedy girl I am.'

'Is he there now?'

'Who, Gary? God no.'

'Or Mr Macho?'

'It was just a one-off.'

'Where did you find him, by the way?'

'Who, the stripper? These people have agents. I just called his agent.'

'Does he look good in a suit?'

'Hmm ... better without, don't you think? Weren't you tempted?'

'No – yes – no.'

'Let's have lunch tomorrow. My treat.' Angela wanted to build bridges.

'Great. Usual place. And, Angela, can you bring the photos from the shoot?'

'What for?'

'They'll be ready, won't they?'

'Yes.'

'I'll explain tomorrow.'

'See you then,' Angela said, sounding a little puzzled.

The doorbell rang as she put the phone down. At the same time there was another cloudburst.

Rain poured out of the sky in huge drops, bouncing noisily off the patio outside the window.

Clare opened the front door. In the short journey from his car to the door Gary had been soaked. He stood on the front path with rain running down his face, his T-shirt already transparent from the wet.

'Hi,' he said.

After the conflicting emotions she experienced last night, Clare had expected her reaction to seeing him to be mixed. It was not. Last night, despite the fact that his erection had been buried in another woman's mouth, her desire for him had been overwhelming. She felt the same reaction now.

'You're soaked,' she said.

'It would be nice if you'd let me in.'

She stood aside and let him into the hall, closing the door behind him.

'Wasn't sure I'd be welcome.'

'You're not.' She threw her arms round his neck and stretched up to kiss him on the mouth. She kissed him passionately, hungrily, as though she hadn't had sex with him for weeks. 'I never want to see you again,' she said, before crushing her lips against him once more. His tongue invaded her mouth. She sucked on it. It was hot and wet and made her body feel weak.

'Yeah, I can see that,' he said, breaking away. Effortlessly he hooked his hand under her knees and scooped her up into his arms.

'Never,' she said, as he carried her upstairs. 'I despise you. You disgust me.'

He strode into her bedroom. She kissed him again, gnawing on his lips, gnawing on his tongue.

'You'd better throw me out, then,' he said,

lowering her on to the bed.

She was wearing a baggy white T-shirt and a pair of white panties. He caught hold of the bottom of the T-shirt and pulled it over her head. She wasn't wearing a bra. He pushed her back on to the bed and dropped his mouth to her left breast, sucking on her nipple.

'I am going to throw you out, you animal. You can't possibly imagine I ever want to have anything to do with you again.' She struggled to sit up and attacked the belt of his jeans. Unzipping his fly, she freed his cock. It was erect, big and hard. She felt it throb as she curled her hand around it and squeezed it as tightly as she could. Her own sex was melting, so wet she was sure her juices were already soaking her panties. She had never wanted anyone as totally as she wanted him.

'You only want me for my body, don't you?' he said.

'Of course.'

He pulled the crotch of her panties aside. Once again there was no time to get undressed. The need was too urgent, too all-consuming. He threw her back and plunged his cock into her, filling her, giving her the instant gratification she only ever experienced with him.

'Just a bit of rough, that's all you want,' he said between clenched teeth, his cock powering into her, breaking the secret barrier in her sex, and ploughing beyond it.

'Yes, rough trade,' she managed to moan as she felt her vagina contracting around his erection, her body quickly giving into the inevitable.

Inspiration

Stephanie Ash

To Angélique,
who taught me
all I know

Chapter One

BEAUTY ARTICLES IN glossy magazines always say that the best way to match a foundation to your skin is to try it out directly on your face, rather than on your wrist where the skin is, quite simply, a totally different colour. It's a great theory, Clare thought, applying the rules of Max Factor to the medium of Monet, as she daubed a little more paint on to her model's cheeks. He twitched nervously – and excitedly, she hoped, since it wasn't the cheeks of his face that she was trying to match.

'That's cold,' he complained.

'Perfect,' Clare exclaimed, ignoring her model's little moans. She dashed back to her canvas with palette in hand and added another sweeping stroke to her latest nude. They were selling like hot cakes. Flying out of the studio to be hung on the walls of the rich, famous and voyeuristic.

'Stunningly realistic,' said the reviews. 'Remarkable use of colour.' And quite right too. She wouldn't have imagined that there were many artists who would go to such great lengths to perfectly match a skin tone.

'Just one more session and then I think we'll be finished, Michael,' Clare told the model as she neared him and his beautifully tanned buttocks quivered expectantly. 'It's OK. I think I've mixed enough paint now.' Was that a sigh of disappointment she heard? 'Well, I suppose I could always . . .'

Clare traced a line down her model's back, from the nape of his neck, right down his left leg, with a soft clean brush. When she reached his strong, brown calves, he slowly rolled over so that he was lying on his back, ready for her to continue her journey. As she drew the brush along his instep his toes scrunched in delight.

'That tickles,' he moaned.

'I'll show you what tickles,' Clare told him, a devilish glint in her eyes.

She threw the brush down on to the floor and clambered on to the couch so that she was balancing precariously at its end. Where the brush had left off, she picked up with her tongue, circling the bone of his ankle before attempting to find the least hairy path up his shin to his thigh.

Softly, softly. Clare held her long dark hair out of the way so that the only part of her that touched him was the tip of her tongue. Every slow inch or so she took a break and looked up to see his reaction. His eyes were shut. Eyebrows raised in a gesture of pleasure. But when he felt she had been looking and not licking for too long, he opened his eyes to implore her to continue. And what incredible eyes they were. Green flecked with ginger, like the eyes of some kind of mythical creature that had just come in from the woods.

Clare's eyes met his. Then his gaze dropped to something which was starting to come between them.

'Do, please, carry on,' he murmured with a smile.

She didn't need asking twice.

Clare lowered herself back on to her path and it wasn't long before she found that it was going vertical. She rested a while. The tip of her tongue hovering at that spot where the balls join the dick. His hips skewed slightly to one side, then he dropped one leg off the couch so that she was able to settle herself into a more comfortable position to finish what she had started.

The model ran a hand through his thick tawny hair, then wiped away the sweat that had begun to gather on his brow. Clare liked to have her studio hot. A single dewy bead glistened at the eye of his penis. She longed to know if he tasted as good as he looked. Like a chameleon, she flicked out her tongue and hit the spot. An involuntary groan of delight escaped his lips.

Having reached her destination, Clare decided that it was about time she backed up the work of her tongue with her hands and wrapped her paint-smeared fingers around his now impressively large shaft. But her model was tired of this one-sided teasing. Suddenly, he had risen from his prone position and it was Clare who was on her back, her head dangling over the end of the chaise longue, throwing her throat open to his expertly light kisses. Deftly he unfastened the silk kimono which she always wore to paint since it gave her such freedom of movement. For a moment, he merely appreciated the view.

'You are so gorgeous,' he breathed, running a soft hand along the pale pink contours before him.

On the wooden floor beside the couch was a bottle of olive oil that Clare used to add to her oil paints from time to time to give them a slightly smoother texture. As her arm dropped from the side of the chaise longue, her hand brushed against it. Involuntarily she looked towards it. But it was too late, her model had spotted the bottle too and Clare rolled her eyes as he picked it up and began to pour a little of the viscous golden liquid into the palm of his hand.

'Warm that up!' she demanded. Too late. His hand came face down on her belly and she breathed in sharply at the shock of the cold virgin oil against her skin. But it was quickly abated as he slid his hand around in a circle three or four times to spread the oil out. He looked deep in thought for a moment and she shivered as he drew a finger across the shiny surface he had made of her skin. He drew a line from her breastbone to her navel, which ended in a quick exploratory dip into that oil-filled orifice.

Then, ever so slowly, he began to slide both palms up the centre of her body, spreading them out when he reached her breasts, smearing the oil all over them so that they shone like burnished bronze. An involuntary moan escaped her lips as his palms brushed lightly over her fast firming

222

nipples. And then he was moving down, down. Drawing his hands back over her belly and down to her thighs, one hand on each, wrapping his fingers around their curving muscles. Long, fast, hard strokes from her hips to her ankles made the blood begin to zing around her lower body.

Clare was covered now from neck to toe, shining with oil, and the beginnings of a sweat as the feel of his hands and the sight of his concentrated expression aroused her circulation in all the right areas. He, too, was glowing.

'Feeling good?' he asked.

She nodded.

His hands were steadily creeping up the insides of her satiny, glistening thighs, which tensed with anticipation. He stopped, the tips of his thumbs just an inch or so away from her lips. Their eyes locked again, his narrowing with mischief. As her thighs tensed, when he moved his hands ever closer to her vagina, she felt her own wetness, oozing out on to her skin.

'Aaaah.'

He slipped a single finger into her vagina. The delicious sensation of penetration. The walls of her vagina rippled in pleasurable reply to his gentle thrustings. As he thrust, he stretched up to kiss her, first on one nipple and then the other. Sucking each hard, pink bud into his mouth until she felt the pressure of his teeth and it almost hurt. Between his kissing lips and thrusting finger, her body was alive with sensation.

Then he moved up Clare's body, taking his hand from her pussy and instead cupping it beneath her head, to stop her from falling off the couch. His body was now full length on top of hers. As he shifted position, she could hear little slurping, sticking sounds, of the oil between them. His neglected penis now lay impatiently between her closed thighs. She opened them awkwardly beneath his weight and his dick sprang into the gap like a missile dropping from the hatch of a bomber. He was still kissing her mouth, licking it, biting it gently, as he rocked and ground his slim hips against hers and his still stiffening dick nudged at her other lips.

'Can I?' he asked, gazing into her eyes. His pupils were so dilated with desire that his green eyes looked almost all black. Clare nodded slowly, and slid her hands around to his buttocks. Even as she was nodding, she could feel him suddenly increase the pressure of his rocking against her body. She opened her legs wider still and pressed his body towards hers.

'Aaaah.' The first thrust. The magical feeling of yielding to pleasure. Clare held him tight to her for a moment, to stop him from moving again while she savoured the sensation of the first thrust of their first fuck.

The ringing of the telephone broke Clare's concentration – and burst the bubble of her daydream. The luscious nude she had been painting in her mind once again became a washed out sea-scape. Her buttock palette, an old plastic egg box. She quickly wiped her paint smeared hands on the seat of her jeans and dashed from the studio into the lounge to take the call.

'Hello,' she trilled, full of expectation.

'Well, hellooo darling,' replied the caller. 'It's Graham from the Dragon Gallery.' That much Clare had already guessed. The sigh that she now exhaled as she shifted the phone to her other ear was definitely one of disappointment.

'What's up with you?' Graham asked.

'Just tired.'

'Up all night, eh?' His laugh made Clare feel as though someone was tying her insides in a knot.

'I wish.'

The dirty laugh again.

'What do you want, Graham?' She tried not to sound irritated.

'I've sold six of your paintings this week . . . To an American woman who wanted to take a little piece of England back to all her friends. She wants some more, as well. She's got a gallery in Houston. She reckons she can take at least – twenty. They've got money to burn, those Yanks.'

'Cheers, Graham, I happen to think my work is worth buying.'

'Oh, I didn't mean it like that. You know I think you're priceless. You can come in and collect the money whenever you want. Or if you can't make it in during the day perhaps . . .'

The last thing Clare wanted was to see Graham from the Dragon Gallery during the hours of darkness, so she quickly said, 'I'll pop in just before lunch.'

'Lunch – that'd be great.'

'Lunch with Daniel,' she added, firmly.

'Haven't you got rid of him yet?'

'When I do, you'll be the first to know.'

'Oh well,' more sighs of disappointment. 'I'll see you in a bit, then.' Graham hung up. Clare felt like washing the ear that had been next to the receiver.

'Who was that?'

'Good afternoon, Daniel!'

Rip Van Winkle had finally awoken. Daniel, Clare's boyfriend, stood at the door of their bedroom, rubbing his eyes.

'Graham from The Dragon.'

Daniel made a face that echoed her feelings about the gallery owner who was definitely more interested in seeing her panties than her paintings. 'What did he want?' asked Daniel.

'He sold six paintings this week. Two of them big ones. That means we can get the car fixed.'

'That's great, really great ... Did he sell any of mine?'

She shook her head.

'Oh.' A shadow of jealousy passed quickly across his face to be replaced by a slightly strained smile. 'Hey, well, I guess I'm just following in the footsteps of Van Gogh. I'll sell for millions when I'm dead.'

There was no laughter in Daniel's voice as he told his self-mocking joke.

'Come back to bed,' he said, curling his arms around Clare's waist and nestling his face in her shoulder. She squeezed him back momentarily. 'You look like you need a good fuck.'

Clare blushed. She was probably still flushed from her day-dream. 'I've got to get some paintings done,' she told Daniel as she unwrapped his arms from her body. They sprang back, in a

226

tighter grip. Daniel nuzzled more ardently.

'Work later . . . later,' he whispered.

'No,' Clare protested. 'Work now.' Daniel was tousled and smelly from eleven hours sleep. 'I've got to do this now. The American woman who bought those paintings wants some more, for her own gallery back in the States. It could be the start of something big.'

'So could this,' Daniel pulled her hand down to the front of his shorts where the cotton was beginning to stretch and tighten over his hardening dick.

'I'll wake you up for lunch,' Clare said, wrestling her hand away. She popped herself out of his arms and fled towards the studio they had made of the spare room. Daniel didn't make it back to bed either. Grumbling, he slumped down on to the sofa and flicked on the TV.

Clare made her living as an artist. Her boyfriend Daniel was an artist as well – probably a better one than she, but about as commercial as an electric blanket in Death Valley. They had met at art school, getting together almost as soon as they started their course, and had been together ever since. Clare had been captivated by Daniel's brilliance, his originality, his imagination, which was as evident in him as it was in his pictures. And he also had a great body, well-muscled and lithe, usually clothed in black; he had dark, wildly curling hair and pale grey-blue eyes like those of a timber wolf . . . She sometimes thought that he had hypnotised her into bed with him.

After leaving college they moved to St Ives. For the light of course. The perfect light for painting which tempted so many people, who should have stuck to painting their dining room walls magnolia, to hang up the rat race for a stipple brush. Fresh out of college, they were used to being penniless and keen to continue being penniless in somewhere a little less polluted and materialistic than London.

Money doesn't matter to us, they would tell each other while they were still at college. We only need our artistic integrity . . . and each other. One or the other of them always seemed to add that as an afterthought. They were fiercely independent of each other, or at least it was fashionable to appear that way, but secretly Clare was overjoyed at the prospect of being in a strange town where she knew nobody but Daniel, the man of her dreams. Where they had only each other for company. And she thought that he was too. He needed her more than he could have admitted, she was sure.

The first few weeks, perhaps even the first two months, in Cornwall passed in a happy whirlwind of coastal walks and Cornish pasties. The sun shone. It was the hottest summer in four years. And both Clare and Daniel found part-time work very easily. Clare waited tables in one of the nicer guesthouses while Daniel pulled pints in the pub next door. By the time Clare had finished serving dinner and washing up, it would almost be time for Daniel to finish his shift too. She would wait for him in the corner of the lounge, sipping an orange juice, watching him work, listening to the happy chat of holiday makers and thanking her lucky stars that she had ended up in

Cornwall with him, rather than in London, slogging her guts out, designing silly patterns on cheap material to be turned into cheap dresses for a cheap chain store or painting fluffy animals on to cheesy birthday cards like so many of their art college friends.

But so much for artistic integrity. They certainly didn't paint much in those first two months. Just sleeping, serving in the restaurant . . . oh, and having sex. The novelty of their own flat, with a double bed! They had to make up for three years of sharing hot, restless nights in one of their single beds in the halls of residence. Hot and restless because the beds were too damn small and creaked too loudly, next to walls too paper thin to allow them to really let go when they were making love.

Oh, the joy of being able to moan in pleasure and know that you wouldn't have to face the textiles student in the room next door doing an impression of your passion over breakfast! One particular prat, called Darren, was always quoting clichés shouted at the height of passion. A girl on Clare's floor would always regret having screamed 'Oooh, baby, you're the pneumatic drill and I'm the pavement,' though Clare thought it was stranger that nobody asked Darren how he managed to glean all these gems of aural sex!

Anyway, the first two months in St Ives were great. But then the summer ended.

Daniel lost his job first. The landlord had warned him that it would only be for the summer, though Daniel had hoped that he might be kept on when the tourists went home. But the recession had bitten badly. Unfortunately, it was a case of last in, first out. As for Clare, she lasted just a little longer at the hotel, but as soon as the 'Vacancies' sign went up in the window again, she was looking for a vacancy of a different sort.

Never mind, they consoled each other. They had saved a little money. Clare had done quite well for tips and had been carefully banking them at the end of every week. They'd sign on. They'd get by. After all – hadn't they come to St Ives to paint? To follow a vocation?

Daniel took up his brushes with a vengeance. The passion that they had recently shared in bed exploded on to his canvasses in bold swathes of blood red and roman candle explosions of orange and yellow.

But those pictures, the pictures that Daniel and Clare wanted to work on, canvasses that meant something to them, just weren't going to sell in this town. Joe Public would probably pronounce them a 'bit too modern for my tastes'. They wanted something to remind them of their holidays; a nice landscape, fishing boats by the sea. Something that would look 'very nice thank you' on their apple white walls and not grab them by the throat when they were walking around the house bleary-eyed in the morning.

So Clare painted some 'very nice thank you' stuff, while Daniel insisted on grabbing throats and Clare's fishing boats sailed out of the galleries, while his red, black and raucous canvasses stayed firmly put, week after week after week. Daniel accused Clare of having sold out . . . and she paid the rent.

Daniel was still lying on the sofa, snoring gently, when Clare emerged from their makeshift spare bedroom studio two hours after Graham's call. She flicked the TV off. If he awoke to the sound of the Neighbours theme tune he would watch that, and then Home and Away, then two or three quiz shows, and then the children's programmes, but if he woke up and the TV wasn't on, he might just be tempted to pick up a paintbrush instead.

Clare smoothed his fringe away from his sleeping eyes. He smiled in his dreams. He was still the most beautiful man she had ever seen.

Chapter Two

THE DRAGON GALLERY was just about the best place to have your work displayed in town, next to the new Tate of course. It was near enough to that more famous gallery to ensure a steady flow of customers who were slightly more interested in art than average and therefore slightly more willing than average to pay for it.

Graham, the gallery owner, greeted Clare with that grin of his that always made her queasy. He held out the money from the sale of her paintings in a brown envelope and moved it backwards as she reached for it, forcing her to topple forwards so that her nose ended up buried in his sleeveless maroon jumper.

'Oops,' he exclaimed, helping Clare regain her balance by pushing her upright by the tits. Clare brushed herself off, snatched the money and tried to laugh light-heartedly. She couldn't afford to have him put up his commission for the sake of a little painful flirtation.

She counted out the money.

'Don't you trust me?' he asked, slipping an arm around her squirmmg waist.

'I don't trust myself when I'm near you, Graham,' Clare quipped. He seemed pleased. Money counted, she slipped it back into the envelope and then into her bag. She gave a 'see you when I see you' kind of wave and started to make for the door.

'Hang on,' he called, 'I need you to sign something to say that you've had the money and I've also got something rather special to give you, oo-er.'

Clare cringed and stopped, but waited right by the door, holding it slightly ajar, ready to make a quick getaway. Graham scribbled a makeshift receipt.

'So, how's your boyfriend?' he couldn't help asking as he wrote.

'Fine.'

'Where's he taking you for lunch?'

'Somewhere romantic.'

'So you're not planning to leave him and come and live with me yet?'

'No,' Clare said flatly, adding to keep him sweet, 'At least, not until you leave your wife.' She was studying Graham's thinning hair. He was mesmerisingly ugly. Everything in the wrong proportions. He looked like the FA Cup. In fact the only thing right about him was the number of eyes he had. As she focused on a lightly hairy mole on the side of his neck Clare remembered a girl at college who had read in a psychology book that if you look at anyone, and that is absolutely anyone, for long enough you will find yourself falling in love with them . . .

'Hey dreamer,' Graham purred. He had caught her looking at him, studying his neck. He probably thought she was sizing him up for a love bite. A little self-consciously he ran his fingers through what remained of his hair. He proffered the receipt and Clare signed it with the flourish that she would one day use to sign limited edition prints of the biceps and buttocks of the rich and famous. 'Well . . . don't spend it all at once!' Graham joked, 'unless you're stocking up on sexy undies for me.' Clare groaned. 'And I'd like a couple more of those water colour harbour pictures, if you have the time.'

'For you, Graham, I'll make the time.'

'Hey, don't forget this.' He handed her a small white envelope. She opened it and drew out a white card, with the dragon logo of the gallery embossed upon it in gold. 'The gallery's been open for ten years, so I'm having a party on Thursday to celebrate. You know, champagne and caviar! I'd like you to come . . . In fact, I'd love you to come.' He placed unnecessary emphasis on that last word.

'Mmm,' Clare thought, 'a party at the Dragon Gallery? Great venue. Champagne and caviar? Wonderful. But champagne and Graham? That could be a dangerous combination.' She'd probably have to have toothache on Thursday night instead.

'The wife is going to be at her mother's,' he added.

Did he think that was an incentive? Clare would definitely have toothache that evening now! But instead she told him, 'I'll try and be there . . . And I'll bring Daniel too, if that's OK?'

Graham sighed. 'I suppose so. Have a nice romantic lunch. Maybe one day I'll show you what romance is really about.'

Clare stepped out of the gallery laughing but her good mood didn't last long. Romance! What a joke. At best, her romantic lunch was going to be a couple of salad cream sandwiches at a paint-covered table, opposite a guy who, having given up on painting, was now determined to make sulking an art-form. She was nearing the flat, one hand on the front gate, the other in her pocket searching for her key, when she decided, 'Sod this!' Clare was going to treat herself. She glanced up at the window. She couldn't see Daniel so she figured that he hadn't seen her nearly arrive home. Clare would go to the vege-tarian restaurant by the harbour that she had drooled over so many times, and then she would go and get her hair done, and a facial, and perhaps even a manicure. She had the cash in her pocket. If she went home now she would end up going to the pub with Daniel, to drown his sorrows with her money.

Clare closed the gate carefully and quietly with a bit of a sigh. It didn't seem that long ago that she wouldn't have dreamt of not wanting to spend lunch time, or any time, with Daniel. She remem-bered her birthday a year earlier, when he had surprised her with a champagne picnic lunch in Hyde Park. Even though it had begun to rain cats and dogs just seconds after they opened the first bottle, they hadn't minded. They had turned the picnic blanket into a rather ineffective tent and spent the afternoon beneath it, kissing, cuddling and catching colds.

It was hard to imagine that the Daniel she had left behind at the flat that morning was the same guy. Cornwall wasn't working out for him. Clare loved it. She was inspired. But she thought that perhaps Daniel felt dampened. Depressed by the lack of insight people here in Cornwall were showing into the way he painted. He needed to be in London. But she didn't need to have him taking out his frustrations on her.

Clare tried to put her worries about Daniel out of her mind.

On the way to the cafe she swung by the newsagents and picked up a glossy magazine so that she could pick a new hairstyle while she ate her lunch. She flicked through it as she walked along, reading the headlines.

'Every woman deserves a sexual adventure!' screamed the big pink letters on page five.

'My sentiments exactly,' she heard herself exclaim to the gulls wheeling in the grey sky.

In the tourist season Clare would have had to queue for about three days to get a seat in the haven of dried flowers and Viennese blinds that was Muffin's, but now, in October, it was almost empty. Two elderly ladies with hair dyed to match their pastel outfits sat at the best table in the window. There was just one other customer, towards the back of the shop. A guy, about thirty-five, reading a paper, looking incongruously sophisticated against the tea-shoppe kitsch. The waitress placed a double espresso in front of him, smiling widely as she did so. He looked up briefly to thank her and Clare couldn't help straining over the refrigeration cabinet which blocked her view to see if his face lived up to the overall impression, which, for a man in St Ives outside the holiday season, was not bad at all.

'What do you want, love?' the woman behind the counter asked Clare as she was in mid gawp. Embarrassed, Clare looked back to the cabinet and picked out a pasta salad, which looked reasonably healthy, and a large piece of strawberry shortcake to reward herself for being so restrained in her first choice. And a cappuccino. As the woman behind the counter revved up the coffee machine and poured that out, Clare glanced around the room. Seconds later, she found her gaze drawn back to the man with the espresso. He looked interesting, intelligent. As he studied his paper, his brows were drawn together in concentration. Who was he? What was he doing here in this Laura Ashley nightmare of a place? Would it be terribly unsubtle to go and sit at the table next to him? There were about nine other tables in the shop but she decided what the hell, she would sit there. He was so engrossed in his paper that he probably wouldn't have noticed if she sat on his lap.

But he did notice when Clare spilled her coffee there instead.

She flew into a panic, blushing furiously, apologising and dabbing at his pale blue shirt with a paper napkin. Suddenly he grabbed her wrist, to stop her frantic fussing. Their eyes met and for a moment she couldn't tell what he was thinking at all. His eyes were of such a dark brown that you could hardly see where the irises ended and his pupils began. They were expressionless for what seemed like an age, then they began to crinkle at the corners and what could have turned into a snarl became a smile.

'Stop fussing,' he told Clare in a low, quiet voice. 'It was my fault since it was my case that you tripped over ... This shirt could do with a wash anyway, and it was your coffee that was spilt. Sit down and I'll buy you another one.'

Clare sat down next to him in a daze and he clicked his fingers to summon the attention of the girl behind the counter who practically flew across the room to do his bidding. As the waitress neared, he took off his coffee-stained shirt, since the quickly cooling wet patch was making him uncomfortable, and revealed a tight sleeveless vest. The woman who owned the café tutted in disapproval.

'Do you think they have a dress code here?' the man laughed.

Clare's eyes met those of the girl who was taking their order over a well defined bicep. She raised her eyebrows and smiled conspiratorially.

He was indeed something to raise your eyebrows about. Though slightly older than Clare had first imagined when viewing him from the back, he obviously took very good care of himself. The muscular arms, which were now folded on the gingham tablecloth, were matched by a pair of equally muscular legs in close-fitting blue jeans. His hair was just long enough to be sexily unkempt. The fringe flopped into his eyes from time to time to be pushed away by light tan fingers with beautifully manicured nails. His eyes were extraordinary, and Clare was surprised to get the feeling, which she had found in the past rarely to be wrong, that it wouldn't be too long before she saw them closed in ecstasy. She found herself wishing that she had gone to get her hair done before having lunch as she casually laid her left hand over a paint stain on her right sleeve.

His name was Steve. He was in property, he told her, in St Ives overseeing the conversion of a few big places into little holiday flats before the next season began. Home for him was normally London so they found common ground there talking about the pollution, the traffic, the stress. And blood pressure. Clare's, at that particular moment, seemed much higher than usual.

Clare said that she was an artist and he seemed genuinely interested when she told him about her artistic ambitions, even nodding knowledgeably when she mentioned a couple of the painters she emulated – names which normally drew nothing more than a blank look. He asked where she was living and she told him but when he asked who with she found herself saying 'just a friend'. As soon as she had said that she lowered her eyes as if he would be able to look into them at that moment and see the lie. Clare swirled what was left of her coffee around in the cup. She had picked nervously at the pasta salad and couldn't even start the shortcake.

'You've got a little way to walk to get home,' he said, when they had both finished. 'I think I may be going that way. Can I give you a lift?'

Clare said yes. The eyes of the women behind the counter seemed to be burning into her back as they left, but what the hell? She was only accepting a lift after all and he was such an interesting guy, she wanted to talk to him for just a little longer.

Clare tried not to look too pleased when she saw his car. A sleek racing green sports model, upholstered in creamy leather stood with its top down in the tiny car-park. He opened her door and she slipped inside.

'Nice car,' Clare breathed. Thinking to herself, 'I could get used to this.'

'Looks even better now,' he replied, smiling at Clare's legs as her long wrap-around skirt took that opportunity to get caught in the door and pull open.

'What make is it?' Clare asked, running her fingers along the dashboard, and making it clear with her eyes that she'd like to be running her fingers across Steve.

'It's a TVR Griffith,' he told her as he started up the powerful engine. 'But I call it Frankie.'

'Frankie?'

'Long story.'

Steve began to drive and Clare felt guiltily disappointed that he headed straight back to her place and didn't attempt to spin the journey out. She got him to drop her on the corner of the road where she lived. The last thing she needed was for grouchy Daniel to see her getting out of some green mean machine, so she told Steve that it would be easier for him to stop there. As they said goodbye there was an awkward moment between them. Clare contemplated asking him in for a coffee, sure that Daniel would enjoy talking to this guy as well, but something prevented her. The promise of something other than a friendship in the way he kissed her hand in farewell.

'Well, it was lovely to talk to you,' he told her.

She nodded.

'I'll see you around, I hope,' he said.

'Maybe,' Clare replied.

She watched as he drove off. The nervous tingle which had been with her at the café had still not abated. Neither had the disappointment that he hadn't taken the opportunity to whisk her straight off to some deserted hill-top car-park, but, as she stepped out of the car, Clare had noticed a familiar little white envelope, out of which poked a gold-embossed invitation. It had been tucked down the side of the passenger seat. Perhaps she would be going to the party at the Dragon Gallery after all . . .

Chapter Three

'DO YOU WANT to come to Graham's party?'
Clare asked Daniel as she slicked on another layer
of deep plummy lipstick. 'I feel that I've got to go
because Graham has been so good about taking
my paintings but it'll just be full of people from
the art society talking about their children's piano
lessons and mortgages and . . .' Daniel was
already shaking his head. A thrill of excitement
raced through her. She was going to the party on
her own.

'You look very pretty,' Daniel said as he
wandered into the bedroom. Clare smiled her
thanks, feeling a little guilty over the effort she
had been making. But she didn't have anything to
feel guilty about, she reminded herself . . . yet.

'Shall I help you do that up?' Daniel began to
button up the back of Clare's long red silk dress.
It was stunning, but not in an obvious way, clinging tightly to the contours of her breasts and her
waist before flaring gently out in a sweep of fabric
that reached her ankles. She felt covered and yet

revealed. The feeling of the silk around her legs as she walked was like the caress of soft hands. Daniel fastened the last button and then ran his hands down the line of her body in appreciation, giving a low whistle as he did so.

'Do you think I should wear my hair up?' Clare asked. 'With this dress?'

'I don't know,' said Daniel, smiling. 'I can't have you going out looking too beautiful.'

Clare began to pin her long, gently waving hair up away from her neck.

'Ah well,' Daniel sighed, stroking a finger lazily up her exposed nape. 'I suppose I'll just have to hope you're going to let me help you take all this off later on.' Clare kissed him on the tip of his nose, leaving a bright ring of lipstick there.

As Clare walked through the town, down the steeply sloping streets to the Gallery in the chilly night air, she found herself humming an old tune she always used to play on her stereo when she and her best friend, Anna, were sixth formers, getting ready to go out and do some under-age drinking in one of their grotty home town pubs. They would have been planning their Saturday night all week. Even co-ordinating their outfits so that they complimented each other and didn't clash. They would start putting their make-up on at five in the afternoon! But that was part of the fun. Saturday nights were always full of promise, the air heavy with hairspray and expectation. Whether chatting up someone gorgeous or putting down someone grotesque, they always had a brilliant time. Walking to the Gallery, she felt that Saturday feeling. How she'd missed it, going out with Anna and the other girls. At college, the social scene had been all couples. Clare wanted a bit of flirtation again ... seduction.

She would give Anna a ring the very next day. See if she wanted to come down for a weekend. Clare could ship Daniel off to one of his mates in London and she and Anna could relive the wild time they had had in Cornwall after finishing their A Levels. They had spent a week in Newquay, while the Hot Tuna Surf Championships were taking place. The weather had been great; they sat on the beach all day and in some pub or other all night. They'd scored left, right and centre. In fact, Anna had managed to pull a really great guy who turned out to live just nine miles away from their home town. They were still together. They had a mortgage now. In fact, getting Anna to leave her Ikea-clad pad and come to Cornwall for a wild weekend would probably be just marginally easier than squeezing blood from a stone these days. Clare stopped just in view of the Gallery and looked up at the stars. Was that what she and Daniel had in store now that they had left college and were officially living together? Better furniture and less sex?

The face of the man she had met in the café slipped in amongst her memories and she found herself smiling in anticipation of seeing him again. Nothing would come of it, she told herself, but it would be nice to flirt. Nice to have someone new and different appreciate the way she looked. See her first and foremost as a woman, rather than as an artistic rival and an unpaid maid, which was how she felt Daniel sometimes saw her these days, and not necessarily even in that order. A street away from the Gallery she stopped and checked her lipstick in the wing mirror of a car. No smudges, still a perfect outline. Kissable, she thought, just kissable.

Graham smiled warmly as usual when Clare walked through the door into his party, but his face positively rivalled the Blackpool illuminations when he realised that she had no boyfriend in tow.

'Lovely to see you,' he trilled, wrapping an arm around her silk-clad waist and ushering her into the main room. 'Where's your boyfriend?' he asked, as if he really wanted to know.

'Where all good men should be. He's chained to my bed,' Clare winked and thought that Graham might even have blushed.

Graham made a few quick introductions which she didn't really take in. She was surprised to see that so many guests had already arrived. She scanned the room hopefully, nodding hellos to familiar faces, but she was disappointed to see no trace of Steve. Perhaps he was in the adjoining room, from which people were emerging with glasses of champagne and punch. As soon as it was humanly and politely possible, Clare would excuse herself from the little group of aspiring watercolourists to whom she had just been introduced, and head for that room. Her pulse quickened a little at the thought that Steve could be just behind that door.

'A drink, Clare?' Graham asked. 'Champagne? Punch?'

'Yes,' she said eagerly, 'but don't worry about me, I'll get it.'

Clare made a dash for the other room. Of course Steve wasn't inside. She glanced at her watch. It was quarter past eight. The party had only started at half past seven. He was the kind of person who would probably turn up to one of these dos later rather than as soon as the door opened. But how much later? She'd been at the party for five minutes and had already exhausted all the conversation she had for any of the other guests. It crossed her mind more and more frequently that he might not even come at all. Just because he had an invitation . . . After all, before Clare had seen his invitation and thought that he might be at the party, she had been going to try and give this evening with Graham a miss.

Clare wondered how Steve knew Graham.

'Clare, Clare,' Graham was calling, 'There's someone here I'd like you to meet.' Steve perhaps? She poured herself a glass of the champagne punch, in which rose petals floated for extra effect, and strolled back into the main room, smoothing down her hair and plastering on her best smile.

'Clare, meet Henry.'

Clare struggled to keep the warm smile on her face as a tall, thirty-something guy with a floppy fringe held out his hand to her. His hand-shake was as limp as his hair and once the formalities of introduction were over, he just stood there in front of Clare, saying nothing, watching her avidly as if the true meaning of life was about to come from her lips. Graham had disappeared to circulate. He must have introduced me to Henry deliberately, Clare thought – a ploy to make her so desperate by the end of the evening that Graham's limited charms would be as irresistible as Harrison Ford's.

'I need the loo,' Clare told her new acquaintance, two minutes later, when she had finished her potted autobiography and he still showed no sign of starting his own. Henry nodded enthusiastically. Clare sloped off with the intention of spending fifteen minutes reapplying her lipstick before she slipped back into the room and made a bee-line for the corner opposite the one in which Henry was lurking. When she emerged twenty minutes later there was still no sign of Steve. How long should she give him? How long could she stand to give him, more to the point? Henry was scanning the crowd as well . . . for Clare. It was unbelievable to her that there should be a man in the room she wanted to be with even less than Graham.

'Graham, Graham!' Clare called, as Henry finally got her in his sights. Graham was wandering past with a couple of glasses of punch for his guests. When he had delivered them, he shot straight back to Clare and wrapped his arm around her waist again.

'Having a good time?' he asked.

'Oh, yes,' she smiled graciously, it was almost as good as her sixteenth birthday party, when Susie Powell had turned up in exactly the same dress and scored with Clare's boyfriend, who claimed that he was drunk and confused. 'But please rescue me from that dreadful man . . .' Graham was only too pleased, and immensely flattered.

It was half past ten. Steve still hadn't turned up. As Clare sipped a third glass of champagne punch – she'd been taking it slowly, because if Steve wasn't going to turn up, she certainly didn't want to be at the mercy of Graham – she wondered how she could make her escape. Graham was showing a couple of insipid prints to the wife of a local councillor. While he was so engrossed, Clare could just slip out of the door. It would be a little rude not to say goodbye but every time she had tried to say goodbye so far that evening, he had introduced her to another local art world bigwig and she'd been forced to prolong her stay. What a great night, she thought sarcastically. She was feeling slightly less spectacular in her red silk dress now. Some idiot had managed to spill punch down her back.

The councillor's wife had dragged Graham on to explain another painting that was further still from the door. Slowly, Clare crept backwards, like a child playing a game, not turning round until the last moment so that, should Graham look towards her, it wouldn't look as if she was making a bid for freedom at all. It was while she was walking backwards, not looking where she was going, that she crashed straight into a familiar back, sending a drink swirling through the air in an arc, to land, once again, on an expensive clean shirt.

'Oh my goodness,' Clare exclaimed in delight as she joyfully recognised her victim. 'Steve, I am so sorry.'

'You again,' he smiled, his face mirroring the pleasure on hers. 'I might have known. Where were you going, walking backwards like that?'

'I was making my escape,' she muttered sheepishly.

'Good idea.'

'You been here long?'

'Ten minutes or so.'

'I've been here since eight.'

They laughed conspiratorially. Graham looked over when he heard the sound of their laughter over the quiet hum of conversation.

'Look serious,' Steve told Clare. 'The last thing we want is for Graham to think we're having a good time and come over to join us.' Clare pulled a mock grave face.

Graham returned to his deep discussion with the councillor's wife.

'I really think I'm going to have to go now, Steve, before I become one of the permanent exhibits,' Clare told him. She was acting casual as she tried to put the idea of joining her into his mind.

'Are you heading home or heading on?' he asked. 'Can I join you?'

It had worked. Easy! 'I suppose so,' Clare shrugged. 'We could go for a walk on the beach.'

'I could certainly use the air. Right –' Steve grabbed her arm – 'We'll walk backwards towards the front of the Gallery, I'll start to push the door open and when I say go, we'll leg it.'

Clare nodded, and they began their retreat. 'Go,' Steve hissed when Graham's back was safely turned. They tumbled out into the car-park, giggling like children. 'Quick, let's get into the car!' Frankie the TVR was waiting, this time with its top up. Clare clambered inside and they sped off, tyres spinning in the gravel, just as Graham appeared at the gallery door, to bid another, more polite guest goodbye.

'He'll be so offended,' Clare said, looking out of the back window at the shrinking figure of their host.

'He'll get over it.'

'How do you know him, the gorgeous Graham?'

'Gorgeous? Surely you mean "gargoyle".' Steve laughed. He hesitated momentarily before he told her, 'I met him about five years ago, through a friend . . .' Clare didn't notice the way his voice tailed off.

'Some friend,' she smiled.

Steve pushed a compact disc into the player and suddenly the car was filled with the strains of stringed instruments and a girl singing about lost love.

'Where to?' he asked.

'Surprise me,' Clare replied, surprising herself. This time Steve wasn't going to be driving her straight home. She glanced at her watch and wondered how long she could risk staying out before Daniel started to worry, then, satisfied she had a couple of hours, she settled back into the deep, leather seat and gazed out of the window at the passing scene, then gazed inside the car at the profile of its driver. So beautiful. Better than she remembered. He had such a powerful profile. His lips were parted as he murmured along with the song.

Steve turned to smile at her. He slipped the car into fourth then his hand left the gear lever and alighted gently on her silk-covered knee. His eyes checked for a positive reaction while Clare felt almost breathless with the realisation that, if she wanted it, then this was it. Her cheeks prickled with heat as the exploratory hand began to move up her thigh.

'My hotel?' he asked quietly.

Clare took a deep breath and nodded her assent. His hand squeezed her thigh tighter in approval.

'Every woman deserves a sexual adventure,' Clare reminded herself as she watched the lights of the Gallery get smaller and smaller until they were gone.

Chapter Four

WHEN CLARE GOT back to the flat in the early hours of the morning, Daniel was already in bed. When he asked where she had been she told him that she had stayed behind, with a few of the others, to help clear up after the party. Then, she continued, they all went back to Graham's house for a night-cap. Clare claimed that a girl Daniel didn't know had given her a lift home. He didn't question her any further.

'Come to bed,' he murmured, stretching an arm out from beneath the duvet.

Clare shook her head. 'I want to get some painting done while I'm still in the mood,' she told him. 'Graham wants some more boat pics for the weekend.'

'But it's the middle of the night!' Daniel exclaimed. 'And I've been waiting and waiting for you to come back so that I could help you off with that dress . . .'

A guilty shudder ran through her but Clare gaily shrugged her shoulders as she reminded him, 'You can't choose when you're going to get hit with a flash of inspiration.'

'See if I care,' he grunted.

Yes, things had been getting a bit 'like that' between them lately, blowing hot and cold depending on whether or not Daniel felt he was getting his own way.

Clare wandered into their 'studio'. A canvas that Daniel had obviously cut up in anger while Clare was at the party was in bits all over the place. Any other night it might have bothered her, but not that night. She kicked some of the larger pieces of debris into a corner and set her own work up. She had a wonderful piece of canvas, larger than she usually used for the tourist paintings, which she had kept in reserve for the moment when that fickle muse struck. He had struck that afternoon in the café and again, tonight, at Graham's party. As Clare picked up her brush to make the first few marks she remembered the first touch of Steve's hand around her wrist. The wave of fear and excitement that had washed through and over her as she looked for the first time into those fascinating eyes. The evil anticipation of what she knew she was inviting when he asked her who she lived with and she told him 'just a friend'. And the illicit thrill of accepting a lift from a party, with a virtual stranger, after dark, that Clare knew would take her nowhere near home.

Her brush traced the outline of a strongly muscled shoulder.

They had skipped a late-night drink at the hotel

bar and tripped stealthily through the quiet corridors to Steve's room that overlooked the churning sea. Outside a light wind was whipping up tiny waves that speckled the blackness of the sea with white when the moon shone through a gap in the clouds. Standing by the window, looking out at the white horses and the reflection of the moon on the sea, Clare had shivered and Steve had put his arm around her, to keep her warm. Her skin was electrified as his fingers closed around her narrow shoulders.

His lips traced a path from the lobe of her ear to her shoulder. Instinctively, Clare turned around so that she was facing him, her forehead level with his lips. He took her chin in his hand and tilted her head back a little so that he was looking into her eyes. From deep within her, Clare felt the first ripple of anticipation, spreading out below her waist and up to her neck, making her nipples harden slowly so that when he asked her to lift her arms and carefully pulled her dress up over her head without unbuttoning it, they were already poking suggestively forward through her thin camisole. If Clare's mind was having doubts about the seduction of an impossibly handsome stranger in a hotel room, it was obvious that her body had already made its decision.

Steve ran two curious hands over the outline of Clare's cream silk-clad torso, his thumbs gently brushing across the unfaithful pink tips of her nipples. He leant forward to kiss her on the lips, softly, just once. It was hardly even a kiss at all, but the prelude to a kiss, before he quietly asked her to raise her arms again and discarded the camisole in the same direction as the dress.

A whisper of wind lifted the gauzy curtain from the window so that it brushed against Clare's back as Steve's lips brushed against the pale winter-white flesh of her belly. Clare shivered again, not with cold but delight. It was as if she was being seduced by a ghost and she wondered how long she would be able to stand these half-caresses before the wetness which was gathering between her legs made her beg him for something more.

It was as Steve knelt to explore her navel with his long probing tongue that Clare felt she could stand it no longer. She grabbed his golden brown head in her hands and pulled him up towards her lips. That tongue, at least, should be exploring the inside of her mouth.

As they kissed, hard, they staggered backwards towards the bed. Clare, almost naked. Steve, still fully clothed, though now slightly dishevelled. Clare scrabbled frantically with the buttons of his white shirt, with its red wine stain like a gunshot wound through his heart, and began to pull it away from his shoulders. He kissed her ever harder, squeezing her right breast with one hand as he used the other to pull down her smooth silk knickers. As soon as they were out of the way, he made just one quick circuit of the silky brown triangle of her pubic hair before returning, tantalisingly, to toy with both her breasts.

'Put something in me,' Clare pleaded. 'Something, anything!'

She felt she could drown in her own wetness. Never had she come so close to an orgasm while her clitoris remained so neglected. Steve continued to kiss her as if he had been starving for her mouth, but now, at last, his hand ventured lower.

There was no need for him to trace playfully around the lips of her vagina now. She was wet, open, ready. He slipped a finger straight inside and began to bring her to the point of no return with long, deliberate thrusts. The knuckle of his thumb, meanwhile, was hard against her clitoris, massaging hard in a way she had never before experienced. Clare's breathing was more shallow now, ragged, as each stroke took her by surprise.

The sensation was incredible. Unbearable!

Waves of tension flooded towards her vagina, building up like a sneeze that never, ever came. Clare couldn't come . . . or was she already coming? His thumb moved faster as the finger slid in and out, in and out, keeping the rhythm. The wave built up to her vagina again and spilled over . . . but not in the usual way. She could feel a shuddering gathering in her legs which made her want to draw them up to her chest and hug them until the feeling passed away.

'What are you doing?' Clare asked him breathlessly as she writhed on the silky sheet. The muscles in her stomach were contracting now, connected to the circuit. Waves of electricity were shooting up and down the side of her rib-cage, making goosebumps as they passed. Her hand instinctively flew down to where he was playing. If this next wave broke over the barrier she couldn't be held responsible for the number of innocents drowned!

'Stop,' Clare groaned, pushing his hand away

from her pulsing vagina. The intensity was just too much. But he was stronger, keeping his fingers in place while using his other hand to hold her own protesting one away. His finger advanced inside her again while his thumb continued its own game on her clit. The feelings he was producing were so intense that Clare wasn't sure whether he had a finger in her anus as well. From the waist down she was afire. 'No, Steve, please. Stop.' She writhed her body away from him and in doing so helped him drive his finger further in again.

'I have stopped,' he told her. A twitch at her G-spot said otherwise.

'Stop properly, take your hand away. I don't think I can stand it . . .' Her words were lost as she panted for breath.

'Do you really want me to?' he asked, his mouth touching hers as he whispered. She nodded, she couldn't say anything. 'I'm not moving my hand at all,' he continued. But Clare could still feel something, a pulsing deep inside her. 'It's you that's moving.' Then he commanded, 'Tighten your muscles around my finger.'

Clare did as she was told and the sensation was suddenly amplified. 'Again,' he whispered, 'Again'. The muscles of her vagina rippled, caressing his finger. She enjoyed it. She was beginning to enjoy it. She was in control. Her vagina was caressing his finger! And each time she contracted it was as if he was plunging it deeper into her!

'I'm not doing a thing,' Steve laughed. 'Do you still want me to stop?'

'No,' Clare squealed, as the barrier finally

broke and she had to bite into his shoulder while her body rippled like a crazy concertina on the inside and the outside and she soaked the sheet with come.

'I think I just had my first multiple orgasm.'

It wasn't long before she was ready for her second.

Clare lay on her back looking up at Steve's concentrated face. Now he was kneeling between her legs and had finally slipped off his trousers and stripy shorts so that when she cast her gaze down his body, it met with the picture of the perfect penis. Thick and long and pointing straight back at her. And just above it, nestling where his thigh smoothly became his groin, a tattoo, a blue and green serpent. He saw her look at it, pleasantly surprised.

'I was eighteen,' he said. 'It was my nickname.'

'The serpent?'

'Well, Steve the Snake actually,' he blushed.

Laughing with him, Clare reached out to trace with her finger the little picture. His cock bobbed for attention.

'That tickles.' Steve shuddered as his words made her trace the snake again, this time with a nail.

'I bet you had it put there for exactly that reason,' Clare told him.

Less patient with teasing than she was, Steve took hold of Clare's wrist and guided her wandering hand to his cock, which was smooth and hot to her touch. She curled her fingers gently around its pleasantly full girth and slid her fisted fingers slowly down over the shaft, which was already sticky with its own emission. Clare slid her hand down his cock just once and when she took her hand away it twitched convulsively upwards again, as if in indignation. Steve took her face in his hands again and kissed her full, blushing lips.

'Carry on,' he whispered.

Clare slicked her hand upwards again, gradually building up a rhythm. Beneath her fingers, she could feel him getting harder and harder. With her free hand she tickled his balls.

'Stop,' he said suddenly. 'I feel like I'm going to come.'

'Then come,' Clare replied.

'No, I want to do something different.' Quickly, Steve began to roll on a condom, his face concentrated into a frown. Clare continued to tickle his balls to remind him she was still there. Within seconds the condom was on and he slid himself down again so that he was supported now on his arms, his legs between her shivering white thighs.

'Are you sure you want to do this now?' he asked gravely.

Clare had never been more sure of what she wanted in her life. She kissed his lips in reply, pulling him closer to her with one arm around his neck as her other hand slid down between them to guide him in between her longing lips. Her legs trembled in anticipation of this moment. As she touched her inner thighs in passing she noticed that they were still damp from the climax he had just made her give herself with his hand.

Steve's penis hovered temptingly at the lips of Clare's vagina. He moved himself up and down slowly, just grazing her lips as she scrabbled to take hold and bring his penis home.

'Let's do this slowly,' he purred, as the first, joyful inch slipped in and was withdrawn.

'Don't tease me,' Clare hissed.

'I never tease,' he lied, teasing her again with another shallow dive. And another and another. Just enough to make her sigh with disappointment as she felt all too short a length being withdrawn.

'I can't stand this.'

'Do you want me to stop?'

'No, no, I don't.' For a second he was hovering around the edge of her vagina again, then she took his buttocks in both her hands and lifted her thighs, pulled him right into her, and drove his penis home. Now she sighed with ecstasy and the pumping could begin in earnest, his energy driving her down into the soft white sheets while she clutched him to her and drew her fingernails up his back. Her heart was pounding so hard that she was sure that he could feel it too, pumping through her flesh and through his. She tried to keep her eyes open and focused on the face that loomed above her. His eyes were closed, his mouth open as he breathed more and more heavily as the movements of his pelvis became faster, more urgent. Clare suddenly lifted her trembling legs from the bed and wrapped them around his slim waist. She pulled his cock deeper inside with her muscles, squeezing as he had showed her before. 'Aaah!' the delicious extra pressure

260

on his dick was bringing his climax too close now, he couldn't hold off any longer and his firm strokes began to lose their rhythm. Clare ground her pelvis against him, exerting as much pressure on her clitoris as she could in that position. She too was beginning to lose control. The moment had taken over and Clare's whole being was trying to pull him closer, closer, further into her body, until the spasms that she could no longer hold back forced him to empty his passion into her, his head jerking backwards with each jet he spurted inside her. Eyes screwed tightly shut, his face the perfect picture of the peculiar agony of sex.

Back in the studio, Clare stood back to take a good look at the painting she had been working on. The man stood with his back to her, but the shadow, the outline of Steve's body was unmistakable. The strength in the shoulders, sweeping down to the slim waist around which she had wrapped her arms as she had kissed and tongued his cock so greedily. Clare could almost smell him. The sensual smell of sweat, soap and sex. Smells of the sophisticated man and the primitive creature within him. The taste of salt as she licked a line from the base of his balls to the tip of his penis where a silvery drop of semen had gathered in anticipation of the arrival of her lips at his most sensitive part.

Clare had wrapped both hands around it, holding it like a bottle of water, precious after a long, dry walk across the desert. He had moaned as she let her tongue touch just that drop of semen, tasting it, savouring it. Just the tip of her tongue had reached out again and again to him, tantalising the delicate ridge as her hands carefully roamed over his balls. In a moment of mischief she had blown on to them, making them contract and stir in the coolness.

Clare's own hand now traced the line down her body that Steve had followed with his hands. Slowly, she unfastened her dress and slipped her hand inside. She wasn't wearing her camisole. In her haste to leave the hotel and get back to the flat, she had stuffed all her underwear into the voluminous pockets of her baggy jacket. So now, her fingers touched achingly bare flesh, a nipple already hardened and sensitised by the silk of her dress that had been rubbing against her breasts as she painted. Clare rolled her nipple between her fingers exactly as Steve had done, then she moved her attention to the other. She didn't want any part of her body to feel left out . . .

Suddenly Clare was aware of someone standing behind her. She turned around slowly. Daniel had got himself out of bed and was leaning against the door frame, silhouetted by the light in the kitchen. He was holding two glasses, clinking with ice, as he stepped tentatively across the room, avoiding the debris of his own canvas.

Chapter Five

'THOUGHT YOU MIGHT be thirsty,' Daniel said, handing Clare a vodka on the rocks. He looked as if he had been crying.

'What did you paint?' he asked. Clare had thrown a sheet over the wet canvas at his approach.

'Nothing good. It went wrong,' she told him. He was almost lifting up the corner of the sheet. 'Don't look at it,' she implored him softly. 'You know I hate letting you see stuff that I'm not happy with.'

'I'm sure I would be impressed,' he assured her but he let the paint-splashed sheet drop again. The next day, Clare decided, she would have to get rid of her latest masterpiece.

'I'm sorry about earlier,' Daniel told Clare as he stood with his back to her, surveying the mess of his own ruined painting.

'No worries. It was my fault too. The fickle muse, eh?' Clare replied, knowing that his temper tantrum should be far outweighed in the guilt stakes by what she had just found herself doing. 'Let's go into the other room.' Even covered by a sheet, the portrait of the lover she had just painted burned into her mind, and her clitoris still pulsed gently in anticipation of a favourable climax to the self-pleasure she had just begun to give.

Now Clare felt strangely shy of this man she had known for so long. She sat on the sofa with the glass in her hands, swirling the liquid around nervously, avoiding Daniel's eyes as they talked about mundane things. What they had been doing that week. The football. Could he tell, she wondered. Did she look different? Did she smell different? She had only had time for a very quick shower before leaving the hotel, telling Steve that she had to go home because her housemate was returning from London at about five in the morning and had forgotten to take his key.

Daniel was perching on the coffee table opposite Clare on the sofa. He had opened his legs so that her knees were caught between his. Suddenly, as she was looking to the honey-coloured floorboards again, racking her brain for some sporting event to discuss, he took the glass from her hands and raised her fingers to his lips. His mouth trailed across them, one after the other, and then, drawing Clare closer, his lips touched her lips and they broke the ice that had formed between them with a kiss.

A tender touch for just a moment and then they began in earnest. His tongue forced her lips apart. Clare opened her mouth wider to let him probe inside. He traced her teeth with the quivering tip.

His tongue was penetrating her, echoing the actions he longed to make with other parts of his body. His hand on the back of her head, first gently guiding and then bringing her firmly towards him. A handful of her hair grasped in his fist. Causing Clare no pain but giving such a wonderful impression of force. Clare was melting into him.

Then, suddenly, a cold slash of sensation across her leg. They were sliding together, from the sofa to the floor and on their lustful journey had knocked Clare's half full glass over with them. Clare's body shuddered, but she was grateful for something so cool in the midst of all the heat that they were generating.

Now they writhed on the floor in a puddle of ice. Daniel clutched up a handful of it, eager not to waste any sensation. The top of Clare's dress was rolled down out of the way and he made straight for her nipples. Tracing delicately around the hardening, rose-pink tips until the ice was barely big enough to hold anymore and instead he massaged one breast fully in each cold palm while the slivers of ice became cold water that mingled with her sweat. Clare's back arched upwards, pushing out her firm breasts for more, searching for Daniel's lips and tongue. But he was sitting back on his heels again.

'One left,' he announced. A solitary ice-cube had not escaped the glass which now lay on its side. Daniel picked it out and held it tantalisingly between thumb and forefinger. 'Where do you want it?'

Where did Clare want it? Where didn't she want it?

'You know where.'

A smile flickered across his long-lashed eyes as he lifted the hem of Clare's skirt and dropped his hand to her mons, which was already thrusting up to meet him halfway. Now he was tracing again, but this time across the lips of her sex, still burning with the passion of her liaison in the hotel. She felt sure that Daniel would notice, that they must be glowing red, but he had restoked the fire which had yet to die down properly and Clare suddenly didn't care. The ice-cube salved them for a moment. Melting water trickled gently down between them.

'Does that feel good?' Daniel asked, as he watched the expression on her face change. Her mouth opened slowly in a silent gasp of pleasure.

'Yeeeesss!' Clare shivered. The sensation was incredible. The ice-cold water felt like liquid gold to her.

'But you must be feeling very cold now,' Daniel continued. 'I think you need something to warm you up.'

While Daniel had been turning ice-cubes to steam on Clare's body, she had been struggling to rid him of the boxer shorts he had been wearing when he went to bed. Now he had given up resistance and she could already feel the tip of his penis nudging at her opening as he licked the salt of sweat from the edge of her mouth. The nudging became more insistent, and her lips began to be forced inwards as Daniel fought to make his way in. Clare went to help him with her hands.

'No don't,' he said. 'Enjoy the friction.'

Just two more pushes and he was in. Clare inhaled sharply at the first delicious full thrust.

'You ... feel ... so ... good,' he told her. A word for each time he entered her. He placed a hand beneath the small of her back to protect her from the hard floor and to lift her pelvis higher so that he could drive deeper. She pushed down through her legs to help him on.

'Deeper, deeper,' Clare moaned, wanting more and more of him inside her still. His balls tapped against her perineum, intensifying the sensation, and her fingernails dug into the firm, twin cheeks of his bum as they tensed and relaxed, tensed and relaxed. Each time he plunged into Clare, he let out a small, animal-like grunt of pleasure, which transferred that pleasure to her. They became faster and faster, a grunt for each thrust, a thrust for each beat of her heart until, suddenly, the rapid thrusts became one long plunge. Daniel held himself in position against Clare's body, raised on his arms, his head thrown back, his mouth open, gasping for air, as his loins jerked convulsively.

Clare pushed up against him, willing his climax to continue forever as he flooded her with hot sticky come.

Afterwards, as they lay together on the rug, Clare couldn't stop a smile from passing across her lips. Daniel kissed it, thinking he had made her happy. But as Clare dreamily watched a spider walking across the ceiling, she was already thinking about the next time she could engineer a meeting with Steve.

Later Clare would ask herself why she didn't just throw that painting away. Things could have been so different. But when she woke up the morning after painting it and saw that Daniel was, thank goodness, still smiling, she figured that her soul probably hadn't been laid as bare by those brush strokes as she thought.

Graham at the Dragon Gallery raised an eyebrow as he eagerly tore away the brown paper in which Clare had wrapped the painting for the journey. He was expecting boats, not a butt. He held it at arm's length and turned it around and around, looking for the right way up, which, Clare supposed, wasn't entirely obvious.

'Is that your Daniel?' he asked.

'No, it's a fantasy work. Your party really fired my imagination.'

'What's it called?'

'It's called Graham. It's based on the way I imagine you must look beneath that mild-mannered maroon number.' Clare's liaison with Steve must have also fired her with a need for danger. She was actually flirting with Graham.

'Well, yes,' he blushed. 'I don't know if I'll be able to sell this one. It's very . . . er . . . erotic.' He turned it around again to catch the composition from another angle. 'But I guess I'll hang it. Since you named it after me.'

'So you enjoyed the party?' he asked as Clare watched the dark, brooding canvas take its place on the wall above a pastel portrait of a fisherman she had done a few weeks earlier. Clare nodded. 'I didn't see you leave,' Graham continued, 'Did you manage to get home all right? I was going to offer you a lift.' She nodded vacantly again. He wasn't going to draw anything out of her. 'Well, good. I don't like the thought of a girl going home on her own. You've got to be careful around some guys these days . . .'

Clare wasn't taking much notice. She was still gazing at the picture. It made her smile. Steve had touched something more in Clare than her G-spot. She was painting again. Really painting.

She was inspired.

'I think the American woman I told you about really liked the style of your landscapes . . . Keep them tasteful, eh?' Graham looked curiously at the girl's strange expression. 'Are you going to be able to get those done?'

'Mmm?'

'I said, are you going to be able to get those landscapes done for me?'

'What? Oh, yeah,' Clare suddenly refocused on Graham. 'Yeah. I feel like I could paint the Sistine Chapel today.'

'Really?' said Graham.

Clare tripped happily out of the gallery and went straight to the café where she and Steve had first met. She ordered exactly the same meal as she had that fateful day, for luck. She waited from twelve until two . . . but Steve didn't come.

Clare told herself that it was probably for the best. And anyway, if she grinned much more her face might have fallen in half.

Chapter Six

'GET THE DOOR would you, Clare?' Daniel screamed. Clare was painting in the studio, he was painting at their bedroom window, finally deigning to take some inspiration from the quaint little houses which spread out below. The door-bell chimed again. Clare and Daniel were engaged in a battle over whose work was less important, who could afford to put down their brush on the off-chance that it wasn't the Jehovah's Witnesses. Clare lost.

Clare opened the door to a petite blonde, about her age, but considerably better dressed, in a pastel blue suit. She offered Clare a hand which wore two subtly expensive rings and smiled to show a row of equally expensively cared-for teeth. Clare wiped her hand, complete with bitten nails, clean on the seat of her jeans and they shook.

'Clare?' she asked.

The dark-haired girl nodded.

'I'm Francesca Philip. I saw your paintings in

the Dragon Gallery. I do hope you don't mind my coming here. I'd like to commission you to do a painting for me. Graham gave me your address. I hope I'm not disturbing you.'

'Of course not,' Clare smiled, then she realised that her visitor was still standing on the doorstep. 'Come in.'

Daniel was standing at the door to the studio, eager to see who was coming in. Clare gave him a stern look as she saw his eyes light up at the entrance of the petite blonde. The petite blonde who didn't seem to notice him standing there. 'What an unusual place you have here,' Francesca said as Clare made coffee. She perched on the edge of the sofa, too shy or polite to move out of the way the books and brushes that cluttered it. While the kettle boiled, Clare made a quick search of the lounge for a reasonably intact and unstained mug, since all those left in the kitchen were missing handles or other vital chunks. A pair of knickers, discarded several nights before, lay by the side of the sofa. Clare swiftly kicked them beneath it before Francesca had time to notice the extent of her bohemian slobbery.

'What kind of thing are you looking for? Boats a speciality,' Clare joked.

'No,' Francesca said, missing the joke. 'Your boat pictures were very nice but I was hoping for something more along the lines of your portrait. The one called "Graham". I must say I didn't realise that he was such a dark horse . . . It was a very sexy picture.'

Clare almost spluttered out the gulp of coffee

271

she had in her mouth. Just the memory of that particular canvas made her prickle with a blush but the thought that Francesca believed Graham had been the model was enough to make Clare really choke.

'What I want,' Francesca continued, 'is a special present for my husband. He's going to be forty in three weeks.'

A sugar-daddy, Clare laughed to herself.

'I think he'd like to have his portrait painted. I've got some photos that you can work from.' Francesca pushed an envelope towards Clare across the coffee table. Clare pushed a mug of coffee back towards her. 'I'll pay the going rate.'

As Clare opened the envelope, she played a game with herself. Trying to imagine what Francesca's husband would look like. Forty years old, knocking about with a girl at least fifteen years his junior who looked as though her hair was made of candyfloss. Fat, balding. Successful but short. Showering her with gifts as long as she was prepared to put up with him dressing up like a baby in bed.

'It should be quite an easy job since he's rather more symmetrical than Graham. He's very handsome, in fact,' Francesca assured the artist.

Clare nodded indulgently as she pulled out the first photo. The printed side was away from her. Clare turned it over and her jaw dropped. 'Don't you think so?'

It was Steve. The woman's husband was Steve. Unmistakable.

Trying not to get too frantic about it, Clare pulled the other photos out of the envelope. There he was in the shirt she had spilled coffee down! And again, in front of an ivy-clad house, sitting on the bonnet of the very car in which he had driven Clare to the hotel where they had made love.

Frankie the car!

'What do you think? Are the photos clear enough? Do you think you can do it?' Francesca fired questions one after another.

Didn't she realise that Clare had already done it? Francesca had been attracted to Clare's work by her mind's eye portrait of Steve. Hadn't Francesca recognised him? Clare was beginning to be swallowed up by the horrible feeling of breathlessness that creeps up in the shadow of a shock. Her chest was tightening.

'Are you OK?' Francesca was leaning forward. She had laid her delicate hand on Clare's arm.

'Yes,' Clare told her. 'Yes, it's just the smell of the turps in here. Sometimes it makes me go a little faint. I really ought to get this room better ventilated.' Clare extricated herself from Francesca's concerned hold on her arm and swayed across to the window.

So it was Steve. So what? They'd met twice. Made love just once. No, you could hardly call it making love. They'd just had sex. Clare was living with a man she was supposed to love and Steve was married to some bimbo. It didn't matter. Clare struggled to compose herself. She needed the money she could get from this painting.

Clare took a few deep breaths of sea air while Francesca muttered something about the photos perhaps not being clear enough.

273

'No, no, they're clear enough. How do you want it done?' Clare asked, not listening as Francesca reeled off her requirements one by one.

'I'll need money for materials.' Francesca was already writing out the cheque – with the number Clare had thought of and another nought. She signed it and handed it over, grinning widely. The name at the bottom of the cheque swam before Clare's eyes. 'Mrs Francesca Philip.' Clare hadn't even known Steve's surname until then. She didn't know anything about him! But Steve the Snake suddenly seemed a very appropriate nickname indeed. 'Can I see it at various stages?' Francesca asked shyly.

'Yes,' Clare said. 'Of course.'

Chapter Seven

AFTER FRANCESCA HAD gone Clare stood at
the window for a long while, just looking out
across the houses to the sea, thinking. That
evening the sea was very calm. Just a few wispy,
cotton-wool clouds crossed the pinky blue sunset
and were echoed by the tiny white horses riding
the waves. The beach was deserted but for a boy
and his dog. The boy threw a stick and the dog
barked, the distant noise carried up to the
window by the wind so that it mingled with the
calling of the gulls constantly wheeling overhead.
The view from the flat where Clare and Daniel
lived was almost the same as the view from
Steve's hotel, though their flat was a little lower
down the hill.

Steve, Steve, Steve. What had Clare been
doing? She had never slept with a married man
before and had always thought of the guys who
had affairs as rats. In fact she had decided never
to do the dirty on another girl right after the
birthday party where Susie Powell stole her man
and her pre-pubescent self-esteem. But at the

same time, when Clare heard about people she knew and their affairs, she had also always assumed that the women these men cheated on must be doing something wrong. Not paying the guy enough attention. Letting themselves go in all the wrong ways. But Francesca? Francesca hadn't let herself go. She looked more like the kind of girl that wars were fought over, not a downtrodden wife. Bizarrely, Clare found herself recalling Francesca's face, and not her husband's.

Oh God, thought Clare, I should just forget it ever happened. He probably has.

Daniel had turned up the heating in the flat far too high and so the slight breeze which floated inland across the waves was welcome. As Clare leaned a little further over the ledge, the top of her navy crepe wrap-around dress pulled open. She didn't do it back up but let the breeze play in over her breasts, caressing her nipples to stiffness. Why should she be bothered that Steve was married, she asked herself again. She was in love with Daniel. They had been going through a bit of a rough patch and she had wanted affection, well, not affection – action, passion. And the incident with the ice-cubes had proved that Daniel could still give her that!

A floorboard creaked in the room behind. 'Stay there,' Daniel told her. 'You look so beautiful.' He came nearer and soon he had slipped both his arms around Clare's waist. His chin rested on her shoulder as he too watched the soothing waves.

'Are you glad we're here and not in London?' he asked her.

The answer Daniel wanted wasn't totally clear

and so Clare gave the answer which was always in her mind when she looked out on to the sea instead of a railway track and a scrap yard. 'Yes,' she said. 'Of course I'm glad we're here.'

Daniel kissed her lightly on the cheek. 'Good. Well, I guess I ought to get back to work.' But the brief squeeze he gave her in parting couldn't help but become something more, an odyssey around the curves of her body. His lips hovered at the back of Clare's neck, while from her waist, his hands began to glide gently down over her hips. From the back to the front. He cupped one breast in each hand. First through the material of Clare's dress, then slipping his left hand inside to feel her skin.

'That's cold,' Clare exclaimed as her nipple leapt to attention.

'Sorry, I'll warm my hands up.' Daniel took his hands from her breasts and began to slide them down her body again, lingering at the curve of her waist. Soon he was at the hem of Clare's skirt, then under it. Sliding his hands back up her body on her bare legs. Clare stood still and silent as though none of this was happening, inwardly beginning to enjoy his gentle touch.

'This seems like a warm spot,' he whispered. Daniel's right hand had come to rest between her upper thighs, cupping her mound like the breast of a dove. Clare squeezed her thighs gently together in approval. His fingers carefully kneaded her for a moment or two. Then he was tugging at her white cotton panties, moving them out of the way before replacing his hand in that soft position. His fingers twisted a little of the silky dark hair.

Clare sighed. Daniel moved forward to kiss her

again on the back of the neck, his hand still between her legs. His fingers were moving somewhere else now. Tracing the line of her body from front to back. Teasingly skirting around her labia. Clare thrust her bottom backwards and up to help him find what he was looking for. As the first finger entered her vagina, Clare was already moist. But Daniel entered her so slowly, just a centimetre at a time. She found herself contracting each time he entered, trying to pull him further in.

'You hungry?' he quipped.

Clare laughed. She had had her eyes shut but now looked down on to the street below. A middle-aged couple ambled along, taking in the fresh evening air with their dog. Daniel suddenly thrust his finger a little harder, making Clare gasp out loud. The woman looked up at Clare's exclamation. She tried to retreat inside, but Daniel was hard behind her, blocking her escape.

'Daniel!' Clare hissed. Her right breast had earlier been freed by his hand. She tucked it back in hurriedly. 'There are some people walking past. They'll see.'

'They can't see below the level of the window-sill.'

Suddenly Daniel jammed Clare forward against the window-ledge with his hips. The couple were still passing, slowly. Daniel flicked up Clare's skirt so that it lay across her back, baring her ass to the room behind.

'Beautiful!' He kissed the pale smooth skin on each cheek. Then without further ado, he began unzipping the trousers, from which his hard-on had been planning its escape for a couple of minutes. He pressed his rigid shaft against her, making her giggle as he rubbed it up and down the cleft between her cheeks. Then, without speaking, Daniel parted Clare's lips and pushed the first inch inside. Though she was dripping with moisture at the thought of this first thrust, the friction still surprised her. Clare had to bite her finger in an attempt not to make any noise that would attract the attention of the people passing below. But as Daniel made a second thrust, so that his balls brushed right against her, pushing the air out from her lungs, Clare couldn't help but call out. The woman looked up again. Clare tried to dodge from her view but Daniel pushed her further forward over the ledge, and thrust and thrust.

'Stop it,' Clare hissed. 'Stop it now.'

'They can't see us,' Daniel told her as she tried to stop herself from popping in and out of the window like a demented cuckoo each time he entered and withdrew. With one hand Clare struggled desperately to keep her dress from falling away from her shoulders completely, while the other tried to stop her from flying straight out through the window. But it was clear that Daniel wasn't about to stop and soon one hand was joining in the fun, reaching back between her legs to stroke Daniel's balls, whenever his thrusting brought them bumping against her inner thighs.

'Are they still there?' he asked breathlessly.

'Yes!' Clare replied. The man was doing up his shoe as his wife tottered on. Clare could see him glance up surreptitiously and had to suppress the urge to wave.

'Are they looking?'

'The man is,' Clare panted.

'Good,' Daniel said. 'Give him a flash of your beautiful breasts.'

'Daniel!' Clare shrieked, half laughing. Whether she had decided to or not, the next thrust was so powerful that she had to use both her hands to stop herself from falling right over the ledge and into the old man's lap. Without her hand to keep her dress on her shoulders, she found that it promptly slipped off so that her breasts hung down like twin pink balloons.

She just had time to savour the astonished look that filled the man's eyes before Daniel pulled her inside to finish that fuck on the hard, shiny wooden floor. Still remaining inside her, he performed some kind of yoga move to grab a cushion from the settee and place it where the small of her back would be before he slammed Clare on to the boards, having managed to get from behind her to on top of her at the same time. Clare's stocking-clad feet were slipping on the varnished floor and, noticing this, he swiftly ripped the stockings off her legs, ruining them as he did so – not that she cared at the time. Before Clare knew what was happening, Daniel had used one of them to bind her hands together above her head, and then to bind her joined hands to the leg of the heavy dining table that sometimes served him as an easel.

Daniel slowly withdrew his prick and sat back on his heels to survey his handiwork. He unfastened the wrap-around dress so that her body was laid completely bare. With his strong hands on her parted thighs he pulled her so that her arms were stretched full length, giving him a better view of her chest, which was heaving with exertion and excitement.

'Mmm,' he smiled slowly. 'What am I going to do with you now?'

'Let me go, you b—' Before Clare could finish her sentence, Daniel had deftly tied the spare stocking around her mouth, preventing her protests. By the way her eyes were crinkling up at the corners he could tell that any protest was only for show anyway. Still holding on to her thighs, Daniel uncurled his legs and lay down on his front so that his mouth was level with Clare's sex. Her hips twisted away from him as his tongue made a first exploratory dip between her labia. Then he brushed her clitoris softly with his tongue.

'Nnnggh,' Clare grunted.

'I take it that means I can carry on?'

Daniel's tongue began to cover the length of Clare's now shiny vulva with hard, strong strokes. Her clitoris was achingly hard, her labia swollen and tingling. The strokes were slow at first, and made all the more pleasurable by the fact that Daniel's nose brushed against her clitoris as he licked. She closed her thighs tightly around his head to hold him there when the pleasure became particularly bad.

'Miss Nutcracker!' Daniel laughed as he unclamped her thighs from his ears and slid his body back up hers so that his lips were level with her gagged mouth. She could feel his penis nudging at her vagina again. Sliding in so easily between her lips soaked with desire.

'I want you to come with me,' Daniel was whispering in her ear as he moved his hips in and out. 'Come with me, Clare. Come with me now.' The strokes were getting faster. Urgent.

'Come, come, come,' he commanded her with each thrust.

Clare screwed her eyes tightly shut as the sensation continued to build within her.

'Come, come.'

Her inner muscles clamped hold of Daniel's dick as it reached for the entrance to her womb. She wanted to cry out loud, needed to scream something in ecstasy but the silken gag kept her silent.

'Come with me,' Daniel spoke in the voice of a body on the brink of delirium. His thrusting was uncoordinated now, his breathing taking on that familiar pattern. Clare's body tuned into his for the count-down, as she grunted in unison through her bondage.

'Come, come, aaaahhh!' An overhard thrust sent Clare knocking against the table as Daniel began to pump furiously into her body. Clare's open eyes saw a small pot of paint make a graceful arc through the sky to land with an indelicate plop on her chest as Daniel reared back from her body in orgasm.

It was too small to hurt but the hilarity of the moment somehow set Clare off and, while she laughed at the sensation of the red paint dribbling slowly across her breasts and beneath her armpits, her hips bucked with their own release.

Daniel withdrew, also laughing, and surveyed the damage. He untied the gag and kissed Clare's lips gently, getting smeared with red paint as their bodies touched. Then he sat back, still panting, and lazily traced a heart on her chest. He pierced it with an arrow and added the initials C & D.

Chapter Eight

CLARE STARTED WORK on Steve's portrait the very next day. She chose to work from the picture of him sitting on his car outside the ivy-clad house, his family home. She chose it because he was wearing a forced, for-the-camera smile. It wasn't an expression Clare had seen on his face in the flesh and thus it was the nearest she could come to finding a picture which didn't remind her of his naked flesh every time she referred to it for her preliminary sketches.

After an hour or so Clare had produced a vague, compositional outline. She stood back and appraised her work. She felt no urge to slip her hand inside her blouse today. The picture wasn't working. It wasn't Steve. But so what? Francesca would think it was him, Francesca would see the jumper and the car and remember snapping the shutter on that strained smile and for her it would be Steven. Daniel wandered in and out of the studio with cups of coffee as Clare painted. He wasn't painting. He was having another off day.

'Mmm, nice jumper,' he said sarcastically as Clare started to add some colour.

'If only you knew,' she muttered.

'What?'

'I said, I need more blue,' Clare smiled.

Blues and greens. The painting was so cool. So different from Clare's much more passionate daub, made in the afterglow of love-making. Cool was how the Steven in the photos made Clare feel. Was this how he made Francesca feel? Detached. Indifferent. Cold? Or was it how he felt about her? A shiver of pride at her ability to have transformed the man into something altogether hotter ran through Clare. But what was going on in her life? The night before, when Daniel and Clare had made love by the window it was with the same intensity and passion as when they first made love years before. There was nothing wrong with that part of things.

Graham rang later that day to tell Clare that he had sold another three of her paintings. Clare wasn't in a hurry to get the money as Francesca's advance had been more than generous, but since Daniel was in one of his moods, mooching around the house like a storm just waiting to break, Clare felt as though she could use the walk. She didn't even look into the café where Steve had first appeared in her life but walked by quickly, breathing deeply to clear her lungs and her head.

Graham's wide smile failed to provoke any similar reaction from Clare's face.

'Hey, what's up, beautiful?' he asked, using her frown as an excuse to sling a fatherly arm around her shoulders. 'You look like you could do with a nice cup of tea and a chat with your old friend, Graham. Boyfriend troubles, eh?'

He sounded hopeful.

'Well, yeah,' Clare recalled the row she had with Daniel the night before, only hours after they had made love so passionately. His jealousy that her paintings sold while his didn't. His claim that she was growing distant, that while they still seemed to be making love all the time, she never initiated sex any more.

'Tell me all.'

'Oh no, Graham,' Clare said, recovering her composure and extricating herself from his tightening embrace. 'You really don't want to know.'

'But I do, I do . . .'

'It's probably just pre-menstrual tension.' Clare lied. There was nothing like the hint of 'women's problems' to make most guys of Graham's ilk cool right off. When Clare was assured that his bubble was safely burst, she accepted his offer of tea.

'Did my lovely young friend Francesca come and visit you?' Graham asked as he stirred three spoonfuls of sugar into his own cup. 'You're sweet enough aren't you?' he had said, when Clare declined sugar for her own.

'Yes, she turned up on Tuesday,' Clare told him. 'She wants me to do a painting for her of . . .'

'Her husband, Steve,' Graham picked up with the words Clare could hardly bring herself to say. 'Interesting chap, Steve, though far too good-looking for my liking. He was at the gallery party . . . briefly. Did I introduce you to him?' His eyes sought hers.

'No.' Clare stared at the steaming brown liquid in her cup.

'Funny, I thought I saw you two talking . . . Anyway, I don't know him that well. I only met him when he married Francesca – actually at their wedding in fact. Her elder brother was in my class at school . . . Yes, I remember Francesca when she had pigtails; we all teased her mercilessly about her frizzy hair and braces while she was growing up but when she hit eighteen – talk about the tale of the ugly duckling. We all fancied her, but Robert, her brother, wouldn't let us anywhere near. I guess he'd heard us all talking about the other girls we'd seen and didn't want her to be discussed in the pub as another notch on the bed-post. It wouldn't have been like that though . . .'

Graham's eyes looked into the past.

'Anyway, we were all horribly jealous of Steve,' he suddenly snapped back to the present and fixed his eyes on Clare's. 'And all Robert's fussing about not wanting any of us scumbags near her seemed a bit pointless when she went off and married a twice-married thirty-five-year-old anyway.'

'Steve had been married before?' Clare asked, realising even as she spoke the words that she was showing an inordinate amount of interest in the personal life of a man she was claiming never to have met.

But Graham was only too pleased to let her have the details. 'Yes, he was. Quite spectacularly, in fact. His first wife was that American singer, Laura Bollinger. I can't think of anything she actually sang, but she always seemed to be opening gold envelopes at award ceremonies. She was twenty years older than him and worth a fortune.' Graham rolled his eye to emphasise just how much of a fortune. 'He met her in the French Alps, at Chamonix, while she was learning to ski, apparently. He was her ski instructor.' Graham gave a little snort of disdain and took a slurp of his tea before carrying on. 'Ironically, it was on a skiing holiday two years later that she fell and broke her neck . . . His second wife, American, affluent, and just twelve years his senior, had a swimming pool accident.' Graham added nonchalantly. 'Still, third time lucky eh?'

Clare nodded, hardly able to believe her ears. What was Graham suggesting? That Steve the Snake had a bite to match that of his namesake?

'So, now he's in town overseeing the development of a new holiday accommodation complex. That was Francesca's father's business; but he died earlier this year leaving the job unfinished. Robert, Francesca's brother, has emigrated to New Zealand – he met a nice Kiwi girl – so he couldn't take the project on. Steve was at a loose end, since his own business had just folded. Now, that was a strange affair . . . But anyway, as I said, I only met Steve at his wedding, so I haven't really known him long enough to cast aspersions.'

Clare raised her eyebrows – what had he been doing thus far?

'It was a great wedding.' Clare was sure that he was placing emphasis on that word and then checking her eyes for a reaction. She smiled and nodded as if he were an auntie telling her about the price of cabbages. 'I was an usher,' Graham continued, 'and I nearly raised a "just impediment" when the vicar asked, but that's yet another story . . .'

Clare didn't press him to hear it. Something told her that a conversation about the wedding of Steve and Francesca Philip would be almost as unbearable for Graham as it was for her.

'Francesca is a very beautiful woman,' Clare said to close the subject.

Graham nodded. He was far away again.

Chapter Nine

FRANCESCA CAME TO see how the painting was getting on just a couple of days after Clare started to paint it. Clare was alone in the flat, Daniel having driven back to London for a couple of days to try and persuade some galleries to display his work there. Francesca explained that her husband was in the area on family business, turning some houses into flats for the tourists. She could only come down to see him occasionally because she had a business of her own these days, a boutique in Chelsea.

Bought to keep her out of the way, Clare thought unkindly. She could imagine what it was like. Full of the kind of peachy pale clothes Francesca was wearing now, populated by bored housewives who giggled like schoolgirls and snatched up sequinned numbers for parties while their husbands were seduced by girls who wore jeans.

Francesca stood behind Clare for a while as she painted. The blonde girl had one arm wrapped protectively around her body so that her hand caressed her hip, while the other played nervously with a well-glossed lip.

'What do you think?' Clare asked, stepping back from the canvas so that Francesca could have a better view. She was blinking rapidly, obviously fighting back tears. 'It's not that bad is it?' Clare joked nervously.

Francesca shook her head vehemently, but it was too late. The flood-gates burst open and suddenly tears were streaming down her prettily made-up face, rivers of salt water stained blue and pink with mascara and powder. Her shoulders shook as she stood there, desperately trying to stem the flow with her little hands.

'What's wrong, what's wrong?' Clare took hold of Francesca's shoulders instinctively and used the towel that she had been wiping her paint-stained hands with to dab away at Francesca's face. She didn't push Clare away but wrapped her arms around her and buried her face in Clare's sweater as though she were an old friend and not, though Francesca had no reason to know it, a woman who had so recently laid her husband. Clare guided Francesca through into the sitting-room and cleared a space so that she could sit down. As Clare sat down next to her, Francesca clung to her again and Clare started to stroke Francesca's flower-scented hair as words finally began to tumble out with the tears.

A tear lingered on Francesca's cheek, a perfect half-sphere waiting to elongate and fall. As she burbled on, the tear still hovered there, unmoving. Clare was transfixed by the tiny orb, in which swirled rainbow patterns, and it was almost unconsciously that she leant forward to kiss it before it had time to run away.

Francesca drew away, still holding on to the tops of Clare's arms, and looked at her, eyes wide.

'I'm sorry,' Clare said, blushing.

'No, no, I am,' Francesca dabbed at her tears. 'I shouldn't be bursting into tears on you like this.' She leapt up from the sofa and paced the room, searching frantically through her handbag for a tissue that wasn't sodden with salt water and mascara. Her shoulders were still shuddering with the emotion.

'What exactly is wrong?' Clare asked again.

Francesca sank back down on to the sofa again and hesitated for just a moment before throwing herself back into Clare's arms.

'I just don't know what I do wrong,' she sobbed. 'I just don't know. He spends all his time away from me looking for new places to buy and do up and when he comes home he just locks himself in his study. He isn't interested in me any more. I just need someone to make me feel . . . well, feel anything again . . . I feel like I'm bloody dying for someone to touch me.'

Their eyes locked. Francesca was studying Clare intensely, as if her last exclamation had been not an observation but a challenge. A challenge to Clare.

Clare swallowed nervously as Francesca's gaze continued to pierce her eyes. The muscles at the back of Clare's neck twisted with the tension of this endless moment while each wondered what to do next.

Moving closer, Francesca brushed her lips across Clare's cheek and the sensation of this unexpected return of affection was not of the lightest of kisses but of a burning firebrand in the shape of her lips.

Francesca sat back to look at Clare once more and a moment of silence and stillness hung between them again before she finally drew Clare's lips to her own.

Clare had never kissed another woman before and had been genuinely embarrassed when the tear on Francesca's cheek had tempted her to touch the blonde girl in anything other than a friendly way. As Francesca placed a slender, well-manicured hand on Clare's knee; Clare's first instinct was to pull away. But for Francesca, Clare later thought, this was definitely not a first time. The surprise Clare had seen in her eyes was merely pleasure at the arrival of an unexpected opportunity. She passed a hand over Clare's hair as though she was calming an anxious pet dog.

'Don't think about it,' Francesca whispered. 'Just let it happen.'

Clare closed her eyes, shutting out the looming face. Francesca kissed Clare's jaw, her chin, her nose, her ears, her eyelids, her forehead and then her lips again. Finding Clare's lips still tightly shut, Francesca made a little noise of amusement before she set to work at prising them open with her tongue. Moments later Clare's own tongue poked tentatively out to touch the tip of Francesca's, and they wrestled them for a moment like the teenagers in boarding schools, experimenting with 'how to kiss'. It was different from any kiss Clare had experienced before. Francesca's touch was lighter and gentler than any man's touch . . . And she had no stubble!

Her tears had all but dried now and when she drew away from Clare again, to check her eyes for surprise, Francesca was laughing slightly to herself.

'What are you laughing about?' Clare asked her.

'Oh, I'm not laughing about anything,' Francesca replied. 'When I laugh it's just because I couldn't possibly smile any wider.'

She leant towards Clare and gently pushed her backwards so that she was lying on the sofa. Clare's body was so stiff with tension that Francesca was reminded of a wooden doll. As the kissing continued, Clare kept her eyes tightly shut, still wrestling with the fact that she was being seduced by a woman. But soon a warm hand was creeping beneath Clare's sweater, caressing a nipple through her bra. It hardened in spite of Clare's misgivings. Clare let Francesca's hands wander curiously over her body for a moment or two, unsure of what she should be doing in return. Exactly the same as Francesca was doing to her, Clare guessed, but the move from kissing to actually caressing another woman's body seemed just too great to make. Francesca was patient, nuzzling Clare's cheeks, whispering encouragement until she felt arms close around her back. She struggled out of her top at the earliest possible opportunity and laid her half-naked torso against Clare's. She had pushed away Clare's clothing so that their bodies rested in some places skin to skin.

'Touch me, Clare,' Francesca murmured.

'Touch me.' Her words were softened by her quickening breath. Clare moved a tentative hand from Francesca's back. Francesca shifted to make herself perfectly accessible. She held herself slightly above Clare, to her side, jutting out her chest so that the target couldn't be more obvious.

Francesca's breasts were smaller than Clare's, encased in a peachy lace-edged bra that was almost invisible against her lightly sun-kissed skin. Clare began to caress them, in the way that Francesca had caressed her, but she was obviously taking too long about it because, before Clare could steel herself to tucking her hand inside the bra and actually touching Francesca's delicate nipples, the blonde girl had reached around and unhooked her bra herself.

'Kiss them,' Francesca begged her nervous lover. 'Suck them.' Tentatively, Clare lifted her head to the proffered breast and flicked out her tongue. Francesca's tiny pink nipples stiffened immediately at the mere suggestion of Clare's caress. She pulled Clare's head closer to her breast and thrust one of the quivering buds into Clare's mouth. 'Bite it,' she commanded. Part of Clare's mind still fought against the suggestion but she gently closed her teeth together on the stiff little bud. 'Harder,' Francesca rasped. 'Harder.'

As Clare paid attention to her breasts, Francesca's hands had crept lower. She was wrestling with the belt of Clare's jeans, deftly unfastening the button fly. Suddenly noticing the shift in focus, Clare tried to push the fiddling hands away.

'No, don't,' she pleaded. 'I really don't think I want . . .'

'This?' Francesca had already broken down her defences. The hair of Clare's pussy seemed to stir with excitement as Francesca's fingers brought her up in goosebumps of nervous desire.

Clare closed her eyes as Francesca's fingers tangled in her hair, waiting for the inevitable. Soft fingers on her clitoris made her bite her lip and sent arrows of tingling electricity all over her body. Francesca kissed Clare again, thrusting her tongue inside Clare's sweet mouth as her fingers echoed the action down below.

'Aaaaaah!' Clare broke away from her lover's mouth and threw back her head.

'Shhh,' Francesca whispered. 'You're so nice and warm inside. So wet. You're enjoying this. You really are.' A peculiar tingle ran down Clare's spine at these words. 'Just lie back and relax. I'm going to make you come . . .'

Automatically, Clare raised her hips so that Francesca could pull her jeans completely out of the way. She had been wearing no knickers under her painting trousers, as she often didn't. Francesca smiled her approval and now licked her lips as she contemplated the task ahead and ducked her head down between Clare's thighs.

With the first flick of her tongue Francesca found Clare's clitoris. She bucked her hips upwards with the surprise. While they were thus raised, Francesca grabbed her lover's buttocks and used them to lift the girl still further, so that she could more easily reach her target. Her tongue moved more slowly now, up and down the shiny shell-pink of Clare's vulva, tantalising her clit. Her eyes fixed on Clare's. Every cell in Clare's body was beginning to vibrate.

'Let go.' Francesca demanded. 'Let yourself come. I can feel you're almost there.'

She was wet from her nose to her chin. It wasn't all saliva. She returned to her frantic tonguing. Clare's hips bucked ever higher again, to drive Francesca's tongue into her. Clare grasped the blonde head, forcing it further between her shaking thighs. Francesca didn't have to ask Clare to come again. Suddenly, her body took over. Every muscle was tensing and relaxing, tensing and relaxing so quickly, it was as if she had been plugged into some ecstatic source of electricity. Clare's mind sat back to watch as she shuddered and covered Francesca's face with sticky sweet come.

The orgasm over. When Clare had finished shaking with its tremendous power, Francesca crawled up the sofa and kissed her gently on the lips. Slowly Clare licked them dry, tasting her own love juice mingled with Francesca's sweet tongue.

'Good?' Francesca asked.

Clare nodded in reply, her eyes still closed. Still breathing heavily.

'Really good?'

'I think so.'

'Right. Now it's your turn,' Francesca said. 'Let's go to bed.'

Clare had never seen another woman's vagina. Francesca reclined on the bed nonchalantly, her legs slightly parted, waiting for Clare to come between them. Her pubic hair was slightly darker than the hair on her head – as if Clare hadn't guessed that Francesca's fluffy blonde locks were dyed! – and the darker hairs were already slightly damp. Clare found herself strangely pleased to see that she hadn't been the only one to enjoy her first Sapphic orgasm!

'What are you waiting for?' Francesca asked, eyebrows raised.

A picture of Daniel lying on that same bed flashed briefly in Clare's mind. She could tell this woman to go now but Francesca slid forward so that her feet touched the floor and her sex was at the edge of the bed. She reached out her hand and twisted a little of Clare's long brown hair between her fingers. Francesca's face was glowing with desire. She communicated a message to Clare which she couldn't ignore now.

Clare knelt between Francesca's open knees and stared in wonder for a moment at the gently swelling clitoris and labia which were becoming more prominent through the hair even as she drew nearer.

'That's right,' Francesca breathed. She pulled gently on Clare's hair to bring her closer still.

Clare gazed at the picture before her. What should she touch her with first? Her fingers or her tongue? Like a baby, which puts every new discovery into its mouth, Clare chose her tongue.

She began by carefully taking some of Francesca's soft brown curls between her teeth, nibbling and pulling them gently, not so hard as to cause any pain. Francesca moaned contentedly and her hips rose slightly from the bed – Clare

298

was doing OK. The musky female aroma that Clare had smelled on her own fingers after masturbating was rising gently towards her from Francesca's vagina, enticing Clare further down. Taking Francesca's slender hips in her shaking hands, Clare made the dive, stretching out her tongue to its full pink, hard length, licking and then penetrating. Tasting that familiar perfume and being delighted by it, Clare licked and licked, faster and faster in response to the excited moans which came from the girl on the bed. Her enthusiasm soared as Francesca writhed on the sheets, just as Clare had done on the sofa. Clare continued her actions, now more confidently and harder until Francesca's hands clutched her head and she cried out.

Up and down Francesca's hips bucked, so that Clare felt her tongue was fucking the girl. Then Francesca pushed Clare away from the centre of her pleasure and pulled her up on to the bed so that they were level and their mouths touched. Flipping Clare over on to her back with surprising strength, Francesca ground the mound of her pubis against Clare's, and they rocked back and forwards, Francesca's hands grasping for Clare's breasts, Clare's hands sweeping up and down Francesca's back, streaking them with lines that went first white and then pale red. Francesca was moaning, sighing, desperately clutching her lover's body to her own. Clare put just one finger into Francesca's vagina. The muscles there were opening and closing like a hungry mouth as Francesca soaked her hand. 'I'm coming, I'm coming,' she screamed. Clare pumped her finger in and out of the pulsing vagina and could hardly believe what she had done.

Afterwards when Francesca lay still on the shambles of a bed, her eyes closed in a contented doze, Clare wandered over to the dressing table and sat down. Her mouth and chin were smeared with Francesca's vibrant pink lipstick. Clare studied the figure on the bed for a moment. Francesca's arms were raised above her head. She was a smooth unbroken curve that ran from the tips of her fingers to the soles of her feet, gently undulating where a tiny waist became a swelling hip. Clare walked over to the bed and sat down beside her. Francesca's eyelids fluttered as the bed dipped slightly beneath Clare's weight. Clare let the back of her fingers follow the line she had made with her eyes.

The gentle touch awoke Francesca, smiling, from her sleep, and she wrapped her arms around the other girl's waist, pulling her down beside her on the bed. They looked at each other for a long time, noses almost touching as they lay face to face, gently caressing each other's hair, earlobes and cheeks. Clare marvelled at the fragility of the body that had just given her such strong pleasure. Outside it was just beginning to rain.

'Are you okay?' Francesca asked. Clare's expression was still that of someone who was not sure that she had done the right thing.

'I'm fine.'

'Can I stay?' Francesca continued. 'I mean, your boyfriend won't be coming back and if he does come back unexpectedly, you can always say that I came round drunk and you were obliged to offer your benefactress a place to stay. He won't think . . .'

No, thought Clare, no one would think . . .

'But won't Steven be expecting you?'

'He thinks I've gone back to London,' Francesca hissed. 'And he's probably gone out to pick up some local tart anyway . . .'

Her words made Clare wince. If only she knew. But Clare had made up her mind about one thing now anyway. After that afternoon, she would never be able to see Steve again.

'Okay,' Clare told her companion, 'you can stay. But you'll have to go first thing tomorrow.'

Francesca nuzzled Clare's neck in appreciation and pulled her slender body closer. She was asleep within minutes, contently moulding her belly to her lover's back. Clare gazed open-eyed into the darkness of the night.

Chapter Ten

LIFE IS WHAT happens when you've made other plans. The next day, when Francesca had finally gone back to London, Clare wandered down to the harbour, diligently avoiding the fatal café on her way. Since she couldn't find her foldaway stool in the chaos of the flat, Clare doubled up her jumper to make a seat on the cold, grey stone wall, and balanced the board she used for an easel on her knees. Graham wanted still more sea scenes. The woman in America was ordering them to be sent all over the place for Christmas. Clare mixed up a job lot of sea-green on the inside of her paint-box lid and began to work on three small scenes at once, like a factory production line. She hadn't got much further than three wishy-washy horizons when he appeared.

'Fancy meeting you here.'

'Yes, fancy.' Clare replied.

Steve was swaddled against the cold in a huge cream fisherman's jumper. He sat down beside her on the harbour wall without being invited and cast an eye over the paintings.

'Hmmm,' he said. 'Not bad.'

Clare didn't say anything. She continued to paint. A seagull appeared on all three paintings, then a fishing boat, so far out to sea it was just a streak. He must have thought her silence a little odd, but what could she say? – 'Hey, Steve, since we were last together I've learnt about your first and second wives and been to bed with your third wife – and do you know what the really funny thing is, she was easily as good as you . . .'?

It was Steve who broke the silence. 'Shall we go for a coffee?' Clare shook her head and continued to paint. She copied the colours of a nearby fishing boat.

But Steve remained beside her, smoking a Marlboro light and flicking the ash into the murky green water that swirled below them, until, finally, she just couldn't help asking: 'So, where have you been lately?'

Steve took a long drag on his cigarette. 'Here, there and everywhere. I've been very busy.' Of course he didn't say that he'd been hiding out of the way while his wife was in town. 'I saw you from the window of a house the estate agent was showing me around, just over there. I'd been hoping that we would bump into each other again. You didn't give me your number.'

'I don't have a phone,' Clare replied.

'You should get one. I've missed you.'

'I'll bet you have.'

But the anger that she felt towards him for having lied to her – well, for having been economical with the truth – was quickly ebbing away even as they sat there, getting numb bums on the wall. Clare knocked over the jar of water that she had been using to rinse her brushes and as they both reached to right it at the same time, their hands brushed together. The electricity was most definitely still there. Clare set down her easel by her side and turned towards him. He searched her face eagerly for the words which played on her lips.

'Shall we go and get that coffee?' she said finally.

He smiled broadly. It was a goal to him, Clare guessed.

Clare reached out to push the golden brown hair from his forehead. So, he was nearly forty, eh? He didn't look it. By the time she was sitting opposite him in the café, she was already undressing him with her eyes. Tracing a path with her tongue down to the snake tattoo on his hip. As if he sensed that the chill was abating, Steve took the hand that had smoothed his hair and gently bit Clare's forefinger as he stared straight into her eyes.

'You've got such pretty hands,' he told her. 'Dangerous nails.'

She thought about scoring passionate lines up his back and wondered if she had left any marks the last time they were together. She smiled.

'Tell me about yourself,' Clare said suddenly, daring him. 'I feel like I don't know anything about you . . . Who dubbed you Steve the Snake? When did you lose your virginity? How old are you? Have you ever been in love?'

'Questions, questions.' He significantly chose to ignore the last one. 'I'm twenty-one.'

Clare rolled her eyes. She wasn't going to get

anything out of him. And what good would it do anyway? If she asked him whether he was married, if she confronted him about Francesca, he'd hardly be inclined to take Clare back to his hotel room again. And that afternoon that was definitely what she wanted, no matter how much she told herself it was wrong.

'Do you want to . . . ?'

Clare nodded before he could finish the sentence and they headed for the car.

'Your place or mine?'

'Yours,' Clare said, adding quickly, 'My place is a tip.'

To his credit, the boy on the reception at the hotel retained an exceptionally discreet demeanour as Steve rushed the dark-haired girl through the door. They began to kiss in the sumptuous gilded and mirrored lift and Clare couldn't help opening her eyes just slightly to enjoy the spectacle of their kiss from all angles. This time there were going to be no torturous tickling, featherlight touches. Clare's jeans were undone before Steve's key was in the lock.

'I really have missed you,' he murmured into her crotch, rubbing his chin against her pussy like a real cat eager to be fed. He hoisted Clare on to his shoulders and started to nibble at her clit, while his fingers began their excellent play. His stubble tickled against the inside of her thighs. But this wasn't going to last long. Steve was just too hot and had hardly begun to waken Clare's body when he started fumbling with the belt of his own jeans.

'Condom!' Clare reminded him with a giggle as he stretched himself full length along her body and began to push against her urgently. He cursed, rolled off Clare and rolled one on. He came back to the bed and threw himself backwards on to it.

'Right,' he said, 'your turn on top!'

Without hesitation, Clare straddled him and hovered above his dick but first playfully placed her own finger in her crotch. 'Ready?' she asked. Steve's cock twitched as if in reply, then stood to attention, like a glorious pole on which there really should have been a flag. Slowly, tantalisingly, Clare began to lower herself on to him.

At first, she took only the tip inside her, waited for a moment, then began to slowly ease herself up again. Steve shuddered at the sensation. The next time, Clare went a little deeper, her thighs quivering with the effort of resisting the urge to plunge him into her, right up to the hilt. Steve's hands began to creep up her legs. His eyes were closed in delirious pleasure.

By the time she made her third journey down, it had already become too much. Clare sighed in ecstasy as her bottom brushed Steve's balls and he pushed upwards at the same time, driving into her, impaling her, filling her with his gorgeous cock. Clare's body was racked with a delicious quaking, every nerve ending vibrating, singing with joy. She arched her body backwards and held the position, relishing the feeling before she carried on.

Steve's eyes were still closed. Beads of sweat were beginning to gather on his forehead as

Clare rocked on his prick, her once measured breathing now coming in shorter and shorter gasps. Determined to heighten the sensation still further, she reached behind her and teased his sac with a careful stroke from her long fingernails. He moaned urgently. His shaft reacted by twitching inside her. Her pussy tightened in response.

'You feel just too good!' he told her, grasping hold of her waist with both hands to help her move up and down even faster. Clare grasped handfuls of her own hair as the pleasure began to reach a dangerous intensity. Her vagina grasped Steve's penis.

'Slow down, slow down! I'm going to come,' Steve groaned as his hips drove him further into her one more time. But it was too late to slow down now. Clare's pussy contracted again and again, and her orgasm burst from her like a peal of laughter, pumping the hot come out of him while her own love-juices trickled down the inside of her thighs.

'I have to spend more time with you,' Steve panted as Clare collapsed on to the bed beside him. 'This weekend. What are you doing this weekend? I'm not going to have to work . . . we could go Barcelona—'

'Barcelona?'

'Yes, come with me.'

Clare figured that she had probably had all the sexual adventures she deserved that week, but she told him that she'd love to. She wasn't really in the right state of mind to ask herself how.

'Why am I saying "yes"?' she asked herself out loud.

'Because I've put a spell on you,' he said.

Steve dropped Clare off on the corner again and she walked the rest of the way to the flat. Daniel's car was parked half on the pavement outside the flat. She hadn't expected him back so soon, but the last thing she'd thought to find, when she let herself into the flat, was that he was sitting drinking tea on the sofa with Francesca.

Clare froze at the door.

'Daniel let me in,' Francesca said cheerfully, nonchalantly, chirping as she had done on the day she first came to commission the painting. 'I hope you don't mind but we took the liberty of looking at the picture while we waited . . . I love it, it's really very good.'

Well, Clare thought, I haven't added anything to it since I saw you this morning but 'I'm glad you like it' was all she could manage out loud.

'I'll make you some tea, shall I?' Daniel asked as he headed for the kitchen, leaving Clare alone in the sitting-room with Francesca.

'Where've you been?' Francesca hissed. 'I've been here for hours . . .'

'What are you doing here?' Clare countered.

'Well, first of all I wanted to see you but also I left my credit cards at the hotel. When I got here I found you weren't in and then, when I went back to my car, the damn thing wouldn't start so I couldn't go up to the hotel – it's too steep to walk in these shoes . . .'

Thank God, Clare thought.

'Daniel's been trying to help me to fix the car but it's really totally knackered. I don't see why I should drive a Volkswagen when Steven swans around in that bloody TVR of his. I rang him at the hotel to see if he'd come and fetch me but he wasn't answering his phone. The lads at the site said he'd gone back there . . .'

'Probably with some tart,' Clare laughed ironically, remembering how Steve had taken the phone off the hook after the first twenty rings, before they spent another hour in each other's arms.

Daniel came back into the lounge with some tea. He was smiling soppily at Francesca. Besotted. A strange, jealous spike twisted in Clare's heart and she wondered if she should tell him that the vision of loveliness on the sofa wasn't a real blonde. Francesca was smiling soppily back at Daniel and carefully crossed her legs to give maximum exposure to her well toned thighs, while appearing to remain totally innocent to the effect this was having on the assembled company. It was strange how very different she was in public and in bed, Clare thought.

'Well I suppose I had better be getting back to the hotel,' Francesca sighed after a few minutes of strained conversation. 'Are you sure it won't be too much trouble for you to drive me, Daniel?'

'No, I'll drive you back,' Clare butted in. 'Daniel's been driving all day.'

Daniel opened his mouth to protest, at which Clare shot him a look that suggested she thought he was the one who would get up to something if he was left alone with this girl. He closed his mouth. Francesca raised a flirtatious eyebrow at Clare. As they left the flat, Francesca stood on tip-toes to give Daniel a kiss on the cheek. When she pulled away, a cerise circle marked the spot where her lips had been. Daniel was enchanted, charmed, grinning like an idiot from ear to ear. Clare gave him a little kick in the shin as she passed.

'Are you angry?' Francesca asked her when they were safely in the car. 'I got about ten miles down the road when I thought that I just had to come back and see you again. I didn't think your boyfriend was going to turn up so soon. I thought we could spend the afternoon in bed and . . .'

'Francesca, I . . .' Clare didn't know what to say but she had an awful feeling that her life was about to get horribly complicated.

'My mind has been racing all day,' Francesca continued, 'and I've had a fantastic idea.' She paused for effect. 'I want you to come away with me, this weekend. I've got to go to a knitwear show in Paris to get some stuff for the shop. The show's on Friday. We can fly out in the morning and come back on Sunday.'

'I can't,' Clare said flatly.

'Why not?'

'I've got things to do . . .' Like spend a weekend in bed in Barcelona with your husband, Clare didn't add. It had suddenly become clear why Steve was going to be unexpectedly free from business meetings and rounds of golf. Barcelona with the husband or Paris with the wife? It wasn't the kind of choice Clare had to make every day.

'What things to do?' Francesca persisted. 'What

can you have to do that would be more fun than spending a weekend in Paris with me? Think of it, Clare. All that shopping!'

Clare rolled her eyes. 'I'm not sure I . . .' She chickened out of voicing her hesitation about their relationship and said instead, 'How would I explain it to Daniel?'

'Easy,' Francesca gushed. 'Just tell him that a girlfriend of yours has won a weekend away and that she's got no handsome beau to go with. I'll ring you up to make it sound kosher.' She'd thought of everything. 'Just imagine it, Clare. The Louvre, the Champs Elysees, Notre Dame . . . Galéries Lafayettes!'

'He won't believe that.'

'Of course he will. Steven would believe it.'

Yes, Clare thought, but he had his own motivations for wanting Francesca out of the way.

'*Please.*'

'I can't afford it,' Clare said at last.

'You don't need to afford it. I've already got the air tickets. It's you or my PA – and she's got a fear of flying and a hairy upper lip. Come with me. Please. Please. Please.'

'Okay. Okay.' What was Clare letting herself in for? What was she going to tell Daniel? What was she going to tell Steve?

'Right, we're flying from Gatwick. Here are the details.' She handed Clare a slip of paper. 'Can you meet me there?'

Clare nodded.

Francesca was clasping her hands together in joy. 'You won't regret it,' she said, 'This is going to be incredible. We are going to have so much fun.'

Suddenly Clare realised that she was automatically driving in the direction of the hotel she had left just an hour or so earlier, so she asked Francesca where they were supposed to be heading. On the way there they passed the building site Steve was working on. Clare prayed that he was still there and not back in his room at the hotel. Fate, fortunately, was on her side.

Chapter Eleven

STEVE WAS DISAPPOINTED when Clare told him she couldn't make it to Barcelona after all. When she said that she was going to Paris, on a ticket won in a raffle, with a friend from school that she couldn't let down, he remarked, 'That's a real coincidence, my . . . friend is going there as well this weekend.' He told Clare that he could cancel the tickets anyway and that he could always use some golf practice. Daniel was far less happy.

Francesca, as promised, had telephoned the flat pretending to be an old girlfriend from school. Daniel was confused as to why Clare should want to spend a weekend away from him with a girl that she hadn't spoken to for four years. Clare assured him that they had actually kept in touch. But to Paris? he moaned. He asked why this schoolfriend couldn't drag up some willing man to see some of the most romantic sights in the world with. He begged Clare not to go. Promised to take her there himself one day and when she refused to give in he went into a sulk which lasted the whole weĕk and hadn't let up by the time Clare got him to drive her to the station, where she was catching the train to Gatwick.

Clare made it to the airport with plenty of time to spare and sat in a café, drinking coffee and wondering if she was doing the right thing. What a crazy situation! Before meeting Steve, Clare thought she would never get involved with a married man, let alone a married woman. Not just a married woman, but a woman she hardly knew. If her mother could have seen her! If Daniel could have seen her, she thought a little sadly. Maybe a weekend away from him would actually help them both, give them a chance to miss each other, see what they had been taking for granted. On the other hand, it could be a complete disaster.

An hour after Clare arrived at the airport, just as she was entering another 'this could be a complete disaster' phase and about to give up the game and go home, Francesca materialised from the midst of a crowd of giggling children. She was carrying three cases, as opposed to Clare's one, rather scruffy bag.

She was effervescent, smiling benevolently at the kids as they got under her feet and in her way. She dropped her bags and kissed Clare on both cheeks.

'*Bonjour, ma chérie,*' she trilled.

'*Bonjour,*' said Clare.

'Have you already checked in?' she asked, eyeing Clare's conspicuous lack of luggage.

'No.'

'Oh. Well, come on then,' she said briskly. 'You can take one of these bags. I want to make sure we get a non-smoking seat. Travelling in the smoking section is just such a nightmare . . .'

Clare nodded but wondered if she would be able to get to Paris without needing a fag to calm her nerves. She had only flown a couple of times before.

'I'm so excited,' Francesca said, bouncing up and down. 'And the hotel I've booked is fantastic. You'll love it. I got a suite. Our rooms both connect on to a central area so you can go off and do your own thing if you want . . .'

'My own thing?'

'Yeah, French guys are just so sexy. They only have to open their mouths to say something in that accent and . . .' Francesca gave a little shimmy.

'I know just what you mean,' Clare laughed. She couldn't help feeling a little relieved. She had not been sure that she could have amused Francesca on her own all weekend long.

Francesca was right. The hotel was fantastic. As she gabbled incomprehensibly in French to the receptionist, Clare stood with their luggage and gazed around the entrance hall. On her last trip to France, a weekend in Boulogne with the sixth form French group, Clare had stayed in a cockroach-infested fleapit of a youth hostel. Now here she found herself in a five-star hotel near the Champs Elysees, in a road just off the Rue François Premier, one of the most amazing streets in Paris. As they had been driven from the airport

315

in a taxi, Francesca had pressed her nose to the window, pointing out the boutiques as they passed. 'Nina Ricci,' she gasped, 'Chanel. Oh, my goodness, there's Inès de la Fressange's place. I read about that boutique in Vogue. We'll go there tomorrow. Sells very classic clothes apparently. She's bound to have something that's you . . .'

'Yeah, but not something to suit my bank manager.'

'Who cares? It'll suit Steven's bank manager. Emotionally he's a wet fish, but financially . . .' Francesca laughed and flexed a plastic card.

Clare had barely recovered from the marbled splendour of the lobby when she had to begin gazing in wonder again at the room Francesca had booked for the weekend. It was quite unlike all the Holiday Inn-style hostels Clare had stayed in before, where the decor was uniformly beige and the only extravagance was an extra carton of cream by the teasmade. This room was a riot of colour! And it wasn't just a room! The suite Francesca had promised had two bedrooms, a lounge and even a tiny kitchen with a freshly stocked minibar. In the communal area, a green leather suite dominated. Francesca kicked off her shoes straightaway and leapt on to it, testing its bounce. The walls were hung with limited edition prints. Clare lovingly fingered one of an abstract still life that she was sure she had seen and admired in a London gallery a couple of years earlier. Francesca didn't seem quite as fazed by the decor as Clare was, wrapping the scarf she had been wearing on the plane round the neck of a large, black marble panther that guarded the door. She was now reclining on the rich green leather sofa, pointing the remote control at the widest television screen Clare had ever seen, which brooded in the opposite corner.

'They've got a great porn channel here,' Francesca commented. 'Just in case we can't think of anything better to do . . .'

A bottle of chilled champagne was waiting in a silver bucket on a glass-topped table. Clare popped the bottle open and poured two glasses.

'*Vive la France*,' Francesca sighed happily, raising her glass to the view. 'I love these big windows, don't you?' She had leapt up from the sofa and was now drawing back the raw silk curtains and looking down on the street below. 'And Paris is the perfect place for big windows. Look at the view, Clare. That woman with the dog down below . . . I'm sure it's even wearing a Chanel collar – everyone here is just so chic!'

Clare joined her at the window and couldn't help recalling the woman with the dog who had walked past the window in St Ives . . . and her surprised husband.

'Kiss me,' Francesca commanded. They were still at the window but Francesca just didn't care. Clare dutifully took the pale face in her hands and caressed the waiting red mouth with her tongue. This was going to be one hell of a weekend.

They dressed for dinner. Clare didn't have anything which Francesca deemed suitable for her plans that evening and so she lent her lover a green dress. Clare had never worn green before but Francesca assured her that, with the natural red highlights in Clare's hair, which she insisted was worn up, it looked great. So great, Francesca told her, that she was torn between letting Clare out at all or keeping her to herself in bed. They had already shelved the idea of an afternoon at the knitwear fashion shows in favour of that. Francesca was wearing cream. A tightly-fitted suit, beneath which she wore nothing but a push-up bra that gave her a fairly respectable cleavage. Her hair was also piled up and pinned with pearl-studded grips, revealing the soft line of her long neck.

'Classy,' Clare whispered as Francesca emerged from the bedroom, still applying her lipstick.

'Should be,' she replied, 'it's Yves Saint Laurent.'

'Are you ready?' Clare asked, pulling on the gorgeous grey cashmere coat that Francesca had also lent her for the occasion.

'Almost,' came the reply as Francesca disappered into the bathroom again.

Clare slipped the coat back off and turned on the television.

At once she was hit by a barrage of high-speed French. She used the remote control to flick through the channels to find something she could summon up the interest to attempt to understand. The news looked depressing. On one channel there was a comedy programme that she had seen on television in England a year earlier. It was dubbed. Clare watched that for a few moments, amused more by the poor synchronisation between sound and vision than the programme itself. That programme finished. Francesca was still in the bathroom. Clare continued to channel surf.

Suddenly the screen was full of moving parts which Clare couldn't quite relate to anything she'd ever seen before. It took a couple of seconds for her to realise that she had stumbled upon the porn channel Francesca had spoken about. On screen was a close-up of an impressively large penis penetrating a shaven vagina, accompanied by sounds of moaning that could have been in any language but were probably Swedish. Clare was so transfixed that she hardly noticed when Francesca finally emerged, looking no different from when she had last paraded for Clare's approval, and sat down beside her on the green leather couch. She slung an arm casually around Clare's neck and settled in to view. They wouldn't be going out for a while longer.

The scene cut to a hilarious routine with six thirty-something porn stars cavorting across a hockey pitch in gym-slips that just barely covered their frilly white knickers. The girls on the sofa collapsed into hysterical laughter, especially when Francesca suddenly burst out, 'That's exactly like my old school uniform!'

'Oh no,' the tears of laughter rolled down their faces as they thought about it.

'But if we'd flashed our knickers like that we would have been in detention for a week!'

'We had to wear those disgusting thick blue gym knickers over our normal pants whenever we were on the hockey pitch,' Clare told her companion.

'At lunch-time, I used to do handstands deliberately to show mine off whenever the boys from the school up the road walked past.' Francesca said.

'Was it an all girls' school?' Clare asked her.

'Yes, a convent actually,' she replied. 'And I boarded.'

'You? A convent girl? I can't believe that. What a nightmare!' Clare sympathised.

'What do you mean? I loved it. I've only got a brother, so the girls at school were like the sisters I always wanted to have . . .'

'Was that where . . . ?'

'Was that where I first got off with a girl?' She completed Clare's question, her fingertips sliding gently down over the bare skin of Clare's neck to her collar-bone. A delicious shiver ran through Clare's body at her touch.

'Yes, it was. I had a crush on the geography teacher for years. She was fresh out of teacher-training college when I arrived in my first year and compared to all the crusty old nuns she was a goddess in her thick glasses and crepe-soled shoes.'

Clare laughed.

'I think what attracted me to her was the fact that she seemed something of an adventuress. She'd spent a year in South America between university and teacher-training school, building fishing pontoons for the natives or something worthy like that. And she had nice hair. Dark with red bits . . like yours in fact.' She ran careful fingers over Clare's neatly piled-up hair. 'But that whole affair came to nothing – except for a grade A in O'level geography.'

Clare groaned. 'I got a C. Our geography teacher was an old bag. But that's beside the point. Tell me. Tell me who it was and how it happened.'

'OK.' Francesca had returned to the business of gently stroking the other girl's neck. Clare relaxed back into the deep soft sofa and Francesca's arm. 'Well. In the sixth form we finally got to move out of the main boarding house which permanently smelled of sweaty feet and Dettol, and into a building on the other side of the playing fields. We had our own rooms and shared a study with one other girl. My best friend, who was as thick as the proverbial planks, had left school at the end of the fifth form to do the Season and all that crap. So, I was left without a study mate and wound up with a girl called Anna. She was a year older than me. Had spent most of her life in South Africa, so when she returned with her family she was a year behind at school. Just a year older, but somehow she really stood out from the rest of the girls in our class. She had a real air of sophistication. We were allowed to wear our own clothes in the sixth form and instead of slavishly following fashion, she was always so classically stylish. While the rest of us were just recovering from disastrous perms which were the craze in our fifth form, she had long straight white-blonde hair that hung down her back in a plait like a rope. By the time she arrived at school, I was completely into boys, having a "relationship" with a boy from the local grammar on Saturday afternoons when we were allowed into town in threes. I gave him a blow-job in the ladies' loos at the bus station.

321

'Boys were definitely becoming more interesting. I had grown out of the geography teacher thing and took great pleasure in pillorying the "real lesbians" with the rest of the girls. But Anna was just so beautiful, so serene. She made me blush when she spoke to me. I was getting that kind of reaction to men but to a girl again . . . that really freaked me out.'

Clare nodded, understanding the confusion Francesca must have felt only too well.

'Did you ever feel like that at school?' Francesca pulled back from Clare a little to study her reaction.

'Well, no actually. I was always very much into boys.'

'Complacently heterosexual until you met me, eh?' Francesca laughed. 'Oh, do you really want to hear about this? It's nearly eight. We should really be going out.'

'No, carry on. I'm intrigued!'

'OK. But don't blame me if you start to feel jealous.'

Clare gave her a playful punch on the arm.

'So, we were sharing a study, Anna and I, except that for me, studying was now becoming quite out of the question, because her being there totally robbed me of my ability to concentrate. The study was a sort of sitting-room as well, with two big armchairs that had springs poking out to jab you in the kidneys if you tried to get too comfortable. She would sit in the one by the window and I would sit in the one by the book shelves, watching her as she read. Always sitting perfectly, with her back straight while I sprawled with my legs across one of the chair arms. Sometimes I used to watch her for what seemed like ages, thinking that she didn't notice me because the sun which came in through the window slightly obscured her face. But, of course, she had noticed me watching and one day she asked me why. She just came straight out and asked me if I fancied her. Of course I wanted to crawl under the threadbare rug and die when she said that. I denied it. Reminded her that I had a boyfriend – boy being the operative word, and told her that I wasn't staring, it was just that I was gazing into the distance while I tried to remember the conjugation of some French verb.

'By the time I had garbled all that, she was standing right in front of me. She put her book down on the table and sat on the arm of my chair. She reached up and unfastened her plait like the heroine of some film, letting her hair fall around her face. She stroked my cheek with her long-fingered hand and then pulled my face towards hers.'

Francesca fell silent.

'What happened then? Did she kiss you?'

'Yes.'

'And then?'

'I don't know. I can't really describe it, I . . .'

'Show me instead.'

Clare shifted position so that she and Francesca were eye-to-eye.

'Show me from the beginning.'

Without further prompting, Francesca cupped Clare's face in her hands as Anna had done hers years before and planted a very gentle kiss on the smiling lips. They pulled apart and studied each other for a moment. Then Francesca leaned towards her lover again and repeated the action, lingering there this time until Clare's mouth opened under the exquisite pressure of her fluttering tongue. Clare's hand tangled in Francesca's golden hair.

'Mmm,' Clare murmured. Francesca's mouth tasted of the freshness of toothpaste and was cool from the water she had been sipping as she spoke. Their tongues stroked each other languorously. 'Then what did she do?'

Francesca finished kissing Clare's mouth and began to let her lips wander over her cheeks instead. She moved up to Clare's eyes and kissed her carefully on her fluttering eyelids. Then down the side of her face. Kiss, kiss, kiss. Clare instinctively leaned her head to one side so that her neck was more exposed to Francesca's travelling lips, which were hotter now, much, much hotter. Clare's back prickled with pleasure as she felt Francesca's teeth close gently on her throat.

'Then what did she do?'

Clare could hardly speak now as Francesca bit carefully at the nape of her neck, where her hair began. Momentarily she felt almost paralysed. Streamers of prickling desire unfolded to either side of her spine.

'Oh, my . . . that feels incredible. . .' Clare murmured.

Francesca began to fumble with the zip at the back of Clare's dress, tugging it down until Clare's shoulders slipped free of their covering.

She pushed away the straps of Clare's cream silk slip so that her shoulders were completely bare, ready to be kissed. Francesca kissed along her lover's breastbone until she came to the centre. With just a little more persuasion, the dress slipped right down, taking Clare's underclothes with it, and her breasts rose up to greet Francesca's descending lips. Her nipples were erect; had been erect for some time.

'Then what did she do?' Clare's voice was barely a whisper as Francesca encircled first one nipple and then the other with her mouth. Her tongue flicked lightly across the reddened buds, while her hands cupped the full orbs of Clare's breasts and stroked them lovingly.

'More,' Clare insisted when Francesca began to move away. 'More. Don't stop.'

Francesca continued to tongue her lover's nipple, by turns biting it teasingly, but her hands had another purpose now. They were creeping up Clare's stockinged legs, under the fluid jersey hem of the dress. Francesca reached Clare's suspender belt and moved her hands beneath the lacy straps which held her stockings up. For a moment or two she savoured the pleasure of having Clare's beautiful, firm thighs beneath her hands, before moving higher still.

A small laugh escaped Francesca's lips when she realised that, once again, her companion was not wearing any knickers. She twisted her fingers in the silky hair, traced them down the warm, waiting labia, then up again, to Clare's aching clit. Lazily she circled the little bud with a finger, watching with great pleasure as Clare closed her eyes and bit her painted lip.

'Carry on,' Clare breathed. 'Please carry on.' She let her legs fall more widely apart. Francesca traced a languorous path between Clare's swollen lips, making her lover sigh with pleasure.

'You're such a tease,' Clare growled.

Francesca's finger found the entrance to Clare's desire and slipped slowly inside. The muscles of Clare's pussy tightened happily around their visitor.

'You're so wet,' Francesca breathed.

'Getting wetter.'

Francesca dragged her finger backwards and almost withdrew, then she slid it back in again, happily feeling Clare's muscles contract.

'Do it faster.'

Francesca obeyed the command and began to work up some speed.

Clare tensed the muscles in her thighs. She pressed her high-heeled shoes into the plush cream carpet to steady herself as Francesca increased the pressure and the pleasure.

'Faster.'

Francesca added another finger. The room was silent except for the wet noises Clare's body made as the fingers slipped in and out and the sound of two girls breathing deeply. Francesca as aroused as she was arousing.

Suddenly, Clare's hand flew down to her pussy and she gripped Francesca tightly around the wrist, helping her to plunge deeper, holding her hand in place. Her breathing had lost its regular pattern. Her lips were flushed deep red.

'Ohmigod!'

Clare's head jerked backwards while her hips jerked up to meet Francesca's hand.

'I'm coming, I'm coming, I'm coming!' she shouted exultantly.

'I know!' Francesca laughed, feeling that Clare definitely wasn't faking. When she had finished, Clare slid from the sofa to the floor and they lay together on the cream carpet, bodies entwined.

'I'm going to have to do my hair again,' Francesca stated flatly after they had been lying still for a couple of minutes.

Clare burst into a fit of the giggles.

They ran together to the bathroom and stripped off their clothes to take another quick shower. As Francesca carefully soaped her hot and relaxed body, Clare asked, 'Did she really do all that to you?'

'Yes,' Francesca replied.

'And did you have an orgasm?'

'Not quite like that one, no.'

Clare was strangely pleased about that.

Francesca knew Paris well, but Clare didn't, and before they went to the restaurant Francesca had chosen for their first evening, Clare insisted that they take a quick dash around the sights in a taxi. Francesca moaned, but she gave in.

'But the Eiffel Tower?' Francesca made an exasperated face. 'It'll be swarming with tourists.'

'I am a tourist, remember,' Clare said, silencing her with a kiss.

Clare let Francesca do the talking. She had spent a few months in France after leaving school, at the insistence of her father.

'To finish me off,' Francesca laughed. 'The best way to learn a language is to have an affair with a native, though I don't think that is exactly what Daddy had in mind for me . . . *Ici, s'il vous plaît, monsieur.*' Francesca had the taxi stop in a street next to the river.

While Francesca fiddled with the francs, Clare clambered out of the taxi and stood transfixed by the beauty of the silently weaving Seine. The river was lined by lights whose reflections glittered and flickered like flames beneath the surface of the water. A large, flat, glass-roofed boat was passing by, bedecked with yet more shimmering lights. It was full of tables, diners, people dancing their way around the Ile de France. Clare tried to suppress a memory which was forcing its way into the forefront of her mind. Daniel's birthday. A cruise on a restaurant boat down the smelly old Thames. She'd worn a stripy jumper and talked with a stupid accent all evening to make up for it not quite being France. He had thought that was hilarious. His best birthday ever – especially the French knickers Clare showed him at the end of it.

'Come on, dreamer,' Francesca caught her arm. 'It's just a short walk from here to *la Tour Eiffel*!' Now it was Francesca's faux French accent that was making Clare laugh. 'We'll go to the top, just for you, I'll point out the red light districts and then we are going to go and have dinner! My stomach is rumbling!'

'Oh, you are such a romantic!' Clare said sarcastically.

As predicted, the Eiffel Tower was swarming

with tourists and there were long queues to go to the top. But Clare didn't mind. It was just so incredible to her that they were there at all. She tipped back her head and looked up through the ironwork to the sky. The struts were glistening with bulbs.

'It's so big,' Clare murmured.

'Who?' was Francesca's automatic reaction.

When their turn came to get into the lift which would take them up to the viewing platforms, Clare made sure that she was by the outer edge of the glass-sided elevator. She didn't want to miss anything, and somehow being able to see out would make her feel less claustrophobic, which was a very important consideration since the guides were packing people into the lift by the dozen. About halfway up she heard Francesca exchanging French words which didn't seem to be pleasantries with a guy who stood behind her.

'He pinched my bum,' she explained. 'I wouldn't usually complain but I didn't fancy him at all.' She manoeuvred herself away from his roving hands and wedged herself next to Clare at the window.

'Fantastic, isn't it?' Clare breathed. 'I can't believe I'm in Paris.'

'Believe it, beautiful,' Francesca whispered. Their eyes locked in a secret smile for a second before the lift doors opened and its contents tumbled out into the cool night air.

It was so cold. Francesca and Clare clung to each other for a little warmth. The wind whipped their hair around.

The viewing platform was closed in by wire

netting which slightly obscured the view, but all the way around it was a desk which bore information about the landmarks you could see out there in the dark. Paris lay beneath them with all its best bits illuminated. The Sacré Coeur was clearly visible, its white majesty lit up by floodlights. Notre Dame was also lit, and though Francesca seemed fairly uninterested in the view, Clare made her promise that the very next day they would visit that famous cathedral. 'And light a candle for our salvation,' Francesca added with a smile.

'And the Louvre, we've got to see the Louvre,' Clare insisted. Francesca nodded. 'And the Musée d'Orsay; some of my favourite impressionist paintings are there, and the Pompidou Centre – that has some great modern stuff – Matisse and co.'

Francesca was covering a mock yawn. 'You can see all that provided I get to go to the Chanel boutique tomorrow and I get my dinner right now!' As if in agreement, her stomach chose that moment to give a impressively loud rumble.

'Point taken,' Clare replied, feeling pretty hungry herself by now. They took the lift back down and flagged a taxi to take them to the restaurant, which was on the other side of town.

The restaurant that Francesca had chosen was an old favourite of hers. It was dark, intimate. The arched ceiling was covered in red velvet! As they entered the maître d' nodded his regards to Francesca as though she were a regular.

'I came here on my honeymoon,' Francesca

explained, and Clare was surprised to feel a thrill of excitement and not hurt.

A young waiter pulled out Clare's chair, a move which always took her unawares and usually resulted in her nearly ending up on the floor. Francesca smiled at the lack of grace and the astonished look on Clare's face when the waiter also shook open her napkin and placed it on her lap.

The leather-bound menu looked bewildering. Clare racked her brains for the schoolgirl French that would save her from ending up with a plate of veal or horse meat. She recognised *les cuisses de grenouille* – frogs' legs – and panicked. They were about the only item on the menu she would be able to pronounce!

'Have snails,' Francesca commanded. 'I think they've got aphrodisiac qualities.'

'No way!' Clare said firmly. 'And they're not aphrodisiacs anyway. You're thinking of oysters.'

'Have you ever tried snails?'

Clare shook her head.

'Exactly. And to think I thought you were the kind of girl who would try anything once ... Maybe I should have brought my PA along after all,' she teased.

'OK, OK. I'll try one,' Clare gave in. They couldn't really be any worse than mussels, she figured.

Francesca ordered for both of them and folded the menu. She handed it back to the waiter who had taken their order with a slow wink. Clare kicked her beneath the table with a pointed toe.

'Pack it in, will you?'

'You're not jealous, are you?' Francesca purred.

The waiter returned with a pair of instruments which looked not dissimilar to eyelash curlers. As he turned to go again, Francesca picked up the shell-holders and chased after his retreating bum with them. Clare clasped her head in her hands in mock embarrassment.

'He was asking for it. Wearing those tight trousers . . .'

The snails arrived, steaming and garlicky, and Clare wrinkled her nose in distaste. She had already changed her mind. Evidently as well versed in molluscs as she was in everything else, Francesca deftly scooped one out of its shell with the dainty fork and held it to her companion's firmly closed lips. She popped it into her own mouth instead and swallowed it with an exaggerated look of divine ecstasy on her face. 'They're delicious,' she purred. 'Like chewing a clitoris.' They fell about laughing. Clare ate three after that.

The rest of the meal was a little more palatable. Francesca had ordered steak, rare and dripping with blood. Clare had gone for fish and left half of it, much to the disgust of their waiter who asked her several times if anything was wrong. Clare could hardly tell him that the thought of the night ahead with Francesca had made her too nervous to eat, though half the time she wasn't sure that the theatrically languorous way in which Francesca took each mouthful was entirely for her benefit anyway.

As they sipped their coffee, Clare's, of course, *au lait*, she noticed that Francesca no longer seemed interested by her at all. Her doe eyes were now narrowed like a cat's. She was scanning the faces in the room and not tremendously subtly at that. The restaurant was full of couples, though Francesca and Clare were the only pair of girls.

'All couples,' Francesca confirmed disappointedly. 'But what do you think of those?'

A pair of young waiters leaned louchely against the bar, moaning no doubt that the customers were taking a long time to leave that night. They looked very similar – perhaps brothers – and were good-looking in that Gallic way. Thick dark hair, darker eyes. Big nosed.

'And you know what they say about men with big noses,' Francesca winked. 'I'll call one of them over to get the bill and we'll ask if *le service est compris*.'

'Francesca! No!' Clare protested feebly. 'They're waiters! And anyway, I don't fancy either of them.'

'You can put paper bags over their heads. I'll have the taller one first and if you really don't like yours, we'll swap over at half time.'

Clare really wasn't sure, but it was too late. Francesca had clicked her fingers and the tall one was already on his way.

Clare focused her slightly drunken eyes on his strong hairy forearm as he leant on the table to listen to what the beautiful blonde had to say.

After a brief exchange in French, which lost Clare as soon as Francesca had said *Bonsoir*, the waiter wandered off again and Francesca rose from her chair in readiness to leave. 'They have to stay behind to tidy up,' she explained. 'But he's

333

given me directions to a really great club and says that they'll meet us there when they've finished. We'll go back to the hotel and change first, if you like.'

'Francesca, I really don't know ... I'm tired. Can't we do this tomorrow night?' Clare was terrified by the thought of being left to make stilted conversation in a variety of pigeon languages with the shorter waiter while Francesca had her way with the other one. What was she getting them into now? Francesca blithely ignored her companion's apprehension.

'I've got a black dress that would look really great on you ...' she chattered on regardless as she guided Clare out of the restaurant and into the night.

Chapter Twelve

BACK AT THE hotel, Clare headed straight for the mini-bar to calm her frazzled nerves. Francesca and Clare had waited for two hours at the club before the waiters finally showed up but now Jean and Bertrand were comfortably ensconced on the green leather sofa, with Francesca between them. She had her leg crossed towards Bertrand, her shoeless foot twitching predatorily, brushing from time to time against his trousered calf. Clare opened another bottle of champagne and filled four glasses. She sat down opposite the other three but wasn't on her own for long.

'See you later,' called Francesca as Bertrand swept her up off her feet and carried her giggling into the darkness of her room. Jean had made his way over to Clare and was now perching on the edge of her chair. His arm snaked around her shoulder and he fixed her with his chocolate-brown gaze. She told him that she didn't normally do this kind of thing but to no avail, since his English seemed to be as bad as her French.

'Let's just kiss.' He had that phrase nailed. He bent down towards Clare and passed his tongue over her lips. Despite herself, she found her mouth opening to let him inside. He tasted wonderful, and Clare had to admit that the way he smelled was starting to turn her on. He used the same aftershave as a guy with whom she had had a passionate affair the summer before going to art school. That guy had taught Clare pretty much everything she knew – except of course, that large chunk of carnal knowledge to which she had been introduced by Francesca.

Unconsciously, Clare began to let her hands wander over this new body, starting by running her fingers through his thick brown hair. Jean, however, was working to a faster timetable. His hand was already at the zip down her back, tugging it open. Clare wondered whether she should protest, but the thought was lost in the persuasion of his kiss. Soon, her own fingers found the buttons of his shirt. She pushed it out of the way and continued to explore.

She couldn't disguise her pleasure at the sight of his bare chest.

Jean was firm, brown, with the well-defined muscles along his torso from his ribs to his belly that show a man who really takes care of himself. His chest was covered with a layer of curling hair against which she just couldn't resist rubbing her face. A line of the hair continued down along his stomach, disappering into his trousers, which were beginning to tighten around the flies with the strain of his contained excitement. She drunkenly followed the line down with hands, teasingly keeping away from his belt buckle.

'Let's go next door,' Jean murmured into her neck as he pulled her to her unsteady feet. They staggered into Clare's bedroom, not letting go of each other. He picked up a bottle of champagne as they passed the fridge, maintaining contact with her silk-stockinged legs as he knelt down to open its door.

'Now we are ready . . .'

Clare didn't need to drink anymore, but fortunately, Jean had thought of plenty of other uses for the bubbly stuff. The green dress had long since been discarded. Clare lay on her back, still wearing her stockings. Jean carefully eased off the knickers Clare had put on to go to the restaurant. Just a little gentle persuasion and she languidly opened her legs. Jean knelt between them, still wearing his trousers, fiddling with the foil around the top of the bottle as lovingly as if it were a foreskin.

Pop!

The cork flew out of the bottle and ricocheted against a chandelier, sending it into a tinkling crystal symphony that continued long after the cork had fallen back to the floor. Just like a mutual orgasm, Clare thought. Hers, of course, being the chandelier, not quite so explosive but much more prolonged.

Now Jean had his thumb over the top of the bottle and he was shaking it backwards and forwards, sending jets of foam whirling up into the air to land on her body which tingled with cold and delight. Clare shrieked and writhed under the fountain of fizz, thrashing her head from side to side, catching droplets in her mouth.

A smile spread slowly across Jean's face. Quickly, he parted her legs again and directed the jet straight at her sex. Clare gasped for air. The surprise of the sensation made her want to snap her thighs together and open them wider still, all at once. But the shock was short-lived. The power of the pressure inside the bottle quickly subsided and Jean had to resort to pouring the champagne over her, dribbling the last of it between her labia.

He licked his smiling lips, a prelude to what she hoped he was about to do next.

'*J'ai soif*,' he whispered, leaning forward to take a drink.

Like a cat drinking milk he lapped at her. His tongue was so strong, Clare didn't last two seconds before she felt the urge to squirm. But more was to come. He sucked at her clit, taking it right into his mouth as no one had ever done before. Clare felt as if it had suddenly sent out a network of nerve tentacles that covered her entire lower body, tracks of ecstasy that reached down the inside of her legs to be raced along by the bolts of electricity that came each time Jean's tongue hit the button. Clare was crawling backwards up the bed, twisting up handfuls of the sheets as she went in the delicious agony of passion. As she tried to slip away from him, Jean grasped her waist in his powerful hands to pull her back down towards his tongue.

'Oh, no, oh no, oh no!' Clare panted. She couldn't possibly wait any longer. But then Jean's tongue was replaced by two fingers. He licked them first, for extra lubrication.

Jean's fingers began rhythmically sliding in and out of her soaking vagina, slowly at first, then faster and faster. Clare thrashed from side to side, moving her hips down to meet his fingers at each thrust. Her breath escaped in short gasps, punctuated by cries for mercy which she didn't want. Opening her eyes briefly, she saw, and heard, that Jean too was panting. His face was flushed, his pupils wide with pleasure, as he continued to work in and out of her, pausing only to massage her engorged clitoris with his thumb.

'Oh no, oh no.' Clare sat up suddenly. She clamped her hand like a vice around Jean's wrist and held his fingers within her as the first waves began to come. Stars danced inside her eyelids. The sound of the blood rushing around her head filled her ears.

'Aaaaah,' her grip tightened as an orgasm exploded within her body, flooding her limbs with pins and needles. Blood raced from one extreme to another until finally her grip on Jean's aching hand relaxed and her body slumped backwards on to the bed.

Such incredible pleasure from one hand. Afterwards, collapsed in exhaustion on the bed, Clare asked him, 'Do you play guitar?' He looked at her blankly. She smiled contentedly. He hadn't even managed to get his trousers off – what a gent!

It was obvious from the noise floating into the centre of the suite that Francesca and Bertrand were far from finished. Clare had wandered out of her room to the mini-bar and couldn't help noticing that Francesca hadn't bothered to shut her door. This was yet another first for Clare after her first Sapphic situation and her first real 'French kiss'. She had only ever seen two other people having sex in porn films and you don't really get to see that much in those. But suddenly she found herself, gin and tonic in hand, standing at the door of Francesca's room, watching her having it off.

Francesca and Bertrand were both totally naked. For a moment Clare just relished the contrast between Francesca's pinky white skin and his which was doughnut brown. Bertrand was lying on his back, his feet towards the door. Francesca sat on his chest with her back to the audience, blocking Clare from Bertrand's view. His erection was incredible. Claire had never see anything quite as big . . . Her mind flicked back to a memory of Francesca's sex. It would be interesting to see how this one went inside.

Francesca raised herself up from her sitting position and shuffled backwards on her knees so that the tip of his penis hovered at the entrance of her pussy like a sacrificial dagger. She reached down and took it in both her hands, guiding Bertrand towards his target which she then opened wider with carefully manicured fingers.

'Oh my . . . aaaaah.'

She had lowered herself down on the first thick inch. The rest of his shaft was still plainly visible between them, as if it were a bar holding them apart.

Francesca lowered herself a little further,

burying another pulsating inch. Then another, and another. Each time she let out a little cry, half pleasure, half pain. Still unnoticed, Clare quietly took another sip of her ice-cold gin.

Suddenly, Clare felt a hand on her shoulder. A hand closed her mouth to stifle any noise of surprise. Now Jean was standing beside her. She had obviously been too long in returning to bed with his drink.

'*Pas mal,*' he muttered when he saw what Clare was watching. He wrapped his warm arms around Clare's waist and rested his stubbly chin on her shoulder, settling in to join her at the watch.

Bertrand had grown tired of that position and now had Francesca on her hands and knees, her bottom waving in the air towards the door. The familiar pussy almost seemed to wink. Now Bertrand's penis stood out straight in front of him. He parted her lips with his fingers and once again took aim.

This time there was no warm up. Bertrand plunged in, straight up to the hilt so that his scrotum swung forward to bump against her. Francesca let out a cry of delicious agony but threw herself back at him all the same as if even his eight inches were not enough. Bertrand increased the tempo of his thrusts. Francesca's head was thrown back, her mouth emitting a throaty groan each time he drove inside. His hands held her hips steady and pulled her back and back and back.

'Keep going, keep going.' Clare could see that Francesca had taken one hand off the bed to fondle her clitoris so that she lurched forward precariously now as Bertrand neared his resolution. Clare recognised the groan which said that Francesca was about to find hers.

Meanwhile, Jean had decided to create his own scene. Clare had hardly heard the unzipping of his trousers over the sound of Francesca's cries, but she soon felt the insistent nudging of his penis at her own overexcited labia. She was at just the right height, since Jean had taken his shoes off and Clare was still wearing a pair of Francesca's lethally high heels. She turned her backside up just a little and made herself steady by taking hold of the door-frame. Though she couldn't see his dick, Clare guessed that like Bertie's, it was bigger than average, because, even after the incredible climax she had just had, his initial entry stretched her just a little more. Clare exhaled in pleasure and reached behind her to hold him tight. After a few luxuriously slow introductory thrusts, Jean all too quickly speeded up to match his best friend stroke for stroke.

Francesca's animal moans were blending into one long squeal. Bertrand was fucking her furiously. In their frenzy they had lost all rhythm and crashed together, heads thrown back, mouths open.

'Hold me, hold me,' Francesca screamed. Bertrand flopped forward over her body, enveloping her in his arms as their hips jerked in ecstasy.

Jean and Clare came just seconds after the other pair. Clare would never forget Francesca's face when she turned around to see where Clare's cries came from. It was such a picture of shock, for just a second, before she burst out laughing and yelled at her spectators, 'You bloody peeping toms!'

Bertrand was still impressively hard when he withdrew his shaft, slick with the mingling of his semen and her come, from Francesca's body. Clare made a mental note to make sure that, later on, she got some of that.

The boys stayed the night at the hotel. Francesca was obviously paying so much money that the manager made no complaint when she rang up to order two extra breakfasts in bed.

'What do you want, Clare?' she called across the room. Clare shrugged her shoulders and let Francesca order. Francesca laughed, 'Oh, I forgot that you'll eat anything that comes!'

The next day, Jean and Bertrand didn't have to work at the restaurant until the evening shift, and while Bertrand and Francesca were happy to stagnate in bed all day, Jean agreed that Clare should see more of Paris, since it was her first time in the city, and he offered to act as her guide.

Strangely, in the daylight, Jean looked far more attractive to Clare than he had done across that crowded restaurant. His brown eyes were so friendly, perpetually crinkled up in a smile.

As they walked, he held her hand naturally and they talked falteringly. First trying to tackle each other's languages, which, on Clare's part at least was an unmitigated disaster, then both speaking English. He really wasn't that bad at all.

He told her he was a student, studying business at a college in Paris, working nights at the restaurant to pay his way. When Clare told him what she did, he looked at her askance. She guessed that in Francesca's Armani casuals, she didn't exactly look the struggling artist.

'I, too,' he said awkwardly, 'I love to paint. I like to show you.' Clare smiled. It was a bit late in their acquaintanceship for him to be inviting her up to look at his etchings, but she agreed to go with him to his flat in the eighteenth arondissement after they had looked around the Louvre. Clare had thought that she needed a little more time to recover from the previous night's exertions, though Jean's hand, gently massaging the back of her neck as they looked at the Venus de Milo, quickly persuaded her otherwise.

They charged around the gallery, paying lip service to the exhibits Clare had always promised herself she would see. In a darkened room full of Egyptian antiquities, Jean's lips brushed lightly against her cheek. His hands grasped her waist as he pulled her across the room to look at a smooth marble cat. Beginning to burn, she sought his lips with hers but he moved out of range, teasingly. It was getting too much. Clare told herself that the Mona Lisa would be there another day and soon they were hurrying back into the cold afternoon and heading for the nearest Métro.

From the outside, the block where Jean had his flat was old, dark and damp-looking. There were about seven storeys, and Jean told Clare that his room was at the very top. She stood in the tiled entrance hall, looked up at the never-ending flight of stairs and shook her head.

'I don't suppose that's working, is it?' Clare looked at the impossibly old lift, but thankfully, Jean was already smiling and leading her inside. It was the kind of lift that she had only ever seen in movies. It didn't have the dull stainless steel doors of lifts in the tower blocks back home, but a wrought-iron trellis that closed with a rattle. You could see the stairs twisting around the lift shaft as they rose to the roof in the little iron cage, and Clare imagined a distraught lover, running round and round down them as the object of her desires took the lift to the ground floor and out of her life. The wonderful smells of evening meals cooking and freshly washed laundry drifted across their upward path from the rooms to either side, and occasionally they heard music, or animated conversation that she couldn't understand. To Clare, the whole thing seemed quite incredibly exotic.

At the seventh floor, the lift door strained itself back and Jean and Clare spilled out on to the landing. The door to Jean's room was varnished a rich coffee brown and on it was pinned a piece of yellowing card with the word 'Artaud', written on it in the peculiarly squirly handwriting of the French. Jean's name, in his handwriting, Clare discovered as he struggled with the key in the lock. It was a very stiff lock, but eventually it gave and the door swung open drunkenly on its ancient hinges. Clare stood in the door frame and gasped in surprise.

A shaft of yellow-red light cut right across the

bare wooden floor like a direct path to the centre of the sun. On their journey up in the lift, Clare had grown accustomed to the darkness and assumed that Jean's room would be equally shady, but here on the seventh floor they were a storey above most of the surrounding buildings and Jean's beautiful large window looked directly west. Clare ran to the window and strained her eyes against the evening glow to pick out landmarks. The whole of Paris was spread before her again, only this time it seemed that it was just for Clare and not for a thousand other tourists jostling her at a rail at the Eiffel tower.

The sight was all too commonplace to Jean. He was busying himself putting things away, tidying up while Clare took in the magnificent view. What a fantastic place this would be to paint in, she thought to herself. There was at least as much inspiration in the colour of this sunset over the city as she had found in the everchanging sea at St Ives. Clare breathed it in, trying to burn on her memory forever the picture of the sky turning pink over Paris in the autumn, before the sun disappeared for the night behind the skyline.

Jean had put on some music. Edith Piaf, her tragically romantic voice the perfect soundtrack for the moment. Without turning round, Clare heard him opening a bottle of wine, pouring out two glasses, walking across the creaking floor towards her. He put his hand on Clare's shoulder and planted a careful kiss on her smiling lips as he passed her a glass. They each took a sip, Clare grimaced at the bitter taste, he didn't, and they chinked their glasses together to toast the dying day. Goosebumps of excitement prickled all over Clare's body as his hand brushed her pony-tailed hair out of the way so that he could kiss her neck.

With the sun finally gone, Clare could now take a proper look at the room. Jean, who had tired of the view first, was sitting on the bed – a sturdy mahogany affair. As a matter of fact, the bed was just about the only thing to sit on. There seemed to be a chair by the door, but it was covered in clothes which had been flung off in a hurry in the race from college to restaurant shift. Above the bed, on a wall yellowed by years of tobacco smoke which must have started before Jean was born, hung a poster for an exhibition. The tiled mantelpiece was covered in postcards and photos. He pointed out his parents in their garden in Normandy, his younger sister. His pet dog.

There was no sign of any painting he had been doing. But then he knelt down and began to fumble under the bed for something. When he finally emerged, he had a sketchbook and a number of large pieces of paper in his hand. He flopped them on to the counterpane and motioned to Clare to look through them.

Clare fell on to the paintings like a vulture on to a cow in the desert. She adored looking at other people's paintings. Three years at college had taught her that you can see so much of a person in the way they paint. When you draw someone else you can't help but draw how you feel about them. Bold strokes for confidence, light strokes for sensitivity. Likewise, a self-portrait is simply the soul laid bare. Hungrily, she sorted through the scraps and sketches that poured from his book. Landscapes, animals, studies of the bricks and ironwork in the very building where he lived.

'Wow,' she enthused as she searched for the right word. 'These are really, really good! *Bon*. I mean *bien*. Oh, you know what I mean.'

Jean, meanwhile, had been under the bed again and now emerged with something new to show her.

'What do you think?' he asked, pushing the piece of canvas into her hands. She looked at it first upside down and then from its side to mock him. But this really was something. A nude, pictured lying on the bed from beneath which the painting had come, Clare assumed. A girl, lying on her side, propped up on one elbow. One arm stretched up and over her head. Her hair falling over the lower shoulder. Eyes closed. The face serene. Clare was surprised to feel what might have been a pang of jealousy. The casual composition, the care with which he had blended the colours, told her that this was someone special to him.

'What do you think?' he asked again.

'Who is it?' Clare asked.

'Oh, no one special.' His narrow, up-down smile said otherwise.

'A girlfriend?'

'She was.'

Clare looked at him. Trying to tell him that he could elaborate if he wanted to. 'But sometimes things don't work out ...' he continued. 'You have to let them go ... Have your life.' He took the painting from her hands again and slid it back beneath the bed. 'Meet new people.'

Clare nodded, slightly hazy from the wine. She suppressed the picture of Daniel which came into her mind. It occurred to her that it was actually the first time she had thought of him that day.

'I would like very much to paint you,' Jean told her.

'Me?' Clare was surprised. No one had ever asked to paint her before, even in three years at art school, not even Daniel. 'Me?' she said again.

'*Oui.*'

'When? I've got to go back to England tomorrow.'

'I start now.' He brought his sketchbook out from beneath the bed.

'Oh no. I can think of better things to do now,' Clare took the edges of his collar flirtatiously.

'No. I want to draw you first,' he insisted.

'OK. How do you want me?' Clare laughed.

'Nude,' he said seriously. She giggled at his pronunciation. 'Take your clothes off in there.' He gestured towards the tiny bathroom. Clare was surprised, but obeyed. When she emerged, he had set up an easel and was sitting behind it, sharpening pencils. She stepped in front of him, where he had arranged a couple of blankets on the floor, and then sat down. He glanced up and put her into the right position with a few hand gestures. She was sitting with her legs tucked beneath her. Leaning on one hand. She wasn't sure that she would be able to stay like that for long . . . or that she wanted to. As she heard Jean's pencil begin to scratch away at an outline, his dark brown head bobbing in front of her.

His eyes travelled the contours of her body and

349

yet she felt as though he wasn't properly looking at her. She pulled faux-sexy facial expressions to catch his attention, which met only with commands to sit still. It was strange and yet so very erotic. He was appreciating her merely as a form.

'I'm starting to get a bit stiff,' Clare said plaintively after she had held her position for a quarter of an hour. 'You're obviously not,' she added sarcastically when Jean failed to acknowledge her complaint. His eyes were now resting on her breasts. Her nipples had stiffened in the cool draught that edged in at the window and came under the door, but she was glad to be a little cold because she liked the way her breasts looked then, taut and firm. It was how she would like them to be immortalised. Her fantasy was to have them cast in bronze, but nobody had ever asked her if they could and she felt it would seem a little vain to suggest it herself. But, she thought, glancing down to see where Jean's eyes had lingered, they were definitely among her best features.

'Nearly finished,' he said, his concentrated expression breaking into a fleeting smile. 'And then I will have to mix some paint.'

'Are you going to use natural colours?' Clare asked him, remembering the painting he had shown her earlier.

'I'm going to paint you how I see you,' he replied.

'Blue with cold?'

The sarcasm was lost on him. Jean's hand was moving frantically again as he shaded something

350

in with a very dark pencil. He sat back from the easel and studied his work. He smiled. It looked right to him.

'Can I see?' Clare asked.

'Not yet.' He had begun to mix watercolours in the lid of his paint-box. He was going to wash colour over the pencil outline. Clare ached. She longed to move, but every time she shifted even a little, Jean would complain that she was disturbing the shadows that he wanted to paint.

She needed to think about something to take her mind off the pins and needles. No, what she really needed was somebody to rub his hands all over her body until she felt as though the blood was moving around it again. Jean had lowered the easel slightly, so that now she could see most of his face. His lashes were so long. They swept across his cheeks as his eyes moved. Clare remembered first making contact with those eyes, in the restaurant, after Francesca had made arrangements for their foursome with Bertrand. Jean had been smiling, or, as she thought at the time, laughing at Francesca's audacity and Clare's markedly contrasting timidity.

Clare's gaze wandered across his head, revelling in the light bouncing off his hair. She looked at his ears – even his ears were cute. He had an earring in one, a tiny yin-yang symbol. She remembered almost having swallowed it the night before. His jaw was stubbly again. He had the kind of dark beard that needs to be shaved twice a day for a squeaky clean look, but she was glad he didn't look like that. The stubble emphasised the shape of his face, the cleft down the centre of his chin. It accentuated the smoothness of his lips. His tongue flicked out across the bottom one in concentration.

Clare closed her eyes and remembered the first touch of those lips on hers, forgetting now the apprehension which had accompanied that kiss. She remembered the taste of his mouth. Coffee, chocolate and champagne. His tongue cool from just having taken a swig from the bottle. The scent of his skin. The cologne he wore which was so familiar to her. The smell of his clean hair. The softness of it as she scrunched it up between her fingers while they were kissing and later, while they were fucking. A friendly feeling was gathering at the top of her thighs as she thought about the man now absorbed in his painting.

Jean smiled when he saw the faraway look on Clare's face. Her mouth had opened slightly. Her lips were a deeper red than they had been a few moments before and glistened with moisture. He liked them even better now. Her cheeks too were noticeably pinker. At this rate he was going to have to mix all his paints up again. He absently ran a dry brush across his own lips as he studied her. It felt good. Suddenly the girl before him was transforming from the subject of his study into the object of his desires again. There was no point in trying to carry on with the painting. He had been distracted.

Silently, Jean rose from his stool and crept across to where Clare was sitting, her eyes still closed. He got within inches of her, but she didn't seem to notice. Jean held out the brush he had in his hand and traced along the line of her mouth.

The edges twitched up in a smile as she realised what was happening. Her favourite fantasy was about to come true, only this time, she wasn't the one in control.

As if he could read her mind, Jean swept the soft brush from her mouth, down across her chin and on to her neck. From her neck to her collarbone. The slight tickling sensation there made her hunch up her shoulders. By the time the brush had reached the level of Clare's breasts, Jean's mouth had taken up the same path.

His tongue tasted of the red wine they had been drinking and the cigarette he had smoked as they walked to his flat from the Louvre. It was a decadent taste, Clare would think later on, the taste of someone who appreciated all kinds of hedonism. His kiss was hard, crushing her lips, bruising them. Their teeth banged together slightly, making them break contact for a moment with a laugh. Her head tilted backwards under the force of his embrace. This was how she liked to be kissed. Feeling that the other person was stealing something from her each time his tongue entered her mouth. He had dropped the brush, and now abandoned her lips to let his kiss roam all over her face, as if he would never be able to touch her again and wanted to remember the way she was with all his senses.

'Oh . . . you . . .' Clare began to speak but gave up, letting herself melt into his arms which embraced the whole of her, his hands covering her body so well that she felt as if he had more than two. His hands swept up and down her back, then grasped at her breasts, fumbling for her nipples, even hurting them slightly. He was still fully dressed. Clare began the task of undressing him, struggling with the metal buttons that fastened his shirt and refused to pop out of the thick cotton without a fight. Growing impatient, he helped her, sliding his belt out from its loops, unzipping the black jeans that hugged his hips.

The jeans were unfastened. Clare pushed them down over his buttocks, taking the cotton boxer shorts with them. She moved her hands around and around on his backside, grasping the muscles that clenched as he wrestled her on to the floor so that she was lying beneath him.

'Jean, Jean,' she managed to pant. His trousers and boxer shorts were around his knees. His dick, now free, waved from side to side in a stately motion as he raised himself up to position Clare on the rough blankets. She opened her legs so that her inner thighs were either side of his strong, sinewy hips. The anticipation and excitement swelling within her seemed to be filling her chest, making it harder for her to breathe. Jean lowered himself back down, crushing her sensitive breasts. Clare delighted in the touch of the wiry hair on his legs against her own delicate skin. Jean positioned himself to enter her. Clare shifted too, to hurry on the moment. She lifted her hips so that her pelvis was touching his. Jean's hand snaked down between them, helping his dick to find its aim.

'Oh . . .' Jean's first eager thrust made Clare suck her breath in sharply. She tightened her thighs against his body and held him still for a moment while she relaxed and let him further inside. But he couldn't hold off for long and soon he thrust into her again. His face hovered above hers. She looked up at the eyes, now tightly shut. He was biting his lower lip as he pushed himself into her again, feeling the divine resistance of her vaginal walls.

'Ah,' he thrust again.

Clare clasped his buttocks. Clenched her fingers into his hard, firm flesh. He responded with a deeper thrust, a longer moan. She raised her body again and again to meet him. But still it didn't feel deep enough.

Jean stopped his frantic pounding for a moment and pulled her legs so that they were wrapped around his middle. He curled his knees beneath him and rocked backwards so that he was sitting up with her astride him. Clare released her legs and used her own knees to help her move up and down on his glorious cock.

'Aaaah . . . aaah,' he moaned as she rode him. His hands raced up and down her body. Clare twisted her fingers in his hair, the soft hair she had been dreaming of.

'Stop, stop,' he held her down against him, preventing her from rising up again. 'I'm going to come.' It was too soon, too soon, but Clare couldn't just patiently wait for the moment to pass.

'I don't care,' she cried, continuing to ride him. He rolled on to his back, so that she looked down upon his ecstatic face. She was totally, totally in control. She rode him faster and faster, ignoring his pleas for mercy, for her to slow down so that they could come together. She wanted him to be in her control, wanted him to be unable to contain the feelings she provoked in him.

'Come, come,' she incited breathlessly, her words making it harder and harder for him to resist.

His hips were beginning to buck upwards. His moaning began to take on the familiar tone that told her when the crisis was drawing near. His eyes screwed tightly shut, in ecstasy, in pain, desperately trying to hang on until she came too.

'No, no,' he begged her, simultaneously grabbing her hips and pulling her down on to his prick, impaling her with his frantically jerking member. Driving himself as far into her as he could possibly go. Clare threw back her head triumphantly as Jean writhed in pleasure beneath her. His come flooded her body and ran down her legs. She fell forward on top of him, laughing ecstatically. He was one hundred per cent hers.

'I wish you were here for a longer time,' Jean whispered into Clare's ear as he wrapped his body around her narrow frame. The heat of his breath and the sincerity of his words sent a wave of warmth through her body. She didn't say anything in reply but put out a hand to gently squeeze his thigh. He kissed her softly on the edge of her jaw and settled down to go to sleep.

Clare slept so well in Jean's tiny flat that by the time she did wake up, she had almost missed the flight she was due to take home. They raced to the hotel to pick up Clare's things and found

Francesca lounging on the green sofa in her dressing gown, with Bertrand sitting on the floor beside her, his head on her lap. She was languidly eating chocolates, popping them into her mouth one after another. Her eyes were fixed to the television screen. While Clare raced about, grabbing discarded knickers and stockings, Francesca didn't seem at all bothered, since she had already decided that they weren't quite ready to go home.

'I can't be bothered with a race to the airport now,' Francesca sighed. 'Call Daniel and tell him that the flights your friend won were a bit dodgy and that there was no room on the flight originally booked. It's simple.' She was running her fingers through Bertrand's hair as she berated Clare. 'I've already told Steven that I'm going to stay in town to see another show ... He didn't sound too bothered. Probably with some girl. The bastard.'

Francesca thrust the phone into Clare's hand and stared at her until she began to dial. Daniel wasn't in but for once he had remembered to put the answermachine on before going out. Clare waited for the tone and garbled a guilty message.

'Daniel, it's me. Flight's cocked up. Looks like I'm going to have to stay here until ...' She glanced over at Francesca, who mouthed 'Thursday'. Ignoring her, Clare said, 'Tomorrow ... Sorry about this, darling. Hope everything's OK. Miss you.' Clare blew a couple of kisses to finish the message.

'You're a better liar than my dear husband,' Francesca laughed. 'Now all we have to do is think up mystery illnesses to keep these two off work for another day.' She ruffled Bertrand's glossy thick hair as though he were a King Charles spaniel. Jean had settled into the sofa beside her and was grinning from ear to ear.

'Oh, well, let's hit *le vin*,' Clare sighed. Another day in Paris wasn't so difficult to resign herself to.

Jean and Bertrand rang the restaurant and claimed to be suffering from food poisoning. Picked up from another, less reputable establishment of course. Excuses made, Bertrand dragged Francesca straight back to bed, and she squealed in mock dismay until his hands and tongue reduced her to delighted giggles.

Clare stood at the floor-length window, looking down on to the street below. She wondered how Daniel would take the message. Hoped that he wouldn't be on his own when he played it.

Jean was sitting on the arm of the sofa now, dragging lazily on one of Bertrand's cigarettes. He reached out a hand to her and she took it. 'Who were you telephoning?' he asked.

In reply, she told him, 'Just the person I share a flat with. A friend.'

They spent the rest of the morning looking at the paintings they had missed out on the day before and the afternoon trawling around the Père Lachaise cemetery in search of Jim Morrison's grave. The tombs stood in rows like tiny terraced houses and Jean tried everything he could to entice her inside one of the dank ghost homes.

At eight o'clock, Jean fumed to Clare and asked

her whether they should be getting back to the hotel to join the others for dinner. No, she told him, she wanted to be with him alone for a little longer yet. He smiled broadly and dragged her off to a Mexican restaurant where he had once worked. They were guests of honour, seated at the best table. The manager's wife fussed around Jean as though he were her own prodigal son. He was very well liked by everyone, in fact, Clare observed, as he knocked back yet another tequila on the house.

Finally walking back Jean threw an arm around her shoulders and Clare hooked her thumb through one of his belt loops. His hips undulated deliciously as he moved and she couldn't stop herself from sliding her hand across his beautiful ass. Clare thought about dancing with him in the club that first evening. His easy grace, so unusual in a man. She moulded her hand around one squarely perfect buttock. When he seemed to be taking little notice of her attentions, she gave him a tiny, hard pinch.

'You are making it 'arder for me to walk,' he laughed, stopping suddenly in the shadow of a tall building and slapping her hand way. 'Look at this.' He took Clare's hand and placed it firmly over his awakening prick.

'Don't you mean *feel* this?' Clare corrected, rubbing the hardening bulge at the front of his trousers. 'If I'm going to look, there has to be something to see.' She took hold of his zip and mischievously tugged it down. She slipped a hand inside and started to set him free.

'Oh, Clare, *non, non, non*,' he moaned in

half-hearted protest.

They were walking by the river, at a point where it was well lined by tall trees. It being late autumn, the leaves were almost all gone, but the branches still provided quite a screen. The street lamps weren't strong. Immediately, Clare could see a thousand opportunities for an al fresco fuck. But just then a gendarme meandered past. Clare hadn't seen him coming, since she was used to looking out for a completely differently shaped hat. Fortunately, Jean had spotted the impending disaster and swiftly steered her from the bench she had been leading him to.

'Wait until we are back at the hotel,' he told her.

Clare pouted out a petulant lip. 'I won't feel like it then.' The gendarme had walked on by, whistling. Clare began to tug down the zip of Jean's hastily closed trousers again.

'Clare,' he moaned exasperatedly.

'What about down there?' she asked. A few feet ahead of them, the path split in two with one branch going down towards the very edge of the river while the other sloped upwards towards a bridge. The riverside path was overshadowed by the wall which edged the other path. It was dark, unlit, screened from the passing river traffic by trees.

'Okay,' Jean consented.

They wandered off the well-lit path, Clare unable to crush the nervous feeling of dark places which had been with her for as long as she could remember, but finding that the fear only made her want Jean more.

She continued to struggle with Jean's flies as

they walked so that by the time they found the perfect spot his dick was already waving in the air, poised for action. Jean was fully behind the project now that they were out of the glare of streetlights and he crushed Clare against his body, grinding her lips beneath his as his hands roamed up and down. It was as if he was trying to imprint her curves on his memory for all time.

Clare couldn't wait. She was beginning to lift her skirt for him.

'Turn around.'

She did as she was told. Jean grasped Clare by the hips to steady her as she bent forward. He murmured with approval at the sight of her stockings, held precariously in place by an exquisitely lacy belt. She was wearing high-heeled shoes, but these were sinking into the mud and she still had to raise herself up on to her tiptoes to be in exactly the right position. His dick was now nudging at the entrance to her sex, already very wet and welcoming. Clare exhaled in delight as Jean plunged himself into her, right up to the hilt. This first thrust was quickly followed by another which pevented her from drawing a breath. She tottered forwards with the force. Jean took preventative action by turning her and himself so that when the next thrust came, she could brace herself with her hands on the cold stone wall.

'Aaaah,' Clare couldn't stop herself from moaning, though she knew the other path was so close that people passing would be bound to hear. She jammed her right hand into her mouth, biting her fingers hard to stifle the noise. But she soon found that she needed both arms to stop herself hitting against the wall. Jean had found his rhythm now and she could tell that he too was making one hell of an effort to keep it quiet. Accompanying each thrust, he squeezed her bare hips, using them as handles to pull her body closer to him. It felt so good to be making love outdoors like this, with evening strollers meandering by on one side and glass topped boats full of people out to see some interesting sights sailing by on the other. It felt so good, and so bad . . .

A boat's horn sounded close behind them. Clare froze momentarily but Jean carried on. They couldn't really see, could they, Clare wondered. No, the screen of trees was too thick and besides, if they could see anything at all it would be Jean's square bare buttocks, not hers.

But keeping quiet was becoming increasingly difficult. Jean was now clasping her tightly to him. Holding her body upright against him. Panting in her ear and biting into her neck by turns. Her arms flailed out in front of her in a desperate attempt to maintain some balance. Meanwhile, her lower body was letting itself go. Her vagina was burning. The muscular walls clenching, squeezing, grasping. Jean's faltering rhythm told her that he too was about to lose all semblance of control.

'Hang on, hang on,' she begged him. He slowed down as far as he possibly could but he had already passed the point of holding off. With the next thrust he pulled her upper body back against him tighter than ever, letting out as he did so an indescribably animal noise. Clare's breath was forced out of her body. She had the sensation of her heart slipping out through her mouth. Her lungs were empty, she gasped for air. Blackness started to creep in at the corners of her eyes.

'Jean,' she clung desperately to the wall as if she was about to fall off the earth. Jean powered into her Three more long, desperate strokes before his sperm was ripped out from his balls with the power of his ejaculation, pumped out of his body by the eager muscles which surrounded his dick like an avidly sucking mouth.

Clare's fingers scraped down the stone.

They slumped against the wall, still joined together, breathing raggedly. Clare turned her face to meet his. They stood cheek by cheek. He tightened his hold on her, then buried his nose in her loosened hair and breathed her in.

Clap, clap, clap.

Clare looked up to see the source of the slow applause. Yes, they had been screened from the river, but not from the bridge and there stood the gendarme, with two of his friends. Jean straightened himself up quickly and they ran, laughing and stumbling, down the blackening path. They had run too far by the time Clare realised she had left her borrowed stilettos behind in the mud.

Francesca and Bertrand lay entwined on the green leather sofa again. Their naked bodies were lit only by the light of the television which flickered and danced along their complementary curves. When she heard the door open, Francesca looked up but didn't bother to cover herself at Clare and Jean's entrance, as Clare probably would have done in her position. Bertrand also looked up lazily from his resting place between Francesca's silky thighs. He looked knackered and Francesca looked frustrated.

Cursory greetings over, Bertrand was content to settle back down again but Francesca had already wriggled out from beneath him and was tripping across the room. She headed straight for the little kitchenette where Clare and Jean had gone to fix some drinks. Francesca slid to a standstill across the tiled floor and Jean couldn't help but find his eyes drawn to her breasts which still jiggled from her little jog.

'Nice evening?' she asked brightly, insinuating her naked self between Jean and the sink.

'Great,' Clare replied. 'And you?'

'Sort of.' She pulled a face which belied her words. 'A little bit boring actually . . .'

'Really?'

'Yeah.'

Francesca had snaked her naked arm around Clare's fully clothed waist and moulded her body against Clare's side while she cracked ice for their glasses. A splinter of the solid cold water flew off the ice-cube mould and landed on Francesca's bare breasts. She shivered exaggeratedly. Her breasts began to jiggle again. She caught Jean's attention once more and gave him a predatory wink.

Clare had a feeling she knew what was coming next.

Now Francesca slipped her other arm around

Jean's strong shoulders and pulled him towards her under a pretence of keeping warn. Picking up the game, he wrapped her in the folds of his fleecy jacket. Clare pulled a pouty face and offered Jean his glass.

'You're not going to bed are you?' Francesca asked when Jean let her out into the cold again while he took his drink. 'It's still early.'

'Bertie's tired,' Clare said meaningfully.

'Exactly,' replied Francesca. 'But he might perk up if something interesting were to start happening. . .' She tucked herself back inside Jean's coat. Something pleasurably hard twitched against her buttocks through his trousers. 'Isn't that right, Jean.' His eyes pleaded agreement. 'It's not nice to be selfish, Clare,' Francesca added as a final blow.

'I see, so now you've worn out poor old Bertrand you . . . OK.' Clare shrugged her shoulders and wandered out of the kitchenette, leaving Jean in Francesca's more than capable hands. The girlie giggles started almost immediately. Clare ruthlessly quashed the wave of jealousy that began to rise in her chest.

She took her place on the sofa beside Bertrand. He lifted his head like a somnambulant tortoise and let her slide her legs underneath. His eyes were glued to the television. Clare had definitely got the raw end of this deal. She let her gaze travel the length of his body. He was thicker-set than Jean. His thighs were huge, a rugby player's, covered in dark hair. His magnificent dick was sleepily curled between them. Clare let her hand trail nonchalantly across his well-muscled chest,

while she sipped her drink and tried to understand the adverts.

'Mmm,' he murmured. His hand rose to hold
hers straight away and he looked up with a smile
into her eyes. Maybe Francesca was right. Maybe
he was just waiting for something interesting to
happen. He rolled over so that he was on his
front, his amazing taut buttocks to the ceiling. He
buried his face in her cotton-covered crotch and
breathed her in as she stroked up and down his
back. His hot breath between her legs was already
beginning to make her clitoris hunger for attention.

Bertrand's arm lolled over the side of the sofa
and his hand rested on the floor. Then slowly it
began to creep up her leg. Carefully massaging a
foot, then an ankle. Things were beginning to
come to life.

A shrill peal of laughter erupted from the
kitchen. Francesca was having a good time and
Clare was determined not to be left out.

Tired of Bertrand's slow hands Clare manhan-
dled him into a more useful position as best she
could. He was very heavy but at last he seemed to
get the idea. He lurched forward and fastened his
lips on to hers. His kiss was far sloppier than
Jean's and when he started to move down her
neck, Clare surreptitiously wiped off her face.

Bertrand nuzzled the buttons of Clare's shirt,
making strange, feral sounds as he did so. He was
moaning something in French which she hoped
was complimentary, while he relieved her of her
clothes. Not quite Jean's gentle touch, but arousing in its own way, Clare thought.

'Jean, aaaahh!' came a disconcerting shriek. Clare's eyes narrowed. Francesca wasn't just pinching her man, she was putting her off the business now in hand. With this in mind, and since Clare was bigger than Francesca and so took up more room on the sofa, she decided that it was time to drag Bertrand off to the bedroom, like a tigress dragging an antelope home for the cubs.

He swayed unsteadily when he got to his feet. A bad sign. But no, his dick was actually reassuringly alert. Clare remembered seeing him in action the day before. Her sex suddenly became the control centre of her body.

'Come on, big boy.' She pulled him along by her bra which she had hooked around his neck like a lead. His large hands waved in front of him, grasping for her. She tantalisingly kept her body just out of his reach.

Inside the room, Clare whirled Bertrand around and he fell in an ungainly heap on the bed. As she closed the bedroom door, she encountered Jean and Francesca, en route to doing the same thing. Her eyes locked with Jean's momentarily. He gave an apologetic shrug. She stuck out her tongue.

Back on the bed, Bertrand had arranged himself into a sort of star shape. His dick was now poking straight up in the air like a television transmitter. Clare's pussy was picking up the signals. She sashayed towards him, flexing the bra noose menacingly between her hands.

'Come 'ere,'he said gruffly.

Clare climbed on to the bed and knelt with one leg on either side of this thick trunk. She lowered herself backwards so that his prick just touched the twin cheeks of her buttocks. His eyes rolled a little with tiredness and tequila. She wasn't having that, so she used the bra to cover his eyes. Each cup making a lens. He laughed at her ingenuity.

'Now you won't be able to see where I'm touching you,' she said in a low hiss. She straightened out her legs and, using her arms to steady herself, hovered over Bertrand's body so that no part of her actually touched him. She was going to make sure that there would be no comparison between her and her blonde-haired friend.

'Lie still,' she ordered. He didn't. His English wasn't great.

She arranged herself so that her long fine hair now reached down to brush lightly across his gormlessly smiling face. She scuttled backwards like a crab, dragging her locks along him. His hands stirred the air around her. She dodged out of their way. When he had given up his game of blind man's buff, she returned to her task, covering his body with the minutest of caresses like a warm southern breeze. His prick was still giving her a standing ovation.

Tired of that trick, she lowered her body a little further so that now she was gliding across him with her silken breasts. Her nipples, swollen hard, scored the path. When she crossed his face, his tongue flicked out to meet them and missed both. She laughed softly as she dangled her left breast carefully just a centimetre above his mouth. If he could sense its presence he wasn't showing it. Finally she just grazed the pink button against his bottom lip. His mouth opened to let her in again but she had already taken the prize away.

Hair. Breasts. What else did she have to touch him with but her hands? That was boring. It didn't take her long to come up with one final instrument of slow torture. Her legs shuddered as she brought herself into place for this one.

'What am I touching you with now?'

Clare brought her pulsing pussy in line with his curving mouth. Her pubic hair touched him first, causing him to wrinkle his nose as if he were about to sneeze. He recognized the musky smell of her womanhood instantly and this time, instead of reaching out to touch her back with his tongue as he had done when she offered her breasts, he refused. If she was going to torture him it was about time she had a taste of her own medicine.

Clare squatted further so that her clitoris almost rubbed his nose. She felt so wet, wet enough to drip on him if he didn't do something about it and quick.

He laughed a secret laugh. His tongue poked out just a tiny, tiny fraction of a centimetre between his sharp white teeth.

'Go on, go on,' Clare thought to herself.

The poised tongue flicked out, lightning fast to take in her clit.

'Yes.' Clare was very, very pleased.

Bertrand gave up his pretence of helplessness and grabbed her by the hips to help her stay still while he began to lick along the length of her inner labia with smooth, deliberate strokes. She began to writhe, but couldn't move out of his way – his hands held her like a vice.

'Oh, yes, oh, yes,' she moaned, louder and louder, not exactly abandoned to the moment, but hoping Francesca could hear. 'Oh yes, yes, yes.' Her chant rose like praise to the heavens. 'Yes, yes, keep going. I'm going to come, yes, yes.'

From the next room came a similar song, but louder, louder and faster still.

'Yes, yes.' Clare began to bounce up and down a little. Bertrand was having trouble finding the spot. 'I'm going to come. I'm going to come.'

'Yeeesss!' screamed Francesca. 'Yeeesss!'

Suddenly Bertrand pushed Clare's pussy away from his face and shoved her backwards down his body so that her vagina was now directly above his cock. He brought her down on it with such force that she let forth a yell louder than anything she had ever yelled before in her life. Even when she had dropped a brick on her toe, aged three.

He began to move her body furiously up and down with his hands until she picked up the rhythm. Every thrust was accompanied by a note of increasing ecstasy now. The sounds from next door were blurring from her mind. Her focus now was between her legs. Bertrand was raising his body to each down-stroke from hers.

But still this wasn't enough for him. Clare found herself instantly on her back. Her legs first trying to keep her body moving to meet his, then giving up and flailing manically in the air as he powered into her, his huge cock filling her, stretching her.

She began to come long before he did. The

nerves in her body flattening and scrunching. Even her eyes feeling rather than seeing. Bright, brilliant colours played across her eyelids. Her blood thundered in her ears. So loud, so loud. Her blood, his breathing, her breathing, his semen.

Bertrand collapsed on top of her, exhaling a sigh like his last breath.

'Now,' he said, 'I am really tired.'

'Have a good time?' Clare asked Francesca when they met by the fridge.

'Yes, thank you. And you?'

'Oh, wonderful.'

They sipped their cold gin and tonics in silence for a moment. Each regarding the other jealously beneath their tousled hair. Funny how the two random guys they had picked up on the first night had suddenly become so exclusive to each.

Francesca laughed first. Spitting out a stream of gin and tonic with the loud 'ha' that exploded from her body. Clare swallowed hers before she took up the giggle and they fell into each other's sweaty arms.

'Quits?' Francesca asked.

'Quits . . .' said Clare. 'Especially now that I know I'm better than you are . . .'

'What?' The war was back on. 'Qualify that remark.'

'Well, if we had a machine like a clapometer that measured the volume of participants' reactions . . .'

'It was Bertie who was doing the work . . . You came first.'

'I bet I could make you come first.' Clare threw

371

down the gauntlet.

'Choose your weapon.'

'Tongues.'

'We'll need referees.'

Bertrand and Jean were dragged into the lounge and seated side by side on the green leather. Bertrand was struggling to keep his eyes open. Jean flicked idly through the TV channels still on air.

Clare and Francesca knelt opposite each other on the carpet, laying down the ground rules before laying down themselves.

'And orgasms not to be unreasonably withheld,' Clare added finally. 'No thinking of father-in-laws or husbands.'

Francesca agreed.

'Let's get into postion then.'

The girls lay down like a yin-yang symbol, nose to tail. Each nonchalantly raised one leg so that the other could get a tongue in. Jean flicked the television off and did the honours by shouting go.

Each girl began licking frantically at the pussy of the other, Francesca concentrating on the smooth labia, Clare going straight for the clit. As she felt her clit stiffen, Francesca was unable to stifle a moan. The moan was an incentive to drive Clare on but she too was already finding it difficult to concentrate on her task. She was still tingling slightly from the fuck she had just had with Bertrand. She should have waited until she had calmed down totally and not given Francesca the head start.

'Amsterdam, Berlin, Cairo,' Clare tried to think of a capital city for every letter of the alphabet.

'Durban ... no that's not a capital. Aaaah!' Francesca had made some progress. She was playing a similar alphabet game in her mind with the names of famous fashion designers and had got as far as Ozbek. But her tongue was tiring and she cheated, backing her mouthwork up with the surreptitious laying on of hands.

'You're cheating,' Clare hissed, pulling her face away from Francesca's sticky-sweet crotch for a moment.

'All's fair,' Francesca replied, using her tongue like a dick now. Straining with the effort of keeping it straight and hard but very pleased with the obvious results. Clare's head lolled back on the carpet. She clamped her upper thigh down on the side of Francesca's head in a desperate bid to halt the progress of a fast approaching orgasm.

'Give up. I give up,' she wailed. Moaning and laughing all at the same time. But Francesca hadn't finished with her yet. Her tongue vibrated wildly over the stiff little clit which she now almost sucked into her mouth. Clare's body twisted and turned from side to side. Francesca used her hands to keep her target steady. The buttocks beneath her fingers clenched tightly together and a new stream of pleasure was soaking Francesca's mouth.

Clare had lost the bet.

Francesca jumped up from the floor laughing at her vanquished victim who still rolled on the carpet, moaning and groaning as if she had been shot rather than just brought to orgasm. On the sofa, Bertrand had fallen asleep. Jean smiled wryly.

'Last one to bed gets Bertrand,' Francesca said.

All too soon it was Monday morning. As Clare rolled over to gaze in lazy wonder at the brown back of Jean against the clean white sheets she was suddenly hit with a hammer-blow of guilt. She had almost completely forgotten about Daniel. She hadn't even bothered to try and phone him since Sunday to make sure that he had received her message about her late return. He would probably be apoplectic with rage by now! What was Clare doing? She was throwing away everything she had with Daniel on a crazy bored wife and a French guy who really held no appeal for her other than the same aftershave as her first love and eyelashes long enough to shame a cow! Jean murmured and rolled over in his sleep so that he was now facing her. His mouth was curved in a smile. Clare remembered the evening in his tiny attic flat. She was going to miss that smile.

While Jean continued to snore lightly, Clare picked up the telephone beside the bed and dialled home. Two rings and then the answermachine cut in. Same message as usual. 'Daniel and Clare aren't here right now . . .' At least he hadn't erased her name from the tape.

Jean moved closer to Clare in his sleep and threw his arm around her waist. He was still smiling.

'Hi, Daniel,' Clare said to the answermachine. 'Just to say I really will be back later. Not sure exactly when but definitely today. Depends on availability of flights. Leave the chain off the door. Love you.'

Clare put the phone down and settled into Jean's sleepy embrace. The warm scent of his chest enveloped her. She told herself that she might as well enjoy it while it lasted. Daniel had probably spent the weekend boozing and playing football anyway . . . And absence made the heart grow fonder. Didn't it?

But Clare's heart touched down with the plane. She glanced across at Francesca, who looked similarly crestfallen. Francesca took Clare's hand and squeezed it.

'Stay in London tonight,' she pleaded. 'I don't want this to end.'

'I can't,' Clare reproached her gently. 'I'm already two days late! It's not fair on Daniel.' Clare stroked Francesca's face with the soft furry paw of the teddy bear she had bought for Daniel in the duty free shop as a peace offering. 'I'll call you tomorrow. And we'll see each other again soon, I promise.'

'How soon?' Francesca begged her.

'Soon, soon,' was all Clare could say as she steeled herself to go.

Clare had been thinking about her position on the flight home. She had to finish this madness. Francesca was obviously becoming too attached and it could only be a matter of time before she found out above Steve. Besides, there was Daniel to think about. Clare had decided that she wanted to be with him after all and so she had to play by the rules. That meant no more messing about. Within the next couple of days she would make sure that Daniel sat down with her and they talked seriously about where they had been going wrong. They would sort out the problems that their rivalry in work was causing. They could even move back to London if that was what it would take to make him feel happy with himself, and with her, again.

But Clare had also been thinking about Jean. On the coach journey home she took out again and again the scrap of paper on which he had scribbled his name and address and a tiny caricature of himself. Clare wondered if she would ever see him again.

By the time Clare arrived at the gates of the block where she lived, it was approaching midnight. She looked up at the windows of the flat and was curious to find herself relieved to see that none of the lights was on. Daniel was out, or he was already in bed. Either way, he couldn't have been too bothered about her late return.

Clare opened the door quietly, in case he was asleep, and didn't put on a light, for fear of awakening him. She tiptoed into the bedroom and threw herself down on to her side of the bed. He wasn't there. Must be out, she thought. She couldn't be bothered to get up again to turn on the light, so she undressed in the darkness, under the covers because it was cold, and was asleep within seconds.

Chapter Thirteen

SHE MUST HAVE been very tired, because she didn't wake up until midday. The weak winter sun was streaming through the window, but it was freezing and her breath made smoky patterns in the air. And Daniel still wasn't beside her.

Why hadn't he sorted out the thermostat so that the heating came on? They weren't that skint.

Clare pulled on her jeans again without getting out from beneath the duvet and it was as she was doing this that she noticed that the room didn't look quite the same as usual. For a start, it was tidy. There was not a solitary sock to be seen on Daniel's side of the room, which usually looked like an explosion in a Chinese laundry. Something else was odd too ... The walls, usually graced with three paintings Daniel had done when they first arrived in Cornwall, were bare.

'My God, we've been burgled,' was Clare's first thought as she leapt out of bed and ran through into the lounge. But nothing had changed there. And Daniel's painting rucksack was still lying on the kitchen table, so he hadn't left her. Slowly, Clare pushed open the door to the studio and the mystery was solved. A mattress lay in the middle of the floor, and in the middle of the mattress lay Daniel.

The light which streamed in through the open door awoke him and he looked up to see who was intruding on his sleep, his arm shading his eyes.

'What are you doing in here?' Clare asked.

Daniel didn't answer. He just pulled his sleeping bag tightly up to his chin and rolled over so that he had his back to her.

'Why have you moved all your stuff out of the bedroom?'

'Guess,' he muttered.

'Oh, come on,' Clare groaned. 'You can't be mad at me. I was away for four days, Daniel.'

'Five,' he corrected.

'You've been away for longer than that before . . .'

'Yeah. But with my mates, Clare, and not to Paris. Who did you go with?'

Clare sensed an impending crisis. 'Fran, from school. I told you. You spoke to her on the phone.' A voice inside Clare's head asked her why she was trying to justify the weekend to him. It would be far, far better to try and laugh it off than to get into some deep debate about it that might reveal more than she wanted to.

'And who else?'

'No one else. It was a weekend for two . . . We even had separate beds,' she added with a nervous laugh.

'Yeah.'

'Daniel,' Clare pleaded. She dropped down on to the mattress beside him. His body seemed to mould into hers momentarily before he remembered the new status quo and moved further towards the other side. She laid a hand on his shoulder which he quickly pushed away. Clare struggled to contain her frustration. She had thought everything over while she was away and had arrived back in Cornwall longing to see Daniel, to hold him and get things back to how they once were. Now he seemed determined to make things worse.

'Oh, for God's sake, Daniel,' she snapped suddenly, 'stop acting like a spoilt child over this. I needed the break. I deserved the break.'

'And I didn't.' Daniel rolled over so that his steely eyes locked hers. His brows were knitted together in a frown that she had never seen before. 'I thought we were meant to be together forever, Clare. In Lurve,' he mocked the word. 'And then you go off to Paris with some girl that you haven't bothered to keep in touch with for five or so years, to spend a weekend shagging frogs.'

'Daniel, that's not fair!'

'Isn't it? Go and listen to the message you left.'

Clare jumped to her feet and then hesitated. If she was innocent, as she claimed to be, she wouldn't be bothered about what the message said. What had she said? She tried to remember. Daniel had saved the messages. Clare pressed 'play'. Her mother, ringing to ask how she was getting on. Daniel's friend Gary. Then her voice. Clare calling to say that she wouldn't be home.

In the background, Francesca's tinkling laugh. A phrase in French. Incomprehensible, but definitely male. It wasn't even Jean.

Daniel had dragged himself out of bed and now stood at the door to the studio, the sleeping bag draped around his shoulders like a child's attempt to simulate a batman cape. 'Well,' he said, his eyes narrowing accusingly.

Clare's shoulders, which had been tensing up as they rowed so that it hurt to move, now suddenly began to release again.

'It was nothing,' she said, thinking quickly. 'Fran had a friend in Paris, called Bertrand. Her brother's pen-pal I think. He just came up to our room for a coffee. Just to be friendly. He wasn't even as handsome as Fran remembered him to be ...' Clare hoped that detail had sounded light. 'And he definitely wasn't anywhere near as handsome and gorgeous as you.' She took a risk and fluttered her eyelashes at him.

Daniel's face was softening.

'Really?' he asked.

'Yes, really.' Clare felt her voice wobble. 'He was the only man I spoke to all weekend.'

'God. I don't know what's wrong with me,' Daniel said. 'I feel like a fool accusing you like that but you know how much I brood about these things when I'm on my own. And then when I heard his voice ... It's just that I had such a crap weekend without you here.'

The breath escaped Clare's body like steam from a kettle. He was right next to her now. Dropping the sleeping bag to the floor. His arms wrapping around Clare's shoulders as he whispered an apology into her ear. An apology which turned into the lightest of kisses.

'I love you, Clare, that's all. I can't stand the thought of anyone else being near you. Anyone. Anyone at all. I was even jealous of Fran in case she turned out to be a rabid lesbian . . .'

Clare laughed ironically to herself and kissed Daniel softly on the cheek.

'I love you too,' she told him.

Daniel's hand moved up the back of her neck. He dipped his head to place a kiss on her collarbone.

'I've missed you, Clare, really missed you,' he murmured. 'Don't ever go away without me again.'

Clare felt a stinging at the back of her eyes. Love, guilt, worry. She gulped down a sob as Daniel continued to kiss his way down her body, carefully unbuttoning her thick cotton pyjama shirt. She shut her eyes tightly to stop the tears from escaping as his hands slid smoothly across her bare skin to rest on either side of her waist.

But Daniel saw that her eyelashes had become wet and transferred his attention to her unhappy eyes. He let his lips rest first on one closed lid and then on the other, sipping away her tears. Clare's arms, which had been hanging loosely at her sides, now came up to rest around his neck and her lips finally sought his.

The way he held her intensified the thoughts that were racing through her mind. How could she have done it? How could she have been unfaithful to this dear man? This man whose touch could still excite her and was even now beginning to make her feel the urge to grind her hips against his, and pull his body right into her heart.

Playfully, Daniel took Clare in a dancing hold, one arm around her back, the other holding her right hand high. 'One, two, three, one, two, three.' They waltzed into the bedroom. His playfulness brought a smile to her now hopelessly tearful face as he waltzed her right up to the edge of the bed and tipped her backwards on to it.

'Are you OK?' he asked, licking a tear away. 'I've had my tantrum. Everything's fine now.'

Clare nodded. 'Yes. Come here.' She pulled his head down so that his lips met hers. Her tongue teased his teeth apart and she explored the inside of his mouth, tickling and tantalising him.

'I love the way you kiss,' he murmured. He undid the only button which was still fastened and slipped her shirt off her shoulders. Clare wriggled her arms until she was totally free of its restraint, then she reached up and helped to ease Daniel out of his tight white T-shirt. Naked from the waist up, they lay together and continued to kiss for a while. Clare's hands thrilled to the touch of the skin on his back. Smooth and dry. Better than silk.

'I want to make love to you,' he told her. She answered him with the lightest of pinches on his left buttock. Her fingers slipped beneath the edges of the legs of his tight-fitting shorts. She knew he liked that. The feeling of her hands breaching his underwear. His skin was somehow more sensitive at the boundary of being clothed and being naked.

He writhed appreciatively.

He pulled himself up and knelt between her

thighs. He studied her half naked body, prone on the bed, then took a breast in each hand and massaged them slowly, gently. Her nipples hardened as if to command. She trailed her own hands down his chest, her long fingers catching in the light layer of dark hair. She reached his well-muscled abdomen. Played like a xylophone the six muscles that he had worked so hard on and that she was always pleased to see. Her finger circled his deep belly button.

Daniel was echoing her movements. Sweeping his fingers down over her slender torso. Then he stopped and just gazed silently at the body before him. The pale white skin that he loved so much, though he always teased her about her inability to go brown in the sun. Her breasts, just the right size, though he always teased her about them being a little small. Her delicate collar-bone. Her perfect waist. How was she to know that he loved her? He had never really told her often enough.

'I love you,' he murmured now. 'I love you, I love you.' He had said it more times that day than in the whole time they had been together.

The back of Clare's throat prickled to hear it, prickled with the gathering of yet more tears.

'Don't be sad,' he told her, seeing the clouds gathering in her eyes. Secretly he felt glad that he seemed to be having such a strong effect on her emotions. He leaned over her and found her mouth again. Clare kissed him gratefully, grateful to be able to divert his attention from her eyes.

Her fingers found the elastic of his shorts again and this time she tugged them down. His penis, already hard, escaped its cotton confines and now hovered between them. Still echoing her movements, his fingers made short work of the silver buttons on her jeans and they joined his shorts on the floor.

Clare wrapped her fingers around his shaft and coaxed it into maximum stiffness. He fumbled through her pubic hair to find her waiting lips. She was wet; he always made her wet, even when she thought she didn't want to. An involuntary giggle of pleasure escaped her.

Daniel slowly slid his fingers up and down the delicate contours of her labia. He could feel them slowly swelling, parting, inviting him in. He moved his hand so that the heel of his palm was hard against her clitoris, and increased the pressure there while the fingers lay still in her shiny vulva. Clare moved her body upwards, trying to drive him inside. His other hand slipped beneath her and wandered lazily over the firm curve of her buttocks.

Clare sought his lips to kiss him but he moved his head away, kissing instead down the side of her neck. A gentle nip from his teeth made her tense with anticipation. With his hand at her sex and his lips at her neck, she felt as though her body was an elastic band, stretched out to its fullest length, waiting hopefully to be allowed to spring free. Her breath vibrated through her aching body. She was so incredibly aware of everything at that moment, of the hairs raised by goosebumps along the length of her trembling thighs, of the swelling of her crimson lips, the dilation of her pupils, the hardening of her nipples. Her body was literally growing towards him.

Daniel pushed a single finger into her. Clare's back arched, captured by this small invasion. She moaned his name and it came out like a sigh

'Daniel.'

He was sitting astride her legs now. Through narrowed eyes she saw his penis bob with excitement as her body bucked toward him again.

'I love you,' he told her once more. He had withdrawn his hand, his fingers shiny with her wetness. He licked them clean, enjoying the way she still blushed slightly at the sight of his petty debauchery.

'Move up the bed,' he whispered.

Clare shuffled herself backwards with her hips until her head almost touched the headboard. She reached her hands behind her and took hold of the twisted metal arc. The sunray of black tubing was awful, but it served its purpose. Clare knew that she was striking Daniel's favourite pose. She drew her legs up automatically. One on either side of his body. He ran his hands up her calves and lowered himself into position.

Clare released one hand from the headboard and stroked the approaching penis lovingly. Enticingly. Daniel focused on the silky triangle of dark hair at the top of her thighs. He curved his hips. Clare lifted her head so that one of his arms could curl around her neck. He still needed the other hand to guide himself inside.

They groaned simultaneously. Daniel waited patiently while Clare adjusted her position minutely so that any pain was instantly pleasure.

His lips fell on her forehead and tasted the salt of her sweat. Her hot hands closed on his buttocks.

Daniel began to glide in and out of her. Like a well-oiled machine. Noiselessly at first, except for the tiny sounds of sweat on sweat. Then breathing more audibly as he increased his pace. Clare's mouth had opened. Her lips curved into a helpless smile.

'Faster, faster,' she murmured like a mantra.

He did as he was told.

Daniel raised himself up on his arms. Straightening them until the joints locked and he could hold himself there without effort. He looked down at the junction between their bodies. They were polished with sweat. Her breasts perfectly rounded. His muscles defined by the exertion as though they were cut from stone.

Clare gazed at the point where he went into her. On the upstroke, his penis appeared miraculously from the centre of her pubic hair, oiled with her pleasure. The veins stood up all along it. It was so hard. Impossible to imagine that it wasn't always like that.

In, in, in. The sight of his penetration heightened the sensation. Her vagina sang with the friction. She heard the quickening of his breath that meant he was just about to come but instead he slowed right down. Counting to himself. Thinking about the sea. He withdrew almost the entire length. The head of his penis hovered between her labia.

She hated it when he did that, hated it and loved it all at the same time. That upstroke seemed to take forever. An agony like the slow separation of a sticking plaster from your skin.

'Daniel!' she squealed. She grasped his buttocks and forced him back inside. His arms buckled beneath him and he collapsed down on to her chest. His pelvis had already taken over. Thrusting, thrusting, thrusting. Clare's rhythmic moan began to rise and rise in pitch.

'Oh, now,' she mumbled. 'Now, Daniel, come now.'

His eyes were screwed tightly shut.

She used his buttocks to help pump his pelvis against her pubic bone. To speed him up to the optimum. To bring his orgasm crashing into her. She tensed her legs against the bed. Raised her pelvis to his again and again.

'Oh, God. No, no,' she cried.

Daniel buried his face in the pillow beside her head while his loins jerked against her. His muffled moans spurred her own end on. She wrapped her legs around his back and held him captive until the sperm began to dribble out down her thighs.

The sheet beneath them was sodden with sperm, sweat and now, as they lay quietly side by side, Daniel's tears.

'Daniel,' Clare said later, as they were sitting in front of the television, picking at a late breakfast of two slices of toast made from the only remaining bread in the house, 'we really do have to sort a few things out.'

The exhilaration, the tenderness of their lovemaking was slowly fading again. An advert for EuroDisney came on screen and Clare could see Daniel's expression blacken at this reminder of her weekend in France. Had he really believed her, or was he, like her, pretending that nothing had happened, because it was easier tht way?

'Yeah,' he said flatly.

Daniel moved his things back into the bedroom. Clare was relieved to see the red and yellow paintings back on the wall, though in the past they had occasionally been too much for her when she awoke hungover. She straightened the middle one as she passed it.

For the first time since returning from France, Clare wandered into the studio with the intention of picking up her brushes and adding something to the portrait of Steve. She pulled away the sheet that covered it and looked at the painting with a critical eye. The form was there. The composition was good, but still it wasn't quite right. She tapped the end of a brush against her teeth. There was no life in it.

As she pondered her next move, she was aware of someone behind her. Daniel placed his hands on her shoulders and took his own look at the painting. 'Needs more pink,' he said sarcastically. 'And talking of pink, I saw Francesca when I popped out to get the milk. She's got some things to do in town but then, she says, she's coming round. She can't wait to see you.' He parodied her voice. 'So you better make yourself look pretty.'

Daniel left her alone again. He hadn't sounded too impressed. Why had he said she should make herself look pretty for the visit? Clare remembered the tinkling laugh in the background of her answermachine message. But surely that recorded giggle hadn't been recognisable?

'You left these,' Francesca tipped a pair of earrings into Clare's hand. Clare shoved them into her pocket with a warning look in her eyes, but it was too late, Daniel's eye had been caught by the gesture and he was now fully tuned in to their conversation.

'Daniel tells me you've been away,' Francesca said theatrically.

'Yes,' replied Clare, 'To Paris. With a friend from school – she won some tickets in a competition.'

'Oh, how lucky. It's lovely at this time of year,' said Francesca. 'But I do hope that doesn't mean that you've been getting behind with the painting. I need it finished by the fifteenth, remember.'

'Easily.'

'Can I see it?' Francesca coyly twirled a strand of hair that had escaped from her neat chignon.

'Of course.'

Clare led Francesca into the studio. Daniel watched approvingly as the blonde girl's slim legs passed by on their high heels. Once safely inside, Clare pushed the door to. Francesca immediately took her lover's face in her hands and planted a kiss on her lips.

'Don't,' said Clare, weakly pushing her away. 'Not now.'

'When? When?'

They heard the scraping of a chair as Daniel got up in the other room.

'I'm going to get some bread,' he called.

'Now?' came the answer to Francesca's question.

Francesca brought Clare's lips smacking back down on to her own. Clare struggled vainly to resist the embrace, fight the tongue which, as usual, wanted to gain entry beyond her tightly shut lips.

'Kiss me, idiot,' Francesca demanded.

Their tongues wrestled. Francesca's hands covered her lover's body. Taking in the shape of her through her thin cotton shirt and figure-hugging jeans.

'I like you in this colour,' Francesca murmured as she began to lift the shirt out of the way. Clare tried to suppress a laugh.

'Have you missed me?'

'Of course.'

A cold hand slipped between Clare's shirt and her skin. She shivered pleasurably and responded by hugging Francesca tighter. The fingers spread out across her back, then moved around to the front. They found a delicate nipple, and brought it to stiffness with a combination of icy flesh and warm feelings.

Francesca slipped her head beneath the covering fabric and kissed the hardened bud. Clare moaned softly and clasped Francesca's head appreciatively in her hand. When Francesca emerged her hair was dishevelled, single strands standing on end as a result of the static electricity she was creating.

All too quickly they heard the rattle of the lock and the door creak open again. Daniel whistled his way into the house, as if he knew he was interrupting something and wanted to make sure that he didn't actually walk in on it. Francesca began to talk animatedly about paint textures and canvas weights as if she knew what she was talking about. All the time she stood behind Clare, her head on Clare's shoulder, holding a milky white breast in each of her hands. Clare pushed her bottom backwards so that it rested against Francesca's pelvis, and rotated her buttocks gently. Her hands slid down the tailored skirt that covered Francesca's carefully maintained thighs.

'Coffee? Tea? Me?' Daniel was right outside the door. The girls sprang apart as he slowly pushed his way backwards into the room with a tray in his hands. He handed them their drinks and stood with them, discussing the merits of some artist's use of light and shade. He showed no sign of leaving them again. Indeed, Clare thought that she saw a peculiar look of pleasure gather in his eyes as the conversation began to falter.

After a while, Francesca simply had to go. She gave Clare a cursory, polite society kiss at the door and promised to phone. By the time Clare returned to the sitting-room, Daniel had reinstalled himself on the sofa. Clare looked at him askance as she crossed the room to the studio. Her skin was still warm from Francesca's touch.

Chapter Fourteen

CLARE SPENT THE next short day down by the harbour again, absently running off three more paintings for Graham. These watercolours were coming more and more easily to her and she finished them in less than two hours. On her way back to the flat she stopped at a bakery and bought two éclairs.

It was almost dark as she opened the rusty gate. No lights were on in their flat. Clare thought nothing of it, but was a little disappointed that she would have to wait to eat her éclair. Perhaps she would eat hers straight away anyway. Whistling, she pushed open the door, turned on the light, tossed the pastries on to the table and made straight for the studio to put her painting gear away.

There was an ominous crunching sound as she opened this door with her hip. Something must have fallen against the other side. She flicked the light switch with her elbow, and the sight which greeted her this time rooted her to the spot.

A torn canvas was scattered around the floor of the studio. Which one was it? Clare dropped her bag and picked up a couple of the pieces. Immediately she recognised the portrait of Steve. Cut to shreds. And it looked as if it had been treated to the addition of a few big splodges of black paint first.

'Daniel!' Clare cried angrily. What had he done that for?

Fuming, she stormed back into the kitchen to pick up one of the kitchen knives to treat him to a taste of his own medicine by slashing one of his own precious works. The cutlery drawer opened without its usual rattle. There was nothing in it. She opened the crockery cupboard. That too was empty. Had they been burgled?

Confused, Clare raced to the bedroom. His paintings were gone again. And the lava lamp that stood by their bed. She flung open the wardrobe. His side was empty.

'Daniel!' she screamed. This time she didn't expect an answer. They hadn't been burgled. Daniel had gone. He had taken his things and left.

Clare dropped the fragment of Steve's portrait which she still clutched in her sweating hand back on to the floor.

She searched the flat from top to bottom for some kind of explanation, a letter or a note, but there was none. He hadn't left any forwarding address either, or a number to contact him on. He'd left nothing, nothing at all. Taken everything he owned so that he had no reason to come to the flat again.

'I can't believe it,' Clare said to the bare walls. And all this after she had decided that the game was through and that she loved Daniel as she had always done after all. Why had he left so suddenly? She just couldn't understand it. When she had walked out of the flat that morning he had kissed her goodbye, the same as always. They hadn't even rowed the night before. He must have found out about her affair. Why else would he have ruined the picture of Steve when there were other paintings of which she was infinitely fonder?

She spent that day, and the cold night that followed it, sitting on the sofa – one of the few things Daniel had left behind in the flat – waiting for the phone to ring. She longed to hear her lover's voice – not Daniel's but Francesca's. She had tried dialling her number several times that day only to be confronted by an answermachine. Finally her dialling was met with a human response.

'Hello.' The woman who answered the phone sounded older.

'Hi,' Clare replied. Holding the phone with tight fingers. Waiting for the bomb to drop. 'Is Francesca there?'

'She is, yes. But she doesn't want to speak to anyone at the moment.'

Clare's heart pounded within her rib-cage. Why didn't she want to speak to anyone? Clare forced herself to ask, 'She isn't ill, is she?'

'No,' said the older woman flatly, 'but she has had a bit of a shock.'

'A shock.'

'Yes.' The woman wasn't about to elaborate.

A shock could be one of two things, Clare guessed. Either someone in Francesca's family had died, or she had found out that her husband had been having an affair. The woman on the phone sounded tight-lipped as opposed to distraught.

Francesca had definitely found out about Steve.

'Who's calling please? I'll ask her to call you back when she's feeling a little better . . .'

'It's just a friend. I'll call her back. Goodbye.' Clare cut off the woman by pressing the button on the phone as if putting the receiver down wouldn't have been quick enough. She slumped into the sofa and stared at a fragment of the portrait of Steve she had salvaged from the studio floor.

How had they found out? How had Daniel and Francesca found out about her affair with Steve? She hadn't been to bed with him since returning from Paris and before then she had been discreet, hadn't she? Of course she had. They had only been to bed together three times in all. He had never been to the flat, or phoned her there. They had never been seen in public together . . .

Clare threw the fragment of canvas to the floor.

Except for once.

At Graham's party.

Graham had seen them laughing together and he had seen them leave together. He had quizzed her about it when she took the nude into the gallery two days later. Clare remembered the conversation she and Graham had had about

Steve and Francesca. The distant look in his eyes every time he mentioned Francesca's name. The very fact that Graham had sent Francesca to Clare to have the portrait painting was just a way for him to warn Clare off. Graham was in love with Francesca. He had every reason to tell her that her husband was being unfaithful if he thought that it might drive Francesca into his arms.

Clare snatched up her coat and headed for the door. But what reason did he have to involve her in his revenge plot as well? He must have told Daniel. Clare whirled through the streets of the little fishing town like a hurricane bent on pulling up every tree and house in its path until she reached the door of the Dragon Gallery and pushed it open so hard that it bounced back off the wall.

'Hey, careful!' Graham was sitting at the front desk as usual. His eyes widened in horror at the spectacle of the expensive frosted-glass door ricocheting off the stoppers designed to stop it from smashing. Clare stood in the doorway, her beautiful face screwed up in anger.

'Who nicked your rattle?' he asked her sarcastically. She didn't break into her usual smile.

'Can you shut the shop and come into the back room with me, please?' Clare was so worked up that she could hardly speak her request.

'Oo-er,' Graham gave his standard response, eliciting this time not a standard grimace from Clare but a standard, stinging slap across his stubbly cheek. Graham stumbled backwards in shock. 'What have I done?'

'That's exactly what I want to ask you myself.' Clare flipped the sign on the shop door to 'closed' and ushered Graham through to the back. A customer, alerted to the excitement by the sound of Clare's hand making contact with Graham's floppy jowl, took a break from studying the paintings to see the performance art instead. But Clare gave the customer a nasty, narrow-eyed smile which sent him scuttling straight out of the gallery at top speed.

Graham put on the brakes and grabbed Clare by the top of her arms.

'What on earth do you think you are doing?' he shouted at her. If Graham had been surprised by Clare's sudden show of aggression, she was certainly surprised by the way he had suddenly decided to take matters in hand. 'What is the matter with you?' This question was softer. 'Clare, what on earth can have happened?'

'Oh, for God's sake, Graham. Don't pretend that you don't know. I get home to find that my boyfriend has left me and then when I phone Francesca, she refuses to talk to me—' Francesca's name sent him into defence.

'Francesca?'

'Yes, Francesca. You know her. Steve's wife. Why did you have to tell her, Graham?'

'Tell her what?'

'Tell her what?!' Clare mimicked. 'About the affair, for God's sake!' She was no longer aggressive, but desperate, her shoulders shaking as she sobbed. Graham still held the tops of her arms. Clare tried listlessly to push his hands away.

'The affair?' Graham looked at her curiously. 'Explain.'

'Steve's affair,' Clare spat.

Graham's face retained an air of puzzlement. 'I had to, Clare. I love Francesca, I didn't want her to get hurt by that bastard husband of hers ... But, but I don't see why it should have anything to do with you?'

'What do you mean "you don't see why it should have anything to do with me"?' Her eyes flashed with anger again. 'You told Daniel as well that I was having an affair with Steve, didn't you?'

'I ...' Graham released Clare's shoulders and sat down on the edge of his desk. His eyes bored into her face, demanding an explanation from her. 'You?' he said incredulously. 'You were having an affair with Steve?'

The look which now passed across Graham's face threw Clare into confusion. He was acting like he didn't know. No, he wasn't acting. He genuinely didn't know.

'Yes. Well, no. Not really an affair. I just saw him a few times after your party.'

'Oh, God.' Graham scrunched up as much hair as he could find on his head in his hands. 'Oh God, Clare. What a mess this is. What a mess!' The tears were streaming down her face as she tried to comprehend what Graham was trying to let her know.

'I didn't know, Clare. I didn't say anything to Daniel about you and Steve. I didn't think you would get mixed up with someone like him. What did Daniel say?'

'Nothing.' Clare spluttered. 'He didn't leave a note or anything. It's just . . .' She sniffed loudly. 'All his things have gone from the flat and he ripped the painting I was doing of Steve to pieces . . .'

'I didn't tell him, I promise.'

'But why did he ruin the painting of Steve? He must have known. What did you tell Francesca? Why won't she come to the phone?'

'I told Francesca everything that I knew,' Graham continued. 'That Steve has been having an affair with my wife.'

'Your wife?'

'Yes. Apparently so.'

'Oh, God,' Clare threw her arms around the narrow shoulders of the man she had despised seconds before and they clung to each other for support. When they had calmed down a little, Graham dashed out into the front of the shop and locked the front door. He made tea, still sniffing. He had never cried before. Let alone in front of a girl.

'I wrote her a letter,' Graham explained. 'But I didn't sign it, or say who was involved, of course, because my wife and Francesca were supposed to be friends.'

'Graham,' Clare looked at him with sad eyes. 'I don't know what to say. You must feel so hurt. Your wife . . .'

'Oh, it was all over between us years ago. In fact, it was probably even over before it began. I was always in love with Francesca, who never even noticed me, and Jackie was just in love with my money. Or the money she thought I had. She

399

was completely furious when I bought this gallery. Said we would lose all our money and that's when I realised that she didn't love me. She wasn't happy with the idea that having a gallery would make *me* happy . . . She's had affairs before but I was surprised to walk in on her and Steve . . . To be perfectly honest I thought she was a bit too old for his current tastes. But I guess he had you to satisfy those.'

Clare snorted indignantly. 'I can't believe I was taken in.'

'He takes everyone in, Clare.'

'But I don't understand why Daniel would have gone and why he would have ripped up that painting first . . .'

'Perhaps, perhaps he just sensed that it was something you were proud of. Perhaps he was going to go away anyway. He never seemed to be totally at home here . . .' Clare nodded gravely. She knew that Graham was right. 'And his pictures of boats were simply terrible.'

At that Clare couldn't help laughing out loud.

As Clare left the gallery and began the walk back to her flat, she wouldn't have said that she felt happy exactly but she certainly felt different. The gulls screeching overhead drew her eyes upwards. She smiled faintly at the winter blue sky, and breathed in the salt-scented air. St Ives hadn't been their dream, it had been her dream. A romantic idyll which suffocated Daniel and perhaps had begun to suffocate her.

Walking down the narrow cobbled street she began to notice for the first time the cracks in her vision. The plastic flowers in the hanging baskets, the net curtains, the Cornish piskies straight from Taiwan. Perhaps she needed to move on as well. She looked out across the sea. She'd used this place up. She remembered a different view. From Jean's room.

Since Daniel's sudden disappearance, Clare had set the answermachine to audible alert so that she wouldn't miss a message if he ever tried to call. When she opened the door to the flat, her ears were assailed for the first time by the high-pitched beep. She rushed to the machine and pressed play, without taking off her coat, without shutting the door.

'Hi, Clare,' came a familiar voice, 'this is Francesca. Mum said someone called – was it you? I need to chat. Don't really want to speak over the phone. I'll be down later today. Be in . . .'

Clare played the message again. When had she left it? How long did Clare have before she arrived on the doorstep? The ringing of the door-bell answered her question.

'Clare!' Francesca fell into her arms. Clare held her tightly and brought her inside. 'Clare. Everything's been so terrible this last week.'

The story tumbled out and Clare couldn't help remembering the first time Francesca had cried in her arms. The letter had arrived the day after they had last been together, Francesca gabbled between sniffs. It wasn't signed, but the postmark was Cornwall and it said that Steven had been having an affair there while working on the new flats.

'It didn't even say who he'd been having an affair with,' Francesca continued, wide-eyed and vulnerable. 'So for all I know I could have passed her in the street on my way here . . .'

Clare shivered at the venom in her voice. 'But I thought you always suspected him of it. I don't see why you're so upset.'

'I didn't really ever think he would,' Francesca sniffed. 'I always said it, but I was only joking. He always said he was too tired to sleep with me after working such long hours down here. I didn't think he'd have the energy to find someone else. Oh, God. I was just stupid. He had all the opportunity he wanted to play around.'

Clare searched the tear-stained face for a trace of the strong, outrageous Francesca who had taken her to Paris. She wasn't there. Instead, sitting on the sofa was the girl Clare had first taken Francesca for, defining herself by her husband.

'It's changed in here,' Francesca said suddenly, blinking her big wet eyes.

'Yes,' Clare replied softly, 'Daniel's gone.'

'Gone?'

'Things weren't working out,' she said cryptically, trying not to let any pain cross her eyes. 'But look, who cares? In fact I'm glad he's gone, because now you're here and you can leave your ratbag husband and come and live with me.'

'No,' Francesca shook her head, her eye brimming again. 'That's why I had to see you. I've talked to Steven about the whole affair. He says it was just something he did while I was in Paris. He was drunk. She was drunk – and it will never happen again. We're going to try again with our marriage. Really try. Spend more time together. Make it work.'

'Make it work?' Clare was incredulous. 'He's a worthless—'

'Sssh,' Francesca put her finger to Clare!s lips. 'He's my husband, Clare. I can't just give up. After all, it's not as if I've been exactly faithful, is it?' She laughed – a little nervously, Clare thought. 'But I'm going to be now. That's why I'm here, to tell you that we can't carry on like before. We've got to just be friends now.'

'Friends?'

'Yes. Oh, come on, Clare,' Francesca took Clare's sad face in her hands. 'It couldn't have worked out anyway. I mean, look at us! For a start, we're both girls!'

'Ha ha.'

'Things won't really change that much. We'll still see each other . . . through perhaps not quite so much. We shouldn't have done anything in the first place.'

'Francesca, it's not that. It's not physical, not sex. I just can't believe that you're being taken in by him. He doesn't make you happy. He's not going to stop having affairs.'

'He says that this is the first time he has ever been unfaith—'

'The first time? Who is he kidding?' Clare almost screamed. It was becoming harder and harder to wrestle with the temptation to let her have the truth.

'I want to believe him, Clare.' Francesca was suddenly firm again. 'I'll call you.' She rose from the sofa without any of the usual lingering caresses that preceded her goodbyes and walked purposefully to the door. She stood silently as she waited for Clare to let her out. 'I will phone,' she promised.

Clare closed the door behind her.

Two days later, Francesca did call. She sounded happy, too happy, and babbled on about the preparations for Steven's birthday party as if the girl on the other end of the phone was her grandmother and not her ex-lover. Suddenly she asked, 'You will finish the painting won't you?' Clare hadn't told her that Daniel had already finished it off in his special way. 'I want you to finish it,' Francesca added, after a disconcerting moment of silence.

'Yes,' said Clare, 'I will.'

'And,' Francesca took a deep breath, 'I'd like you to come to the party yourself. To deliver the painting in person.'

'I don't think I . . .'

'It's important to me. I want you to meet Steven. You'll be charmed, I promise . . . Oh, Clare, yesterday, when I got home from the gym there were two hundred roses in the hallway! Well, I nearly sneezed myself to death, but the thought! And then . . .'

Clare listened to Francesca's excited babbling without hearing. This wasn't the girl she knew at all. Perhaps she should just let her go. Let her find out in a year or two years that while a snake can shed its skin, it can never alter its fundamental nature.

'So you'll come to the party?'

Clare's attention had drifted to the pile of dirty crockery that stood by the sink.

'Clare, you'll come to the party, won't you?'

'It's such a long way to come. And I won't know anyone.'

'You know me . . . I'll introduce you to some nice bloke.'

'You've swung it.' Clare forced a laugh.

She decided to go for a walk by the sea to clear her head and make some decisions. The beauty of the moon reflected in the sea didn't thrill her that night. She just felt loss. Only a week earlier she had been panicking in the face of too much love. How different things were now.

Francesca was going to give her marriage another chance. Perhaps she wasn't wrong to do that. As she herself had said, the infidelity hadn't exactly been one-sided. She obviously loved Steve. Another part of Clare's mind protested that Francesca was just scared of being alone, scared of losing her stability and respectability. She could only swing with no knickers on the flying trapeze if she had a safety net to fall into.

'Hmm.' Clare let the wind play over her hair. She didn't care. She didn't care about any of them. She could live without them all. After all, a month ago she hadn't even met them. Well, she hadn't met Francesca and Steve. Daniel was another matter entirely. The hole left by four years with him was probably only just beginning to open. She let her knees fold beneath her and sat down. Her skirt spread out around her, like a beached jellyfish floating down on to the sand. Clare was so absorbed by the question of what she should do next that she didn't notice the figure of a man walking in her direction along the black water's edge until he was almost level with her. The figure gave a casual wave.

Clare looked up when the movement caught her attention.

It was Steve.

Strolling towards her in his designer jacket and jeans like the proverbial bad penny.

'Well met by moonlight,' he called as he neared her. 'Fancy meeting you here.'

'You said that last time,' Clare replied wearily.

'Mind if I join you?'

'I'd rather you didn't.'

'How was Paris?'

'Different.'

He had ignored her request to be alone and sat down beside her, picking up handfuls of sand and letting the grains run out through his open fingers. Clare watched his beautiful hands, remembered involuntarily what he could do with them, and then tried not to think about it.

'I was having a drink in the bar up there,' he motioned to the hotel which overlooked the bay. 'I saw your silhouette in the moonlight, recognised you by the way you walk. Couldn't believe my luck. I didn't think I'd ever see you again.'

'Likewise,' Clare huffed in reply.

'I love it down here,' he continued regardless. 'Can't imagine walking by the Thames like this, can you?'

Clare didn't answer.

'I wish I could stay here forever, but the project will be finished next week and then I suppose I will have to go back to London and frighten my tenants there . . . This place is like paradise.'

Clare would have agreed. She gazed stonily at the sand in front of her feet.

'What's the matter with you?' he asked. 'Aren't we friends anymore?'

Friends? Had they ever been friends?

'I just want to be on my own, Steve, that's all.'

It wasn't the answer he wanted. He gave up dribbling the grains of sand back on to the beach and instead dropped a few of them on to her shoe. Clare flicked them off in irritation. Steve replaced them with another handful.

'Will you stop that?' she hissed. She rose to her feet and started to walk back up the beach, the sand keeping her from going quite as quickly as she wanted to.

Steve followed close behind.

'I love it when you're angry,' he told her.

'Oh, you really haven't seen me angry,' Clare warned him.

'What's wrong, Clare? When you left for Paris I thought we were getting on really well. I've been praying that we'd bump into each other again . . .'

Clare tried not to listen. She focused on the reflection of the moon in the waves. This was the man that Francesca was trying to rescue her marriage with. Suddenly his hand grasped her arm.

'Let go.' She tried to shake him free.

He whirled her around to face him, forced her close to him and kissed her protesting lips. He didn't loosen his grip on her until he felt her soften beneath his kiss, felt her lips give way and part. He held her tightly until her angry eyes started to close.

'Don't tell me you haven't thought about me at all . . .' he murmured into her reddening cheek.

Not in the way you think, Clare wanted to say, but she held back. Deep inside, part of her still wanted to see just how far the reformed Steve would go.

His hand moved languorously in the long hair which tumbled down her back. It was knotted by the wind. Occasionally his fingers found the knots and it hurt.

'I've dreamed about your body in the moonlight.' His voice caressed her far more subtly than his hands. 'Your porcelain skin and that beautiful mahogany hair.'

'You make me sound like a piece of furniture,' Clare snorted, fighting his determination to break her resolve.

'All the time I find myself thinking about the way you looked when you were standing at the window on that first evening we spent together. Wearing that red dress. The white curtains billowing around you. The smile in your eyes.'

He kissed her closed eyelids and Clare remembered the first time as well. She remembered his smile.

'Your nipples, showing pink through your white camisole . . .'

He pulled her body closer still to his own. Her arms had nowhere to go but around his back. She breathed him in, the smell of him clouding the anger she had been carrying in her mind, breaking her down like a slow poison. His hand rested on her buttocks, pulled her pelvis towards his. She felt his stiffening dick.

He began to kiss her again. This time her tongue tangled with his. He moaned his pleasure at her silent acquiescence before leaving her mouth to move his lips along the length of her neck. He held her hair up and out of the way. It was like a tent, concealing his furtive worship from the empty beach.

'I can't,' she said suddenly, pushing him away ineffectually with her chilly hands.

'Ssssh.' He kissed her as though his lips were a pacifier. He was using the gentle weight of his body against hers to move her backwards up the sand. Soon they were in the shade of the sea wall. The golden sand on to which they sank was night black.

'Stop,' she said – pleaded.

His hand moved to the front of her body, sliding up and down her breasts, computing the easiest way inside her blouse. The buttons were at the back so the hand untucked her shirt from the waistband and slid beneath it.

The coolness of his fingers against her uncovered belly made her draw in her breath. Their chill was quickly abated as he flattened the hand out, stealing the warmth from her blood. His lips still pressed hers urgently, preventing any more protestations. Her returning kisses defied her brain.

The hand beneath her shirt found a breast and then a nipple. He rolled the nipple between his fingers, beginning to make the soft animal noises of pleasure that he had made when first discovering her body. He writhed impatiently, grinding his pelvis against nowhere in particular, then pushing her over on to her back and lying full length on top of her. She could feel his penis hard against her thigh. He shifted so that it lay between her legs. They parted a little wider to let him comfortably inside.

Her eyes started to sting with tears that he wouldn't be able to see. Her body was responding like a traitor to his overtures, swelling, hardening and moistening to complement his. As he ground his denim-clad pelvis ever harder against hers, which was covered only by thin layers of pretty ethnic print, she could not cut out the fantastic sensation of the friction in her clitoris. Her nipples burned beneath his tongue as he pushed her top out of the way. The breeze coming in from the sea couldn't keep her skin cool now.

As he sucked her nipple up between his teeth, her fingers began to stroke the tense arc of his neck. Without breaking contact between his tongue and her body for a minute, he shrugged off his jacket. Suddenly, he was more visible. The feeble light of the moon captured and intensified by his billowing white shirt.

Clare arched her back in reply to a line of nipping kisses from her breasts, down her side, to the waistband of her skirt. He gently bit the skin again in the place that had always made her groan loudest.

'No, no.' Her protests were lost in the sound of the water dragging pebbles back into the sea, and her hips raised themselves voluntarily to help him shed her skirt. Her tights were dragged down with it, to her calves, exposing her soft, white thighs. One hand on each, Steve used his grip on her to pull her half on to his knees. Her tights were still in the way. He pulled them fully off and repositioned her. One leg to each side of him. Her bottom on his kneeling thighs. Her pelvis pointing towards heaven and her long hair dragging behind in the cold, dry sand. She let her arms fall backwards above her head. Her body was now in a position of total surrender.

His hands slid up the inside of her thighs until his thumbs rested on either side of her mound. She felt a wave of warmth as he leaned forward over her, his shirt touching her bare, sensitised flesh. He kissed her stretched out belly. Rubbed his face against the downy velvet skin. Peach skin. He was moaning softly just from the pleasure of having her to touch. Clare drew her knees higher and squeezed the body between them. His kiss travelled down her as he curled himself upright again.

Regarding her now from his elevated position, he moved his hands over her like a healer, a magician. Quickly, quickly, up and down and in circles. The friction brought heat to her skin again, made it hum with blood. He woke up nerve endings begging for more. Her pelvis thrust itself further upwards, demanding attention. His hands sought it out. His thumbs carefully parted her lips, bringing a slow smile to his face when he saw how wet they were.

A first finger slipped easily inside. He drew it

out slowly, taking pleasure in the feeling of her and the sound of her taking pleasure from him. She sighed. Her pelvis raised automatically to meet his descending finger again. And again. And again.

He worked his hand faster and faster. Using sometimes two fingers, sometimes three. His other hand concentrated on her clitoris. Pinching it, rubbing it. Her sighs were louder, her hips rolling from side to side as she tried to dodge the very maximum sensation that could send her over the edge. Her backside had slipped off his lap and she was rolling in the sand. Her juices ran down between her buttocks to pick up the tiny grains.

'Fuck me,' she said, hardly recognising the gravelly, urgent voice that escaped her mouth. 'Fuck me now.'

'No,' he told her. 'Not yet.'

He slid backwards in the sand until he was lying face down between her legs. She could feel his hot breath on her inner thighs, the coolness of the evaporating wetness that ran from her vagina. His tongue flickered out to taste, and her muscles tensed at the touch.

'No, no,' she moaned. The battle in her mind was now only serving to heighten the sensation in her body. She could feel the ripples beginning, could hold off no longer. Her body began to shudder uncontrollably in his hands. Her breasts rose and fell with the waves, faster and faster as the ripples descended her thighs. Her breath fluttered out of her body.

'Now, yes?' he asked.

Her sex was suddenly cold in the icy sea air. He

had left off his frantic tonguing and was now positioning himself so that he too got some of the pleasure. Her breath quickened still more in anticipation as he fumbled on the condom, cursing the ubiquitous sand.

'Now, now,' she echoed, lifting her pelvis up to meet his. He cupped her buttocks with one hand and used the other to guide himself in. She exhaled with a loud, resonant sigh as he drove into her. Driving her conscience further from her body with each thrust he made.

She closed her eyes against the shadow of his face and let herself be all touch, all sound. The sea seemed to be getting closer. The wind was rising. He lifted the top half of his body away from her and she felt the cold air rush in between them. He closed the gap again and pumped more furiously. When she cried out in ecstasy, the wind stole her words and they flew out to sea.

Afterwards they lay side by side in the sand. Steve was making a pattern with his right arm like a child in the snow. Clare's head was cradled in the crook of his left. She pulled closer to him and tucked herself into the folds of his shirt for warmth. The animal heat of their love-making all but blown away now.

'Come back to my hotel?' he asked, when the wind began to breech his clothes once more.

'No,' she sniffed. 'I can't.'

'Why not?'

'Why didn't you tell me that you're married, Steve?'

A moment of silence stretched between them.

He cleared his throat.

'Married?' he asked. His voice remained steady, without emotion. 'Because I'm not.'

She didn't bother to present him with the evidence. Instead she got unsteadily to her feet, threw her coat over her shoulder and left, without saying another word. He stayed behind on the sand, watching her until she disappeared into the all-enveloping folds of the black night. He didn't even bother to call her name. Steve had suddenly realised that this particular game was over for him . . . but he would easily find another willing pawn to play by his rules.

The walk back to Clare's flat was cold and long, but it was helpful. By the time she turned her key in the door, she already knew exactly what she had to do.

The new painting was finished. Smiling, Clare wrapped the freshly framed canvas in bubble-wrap to protect the glass as she transported it from Cornwall to London, where Francesca had asked her to attend the party. Clare hadn't been sure at first. She imagined Steve's face when she walked in. Would he show even a spark of recognition for the artist whom he knew so much better than any of the guests would have suspected? Misreading Clare's apprehension, Francesca had assured her that she would not reveal that Clare had been anything other than a painter of pictures to the good lady wife of the subject. Eventually Clare had been persuaded, but, she told Francesca, she would have to turn up a little late. She had things to do in Cornwall and wouldn't be able to get away until at least seven. Francesca begged her to send the picture down ahead, just in case, but Clare refused.

'I might have to tighten the canvas in the frame again before I can let you have it,' she had explained.

'You're a perfectionist,' Francesca laughed affectionately.

'Yeah . . . I just want everything to be exactly right for that special moment,' Clare had cooed into the phone.

Now the day had arrived. Clare covered the layer of bubble-wrap with the paper that Francesca had requested for her husband's gift. It was metallic silver, dotted with tiny red hearts. There was a matching gift-tag on to which Clare had written 'To my darling husband Steve, All my love, Francesca' in her most careful calligraphy. The painting lay on the kitchen table while Clare did the last of her chores before she prepared for the party. As she packed a case, she brought the red silk dress out of her wardrobe and held it up to her body. It had been dry-cleaned twice since Graham's gallery do but the faint trace of spilled punch still showed to knowing eyes. Clare folded the dress carefully over the back of a chair and began to work out how she was going to fit all her shoes into one bag.

Packing finished, the cases all safely stowed in the boot of the car she had hired to drive to the capital, Clare walked up to the flat one last time to dress for the party. She had left her cream silk underwear out of the suitcase as well and now she slipped that on over her perfumed skin. She smoothed it flat across the gentle curve of her belly and her softly swelling hips. The perfect background. It was very, very important that everything was perfect that night. Clare sighed as she rolled the first of her stockings slowly up her leg, stretching it up to meet her suspender belt, remembering other occasions when she had taken this much care to dress. She slipped the red dress over her head and shook out the skirt. She locked eyes with her reflection in the mirror as she decided how she would wear her hair.

'Up, or down?' she asked herself. Crazy, crazy girl, she thought. After all, it wasn't as if anyone would actually see her. She would deliver the picture to the hotel and then leave. And anyway, all those hours ahead in the car would be bound to leave her looking a little the worse for wear. But if something's worth doing . . . Clare twisted her hair into a thick, smooth French pleat.

Francesca fussed nervously around the ballroom where a waiter was laying out the guests' name cards according to her grand plan. Six or seven of them were already in the bar, under the watchful eye of her mother. Steven was somewhere in town with his younger brother, who had promised to keep him out of the way until everyone was assembled to maximise the surprise. As she followed the waiter around, double-checking everything off against her personal lists, Francesca realised with horror that she had seated an elderly aunt next to one of Steven's less discreet builder friends and had to rearrange an entire table to compensate for the blunder. She looked at her watch, surveyed the room. The birthday banner in place above the top table. The candles as yet unlit. The empty easel waiting for the centrepiece of the whole evening to arrive. When would Clare arrive with that damn painting? She should have demanded that it be sent on ahead. Francesca began to chew her lip, tasted lipstick and stopped.

'Is there a phone in here?' she inadvertently snapped at the waiter.

He pointed her in the right direction. Francesca picked up the phone and began to dial Clare's number. Four, one, eight . . . She couldn't remember any more of the number she once knew by heart. She dashed back to her handbag to dig out her address book, flipped to the dog-eared page where the letters of Clare's name had been traced over and over, and started to dial again.

'The number you have dialled has not been recognised,' came the clipped electronic tone. Francesca replaced the receiver and dialled again. More slowly this time. 'The number you have dialled. . .' Click. Where was she? Where was Clare? Francesca punched the number into the phone one last time. 'The number . . .' Francesca chewed an immaculate finger. So her phone was out of order.

'I mustn't panic,' Francesca told herself under her breath.

Clare would be on her way. Of course she would. And now that Francesca thought about it, Clare had said that she might be a little late.

The manager of the hotel sidled up to

Francesca across the shiny parquet floor.

'Mrs Philip?'

'What is it?' Francesca was automatically on guard. She saw the manager's face wince involuntarily at her tone. 'Oh, I'm sorry,' she explained, 'it's just that I want everything to be just right this evening.'

'I understand, madam.'

What he didn't understand was that it was her chance to prove to Steven that he was right to give their marriage another try.

The manager continued in his deferential way, 'I've come to say that the bar is getting a little crowded and so I thought it might be a good idea to begin to move the guests in for dinner.'

'Yes, of course. Do ... do whatever ...' Francesca waved at the room vaguely then she fled to the toilet for one last make-up check before the big moment. Her reflection was comforting. She was wearing Steven's favourite dress, the green one that he had picked out for her during a rare spell of good taste while they were celebrating their first anniversary in Paris. As Francesca brushed a stray hair from her shoulder, she suddenly had a vivid picture of another girl in that dress and it took a few moments before she remembered that she had lent it to Clare. And how much better it had looked with Clare's dark, red streaked hair. She'd taken their split so well ...

'Francesca, there you are.' An older woman's reflection had appeared in the mirror beside the blonde girl. 'Jeremy just telephoned on his mobile to say that he and Steven are almost here.

Everyone is sitting down ready. The manager wants to know whether you want to dim all the lights to the room until Steven walks through the door? I think that's a good idea. Do you think that's a good idea? Do you? Dear?' Francesca's mother laid a comforting hand on her shoulder.

'I'm sorry, Mum,' said Francesca, suddenly smiling again. 'I'm just a bit stressed out with all the arrangements . . . yes, dim the lights. That's the best idea.'

Mother and daughter bustled out into the ball-room again to await the arrival of the man of the moment.

Clare missed her turning on the motorway and had to make a twelve mile detour but she was sure she would still make it to London in plenty of time. The hire car was bigger than any car she had ever driven before – when she put her foot down, it actually made a difference. When she had put her foot down in the car she once shared with Daniel, the only danger she had been in was of her foot going through the rusty floor. The stereo pumped out loud fast music. She opened the window so that the wind whipped loose strands of her hair backwards and forwards across her face. The music was almost drowned out by the sound of the rushing air except for the constant bass beat that raced her heart. The red tarmac of Devon and Cornwall was long behind her. A fine mist of rain made the black bitumen ahead of her shine like patent leather.

The room waited silently in darkness as Steve and

his brother made their approach. Francesca strained to hear their footsteps in the lobby. She twisted her hands together, praying that the portrait would arrive in time. A familiar laugh bellowed out at a bad joke. The double doors swung open and the room was suddenly filled with light.

'Ta-daaa!' Francesca pulled a party pose as her beloved husband stood rooted to the spot in surprise. Her terror subsided when she saw him grin from ear to ear. He drew nearer to her through the gaudily decorated room, shaking the hands of friends and relations as he went. The family man, the trusted friend, the husband whom she loved.

'Thank you, darling,' he murmured as he kissed her. His breath told her that Michael had already plied him with drink. 'How did you get hold of all these people, you clever thing?'

'She went through your little black book,' a red-faced man laughed. Steve blanched at the thought.

'Happy birthday, darling.'

Francesca was handing over a huge, flat parcel, just rushed to the top table by the manager's PA. She was beaming from ear to ear. Clare had made it. Thank heavens. As Steven turned the package over in his hands, making a show of guessing what it was for the other guests, Francesca scanned the back of the room for a sight of her ex-lover. She thought she saw a familiar head of brown hair through the double doors and waved tentatively. Why wasn't Clare coming in?

'Open it, open it,' was the whisper around the

table. Yes, go on Steve, Clare thought as she watched the scene through the tiny window in the door, open the can of worms.

Now Francesca's hands were clasped together in anticipation as he ripped away at the ribbons and tore a strip down the paper to reveal only the back of the picture. It gave away nothing more than the name of an artist that he didn't yet recognise. Finally he shook it free of the paper . . .

'Hold it up, Steve!' called an uncle from the other end of the room. 'Show it to us.'

Steve's face in itself was a picture. As was Francesca's. The beneficent smiles were fading, to be replaced by a look of confusion as the significance of the composition gradually sank in.

'What is it?' a solitary voice called.

Francesca was turning away, her hands to her eyes. Steve held the picture at arm's length.

'Is this a joke?' he asked her, his voice shaking. 'Is this a joke?'

In life-like colours with an ultra-real expression, a lover lay on a bed covered by white cotton sheets. A lover with a serpent, a tattoo from his teens, nestling at the top of a well-muscled thigh.

Clare turned slowly away from the scene. Slowly away from the vision of Francesca running blindly down the centre of the room to the door. Steve calling after her. The laughter of the party guests, unable to see the real joke.

Yes, she thought, her latest nude had been a great success. But the brightly lit room with its exotic human contents held no more inspiration for her now. She closed the hire-car door and checked the

421

glove compartment. Her passport and her one-way ticket. They were still there. Her ticket to Paris, France.

Velvet Touch

Zara Devereux

Chapter One

'WE'RE SPENDING THE summer on the Greek islands. D'you have to take that job? Why not come with us?' Jeremy pleaded, using that little-boy-lost expression he had learned at his nanny's knee.

Karen grinned, knowing this ploy worked wonders with female students and lecturers alike. Not with her, however. She recognised their relationship for what it was – mutual lust and nothing more. Not for her the agony of sighing after this handsome, feckless young man, the jealous pangs, the heart-breaking wait by the phone for calls that rarely came.

Thank God he doesn't affect me that way, she thought, resting back against the flat corduroy boat cushions as he poled the punt along the placid surface of the Cherwell. *I can admire his well-shaped head, bleached-blond hair, broad shoulders, slim waist and lean hips, and his tush, balls and cock are ten out of ten. He's fit, muscular and tanned, but I'm not in love with him, whatever that means.*

'By "us" I suppose you mean Pete and half a

dozen hangers-on?' she asked, idly trailing her finger in the river. It was deliciously cool, and she relished the sensual caress of the swirling water on her bare skin, a striking contrast to the hot sun beating down on her head, turning her chestnut hair to flame.

Milton's verse ran through her mind: 'See here the olive grove of Academe – There Ilissus rolls his whispering stream.'

She had enjoyed her years at university, indulging to the full her passion for history, revelled in the rich social life, the plethora of red-blooded males, and had come out with brilliant grades – but it was time to go.

'My parents have a villa in Corfu. They'll be in Miami, and we can use the place as a base.' Jeremy jabbed the pole into the greenish water then lifted it out. Diamond drops sparkled from it at every storke. He regarded her from under thick fair lashes hedging pale-blue eyes. He was sweating, though they had not been out long. Karen was sure his body heat had something to do with the fact that her thin cotton skirt had become wet when she climbed into the unstable craft. It was sticking to her, outlining the curves and angles of her bare legs.

With a smile tugging at the corners of her generous mouth, she deliberately let her eyes rest on the solid bulge straining the zipper of his tight denim jeans and then looked up into his face. So intent was he on trying to make out the dark triangle at the apex of her thighs, he very nearly overbalanced from his precarious perch at the back of the punt.

'Whoops! Steady!' she warned, laughter

bubbling up in her throat. It amused her to see him showing off for her benefit and to guess at the discomfort of his swollen phallus confined by Levi's.

Jeremy Hurst-Pemberton, popular athlete and champion oarsman, the darling of the campus, pursued by a horde of doting women, had tried everything to win her over. Bouquets, champagne suppers, windswept rides in his Ferrari, even a long weekend at his aristocratic father's Scottish castle.

Win her over? She smiled to herself at the old-fashioned phrase. It sounded vaguely Victorian – all hearts, flowers, chaperones and blushing maidens. The reality had been very different.

Karen had seduced him after a select dinner party given by a university professor and his wife whose soirees were renowned in academic circles both for the cuisine and the engaging conversation. It was she who had taken him to her room, eased him out of his tuxedo, lured him into bed and shown him how to pleasure her.

He had been disappointing, she remembered. Though living off a reputation as a stud, his knowledge of female arousal had been abysmal. He wasn't much better now, needing constant reminding that slam-bam-thank-you-ma'am just wouldn't do.

He steered the punt into a secluded creek, screened almost entirely by overhanging willows. After shipping the pole and tying the painter securely, he slid over to where Karen was sitting. He rested a hand on her knee, started to move his fingers up under her skirt, heading towards the damp, cotton-covered mouth of her sex. He was eager to probe the entrance to the liquid centre of her being, but she closed her legs, not ready for him yet. He was always so precipitous, grabbing at her breasts, homing in on her clitoris. She made him wait.

Karen sat up and took the velvet scrunchie from her hair, shaking out the tumbling mane of Medusa curls till they flowed across her shoulders and half-way down her back. Jeremy watched her, biting his lip in frustration. She was like a woman from a Rossetti painting – tall, full breasted, with an almost barbaric beauty, an exotic bloom who captured attention wherever she went, admired, envied, even disliked, but never ignored.

Although he had known her carnally, drawn into the vortex of her tumultuous orgasms, he still shuddered with a feeling akin to awe whenever she was close. He was mesmerised by the enticing perfume that emanated from her skin, frightened by the fierce light in her green eyes, chastened by her intellect and biting sarcasm. Karen was clever, quick-witted and confident. A free spirit who took no prisoners.

Jeremy had only to crook his little finger to summon a bevy of girls panting to have him shaft them. They flattered him, made him feel macho and virile, but none was as exciting as Karen. She was a potent drug, too powerful for all save the strongest personality. The need to convince himself that he could tame her forced him to attempt it again and again.

He took the tartan rug stowed under the seat, stepped on to the bank and held out a hand to her. The willow formed a perfect bower; the blanket spread on the short grass invited fornication. Karen sank down on it, linking her hands under her head and looked up at the bright dazzle filtering through the swaying branches.

How she loved summer; she became listless and droopy during the dull rainy days of winter. Now energy poured through her veins, revitalising her, running like quicksilver along every nerve, inflaming her senses.

From beneath curling dark lashes she considered Jeremy, who sprawled beside her, propped up on one elbow. He leaned over, and his mouth caressed the smooth, petal-soft skin of her cheek. She turned her head and their tongues met and tangled. He grunted and pulled her closer, the tips of her breasts bunching as they brushed against the material of her flimsy blouse. She was warming to his kisses, her juices already pooling at the opening of her vagina, the ripe, sweet scent of her rising into the warm air.

Jeremy might not be a ideal lover, but the afternoon was filled with a golden haze, heavy with langour. The sound of water, the rustle of leaves, the birdcalls and distance voices of other boaters combined to rouse in her a deep and enticing longing for fulfilment, and a heaviness gathered in her groin.

Had she been there alone she would have lifted her skirt, pushed aside her briefs and played with her clitoris, stroking, petting, rubbing it, bringing herself to climax in that entirely satisfying way that no man had yet surpassed. She suspected that another woman might, but had not yet tried, merely fantasising about it sometimes when she masturbated.

She relaxed in Jeremy's arms, and he lowered his mouth, fastening his lips around her nipple, sucking it through the cotton till it stood up in a needful little peak, hard as stone. She gritted her teeth and closed her eyes, drawing in a sharp breath at the delicious friction of his tongue. Her hand smoothed the outside of his jeans, tracing the large, elongated shape of his cock that throbbed urgently, demanding release from its imprisonment.

Gently but firmly she unfastened the metal button at his waistband, then seized the zipper tag between thumb and forefinger. Tantalisingly slowly, she pulled it down, the gap widening till it freed the pulsing member, which sprang out to nestle in her palm. Her hand closed round it and she applied pressure, her touch slippery smooth, enjoying the sensation of the damp, hot hardness jerking and moving as if it had a life of its own, a thing apart from Jeremy.

He opened her blouse. She was not wearing a brassiere. Her breasts bared to his gaze, beautiful in form and colouring, firm and high and lightly tanned, with faint blue veins and luscious nipples ringed with darker brown.

He cupped her right breast in his hand, his thumb revolving on the tense tip. Then he bent his head and sucked it into his mouth, teasing and tonguing it before moving to the other, while Karen moaned her appreciation of this tribute. Such attention was irresistible, but it made her clitoris ache. She wriggled her hips, attempting to rub her inner lips together and put pressure on her rampant nub.

Jeremy responded to her need, one hand straying below her waist, across the flat bowl of her belly and under her panties, easing them down. Karen kicked them aside, and he brushed the abundant tangle of brown pubic hair, a finger finding its way into the deep avenue between. It parted to reveal her labia, swollen now, her clitoris standing out from its hood, glistening like a silver-pink pearl, quivering with want.

Karen closed her eyes, her hand working up and down his engorged phallus, but aware that she must not rouse him too soon or he would lose patience and plough into her, forgetting that she, too, needed orgasm. She slowed the movement, caressed him gently, though lost concentration as she waited breathlessly for him to bring her off.

Jeremy was panting, nibbling at her breasts, his finger dipping into the scented pool of her vulva, then, once moistened, moving upwards along her crevice to spread silkily over the sensitive head of her lovebud. She could feel herself spiralling as he settled into the slick, wet rhythm she so desperately needed to carry her over the edge.

Up she rode, up and up, waves crashing hard on one another. 'That's it,' she whispered hoarsely, clutching at his cock. 'Don't stop! Go on! Go on! Oh – oh! Yes! Yes!'

She was peaking. She was there. Sensation washed over her, tingling from the tips of her toes to the recesses of her brain, glorious release provided by that tiny organ existing solely for delight, her precious, delectable, wonderful clit.

Jeremy pushed between her relaxed thighs, his thick member plunging to the hilt in her warm, convulsing depths. A couple of strong thrusts, and she felt the twitch of his cock as he came, clasping her tightly to him. After a moment, she freed herself from his weight, shifting to lie with an arm across her eyes.

Karen was filled with a sense of well-being, the rolling spasms of pleasure receding, leaving her limp and momentarily satiated. Her thoughts wandered aimlessly. Fragments of music floated in her head – ideas, plans. She was aware of the lovely sounds of nature, the lapping of the river, the fussy cheep of the moorhen calling her fluffy black chicks. Summer in England, and where more summer-like than magical Oxford?

At the same time she was aware of her juices bedewing her thighs and puckered folds. She could smell Jeremy's sharp, male sweat cutting across her familiar female fragrance which carried the odour of seaweed and shells. Sex, raw and untamed. Sex and only sex. She felt a pang of loss, of regret. Was there nothing more?

Poems, music, great works of art all spoke of something deep and meaningful. Whenever she listened to symphonies or opera her throat constricted and tears pricked her eyes. She had not yet found this elusive, heart-stopping element during her congress with men, and her experience had been considerable.

Fastidious and choosy, she had applied her intellect to her experiments with a number of them. Each had been carefully selected, but even so, none had moved her beyond satisfying the yearnings of her loins. There seemed to be an emotional block. She was aware that some accused her of being cold but knew this to be untrue. If anything she was too sensitive, too vulnerable, and this made her afraid to lower her defences. Too often she had comforted women friends devastated by callous males, and she had vowed it would never happen to her.

Karen pulled herself up, leaning back against the bole of the willow, and Jeremy shifted over to lie with his head in her lap. She pushed her fingers through his rumpled curls. A pattern of leaves dappled his face and spilled across his eyes.

'You'll come to Greece?' he asked softly, seizing her hand and running his tongue over her fingers, sucking each digit with absorbed concentration.

Karen frowned, withdrawing her hand. His licking was too canine to be pleasant. 'I can't,' she said. 'I've told you before. There's a post waiting for me in Devon. If I turn it down, I'll never get another chance like that. It's just what I want.'

'Why so keen to work?' He rolled on his stomach, his head to one side, resting on his folded arms, regarding her with a sulky expression.

'It's not a question of keenness. I have to earn a living,' she replied crisply. 'We don't all have rich parents, you know.'

'Yours can't be badly off.' Jeremy was in a perverse mood. She guessed he was annoyed by her refusal, probably more upset than he cared to admit. 'Your mother's just had another book on archaeology published, hasn't she? And your old man appears on BBC2 regularly in those philosophy programmes.'

Karen was decidedly bored by this. When he could not get his own way, Jeremy displayed the less attractive side of his character. She picked up her discarded knickers and stuffed them in her pocket, then scrambled to her feet, parted the peridot veil of leaves and dropped down into the punt. It wobbled dangerously.

'I don't have to explain anything to you,' she said, lowering herself on to the seat. 'Come on. It's time we went back. I've packing to finish.'

In silence they drifted up the river, sometimes hailed by fellow students on other boats. The shadows lengthened and the bells chimed from spires poking admonishing fingers into the plumblue dusk. They left the punt moored under Magdalen Bridge alongside several others, then strolled through the Botanic Gardens towards the High Street. It was busy as always, but with an extra frenetic buzz about it – it was the end of the teaching year; for some, like Karen, the end of an era.

It seemed incredible that it was over four years since she had obtained sufficient A Levels to be accepted at this, the *crème de la crème* of universities. She had spent three years as an undergraduate, finally achieving degrees in history, art and English with an additional familiarity with Latin. This had not been the end, however, for she had stayed on to take a postgrad course in archive administration. This might have led to the position of records manager's assistant in local government of a big company, had not Tony come up with the invitation to work as his aide at Blackwood Towers.

Just because her parents were famed intellectuals, it had not been easy for her. In fact it had been hard – a case of the cobbler's children. They had expected her to do well simply because she was

434

their daughter and had never had the time or inclination to give her extra tuition themselves.

Standing by the archway leading to her lodgings, Karen said goodbye to Jeremy, aware of the cool air breathing on her bare thighs and naked pussy. He was aware of it, too, and she felt the heat of his hand on her backside, curving round the tight globes, pushing into the crease between in a proprietorial way that she found offensive.

'You'll write?' he persisted anxiously, a sullen expression spoiling his near-perfect looks.

'Yes,' she lied. 'Have a good summer, Jeremy. Be happy.' She rested the back of her hand against his cheek in a casually affectionate gesture.

He gripped her arm, tried to stop her going, but she broke free and disappeared into the passageway. Jem, the porter, stuck his head out of his cubbyhole of an office.

'Letter for you, Miss Heyward,' he said cheerfully, handing over a white envelope. She was going to miss Jem, perpetually optimistic despite the weather, the recession, the peculiarities of dons, the behaviour of students. Nothing ruffled him.

'Thanks,' she said with a smile.

'You off then, miss?' Jem lingered to talk. His ruddy face with the bushy walrus moustache would be etched on her memory.

'Tomorrow morning.'

She ran lightly up the dark, winding staircase leading to the rooms she shared with Alison Gray. Alison had finished, too, but she was taking a year off in Boston before embarking on a career.

Karen looked out through the landing window. Below lay the quad, across it the stately buildings that had sheltered aspiring students for over five hundred years. Not women, of course – they were a late addition. At one time no females had been permitted beneath the sacred portals of those male-dominated seats of learning.

Just one more night spent there. It was sad, really. Despite her assertions to Jeremy, Karen was nervous of taking up the position she had been offered. She unlocked the door of the college flat. Inside the cosy panelled sitting room she stepped out of her sandals, padded across to the little kitchen and switched on the kettle. While waiting for it to boil, she opened the letter.

Dear Karen,

Am looking forward tremendously to having you join me at Blackwood Towers. You'll like Porthcombe. Miles of beach, a pounding sea and spectacular cliffs. The library is a mess. I really need your help. It's too much for one person. The late marquis neglected it. He was only interested in the farming side of the estate. But Lord Mallory Burnet is different and wants everything in order. There's enough work here to last us years!

See you on the 20th, Exeter Station, Platform 2, at 2.30 p.m.

Yours,

Tony

Tomorrow, Karen though, folding the letter and returning it to the envelope. *By this time tomorrow*

I'll be there. One door closing and another opening. Dear Tony. He must be keen. We've already settled these arrangements by phone.

My old friend and teacher who got me the job. He's a gentleman and won't expect anything in return, though I'd not say no. He's forty-something, I know, but it was he who taught me how to achieve an orgasm. Before his tender tuition, I was a bundle of ignorance and frustration. I wonder why he never married. The typical bachelor, but what a lover! Jeremy could take a few leaves from his book.

Even remembering those hours spent in Tony Stroud's apartment when, as an unhappy, rebellious teenager she had discovered what sex really meant, made her loins ache and her clitoris pulse. Maybe it, too, remembered its awakening, she thought. The first time it had blossomed and bloomed, rising hard and proud at her teacher's expert caressing. His long fingers, his skilful tongue, her nub sucked and fondled until it reached such a frantic explosion that she had fainted with the shock and pleasure of it, then begged him to do it again – and he had. She recalled achieving nine orgasms during that night with him, a record she had not yet beaten.

The kettle steamed and Karen poured water on to instant coffee granules in a pottery mug and settled down on the shabby cretonne-covered couch, tucking her feet up under her. Her packing was almost done, the evening ahead planned. She had half an hour of rest before she set off – space to herself, a time to get her thoughts in order.

Her books and belongings had been boxed up and waited collection. Most of them would be dispatched to her parents' home in Wimbledon.

The housekeeper would take them in and store them. Karen's father was on a lecture tour of the States and her mother had gone with him. They never liked to be apart, utterly absorbed in each other, still madly in love after twenty-five years, a phenomenon Karen found remarkable, moving and exasperating.

She had always felt surplus to requirements, sure she was an accidental not a planned child. Not that they were ever unkind or neglectful, far from it, but she had been aware, right from the start, that they were so wrapped up in each other that anything or anyone else was considered to be an intrusion. Even a well-loved offspring. Needless to say, Karen had been an only child.

Such an upbringing had made her independent, a loner, living a great deal in a fantasy world. History, literature, antiquities of any sort, these had become her obsessions. Boarding school had cemented her emotional isolation, then university. 'I'm so sorry we shan't be in London when you finish,' her mother had said on one of her recent visits, drifting about the flat in an elegant navy and white Chanel outfit. 'Unfortunately we're off to America.'

'Don't worry, Mother. I'm going straight to Devon,' Karen had assured her, feeling gauche in the face of such perfection, while Alison had obligingly aimed the camera, capturing the three Heywards for posterity.

Now Karen set down her cup and went into her room to change. She stripped, glad to remove her stained skirt, and thrust it into the linen basket. Naked, she prowled to the bathroom and stepped into the shower cubicle.

The jets gushed, stinging her skin with pleasurable little jabs, pouring down her shoulders, over her breasts, across her belly and between her legs. She soaped herself, breathing in the scent of showergel, enjoying the sensation of her own hands sliding across her flesh. She circled her nipples, which rose instantly at her touch, travelled down to her navel, made tiny soapy swirls and corkscrews in her pubic hair and gently rinsed between her pouting lips.

Wrapped in a white towel, she padded into her room with its low, sloping ceiling and black beams, chintz curtains and powder-blue carpet. This had been her home for months. She had taken time to settle but having done so had no desire to move. It was inevitable, however, and a part of her was excited by the challenge – fresh fields to conquer, new people to meet, opportunities, even lovers. She had the urge to snort and paw the ground like a warhorse scenting battle.

She let the towel drop and considered herself critically in the long mirror fastened to one wall. It wasn't a bad body, all things considered. Working out and practising martial arts had kept her in trim, and she was streamlined – tall but slender boned, and her breasts were full, her waist slim and her stomach flat. She ran her hands down the long sweep of her thighs, past the shapely knees and rounded calves to the trim ankles. Her body thrilled at the friction of palms of skin.

Amoral, wanton body, she addressed it sternly. *You don't care who offers you caresses just as long as you can purr under them. Particularly if they culminate on your clitoris, the epicentre, the key to ecstasy, the only organ in the entire human body designed exclusively for pleasure.*

Why had it been put there? she wondered. Was it to compensate the female for the pain of childbirth? Sensible, really, for had the vagina been the seat of orgasm, then it would have been impossible to endure the passage of a baby through it. As it was, the clitoris was well up out of harm's way.

Her hand wandered involuntarily down to part the freshly washed hair and press on her bud's stem, tracing it back to where it joined her pelvic bone. At once a tremor of excitement stirred in her loins, and her honeydew commenced to flow. She wriggled her hips against her finger's sweet invasion while, in the glass, she could see her nipples becoming redder, hardening in response.

Stop it, she chided herself. *Save it for later.*

Karen controlled the urge to bring herself off, smoothed body lotion into her skin, and dusted talc over her mound and between her legs. She sprayed deodorant beneath her shaven underarms and applied a matching haze of *Casmir*.

She glanced at her watch. Ten to seven. No time to waste. White cotton briefs now concealed her genitals, followed by a black tracksuit bottom. A matching sweatshirt was pulled over her head. Her hair was piled high and confined by a headband. On her left breast was a badge emblazoned in red and gold which proclaimed '*Shotokan Karate*'.

After peeling on white socks and lacing her trainers, Karen picked up a tote bag and left the apartment. In a few moments she was cycling through the streets towards the sports centre. This had been the major backdrop for much of her life at college. Here she had practised karate three times a week, played badminton, pumped iron and swum. A fitness fanatic? Hardly. One of the prime instigators of her interest had been the man under whose direction she would train tonight – her *sensei*.

After chaining her bike securely to a stand, Karen pushed through the swing doors into the foyer. The centre was, as always, busy. Young, beautiful people wearing colourful leotards, shorts, legwarmers and T-shirts were chatting as they made their way to the various rooms devoted to their particular sport. Karen walked towards the lofty gym, which had been transformed into a training *dojo* for the evening. She nodded to several students who were already in the changing room, replacing her tracksuit with a white *gi*, the thick cotton unyielding against her skin, the brown belt folded correctly round her waist. Barefoot, she trotted back to the *dojo*, bowing to her master as she entered.

Kan Takeyama was standing by the window, illumined by the sunset glow behind his body. He straightened, returned her bow. 'Good evening, Heyward,' he said, poker-faced. No smile of recognition crossed his impassive features.

'Good evening, *sensei*,' she replied, equally formal, though her nipples tensed under her fighting suit.

His fiercely masculine yet sensual good looks instilled in her a feeling of tranquillity on one hand and awoke her slumbering sexual passion on the other.

His body was perfection. Now, like her, he wore a white *gi*, though his was girded by a black belt, as he was a third dan in the art, but she knew what he looked like naked. Besides being her master in karate, he lectured on oriental history and art. Karen had proved his most promising student. The opportunities for lovemaking had been legion.

In the *dojo*, however, Kan was severe and professional. Twenty novices were put through their paces. First the rigorous warm up, enough to exhaust all but the fighting fit, then from simple groups of techniques the class moved to exacting *kata*, before progressing to sparring.

Karen was paired with a short, stocky opponent, quick and light on his feet but no match for her. She was the star of the *dojo*. But Kan would not permit anyone to think themselves superior to the rest. He took over, giving her no quarter, an exacting taskmaster, intent of pushing her to the limit, for she was due to grade as a black belt soon.

This was a responsible position, and she would be issued with a licence only if she used her hands in self-defence, not attack. Empty hands – *karate*, the name given to it centuries before when disarmed Okinawa islanders found a subtle way to fight their tyrannical Japanese conquerors.

As Kan her *sensei* and mentor, worked with her, she was aware of the tension growing between them, an electric thrill passing through her every time he touched her in correction or instruction. This always happened, always had, always would – and her need for physical contact with him became almost painful in its intensity.

She was volatile as she fought him, every line of her expressing not only the spiritual warrior but the woman, too – her green eyes, her firm mouth, lithe limbs; she was powerfully aggressive, gloriously female; sexuality incarnate. Kan was conscious and responsive to all these things yet did not betray it with the flicker of an eye.

The session ended. Everyone bowed to everyone else. People trailed off to the changing rooms. Karen sat panting, wiping her face with a towel, aware of an echoing wetness between her thighs.

'You're doing well,' Kan said in his quiet, serious way, never giving praise lightly. 'You'll get your black belt. No problem.'

'I'm moving away,' she replied regretfully.

'You'll keep training, and come to Crystal Palace next May. Grade then. I'll arrange it with the judges. We'll keep in touch.'

As usual after training, they wound up at Kan's cool, light apartment. Karen thought of the opera *Madame Butterfly* every time she set foot in there: there were low tables, low stools, a paper screen, artistically arranged flowers, netsuke in a glass cabinet, a couple of gnarled and ancient bonsai trees on the balcony. Taped music of the *samisen*, a three-stringed lute, tinkled in the background.

'Is this new?' she asked, pointing to a delicately executed print of Mount Fuji with a peaceful river and a pine tree in the foreground.

'Yes. I've started a collection. Japanese wood blocks are known as *ukiyo-e*, which means images of the floating world.'

'How lovely,' she replied, a catch in her throat. Soon she would be without her charming, aesthetic *sensei*.

'I'm glad it pleases you,' Kan said, watching her with wise, slanting eyes.

443

'Can I take a shower?' Karen needed to be fresh for him, as if trying to recapture her virginity. This was so divine and pure a setting that she wanted nothing to mar her final experience of it, wishing to be fragrant from top to toe, her flesh masked in silk, which she knew would be appreciated by the beauty-loving Kan.

'Be my guest.' He ran his fingers through his straight black hair, every gesture graceful. 'We'll make love and then I'll send out for some sushi.'

The bathroom was immacluate, the shower hot and refreshing. After she had anointed her body with jasmine-scented lotion, she draped herself in the splendid cream kimono Kan reserved especially for her. Padded and lined with crimson silk, it was rich with embroidered chrysanthemums and applique birds outlined with gilt thread. The hanging sleeves were wide, and she fastened a magnificent obi round her waist. It was the attire of a court concubine, and Karen could feel herself changing, taking tiny steps, moving modestly, eyes cast down.

'I'm too tall to be a geisha,' she said as she glided back into the room.

'You're beautiful,' he replied earnestly, his eyes darkening with desire.

He was kneeling on the *tatami*, wearing a turquoise silk robe patterned with trees set amid snow-covered foilage. Karen sat on her haunches facing him, fingers linked lightly in her lap, and for a moment he did nothing but gaze at her. Then he took her hands and placed them on his thighs, doing the same to her. Silence descended on them, a deep, meditative silence, healing and cleansing.

He sighed, reached for her, drew her into his arms. His kisses were just right, tongue flickering over her lips before venturing between. And his hands cupped her silk-covered breasts, the nipples rising urgently against the crimson lining. He rewarded them with the merest grazing touch. Lust snaked through her like a white-hot flame.

Kan rose, lifting her with him. He released her for a second and slid the gown from his body. His smooth, silky skin was bronze coloured. It had the sheen and texture of polished marble, every muscle honed, unmarked by a single blemish, free from hair except for the wiry black thicket covering his pubis.

This served to accentuate a formidable penis, long, thick, copper hued, curving above a pair of plump testicles hanging in their scrotal sac. His smouldering eyes, his voluptuous lips, exquisite mouth and magnificent prick promised ecstasy and never failed to deliver.

Kan's eyes continued to hold hers, and what she read in them sent a shiver right down her spine to her clit. He took one of her hands, raised it to his lips and licked the centre of the palm with the tip of his tongue, sealing it with a kiss. She sighed, trembled, his every touch a strong aphrodisiac.

His hands as gentle as a woman's, in odd contrast to his reputation as a warrior, he removed her kimono. Her nipples sprang erect with excitement and sudden chill and, standing before her, he took the weight of her breasts in his hands, then lowered his shining dark head to lick over the tips. She could feel the swollen cap of his phallus nudging intimately against her belly.

Leaving her breasts momentarily, he took the band from her hair and let the burnished curls fall across them like a veil.

Karen stood perfectly still, legs pressed together, and Kan stroked her mound of Venus gently, seductively, inserting a finger along the dark fissure which opened like a flower under the knowing caress. He was a master of sensuality, a student of ancient books of all kinds, particularly those that dealt with the language of love. His knowledge of the female body was extensive, and he took pride and delight in playing it like a finely tuned instrument.

Karen closed her eyes, the double action of his lips sucking her nipples and his finger stroking each side of her clitoris, but carefully avoiding the head, lifting her to the brink of orgasm. Kan had no intention of allowing this yet. Her pleasure would be heightened if the tension was built up slowly and gradually.

He lifted her in his arms, and she gripped him round the waist with her legs, her wide open pussy rubbing on the stalk of his cock, her juices glinting against his pubic hair. He carried her across the room and mounted a couple of wide, shallow steps to the area he used as a sleeping place. There she was laid down on a double futon. Pools of soft golden light filtered through the globular paper lampshades, casting a subdued glow.

Kan submitted every inch of her to attention, a man so secure and confident in himself that he could lavish admiration on the woman in his arms. His mouth feasted on hers, while his hands made exciting and passionate love to her breasts, then he kissed between them, his tongue lapping her waist, her belly, dipping into her navel, burrowing lower like a hungry little animal amongst the thick curls protecting her sex.

He paused, his head between her legs, eagerly observing her reaction as he held her labia majora apart with two fingers. The inner ones opened like petals at his stroking, and Karen gasped as he wetted the cleft between with saliva and started to caress her clitoris. Her pleasure was his, it seemed. He didn't hurry, content to have her fondle his cock as he brought her closer and closer to ecstasy.

Karen was hot, slick, the force gathering to roll across and through her. Kan judged her condition, held off for a second, his fingertip hovering over but not touching her tortured bud, then sliding across it once more, back and forth. He stopped and she groaned in protest, then felt him shift down, felt his tongue sucking her clitoris into her mouth, rolling it, licking it. Her climax flared through her body like an electric current, making her shudder and cry out.

While she was still convulsing, he slid his penis into her depths, yielding to the sexual rhythm of passionate intercourse. She embraced him with her thighs, urged him on, impaling herself on his raging prick, till at last he gave a long groan, his spasms echoed by her throbbing vagina.

It was past midnight when he dropped her off. Jem had shut up his office and gone home.

'What about your bike?' Kan had asked as they left the apartment and headed for the parking lot and his Nissan.

'D'you know someone who'd like it? I shan't be

taking it to Devon,' she had replied, feeling sleepy, ripe, languid with sex, her other hunger sated with raw fish, rice and saki.

He promised to find a home for it and kissed her again. Karen clung to him for an instant. 'I'm going to Tokyo for the vacation. Come with me,' he whispered, his hands slipping under her sweatshirt and skimming over her naked back. 'I'll be training with my own sensei. He's an eighth dan. You'd like him. He's very wise.'

'No. Thank you all the same.' It was hard to refuse. 'One day, perhaps.'

Shakily, she fled up the stairs and let herself into her rooms. She could tell Alison was home by the creaking of springs and moans of pleasure coming from the second bedroom. Obviously she was entertaining her boyfriend, the good-natured, reliable, boring Gareth.

Karen's suitcase stood open on the floor, ready to receive the last items of clothing. Smiling as she reminisced, she laid in the cream silk kimono Kan had given her as a farewell gift. It still carried the spicy cinnamon smell of his hair, the personal odour of his body. She would never forget him, but her heart was not bleeding because she was leaving him.

Maybe my critics are right, and I don't have a heart after all, she thought as she climbed into bed and switched off the light. Drowsily, she listened to the distant night sounds of the college building, car doors slamming occasionally, voices, a dog barking somewhere. Soon they would no longer be the background pattern of her existence.

Chapter Two

I DON'T KNOW about fucking in the hay, thought Armina Channing as she proceeded to do just that. *It's scratchy – smelly. Bits stick into one's most delicate and private parts – though you could hardly call mine private.*

The brawny young man who was pleasuring her, head burrowed between her spread legs, seemed to have no such reservations. Hidden in a stall at the back of the stable, they were practically invisible. This would have been a great place to do it if it had been less uncomfortable. Armina revelled in the refinements of life – satin sheets, the touch of velvet against her pampered skin, perfumed bath water – exquisite cuisine, fine wines and decadent luxury.

Yet a bit of rough could be stimulating, and Tayte Penwarden was rough all right – Lord Burnet's head groom. And Armina was one of His Lordship's mistresses, the chief odalisque of the seraglio. But while the cat was away the mice would play, and anything Tayte lacked as a sophisticated lover, he made up for in enthusiasm.

Fit and muscular, his olive skin glowed with health, a hearty young stud indeed. Armina, clitoris fired by the caresses of his fleshy wet tongue, buried her hands in his tightly ringleted hair. Tayte was a Cornishman who had slipped over the Tamar into Devon, but was also of gypsy stock if his swarthy colouring and those black-lashed eyes tilting upwards at the outer corners were anything to go by.

Whenever she looked at him, she tingled at the remembrance of the Carlos Saura movie based on *Carmen* and performed by a Spanish dance company. It was one of her favourite adjuncts to masturbation, a rich, sensual feast of a film, over-flowing with passionate flamenco, smouldering fire, world-weary languor and desirable dancers of both sexes. She often watched it on the video in her bedroom while she used her dildo or fingered herself to climax. The leading male had a body to die for, gorgeous enough to bring a puritan to orgasm.

A critic had described him as having 'wolves eyes. Gypsy eyes.'

Just like Tayte's.

Now, sensing her distraction, he stopped nuzzling her sex and moved upwards, fixing her with that lupine gaze. 'What's wrong?' he asked in his guttural voice.

'Nothing,' she answered in her melodious, cultured accent.

She was frustrated because he had stopped, but she savoured the denial, too. Had he continued she would have spilled over by now. As it was she could look forward to further leisurely, lubricious arousal.

She trailed agile fingers up the well-muscled inner surface of his denim-covered thigh. He wore tattered work jeans, faded blue. Through a hole in one knee she glimpsed his coppery, darkly furred skin. Her juices wetted her labia even more as her hand moved nearer to the generous swell at his crotch. It made her dizzy with anticipation simply to look at it. She thought of the thick brown serpent nestling between Tayte's legs and was overwhelmed by a hot surge of lust.

'That's OK then,' he muttered and stared at her pert breasts. Tiny, like their owner, with wantonly pink nipples, they were as wilfully lascivious as she was, demanding to be fondled, sucked, teased and pinched.

Armina was Tayte's first lady, though not his first woman by any means, and she offered a bewildering wonderland of new delights and wickedly shameless sensations, unbelievable in one so dainty, ladylike and innocent looking.

She had entered the stable that morning on the pretext of an early gallop, wearing a white shirt tucked into the waistband of skin-tight jodhpurs that outlined the division of her rounded buttocks at the back and cut between her plump secret lips at the front. Black riding boots had completed her attire. It had been obvious she was wearing no underwear.

Tayte had been waiting for her, leaning nonchalantly against a manger, chewing a blade of grass. His hands had shot out, seized her with that brutal impetuosity she found so intoxicating and propelled her into the hay. Her jodhpurs had not remained in place for long.

'You know he's abroad,' Armina continued,

lazy with desire, watching as he unfastened his belt, then the top button of his old jeans. Long before he had reached a hand into his pants she had visualised the sight of his curving, iron-hard phallus emerging from its nest of black curls.

'I do,' he said, taking it out, its smooth, red-brown knob poking from between his fingers as he cradled the shaft and rubbed it, sliding the foreskin up and down, excited by having her watch.

'Then there's nothing to stop us doing it in my house,' she said, eyeing him lecherously.

Lord, what a weapon! Thick as a truncheon, stunningly long. How was it possible she could take all of it? Only just, she recalled. It felt as if it reached right up to her waist when he pumped it almost painfully against her cervix. Her avenue was slippery wet, her mouth too, as she imagined it thrusting into her void which longed to be filled.

'Suppose so,' he agreed, looking down at his cock, fascinated as it swelled even more under the familiar touch of his fingers. 'Suppose we could do that even when he's home.'

'I don't think so.' Armina shook her blonde head and knelt before him, lifted her face to his prick and took the head of it in her mouth.

Tayte groaned, thrust his pelvis forward, pushed in further. Armina could feel the blunt tip pressing into the back of her throat, and was delighted by the salty taste and solid feel of it. She played with him as he stood above her, legs tense and parted, back against a beam. Her hand cupped his taut balls, gently squeezing the full velvety sac. Slipping him from her mouth, she hovered with her lips barely touching his cock head, breathing on it, soft as a whisper, then lowering herself so that it entered between her teeth again, sliding across her palate.

Tayte gasped, his strong, sinewy hands gripping her shoulders. His lids were half closed, his expression that of a tortured saint. Triumph flamed through Armina. There was no greater aid to sex than having control over a man. Would he be able to hold back? Or would he suddenly come, his seed gushing out to fill her mouth and cream her face?

This was the novelty of him – he was as yet untried, a virgin when it came to the voluptuous games at which she was adept, games she had learned from promiscuous people far removed from Tayte's simple ken. She had lived and been brought up among those whose extravagant lifestyle allowed them to experiment with sensuality, refining it, glorifying it: the touch of cruelty, the hint of mystery, the realisation that a shiver of fear could give an adrenaline rush as fierce as a snort of amyl nitrate.

Tayte controlled himself with an effort. He moved away from her and lay flat on his back on the straw. Now it was Armina's turn to be mouthed. He held up his arms and she slipped between them, thighs spread open, a knee each side of his body. She still wore her white shirt. The buttons were undone all the way down, breasts jutting from the opening. Tayte supported her above him, examining those tip-tilted orbs. She was as light as a child, fragile seeming as a fairy, randy as a bitch on heat. He lifted his head, groping for her nipples with his lips, sucking hard on the right one, then the left. Armina squealed her pleasure.

Sitting back, facing him, she could feel his penis prodding the crease between her bare bottom cheeks, blindly seeking entrance to one or other of her openings. She was not in the mood for anal penetration so rose slightly, positioned her hips and impaled herself on him, feeling him drive into the farthest depths of her vagina. Closing her eyes, she pumped furiously on the mighty, glistening organ, creamy now with her juices, while Tayte fastened his hands round her breasts, pinching the rosebud teats with his fingers.

Armina could feel the force gathering in her, tingling along her spine to the small of her back, flooding through her womb. She ground herself down on Tayte's pubis, hoping this friction might bring on her orgasm. But it was too harsh a pressure on the sensitive clitoris, dulling rather than sharpening sensation. She needed the delicate mouthing he had given her before. Her body readied itself as she knelt above him, legs opened wide around his head.

Tayte stared at the depilated area, still an exciting novelty to him, the pussy hair removed in a way he had never before seen in a grown woman, her mound silky smooth to the touch, the delicate pink flesh divided neatly, swollen lips fully exposed, clitoris standing up proud. It expressed Armina's disregard for modesty; this flamboyant display of her womanhood was a statement of her defiant, hedonistic view of life.

His tongue was waiting for her when she lowered herself on his face. It flicked unerringly across her nub, tiny, darting, butterfly-light caresses, tip on tip, till she could feel her control dissolving. She moved her hips backwards and forwards, very carefully so as not to disturb the rising excitement as he sucked her love-button, flicked it with his tongue, ravished it with firm, steady strokes. Armina gasped, her groin heavy with need, a light sheen of sweat dewing her Dresden china complexion. Heat poured through her. The stable span in space. She came in a sudden, merciless rush, yowling like a female cat speared by a tom's spiky probe. Tayte shifted her down, even as she clung to him in ecstasy. He worked the head of his enormous shaft along her sex-lips, slick with saliva and vaginal juice, then sheathed it in her. The spasms still roiling through her, she lunged against him, riding him hard, inner muscles contracting joyfully round his bar of solid flesh.

Molten waves fused them together, till she finally collapsed on his chest, his replete and softening cock slipping from inside her.

It was comforting to be met at a strange station, Karen decided, stepping from the corridor to the platform. She was cramped from sitting too long, drowsy, hair ruffled where she had rested against the back of the seat. In all, she was not feeling her best, thinking, *I'm glad it's Tony and not Lord Burnet who'll be taking me to Blackwood Towers*.

There was nothing remarkable about Exeter Station. It was filled with tourists and students seeking temporary employment, with the usual gaggle of goofy-looking train spotters in hooded anoraks and spectacles, on a mission, clipboards and ballpoints at the ready.

455

Karen found the atmosphere nostalgic. Too often she had stood on similar platforms when shunted back to school or off to stay with relatives during the vacations, her parents too busy to be bothered with her. Some people found trains exciting, their fumes hinting at adventure, but they only served to depress her.

Once they had been sooty, dirty, littered. Now some bright spark had ordered a clean up. Freshly painted plastic benches; sterile canteens, toilets and newsagents; large notices proclaiming primly that this was a smoke-free zone and would passengers kindly put out their cigarettes. But no one had been able to stop maverick pigeons dropping their white-grey shit with Rabelaisian disregard for rules and regulations.

'Bloody hell,' commented Tony, a rebel himself, ignoring the edict, a Marlboro held defiantly between his fingers as he took her outstretched hand in his free one. 'How doom-laden everything is these days. We users of the weed are persecuted. "Oh, my God! He's turning me into a passive smoker! Off with his head!"' He bent to kiss her cheek. 'You look good enough to eat, Karen. Better still, good enough to fuck. Are you well?'

'Very well, thank you, Tony, and you're looking positively Bohemian. Doesn't Lord Burnet object to his librarian wearing cutoffs?'

Tony's lips curled into a smile, lighting up his sharp hazel eyes and bearded face. 'He doesn't give a toss as long as I do my job without bothering him.'

He picked up her case and put a guiding arm round her. Soon they were outside, brilliant sunshine slicing through the shadows. Tony slung the luggage in the back of a gunmetal-grey Vogue SE Range Rover, singing out, 'All aboard the *Skylark*!'

'Posh,' Karen remarked, for the sturdy vehicle was shiny new.

'That's nothing, love. There are half a dozen cars to chose from. I thought you'd like a ride in this. I enjoy driving it, anyway. Makes me feel like Indiana Jones, or a genteman farmer, depending on mood and fancy.'

'I was thinking of buying one of my own, something small, you know.' Karen sat back in the passenger seat and fastened the belt as he wheeled recklessly out of the regulation parking area and headed through the streets. They were packed with herds of loitering visitors gazing, mesmerised, at the multitude of gift shops, burger bars and stores.

'Emmets,' Tony sneered disparagingly, jerking his head at them. 'We have to put up with this invasion during the summer. It's far worse at the coast. There we get the others, the caravan clubbers and amateur sailors. Every weekend they come trolling down, towing their mobile homes and boats, cars crammed with children, dogs, grannies. It's enough to drive one back to the Smoke.'

Karen glanced at him from the corner of her eye. He had not changed much, still acerbic, still handsome in a craggy sort of way. His brown beard threaded with grey, long hair pulled back in a pony-tail. He was tall enough to top her, his shoulders were broad beneath a black sleeveless vest. His tanned arms, chest and legs were bare and his supple waist and lean hips were confined in a pair of shorts with frayed hems. These had once been jeans. Tony had simply taken the scissors and performed an above the knee amputation. He wore nothing on his feet.

Karen's clit stirred, warmed by memories. *Once I hero-worshipped him,* she thought. *Hung around after school, just on the off chance of seeing him. Jail bait. But I was sixteen and past the age of consent before I succeeded in persuading him to seduce me.*

The twitch of a smile beside his mouth told her that he was aware and remembering. 'Water under the bridge, Karen,' he remarked.

'Gallons of it.'

'You're not married.' He glanced at the third finger of her left hand, but this told him nothing. She wore large rings on every finger, casual and hippyish in dress, inclining towards flowing Indian cottons, baggy palazzo pants, loose tops and sandals. 'Divorced? Engaged? A regular boyfriend?'

'No. Fancy-free.'

'Good. So am I.'

This could have meant anything or nothing at all, but she was painfully conscious of his bare thigh close to hers on the seat (his shorts really were short) and those sensitive hands with the manicured nails handling the gears with the expertise they had once used on her eager pussy. How sweet it would be to repeat that journey from innocence to awakening, but how impossible.

Karen would have liked to linger in Exeter: the cathedral was reputed to be worth a look. But Tony was hellbent on getting out of the congested

458

traffic. They left the town, skirting a roundabout and driving along the bypass.

'No hurry,' he said. 'We'll take the scenic route. Can't stand motorways.'

The secondary road rose and fell, curved and straightened, presenting an enchanting, picture-postcard vista of valleys sweeping up to rolling hills as graceful and smooth as a young girl's breasts. Their sweet tips were constantly changing from green to blue through to mauve according to the passage of cumulus across the sun.

'It's wonderful,' Karen exclaimed, tiredness forgotten, leaning forward in her seat, waiting eagerly for the next panorama.

'Not been in Devon before?' Tony asked, amused by her enthusiasm and sorely tempted to tackle the button-through skirt of her flower-patterned dress or untie the shoestring straps. The dress was long, flowing between her thighs, pressing against her mound. The skinny girl had been replaced by a queenly woman.

'No, never.' Karen linked her hands in her lap. Beneath them she could feel the ridge of the briefs that barely covered her pubic hair. Already the crotch was wet with her juices, her belly aching for love. This was the effect Tony had always had on her.

'You haven't lived till you've scoffed back a Devonshire tea of home-made scones and straw-berry jam obscenely loaded with cream as thick as bulls' spunk. We'll stop when we find a decent café.' He looked at her sideways, grinning puck-ishly. 'Darling, you haven't changed one bit. Still the wide-eyed ingenue who'd never come till I showed her how.'

459

Karen could feel a blush heating her face. He had an uncanny knack of reading her thoughts. She darted a glance at him, the tip of her tongue coming out to lick over her coral lips. 'Trust you to remind me of that.'

'Sweetheart, don't try to kid me that you've never thought of it.' He reached across and fondled her knee. 'Maybe you'd care to show your old teach what you've learned since.'

'Maybe I would.' She placed her hand on top of his. His grip tightened, his touch evocative, sending shocks through her nipples and clitoris in unison.

One peaked brow shot up, and his eyes twinkled mischievously as he said, 'Meanwhile, light up a couple of cigarettes and pass one over.'

Now the lanes were narrower, lined by thick hedges. Five-barred gates afforded glimpses of lush meadows polka-dotted with buttercups where *café au lait* Jersey cows with heavy udders stood chewing the cud beneath shady trees. The vehicle careered over little stone hump backed bridges spanning gurgling streams and through picturesque villages where irregularly built thatched cottages leaned against each other like besotted lovers.

Tony braked outside one of them. It had a 'Cream Teas' placard propped against its lobelia-festooned dry-stone wall. Seated in the garden at a rickety table beneath a big striped sunshade, they smiled at one another, that easy smile born of friendship, good sex and genuine affection.

'You like living down here?' she asked as the apple-cheeked, beaming waitress went off with their order. Tony watched her retreating, her backside swaying tantalisingly beneath a miniskirt.

'Sure I like it here. It's fine. Quiet off season. The villagers consist of well-heeled professionals who can operate their businesses just as easily in the country, with the occasional foray into town.'

'Tasty women?' Karen loved him for his out-and-out admiration of the female of the species. He liked their minds as well as their bodies, finding them much more diverse and interesting than men.

'Sure, though they all seem to be studying aromatherapy. It's the in thing. Dozens of 'em of all ages, shapes and sizes, eager and willing to practise on one. I think they'd be naughty if they'd only let themselves go. It's also considered groovy to be on the self-sufficiency jag and to join the barter system.'

'What's that?' University had not prepared her for this entirely different culture. She had some vague notion that rural entertainment consisted of baking cakes for church fetes or helping to run jumble sales in the village hall.

'Everyone offers a skill of some sort, like, "I'll muck out your cesspit if you supply me with organic vegetables." Very quaint, my dear. As fashionable as giving up smoking and risking a coronary on the jogging circuit.' There was a sardonic slant to Tony's mobile, humorous mouth. 'The men are keen – when it comes to saving money on the domestic front, I guess. When I was asked if I'd like to add to the list and contribute something, I wrote "Raw Sex". It went down with the husbands like a pork chop in a synagogue.'

461

'I'll bet it did. You're incorrigible.'

'I hope so.'

The waitress sashayed across, arch and flirtatious as she placed the tea things in front of Tony and leaned across to arrange them. Her blouse was semi-transparent and her big, jiggling breasts crowned with nipples like organ stops brushed momentarily against his shoulder.

'It's my charisma,' he explained with a wide smile as the girl reluctantly retired.

Karen knew all about that, honeyed fluid seeping from her sex as she longed to have him toy with her. She put a curb on her wayward thoughts. It was no use. She simply had to be more businesslike in her dealings with him. The situation had changed. Hadn't it?

'What's he like?' she asked, deliberately cool as she cut into a floury, dusky-capped scone. A plate heaped with more stood on the white cloth. The cream was clotted, yellow and delectably lumpy; the jam contained whole, succulent strawberries glinting like overblown rubies in a tsar's crown.

'Our boss, the marquis? Some say he's a hero, others that he's an objectionable, arrogant bastard.' Tony shrugged, pantomiming with his expressive hands. 'He's a pig. He's a saint. He seduces and betrays women. He's an honourable gentleman. He cheats. He's overbearing. Abominable. He's a good mate. It depends where you stand, who you are and what you need from him.' He picked up the brown earthenware teapot. 'Shall I be mother?'

'Please,' she nodded. 'I'll keep an open mind.'

'You do that,' he answered solemnly, passing her a cup of tea. 'We needed you down here

462

because Lord Burnet has some fat-cat American businessman interested in the library.'

'He's not selling?' This was a horrible idea. Karen hated to see any part of English heritage disappearing overseas.

'No, no. He talked to me about it some time ago. Seems he met this guy in California and he's an Anglophile, wants to own some of the more valuable works but is content to leave them where they are. Lord Burnet seems to agree with him that it would be a good idea to open the house and library to the public.'

'He can't need the money, can he?' Somehow she had imagined that a marquis would be beyond financial stress.

'Not in the way you and I think of, but he did have to pay the most crippling death duties when he inherited.' Tony's eyes twinkled as he added, 'The American's coming over and the library has to be got into shape pretty damn quick. Hence your involvement.'

He leaned closer. There was a smear of cream on her lips. He carefully removed it, licking the tip of his finger where it had touched her mouth, the cream still warm from contact with her tongue. She felt her womb contract involuntarily, as though wanting to suck him into her. She glanced down. His arousal was obvious.

Legs apart, he had positioned himself in such a way that she could see the top of his penis peeping out through the fringed hem of his cutoffs. A pearly drop glistened at its single eye; the red glans was swollen, bare of foreskin. Was the shining head less sensitive or more without its fleshy sheath? Karen wondered, never able to make up her mind which she preferred – the cut or uncut male?

Tony grinned, mind-reading again. 'Yep, it's ready for you, girl. Ready and raring to go. I'll take you on a guided tour of my humble abode before we go to the big house. You'll love my antique bed.'

Karen did not realise they had entered the Blackwood estate until they were a couple of miles inside. Then the surrounding area became more woody, and there was a noticeable absence of vehicles. No other living person was anywhere in sight.

They drove along a sandy road surrounded on either side by tall pines, stately beeches, oaks and ash with verdant grass carpeting the avenues and ridges between. A dazzling display of rhododendrons, with blue and pink blooms drooping as if worn out by excesses, sheltered in the arms of leathery bottle-green leaves. There was a momentary glimpse of deer heads raised alertly as they paused before vanishing with a quick white flash of their scuts.

All was silent, except for birdsong. Lord Burnet's kingdom.

'Where's the house?' She was eager to view her employer's domain.

'Further on. I've a cottage near the spinney. It goes with the job. You'll get one, too. Convenient. Not far from the pub.' Tony swung the Range Rover down a shady lane at the end of which stood a small dwelling with ivy swarming over its walls.

Tiny dormer windows stared down like curious eyes watching from beneath a fringe of thatch as he drove through the gates and pulled up on the gravel. Karen was surprised by the well-tended garden with its shell-edged path. There were wild flowers in the borders and geraniums in large clay pots on the cobbles outside the front door. Honeysuckle and roses rioted around the door unchecked, forming a scented arch.

Karen felt Tony's touch on her shoulder, then he unlocked the door and entered first, saying, 'Mind you don't bump your head. The beams are low in some places.'

There was no hall. One simply walked straight into the living-room, and the cosy intimacy of it made her heart thump and her blood quicken. She was a girl again, alone with her teacher. He was forbidden fruit, irresistibly alluring and dangerous.

The cottage was plainly furnished, centuries old with two-foot thick walls and low latticed windows. A fireplace occupied most of one side. Inside it were seats and the pitted cast-iron door of a bread oven.

'I don't use it,' Tony said, moving to the sideboard and picking up a bottle. 'The supermarket does a marvellously unhealthy white sliced loaf. I buy half a dozen at a time and bung 'em in the freezer. Thank God for progress. D'you want a drink?'

'Yes, please.' Tension was coiling tightly in her loins. She could almost see it flowering, a pulsing, throbbing crimson. *My chakra*, she thought. *The core of my being. My sex.*

'The bedroom's upstairs.' He lifted a salver containing glasses, the gin, mixers and a freshly filled ice tub.

Karen nodded and followed him up a winding flight of stairs leading from a doorway next to the fireplace. There was no landing. A few steps, and she was standing beneath the low attic ceiling. The windows were on a level with the uneven floor. They were open. The smell of roses crept in.

It was a strictly masculine room: a mirror supported on a dressing table, a built-in wardrobe, a chest of drawers and a wide mahogany bed, neatly made, the duvet pulled straight.

'You keep your house very tidy,' she commented, remembering vividly the chaos of his flat, the floor strewn with books and papers, the dilapidated settee where she had lost her cherry.

'I've a woman who "does".' He put the tray on the bedside table. Gin and tonic splashed into the glasses, topped with shaved ice and a twist of lemon.

'Here's to my assistant librarian,' Tony said, smiling into her eyes as he toasted her. 'I recommended you for your abilities, not because I expected to screw you, though I'll admit that wasn't far from my thoughts.'

'Wicked, wicked tutor,' she murmured, leaning into him, nipples aching to feel his fingers rotating on their tender tips.

'I am. An unabashed scoundrel.'

He put down his glass, took hers away and nestled her in his arms. His fingers roamed her face, tracing the line of her neck to the lobe of her ear, setting the dangling hoop swinging. Karen sighed and tingled, the caress awakening a pleasurable echo in her epicentre.

'You smell yummy, like patchouli and *chypre*,'

he whispered in that husky, totally captivating way of his. Then he tongued the rim of her ear and kissed the lobe. Karen moaned. She could feel the warmth and quickness of his breath, her increasing wetness dampening her knickers.

He was becoming as excited as her, the solid rod of his penis pressing against her pubis through the censoring denim and her cotton skirt. His mouth was soft, working its way across her cheek to the corner of her lips and resting there. She relished the gentle, seductive warmth, then opened her mouth to him, her tongue like a fiery arrow winging to meet his.

'Ummm,' he sighed appreciatively, removing his lips from hers. 'You always were my star pupil.'

It was Tony's habit to make love with words as well as caresses, and this was one of the most exciting things about him. Karen was warmed right through by his kisses, feeling relaxed and languid. He guided her to the bed, laid her on the pillows, hands hovering over her breasts as if they were ripe fruit about to be plucked from a tree. Karen arched her back, thrusting them up to meet his touch, the chafing of her bodice excitingly acute against the pink, needy crests.

Then Tony proceeded to do what he had wanted to do since seeing her at Exeter Station. Fingers on the front of her dress, he started to open the buttons slowly until her naked breasts were exposed to his admiring gaze.

He cupped one, his thumbnail scratching across the tip. Karen jerked, writhed her hips, strained to meet that tormenting arousal, labia thickening, but thrumming in response, pleasure gathering in her vagina. Not content with having her bare to the waist, he continued with the unbuttoning until the dress fell open either side of her long, slim legs, exposing her narrow waist, flat belly and wisps of chestnut bush showing above the triangle of white cotton hiding her mound. Karen held her breath as he leaned above her, filling his eyes with the sight of her and his nostrils with the aroma of her salty, piscine lubrication.

'You're beautiful,' he whispered, voice thick with desire. 'Very, very beautiful.'

He bent to suck hard at one nipple, his fingers busy with the other, a double feast of pleasure augmented by the tingling rush of blood hardening her clitoris. Concentrating on each breast in turn, he sucked and nibbled, using his tongue, and her nipples seemed to grow larger, as if trying to fill his whole mouth. Karen's hand slid down, pushing aside her panties, unable to resist dipping into her slippery cleft, wetting a finger and fondling her nub that strained out of its tiny cowl.

'Let me,' he said, and she felt his finger fluttering over her pussy, stroking her through the panties, tracing the deep line that scored the centre, then lowering his head and nibbling at it through the fabric.

She surrendered to his hungry mouth, feeling the warm, wet drag of his lips and the delicious frisson of the thin material over her clit head, the brush of his beard against her skin. Her lower lips swelled with blood, the humid heat in her vagina turning to hot lava.

'Do it like you did that first time,' she begged.

She could feel his chuckle vibrating through her and he raised himself on his arms, staring at her from between her legs, chin resting lightly on her mons. 'All this time, and you've remembered, I had an idea you might.'

'A woman never forgets the man who took her virginity,' she assured him, her breathing jerky

'So the pundits say,' he replied. He moved round to the side of the bed and lay beside her.

Karen turned to him, held him tightly, her open-mouthed kisses leaving beads of moisture on his beard. He smelled of her juices, tasted of the nectar soaking her knickers. He bit her lower lip, drew it into his mouth, his tongue sliding inside, skimming along the roof to tickle the back of her throat.

'Oh, yes. That's how you began.'

She was feeling playful, as she had done on that occasion in his flat, playful and fearful all at the same time. Her hands skimmed over his shoulders, dipped into the opening at the top of his vest, teased his crisp brown chest hair, tweaked his small male nipples.

'But you didn't do that,' he gasped.

'Didn't I?' She wriggled against him, tugging at his belt.

He helped her, swiftly stripping away his clothes. His body was lean, sun browned, the body of a mature man; wiry, strong, with hard muscles and firm flesh trimmed by walking and riding rather than faddy exercise routines.

Her hand closed round his erect penis, thrusting from the thick hair coating his underbelly. She was fascinated by its shaft, brown skinned, corded with bluish veins, supporting the massive, gleaming naked head. Her hand moved to cradle his testicles, testing their weight. These were not boyish cods, but solid orbs dangling in their hairy net, ripe with the promise of fulfilment; the balls of an older man who has made love to many women.

Tony laughed with the joy of the moment, tipping her face to his mouth, feeding on her lips. 'You've learned a lot.'

'I have. Now I want to share it with you, but first let's pretend we're back in your flat. Treat me as you did that day.'

Tony smiled tenderly and began to weave his magic. He settled her comfortably on the bed. First her toes were caressed and licked, each one receiving attention, then her ankles, his lips coasting up her calves, across her knees, the insides of her thighs. She quivered, her ultra sensitive skin stippled with goose-bumps, responding to every touch.

When he reached the barrier of her panties he parted her legs slightly and squeezed the prominent swell of the hidden mound, then slipped a finger round one side and rubbed the furry bush. He watched her face, seeing her rapt expression, carefully judging every move.

'Oh, Tony,' she whimpered, clutching him round the neck, burying her face in his unbound hair.

'Hush, darling. Wait – that's right.'

He pushed down her briefs and she helped him, squirming out of them. He trailed a finger back and forth across her sex-lips and kissed her, his tongue relishing hers, till it seemed there was nothing but tongues and tasting. She shivered in the grip of passion, wanted to draw him into her very centre, but more than that she needed him to bring her to orgasm.

Then she felt the compelling combination of tongue and hand as he gently opened her labia, stroking the damp aisle, then sliding a finger into her vagina while keeping his thumb on her pulsing clit, never stopping that enticing friction. She could feel the pre-orgasm tremors flowing along her thighs, and he too was as aware as if they were his own. His fingers sunk in further and she moaned loudly, beginning the ascent, reaching that perilous plateau where it was possible to stick if disturbed. No disturbance or frustration today, however. She was in the hands of a master.

He paid homage to that glorious bud of flesh, tenderly caressing its stem, fondling it on each side to prolong the sensation, and the head ached and swelled, shiny like a gem amidst its plump hood and guardian pink lips. He had positioned himself so that he could look at it, flick it, tease it, have it almost speak its need. They worked together, he and Karen's clitoris, and his timing was perfect. Never for a moment did he allow her to become bored, varying his touch, sometimes feather-light and slow, sometimes fierce and rapid, but always holding off when she began to peak.

'I want it,' she implored, trembling.

'In a while.'

'Now, please!'

'Now? You really want it now?'

'Yes, yes.' Her climax was hovering, waiting for the next slow slide of his finger over her clitoris which would bring her to the peak.

He smiled, kissing the tips of her stone-hard

nipples, hearing her short, sharp cries and rewarding her eagerness with a steady, unstoppable friction. Karen felt the heat surging up, dying back, surging higher. Nothing could prevent her coming, and the spasms poured through her, bringing joyous relief.

As her body shook with pleasure, Tony slipped his eager penis into her, and she heard herself laughing joyfully at the unadulterated perfection of their coupling, a roller-coaster of delight.

Chapter Three

TONY LED KAREN up the meandering, holly-hock-bordered path to a house not far from his own. The whitewashed walls were dappled with ochre lichen and cushiony green moss. He produced a key and opened the oak front door, standing back with a flourish so she might enter.

'*Voilà, madame*! Your very own country retreat.'

'The marquis has given this to me?' It was more than she had expected.

'Not exactly, dear. It's a tied cottage. Part of your wages. If you stop working for him you're out, lock, stock and barrel. Nothing is for nothing. These were designed especially to quarter the lord of the manor's peons – field hands, grounds-men and foresters. Slavery wasn't invented by the Americans.'

It was a carbon copy of Tony's cottage. A basic one up, one down, with the later addition of a kitchen and bathroom built on at the back.

'There's not much room.' Karen humped her holdall up the stairs and set it down on the patch-work quilt spread over the double bed.

Tony followed her, a suitcase in either hand. 'I'm told it wasn't unusual for the serfs to raise upwards of twenty children in one of these. In the summer the older kids were sent out to sleep on the common.'

Karen shuddered. 'And they call them the good old days?'

'Oh, they were – for the upper crust. Still are, my dear. You'll see when you've been here a few days and learnt about Lord Burnet's habits.'

'I can't wait,' Karen said ironically, beginning to resent this high and mighty personage who had not yet deigned to meet her.

The kitchen had every amenity: blue Delftware tiles, a washing machine, tumble dryer, cathedral-style light-oak units and matching leaded-glass wall cupboards. The fridge-freezer was stocked with essentials: milk with a two-inch layer of gold-tinted cream, primrose butter, a wedge of tongue-tingling Cheddar cheese. A farmhouse loaf with a mouth-watering crusty brown top sheltered in the bread bin. There were reliable stand-bys in the larder – baked beans, tuna fish and plum tomatoes – and cleaning materials in the under sink unit.

The bathroom was decorated with whimsical old-world charm. A floral-patterned ceramic washbasin, a free-standing bath on brass claw feet, a matching bidet and a lavatory with a polished wood seat. 'Thank heavens, it's been modernised!' Karen exclaimed, growing ever more delighted with her residence.

'All these new-fangled gismos,' Tony remarked, leaning a broad shoulder against the tiled shower stall. 'What's wrong with using a communal crapper in the back-yard and having a swill under the pump?'

'Shut up! I hadn't noticed you were averse to mod cons.' She went to brush past him, but his arm snaked out and clipped her round the waist.

'What about having a shower together?' he suggested, hands sliding down to fondle her buttocks, a finger slipping between to trace the tight nether orifice.

'What about showing me the big house?' I mustn't get too dependent on him, she thought, though unable to resist grinding her pubis against the swell of his prick. *One fuck with him is enough for today. He may start getting possessive, and I want to be free to explore every possibility.*

'Tonight suit you? Then we'll go down to the harbour for a drink.'

'Give me half an hour to change.'

When he had gone, she took a quick shower, then carried out Kan's meditation technique while making up her face. Dreamily she studied her reflection in the dressing-table mirror as she applied brownish-black mascara to her curling lashes. Not too much make-up; pencil-thin grey eyeliner where the socket deepened, a touch of white powder on the lids, a smear of bronze at the outer corners blended with the tip of her little finger. This served to make her eyes larger, brighter, greener. Carefully she brushed over her lips with rose blusher. She had no intention of going out looking tarty, just in case Lord Burnet had returned from his wanderings.

What to wear? The scarlet-edged evening cast long shadows over the trees, sculpting sepia spaces between them. It was cooler, so she opted for baggy cream and brown patterned trousers in cotton crepe that enhanced rather than concealed the length of her legs, a beige T-shirt plunging in a deep V beneath her breasts and a loose nutmeg waistcoat in fine crochet.

Images drifted through her mind, too formless to be called thoughts. She was determined to get that black belt and intended to seek out a local *dojo*, if such a thing existed. If not, what was to stop her opening one of her own? She knew enough about the art. This would give her an excuse for getting in contact with Kan. The thought of his bronzed body and lusty, uplifted cock made her cunt ache with hunger, juice seeping out to bedew her freshly shampooed pubic floss.

Gritting her teeth against this forceful spasm of desire, she centred her mind on her career. This was of prime importance. Her parents expected her to be an achiever, but she was ambitious on her own account – impatient to get started, wanting to meet her employer.

Where was it Tony said he had gone? To India? To the Seychelles? Feathery palms, white sand, a clear blue ocean lapping a tropical beach floated before her inner vision, and a mysterious man, his back turned towards her.

She asked Tony again when he picked her up half an hour later. 'Where's the boss vacationing?'

'First Goa, then the States.'

He also had changed; a lawn shirt covered his muscular torso, and he wore loosely cut linen pants that fitted his trim waist snugly and seemed to emphasise the fullness behind the fly. Able to afford the best, he wore the latest line in leather thong sandals designed by Gucci.

'Have the mistresses gone too?' She picked up her canvas shoulder bag ever so casually, as if His Lordship's amours were of no possible interest to her.

'The mistresses? How sweetly old-fashioned.' His quirky smile lifted those bearded lips, and she knew he saw through her pretence. 'I presume you're referring to his strumpets? Dear me, I didn't think you'd stoop to reading the gutter press.'

'I developed a taste for the gossip columns when I knew I was to be working here. Didn't you always teach me that forewarned is forearmed? Isn't it true he keeps a dozen women?'

'No. He keeps four at present. The paparazzi have got it wrong again.'

'Ha! Only four? Poor deprived man!'

Tony was finding her reaction highly entertaining. Ever since he had known her she had been a romantic, harbouring dreams of chivalrous knights on white chargers, though she would have denied it with every last breath in her gorgeous body. Presumably she had somehow slotted Lord Burnet into this category and wasn't taking kindly to being disillusioned.

'He hasn't taken them on holiday,' he supplied as they walked to the Range Rover. 'Never does. Goes into retreat at times. An unpredictable person who likes his own company. He has the makings of a recluse, though you'll find that hard to believe.'

The evening was glorious, pouring over the parched land like *après-soleil* milk on a sunbather's skin, soothing away the heat of the day. The fosse-like lane enfolded them in secretive green.

Noisy conclaves of rooks gyrated over the tops of the trees, seeking night-time roosts.

Karen was on the edge of her seat, straining against the belt that crossed and divided her breasts, eager for her first glimpse of Blackwood Towers. The road descended into a broad valley of parkland, and then she saw the house, dozing there as it had done for centuries. It was surrounded by hills and hanging woods. The sunset was reflected in a mass of bayed, mullioned windows, turning them to fire. Blackwood Towers fulfilled all her hopes, blending with the sky, the landscape and the country around it as it it had stuck down roots and grown from the soil rather than owing its creation to man.

Karen fell in love with it immediately, and for ever.

'I've never seen anything like it,' she breathed, enraptured.

'It began as a priory in the sixteenth century, then the land was acquired by the Burnet founding-father, through skulduggery, no doubt,' Tony said as they cruised down the long, gradual slope leading to the front of the house.

'Was he dishonest?' Karen was intrigued, bewitched, already falling under the manor's powerful spell.

'Probably. Descended from Norman robber barons like most of England's aristocracy Anyhow, he knocked down the ecclesiastical buildings and erected this massive pile in the Italianate style. It's way over the top.'

They circled the stone basin of the fountain, where a mighty bronze Titan, flaunting a phallus nearby as big as his trident, sported with adoring Junoesque water nymphs. Gravel sprayed out from under the Range Rover's wheels, and the vehicle rocked to a halt at the bottom of a flight of wide steps. The facade of the house was even more impressive close up. There were larger than life statues of Greek gods and Roman heroes in niches between the windows, and a long balustraded and pinnacled enclosure with domed pavilions at the corners. The front door was huge, set back under a towering portico resembling that of a mausoleum.

'We'll use the tradesmen's entrance,' Tony said. 'The indoor staff aren't here at present. Just a caretaker to tend the burglar alarms.'

He was exaggerating as usual, and the door he used to admit them led to a private stair to the library. 'I'll give you a duplicate key,' he promised. 'You'll be working here without me sometimes. You won't be scared, will you? Not afraid of ghosts?'

'I've yet to be convinced they exist,' she replied, overawed by the magnificence surrounding her. The library was as long and wide as a ballroom, wainscotted in oak, every surface richly carved and inlaid, with an elaborate chimney-piece and pedimented doors.

The tall, recessed casements were hung with damask drapes held back by cords with long tassels. The windows overlooked the formal knot garden laid out like a complicated embroidery, and a sweeping green lawn guarded by sentinel trees.

There were books everywhere, lurking on tables, piled on the floor, snoozing behind the glass doors of specially constructed shelves; old books, rare books, first editions, folios.

'Some are worth the proverbial king's ransom.' There was a touch of pride in Tony's voice, as if he was somehow personally responsible for garnering such a collection. 'So valuable that no insurance company will risk taking them on. It's the only place where I agree with non smoking.'

'Do we have to sort them?' She wandered round, running a caressing finger over the bookcases, craning her neck to look up at the ceiling with its overpowering design of wreaths and straps. As far as she was concerned, this was paradise.

'Are you computer friendly?' He answered her question with one of his own.

'Sure. No graphics, but I can handle a mouse and a key board, data base, spreadsheets and word processing.'

In an adjoining office was state of the art equipment, more advanced even than that which she had used at Oxford. It was odd to see the latest technology standing on a desk that had once belonged to the Emperor Napoleon, in a room hung with Flemish tapestries.

Tony patted the machine fondly. 'I'm tempted to call it Hal – though I hope it'll never take it upon itself to be rebellious.'

'Computers can't think. They're only as good as their programmers,' Karen reminded him sedately, seating herself in the operator's chair, which was upholstered in chocolate-brown leather. It had hydraulic lift and swivelled at a touch.

'Nice,' she added, feeling the upholstery squish

beneath her bottom and drag the seam of her pants tighty between her pouting pussy lips. She savoured the piquant smell of the top-quality animal hide.

'We're on the Net.' Tony perched on a corner of the desk, one leg swinging lazily, the other braced on the Turkish carpet. 'And we can link up with any library or university in the world.'

'Useful. Have you entered any data yet?'

'Some.' He was looking at her speculatively. The rich light falling from the stained glass of an oriel window complemented her colouring. It gave a fierce lustre of her burnished chestnut hair and flushed her skin as he had seen it flush during the little death of orgasm.

Tony's penis rose and hardened in response to Karen's beauty and hot recollections of the afternoon's coupling. He focused on her lips, so sensually perfect. Was it only an hour or so ago she had used her mouth on his cock, lipping, sucking, tasting it? A mouth that had mastered the art of fellatio.

He had never lacked sexual partners, but the memory of his clever, ardent, passionately eager pupil had remained with him down the years. The reality of shafting her again had exceeded his wildest dreams. Now the thought of having her with him day after day was wildly exhilarating, sending the blood pulsing through his stiff organ.

'My God, Karen, just feel what you do to me,' he whispered. Instinctively she curled her fingers around his turgid prick, the heat of it burning tantalisingly through his trousers.

He reached out and touched the tip of her breast. At once it bunched, the taut cone pressing against her T-shirt. He moved closer and, still fondling his bulge, Karen sat back in the chair, one leg thrown over the other, squeezing her thighs together to bring pressure to bear on her clitoris.

There was something powerfully erotic about the glorious interior of Blackwood Towers. Generations of Burnets had fucked there – not only husbands and wives but, no doubt, a multitude of illicit lovers as well. It was as if the tumescence, liquid arousal and violent pleasure of these people from the past had impregnated the walls. She could almost see them dressed in period costume, ruffles and lace, trooped skirts and powdered wigs. Her mind slipped notches, filled with swirling coloured lights and images of fornicating couples.

How on earth am I going to work here? she wondered. *I shall be in a permanent state of excitation.*

'I've something to show you.' Tony's voice brought her back to herself. 'It's the pride of the library. Only the privileged are permitted a viewing. I've orders to take extra special care of such a rarity, particularly in light of the Yankee millionaire's interest.'

He had the key to an inner sanctum, hidden by a door cunningly constructed to look like a bookcase. It was even lined with fake volumes, their spines meticulously engraved and painted. The small room was simply furnished, its only ornamentation a gilt-framed mirror. Tony unlocked a walnut cabinet with a further set of keys. It contained several large, shallow drawers, and from the ton one he lifted a sheaf of yellowing cartridge paper covered with black and white drawings. Karen, tingling with anticipation and curiosity, watched as he spread them out on the surface of a mahogany table of Georgian vintage.

She glanced down at the first and then stared harder, arrested by the subject. 'My God!' she breathed in a husky whisper.

Tony gave a slow smile, his eyes bright. 'I thought you'd appreciate them. They're much more inventive than even Giulio Romano's illustrations of Pietro Aretino's smutty poems, *Sonetti Lussuriosi*.'

'Aren't they just!' She had seen copies of the pornographic Renaissance pictures representing the various 'postures' of sexual intercourse. 'Much later, of course.'

'Eighteenth century.'

'By Hogarth, or James Gilray, Thomas Rowlandson – George Cruikshank?' Her throat felt dry. It was hard to speak. Try as she might to be sensible, lust washed through her in gigantic waves.

'No,' he said, and she knew by his tone he was picking up on her feelings. 'An unknown artist produced these cartoons. He used the pseudonym of Dick Bedwell. No one is sure of his true identity. This leads to much heated debate among connoisseurs, which is strange, considering how few have actually seen the originals.'

The drawings were beautifully executed, explicit and detailed, the nearest thing to photography produced at that time. The first example, coyly titled *The Morning Toilette*, was of a lady reclining on a four-poster bed, skirts hitched high, exposing the dark wisps coating her mons veneris. Her legs were wide apart and her maid knelt between them, while another servant leaned across, fingers toying with her mistress's large bare nipples.

Their costumes were typical of the era in which they had been immortalised; mob caps, low necklines, tightly laced corsets pushing breasts high, crested teats protruding over the tops of bodices, flounced petticoats, stockings rolled below the knee and fastened with lacy garters, Louis-heeled shoes with paste buckles. And, most important of all, they were pantiless, this having been an age when it was considered immodest to wear drawers, which were considered male garments.

The faces of Bedwell's sitters had been captured for all time, lasciviously curved Cupid's-bow lips, heavy eyelids, the kneeling girl ecstatic as she held back the fleshy hood and licked the tip of the recumbent woman's clitoris. This vital little organ was drawn with amazing accuracy, as if the artist had spent much time closely studying how it poked from the embrace of the furled and thickened lips, glistening with droplets of love juice. A handsome young dandy in a queue wig and frilled shirt, his breeches agape, was half hidden by the curtains, stroking himself to erection as he watched them with a lecherous smile.

Despite herself Karen could feel heat spreading between her thighs, her pussy moistening even more. Most cartoons of that period were crudely done, the lowest kind of rude representation intended for the masses, but these were brilliant and subtle. It was as much as she could do to keep her hand away from her pubis, the warmth doubled by the knowledge that Tony was sharing the same almost uncontrollable emotions.

He brought out the rest, one after the other, an exotic feast of sensual delights, each more daring and innovative than the last. There was one of a woman wearing vaguely Eastern dress suggestive of a harem. She was on all fours, bending over so that her pudendum was in full view: the shadowed area between her legs, the plump wet labia fringed with hair. Her mouth encompassed the turgid prick of the youth beneath her. An older man straddled her, about to thrust a truly spectacular twelve-inch cock into the depths of her forbidden rear entrance. A beautiful slave girl lay beside them, fingering the woman's enlarged clit.

Tony watched slyly as Karen's tongue passed over her lips rapaciously and her hands crept up to cup her breasts, cheeks pink as she scrutinised each picture avidly.

There were idyllic gardens with girls on swings, skirts flying high, showing sturdy thighs and the peach-like bloom of dewy pubes amid a froth of white petticoats. Their gallants stood below, admiring the heavenly view while rubbing one another's cocks.

In contrast to the country landscapes of the period, Bedwell had sketched London's gambling dens, squalid dives with card-strewn tables, bottles standing on their sticky surfaces along with half empty glasses. The bawdy gamesters, pricks jutting out of their unfastened breeks, dropped chips down the cleavages of giggling girls. A naked whore, trussed like a chicken, lay on a trestle while they vied with one another, lobbing coins into her wide exposed cleft.

A sketch labelled *Symptoms of Sanctity* showed the interior of a monastery. A bald and very ugly monk was leering obscenely at a lovely young virgin standing before him, head bowed in prayer. The holy man's hand was resting on her bare breast while he fondled his balls with the other. They were surrounded by a rutting crowd of nuns and priests, clothing in disarray, black robes pulled up over nude backsides, each linked with another sexually by mouth, cunt, prick or anus.

The artist's imagination had known no bounds. He had drawn grand ladies entertaining swaggering grenadiers in their boudoirs, where dildoes stood in vases in place of flowers and randy maids and valets watched through window, fondling sex lips and penises. Or coaching inns where female passengers took time out to romp in the stables with well-endowed grooms. A masked highwayman pressed a lady against a carriage, her skirts whipped high as he penetated her with a weapon longer and thicker than his pistol.

The study seemed to vibrate with the heat and grind of passion as Karen viewed the hump backed beast, transvestites, flagellation; dirty old men with grotesque, distended members and huge sagging testicles; beautiful youths with spritely cocks springing eagerly from thick pubic hair, their balls firm and taut. No aspect of physical congress was left unexplored. Women with women, men with men, women with men, every variation under the sun depicted – a seething bacchanalia.

'You see how wonderful they are,' Tony said unsteadily, hand working up and down the outside of his trousers, distended and dampened by his urgent cock-head. 'It's great to look at them with you here. You, of all people, who understand and appreciate them.'

Karen's nipples and honey-pot were burning; the entire surface of her skin had become unbearably sensitive. She struggled for control. This was absurd and most unprofessional, throwing her into an ethical tizzy. She should be able to give a cool, unbiased assessment of the artistic merits of Dick Bedwell's work.

'I can see why they're so valuable,' was all she managed to gasp.

Tony pushed the drawings to the far side of the table. 'Lie down, Karen,' he said in a dark, persuasive tone.

There was no way she could deny him or herself as he pressed her back, the hard table edge cutting into her thighs. He possessed her lips hungrily, and she sighed with satisfaction at the feel of his tongue moving insidiously in the wetness of her mouth. He insinuated a hand into her T-shirt, fingers caressing her bare breasts with exquisite tenderness, then moving down to the elasticated waistband of her palazzo pants. Beneath he found the fragment of saturated cotton covering her mound.

'I'm surprised you're wearing knickers,' he whispered thickly, and wormed his way inside and teased her intimate lips with his fingers, opening the floodgates of desire for her.

Twilight filled the quiet room. Blackwood Towers enfolded them. Guardian angel of lovers, or demon of desire? Karen gave a whimpering sob of longing. 'Touch me. Touch me there,' she begged, her hand reaching down to guide his finger to her pleasure centre.

He pressed on it hard, a fiery current shooting right through her. It was too much, so she took his hand in hers, lifted it to her mouth and wetted his finger with spittle, catching the fragrance of her juices on it, tasting it, rich and fruity. Tony's eyelids closed and he grunted with pure enjoyment as her lips closed around his finger, warmly, wetly, mimicking her lower lips. She guided his hand back down, dropping her pants, the thin material whispering down to tangle round her ankles.

His saliva-coated finger stroked her clitoris softly while she supplemented her pleasure by touching the crests of her nipples, circling them, pinching and rolling them, adding to that desperate need pounding through her veins. Her climax was on its way. She grew quiet as if in a trance, and Tony lifted her by the hips so that she could slide into position on the table, spread legs bent at the knees. He pressed between them, adoring her cleft, paying homage to the jewel in the crown – her gem-hard, pink, hungry clitoris.

His fingers and tongue encouraged it to swell even more, ready to take her higher. With a long moan she reached the summit. She was rising, swirling, tossed into an intense whirlpool of sensation, screaming with delight and release.

Then Tony was on top of her. She was aware of the mahogany against her bare back as he entered her in a single stroke, plunging deep, filling her with his big, powerful dick. She knew his crisis was upon him, feeling him thrust faster, hearing his laboured breathing, seeing his long, strong neck strained backwards, the tendons bulging.

She drew up her legs, folding them round his waist, feeling his furious ride towards completion. Her inner muscles held him, adding to his pleasure as, with a loud cry, he suddenly reached his goal.

Behind the two-way mirror in the priest-hole hidden in the thickness of the wall, Armina lay back in a wing-chair. She had a leg hooked over either arm, every part of her smooth, shiny wet quim exposed. With a hand slipped between her avenue, she worked her clitoris to a furious climax. Waves of molten heat gushed over her as she watched the scene in the next room where Tony and his lovely assistant thrashed on the table in the last throes of ecstasy.

They slumped. So did she, closing her eyes to appreciate fully the violent muscular contractions of her vagina sucking greedily at her fingers. When she opened them again, it was to see him lifting himself away from the relaxed body of the girl, his softening cock anointed by her juices. He wiped it on a tissue before sliding it back into his trousers and fastening up.

Armina grinned to herself, desire beginning to claw at her loins again. She had not realised Mallory's historical archivist had such a magnificent tool. Up till then she had not seriously considered cultivating him, but today's performance changed her mind.

As for the new girl? She was beautiful. Armina's clit twitched as she replayed the image of Tony bringing her to climax. A handsome young savage with the hips of a boy and the breasts of an Amazon, she had bucked and arched against the finger frigging her, moans escaping from her full lips. Did she swing both ways? It would not be difficult to find out. *Fun and games*, thought Lord Burnet's most influential mistress. And there was no time like the present. She had spied on them from a lookout post on the roof when they had arrived at the house, having learned from Tayte earlier that Tony Stroud had fetched his assistant from the railway station. Mallory, in the first flush of their affair, had introduced Armina to some of the manor's underground passages, and she had used one that connected the folly, a mock Greek temple built near the lake, with the priest-hole.

She liked it when Mallory was away, leaving her free to explore the house, poke into corners, rape bedrooms, ransack drawers and help herself to items she was certain he would never miss. She had the instinct of a magpie, unable to resist acquiring bright, sparkling objects that belonged by rights to others.

Armina never saw herself as a thief, more an opportunist. With a private income of her own, she had no need to shoplift but did it for kicks. It excited her as much as sex – the thrill of getting away with it, the powerful rush of excitement as she tripped nonchalantly out of a store with unpaid-for goods in her bag or about her person. She couldn't wait to find somewhere private after one of these adventures, the need to masturbate so extreme that she could have done it in the street with an audience of pedestrians.

Mallory, who had introduced her to the observation room, had told her how it had come into existence. Once a place to conceal priests during the days of religious persecution, it had been shut up for years. Then his roisterous ancestor, the notorious Regency rakehell Marmaduke Burnet, had won the Bedwell cartoons in a wager. Of fertile, lickerish imagination, he had at once seen the potential: open up the secret nook, install a mirror such as he had used to view the whores at work in Mother Baggot's brothel, where he was a frequent client, and bingo! Not only would he have a source of entertainment for his lecherous self, but a profitable sideline, too, charging fellow voyeurs for the privilege of watching those in the sanctum driven to a frenzy of lust, uncontrollably aroused by the drawings.

The whereabouts of this window on sin had been revealed to Mallory when he had inherited, the knowledge handed down to each successive heir to the title and estate. He was circumspect in his choice of intimates with whom to share the secret. Armina, to whom intrigue was the stuff of life, was one of the select few.

A mischief maker, with an eye on the main chance, she could see that it would be a useful aid to blackmail, if circumstances arose. But just for now it provided a fillip for her rampant appetite and helped to keep Mallory's interest in her alive. He was fickle – cunt-struck for about a month after meeting someone new, then needing fresh stimulation.

Many a time he and Armina had amused themselves by standing in the dim, warm confines of the recess, viewing the action taking

491

place on the other side of the mirror and reproducing it. The occupants of the cartoon room had been blissfully unaware that their activities reflected so excitingly in the beautiful antique Venetian glass were being relayed, slavered over and emulated.

He's as wicked as I am, Armina concluded smugly. My lover, my Lord Burnet, my Marquis of Ainsworth.

The library door opened on well-oiled hinges. Karen turned from helping Tony put the precious drawings away and stared at the woman who strolled in as if she owned the house and everything in it.

She was petite, her white-blonde hair cut short, forming cherubic curls round her shapely head, little fronds caressing the nape of her slender neck. Her face was gamine, elfin – big blue eyes, a retrousse nose, full red lips.

There was hardly anything of her dress but Karen recognised it as being couturier designed and ferociously expensive. It was made of pale-blue chiffon and velvet with a scooped neck and a sequined hem, which at its longest point reached halfway down her thighs and at its shortest was slit almost to the waist. Her clear, typically English skin was tanned to pale gold. Her naked legs were exquisitely formed and her feet pushed into high-heeled white satin mules, absurdly laced across the instep.

'Good evening, Armina,' Tony said, with a lift of his brow. 'How did you get in? I thought the house was out of bounds.'

She shimmied towards them, a feline smile

dimpling her cheeks as she answered a shade defiantly, 'Mallory gives me the run of the place.' Her voice was low, husky, thrillingly modulated.

There was a self-satisfied air about her that suggested she had been up to something. Tony wondered what. He knew about Tayte. Who in and around the estate didn't? But he sensed an element of deeper mischief than her rogering the head groom.

'May I introduce my assistant, Karen Heyward? Karen, this is Armina Channing, one of Lord Burnet's friends.'

'Hi,' Armina murmured, extending a perfectly manicured hand.

'Hello.' Karen was disconcerted as she took it, aware of the cling of those cool, slim fingers. By 'friend' did Tony mean 'mistress'? There was no doubt that Armina looked like someone's costly toy.

'She's not been here long. I met her at Exeter Station this afternoon,' Tony replied, considering the two lovely women who fitted so perfectly into the library's ornate splendour, both elegant, both infinitely desirable in entirely different ways.

'Has Mallory put her in one of the cottages?' Armina asked, seating herself on a brocade-covered couch. As she sank into the deeply feathered cushions, her skirt rode up.

Karen quickly looked away, but not before she had caught a flash of a fascinatingly pale, hairless triangle. Armina's smile broadened. Karen knew without doubt that His Lordship's friend had done this on purpose.

A new, exciting feeling quivered along her nerves and centred in her sex. Curiosity, certainly;

a burning desire to touch that depilated mound, to ask Armina why she had removed her down and what it felt like to do so, to probe between the chubby lips, to finger a clit other than her own. She swallowed hard, paced to the window and looked out at the darkening garden. Bats made swooping, noiseless rushes across the lawn and an owl screeched in the woods. Karen could see Armina's dark reflection in the panes, the glow from a reading lamp forming an undeserved halo round her flaxen head.

'She's staying in the one next to mine,' Tony said steadily. Somehow he was always wary when in Armina's presence, choosing his words with care. He followed his intuition and wouldn't trust her further then he could throw her.

'How neighbourly,' Armina cooed. 'So handy if she wants anything in the night.'

'Like what?' Tony was almost sure she knew he and Karen had been screwing. How she knew, he couldn't tell, but there was a darkening of her blue eyes as she looked at him, and invitation in the way in which the tip of her luscious rosy tongue played over her lips.

She lifted her bare shoulders in a shrug, the action raising her nipples above the chiffon, bright and shiny as cherries. 'Who knows? Maybe she'll be frightened? Have you lived in the country before, Karen?'

It was the first time she had addressed her directly, apart from the formal greeting, and Karen felt her voice brushing her ear like a kiss. She shivered as she heard her name, and felt the tender opening of her sex quiver, felt that voice like fingers trailing over her naked skin, touching her nipples and then dipping down to familiarise themselves with her labia and ever-eager nub.

She straightened, drew herself up to her full, graceful height. 'No, Armina,' she replied levelly. 'One can hardly call Oxford University the country. I'm pleased to be here, and am looking forward to meeting Lord Burnet.'

'Ah, I see. You've not actually met him? Well, I can do something about that. Come with me!' She uncoiled her limbs and rose. Karen felt the soft yet firm touch of her hand. It sent fiery shocks up her arm, across her shoulders and down her spine.

They left the library, Tony following behind, walking through seemingly endless corridors until reaching a T-shaped intersection dominated by a large window. Armina nodded towards the passage on the right, pausing to run a hand over the thick crimson silk cord barring the way.

'That leads to the West Wing and Lord Burnet's private apartment,' she said. 'Strictly taboo. No one goes there unless he invites them. We go left. Don't worry. I know it seems like a rabbit warren but you'll get the hang of the place eventually.' More lengthy corridors with vast doorways and tall windows, and then Armina opened a pair of doors and announced, 'The Long Gallery.'

'It's the finest room in the house, baroque in the extreme,' Tony said, as they stepped inside. 'Sixty feet long and forty wide, a perfect example of the Elizabethan penchant for grandeur, but with a practical application as well. On wet days, members of the family would have played carpet bowls here for exercise.

Karen stared round her, overwhelmed by the magnificence. Portraits of every Burnet from the sixteenth century to the twentieth lined the walls: bewigged statesmen, dashing admirals, generals in full dress uniform, red-robed judges and dandified gentlemen of fashion.

Their faces all bore the same stamp of strength, pride and confidence in their God-given right to ride rough-shod over lesser mortals. They were flanked by portraits of other members of their elite family – their wives and numerous offspring, even their favourite hounds and horses.

It was a wonderland of costumes and history, and Karen wandered down its length in a happy daze. She was distinctly aware of Armina at her side. It was as if sexuality emanated from the woman's pores, coiling round Karen, reaching out to her. Karen knew with absolute certainty there was unfinished business between them.

Tony was somewhere behind, paling into insignificance against the silken thread binding her ever closer in Armina's web. She was finding it hard to hide her arousal, and could tell by the brightness of Armina's eyes that she was aware and sharing the same feeling.

The mystery of the softly lit gallery wrapped itself round Karen like a feathery quilt. Its atmosphere was redolent of beeswax and pot pourri, of the wind blowing in from the sea, of old, far-off events, both grave and gay.

This house had seen sons ride off to war, had welcomed them home in triumph or received their coffins to stand in state in the Great Hall before interment in the family vault. It had been the venue for marriages – many brides must have yielded their maidenheads under this roof. Karen hoped they had done so willingly. There had been births, parties and great, costly occasions like a visit from a monarch during a royal progress.

'There he is,' a voice murmured in her ear, scented breath skimming lightly over the sensitive lobe. 'It was painted last winter. Isn't he drop-dead gorgeous? I helped him chose his outfit. The gold velvet slacks are by Van Notes, the black velvet jacket and damask waistcoat created especially for him by Moschino. And the long windcoat came from the Miyake workrooms.

It was a shockingly arresting portrait, hanging incandescent on the wall, a visionary glow of paint. Karen's heart missed a beat, then rushed on again. Every nerve in her body tingled. Her sex ached emptily and her breasts hungered for a touch. Not anyone's touch. His.

It was as if he stared straight at her, was there in the flesh. He was magnificent. Perhaps the most magnificently handsome man she had ever seen. Long dark hair brushed his shoulders, his funky, elegant clothes as modern as tomorrow, yet his features could have graced a Roman coin, classical, timeless: aquiline nose, high cheekbones, tawny eyes and a mouth with a ruthless slant, the upper lip hinting at impatience, the lower full and sensual. He was tall, with good shoulders and strong hands, the arrogant master of Blackwood Towers.

This was depicted in the background, glimpsed through dark, shrouding trees. Two hounds lay at his feet, gazing up at him as if hypnotised, and a hooded falcon rested on his raised right wrist, talons gripping the leather glove, as fierce and dangerous as her handler.

Karen reached out blindly, completely disoriented. Her fingers were met by and enmeshed in Armina's, who pressed against her side, whispering, 'Isn't he lovely? Can you see his bulge? Doesn't the very sight of him make your tits tingle and set your cunt on fire? Come back to my place tonight and I'll tell you about him.'

Chapter Four

THE AINSWORTH ARMS had merited a mention in every good-food guide covering Devon. Though its restaurant was fully booked, the landlord always kept a table in reserve for Lord Burnet or his friends.

The pub occupied a prime position at the top of the main street winding down to the crescent-shaped bay, an ancient hostelry which had opened its doors to travellers since the Middle Ages. That night was no exception. Every room had been taken, the holiday season being in full spate.

Karen was charmed by this fine example of a traditional coaching inn, a place of sooted beams hung with polished horse brasses, and open fire-places that would blaze with logs in cold weather. Gleaming copper warming-pans adorned the panelled walls, and a collection of willow-pattern china, ships in bottles, enamelled signs and a hundred and one curios.

Their table was in the wide semi-circular window looking out over the harbour. The dying sun spread a dazzling copper path across the sea, and masts reared into the gathering night sky, not fishing boats but private yachts bobbing at anchor near the quayside.

The port relied on the tourist trade. Each hotel and house carrying a bed and breakfast sign was chock-a-block, chalets were booked from one year to the next, the caravan park was full and they would be turning away campers on every farm leading to Porthcombe. The boarding-house proprietors, shop keepers and publicans worked like galley slaves, sacrificing their own beds if need be. The season was short, money tight, and a long hard winter lay ahead.

'I'm famished,' Tony announced, scanning the menu. 'What d'you fancy, girls?'

Armina beckoned to the wine waiter. 'I want a Pimms, long and cool and fruity. I drove here, so it's only fair that one of you takes us back, then I can get rat-arsed.'

Tony shrugged good-naturedly. 'OK. I'll do it. Order me a lager, and that'll be my lot.' Earlier he had returned the Range Rover to the garage of Blackwood Towers and Armina had commandeered the vintage Alfa Romeo Sprite she regarded as her own.

The fragrance of cooking wafted from the kitchens. Karen's mouth watered. She had eaten nothing but a sandwich all day, and a buffet-car one at that. There had been no time to think about food, Tony sweeping her away with his enthusiasms and his passion, but now she was ravenous.

A darkly smouldering Italian waiter sauntered across, smiling down at Armina then checking Karen out.

'Two Pimms and a Pils lager, please, Mario,' Armina purred, laying a hand on his arm with lazy intimacy. 'How are you, sweetie? Haven't seen you for ages. We must meet. When's your next evening off?'

Karen could not hear his murmured reply. She felt surprise crossed with resentment at Armina's familiarity with him, especially after the way she had drooled over the portrait of her lover, Lord Burnet. They were screened from the rest of the diners by a trough loaded with flamboyant hothouse plants, but Karen could see Armina running a crimson fingernail across the baton of Mario's cock as it sloped against his inner left thigh, underscored by the close fit of his black trousers.

Yet there was something wickedly attractive about Armina that made Karen forgive her peccadilloes. She defied convention with her skimpy dress clinging seductively to her body, naked beneath the sensual fabric, her breasts pert, nipples poking through the chiffon. Her precious little peach of a bottom tempted and teased with every movement she made.

Mario disappeared to be replaced by an older, plainer waiter who served their order. This was better. Karen was able to marshal her confused thoughts and concentrate on the food. She ate voraciously, though not blind to the way in which Armina's serpentine tongue sipped and tasted with the avidity of a lover sampling her partner's juices. Her every action had a sexual connotation.

The Ainsworth Arms lived up to its reputation: ravioli mixed with lobster and scallops and creamy fish sauce, followed by wafer-thin slices of veal cooked in wine and covered in mush-rooms, mange tout and tiny puffs of deep fried potatoes that melted in the mouth. After this came pudding: glass dishes of magnificent ice cream, a symphony of raspberries, toffee fudge and whipped cream lavishly sprinkled with grated chocolate and almonds.

'Have you known each other long?' Armina directed her question at Tony as she licked a morsel from her lips.

He grinned at Karen, his beard giving him a raffish appearance. With his yoked cotton shirt and full, putty-coloured pants, he might have been an artist or man of letters fresh from Paris.

'I taught her how delightful sex could be and brought her to orgasm for the first time,' he replied, his gaze wandering over Armina's lips and throat and coming to rest on her breasts.

'Very old and close friends,' she murmured with a sultry smile.

She extended a foot in its fashionable mule and nudged him gently between the legs under cover of the table. Her intelligent yet decadently sensu-ous eyes were fixed on Karen's face with an absorption embarrassing yet stimulating in the light of her contact with Tony's testicles.

'Until him, sex for me had been all clumsy boys, a lot of heavy breathing, inexperienced penises, premature ejaculation and crushed breasts,' Karen said, her inner core tingling and moistening as she watched this brazen foreplay.

Had Tony and Armina been lovers? Hot images of them fucking right there in the middle of the restaurant ripped through her mind. Or in the sanctum, perhaps? Maybe he had shown Armina the cartoons, sharing an upsurge of excitement leading to coition?

'I know. Been there. Done that. It's enough to turn a girl lesbian.' Armina, cool as a mountain stream, wriggled her toes against Tony's cock and then withdrew them.

'Even is she wasn't already inclined that way,' Tony purred sarcastically, his voice soft as silk.

Later, coming out of the lavatory in the ladies' room, Karen found Armina gone. She had left her powdering her nose and promising to wait. Where was she? Making a date with Mario? Bonking him against the garden wall? What would he be like in the sack? She had never done a field trial, but they did say Latins were lousy lovers.

She washed her hands, staring at herself in the mirror as she held them to the dryer, tired now, full of food and a tad too much alcohol. She wanted to go back to her little house, tuck under the duvet and sleep. Laurel Cottage. Such a pretty name, such a pretty place, and she must send cards to her mother and Alison, let them know she had arrived in one piece. Jeremy? Maybe. Or perhaps she'd wait till she received one postmarked Greece. The corridor connecting the toilets with the restaurant was deserted. She moved in the direction of the bar, lost in thought and not looking where she was going. A man stepped in front of her. They collided. Clothed entirely in black leather, he carried a crash helmet under one arm.

'Sorry,' he said, steadying her with a large hand. Blue eyes contacted hers and held. 'Didn't mean to sent you flying, miss.'

Her heart jumped. 'That's all right,' she replied automatically.

He was roughly six-two, with broad shoulders under a fringed, metal-studded biker's jacket. Thick, dark-blond hair straggled over the collar, a neatly braided plait behind each ear. Gold sleepers bearing tiny ankhs pierced the lobes. He had, a wide-planed face and short nose. *If he'd been American, Karen thought, I'd have said he came from the Mid-West – a Hollander, like Brad Pitt whom he rather resembles. What a hunk!*

She could not resist glancing down, checking his equipment.

Yes, sure enough, there between his muscular leather-covered thighs lay the prominently thick finger of his phallus. Leather! There wasn't a smell like it anywhere on God's earth. Animal. Feral. Totally sex oriented.

She melted inside, loose and moist as she relived the moment in the library when she had sat in the operator's chair and rubbed her pussy against the seat. Leather combined with male sweat, male aftershave, the strong tang of male sex organs. Wonderful! Juices seeped from her vulva, soaking her panty gusset.

There was a certain rough charm about him, a combination of virile masculinity and innocent boyishness. He looked too wholesome to be a Hell's Angel. How old? She wondered during that long moment when they took each other's measure. Twenty?

'Can I buy you a drink?' His shyness was masked by a veneer of brash self-assurance, his accent West Country, but no country clod with straw in his hair.

'No, thank you. I'd like to but I've friends waiting. Another time, perhaps.'

Damn, she fretted. *I would have liked to get to know him, in the biblical sense, of course. Nothing serious. I've never pictured myself as a biker's old lady.*

'I haven't seen you around before,' he said, with an ingenuous smile.

'I only arrived today.'

'Where are you staying? I'll call for you, take you for a spin on the Harley. I've got another lid.'

A Harley-Davidson. He hadn't taken long to drop that into the conversation. Obviously it helped him pull.

'Laurel Cottage.' She wondered if this was wise but was unable to resist the lure of the huge basket in his leather trousers.

'Up on the estate?'

'Yes. Now, I really must go.'

'I'll call sometime. My name's Spike.'

Get a life! she thought sardonically. *I'll bet it's not; probably something plebeian – Michael or Alan, even Bill. Spike? How priapic, like motorbikes themselves.* She hoped the theory of big bike, small dick didn't apply to him. From what she'd seen, it looked far from small.

He did not move and she pushed past him, hotly aware of their bodies touching as she squeezed through the narrow doorway. She felt a responsive quiver deep inside her, the smell of him irresistibly provocative.

Armina lay on the chesterfield in a circle of lamp light. 'I'm pissed,' she announced. 'Not very pissed, just enough to make me feel horny as hell.'

'You should have brought Mario or Tony along.' Karen lounged in the chintz-covered chair opposite, too indolent to stir a muscle, idly watching the television screen. *The Twilight Zone* was showing, the sound turned down, Vivaldi's *Four Seasons* drifting from the elegantly slender stereo speakers.

'Mario's working till two. Then he'll be bushed. That's no bloody use to me. I'd rather have a vibrator. Wouldn't you rather have a vibrator?' She propped herself up, staring at Karen owlishly. 'Great invention, vibrators. D'you realise there's no longer any need for men? They've outgrown their usefulness. We've enough semen in sperm banks to last for years – and have always had more pleasure from wanking or bringing each other off than having them poke us.'

'I thought you liked men?'

Karen wondered how she was going to get home. Tony had dropped them at the Dower House before driving back to his cottage. He had told her it was within walking distance, but it was dark outside, quiet and eerie. She had not come to terms with the country yet.

'I do,' Armina vowed earnestly. 'I love the brutes, but I love women, too. Variety, change, the element of risk the surprise, the unexpected – these make life worth living.' She uncurled with the ease and sinuousness of a cat. Karen could see her nipples, pink through blue silk. She wanted to stroke them, to feel them bunch under her fingertips.

Restless and desirous, she was haunted by visions of the fat, leather-wrapped package nestling in Spike's crotch. Had he been cut or was he *au naturel*? An intriguing puzzle, which she intended to solve at the earliest possible moment.

Armina's presence encouraged prurience, and Karen was experiencing actual discomfort in her pussy, a tormenting, pulsing need. With a tremendous effort of will, she concentrated on her surroundings.

The Dower House was a delight, pseudo-Gothic and wildly eccentric, furnished in a variety of styles and periods, mostly overblown Victorian, reflecting the period in which it had been refurbished. Once it had sheltered widowed marchionesses, now it housed a marquis's whore.

'You said you'd tell me about Lord Burnet,' she said, quashing her libidinous feelings.

'What d'you want to know? The size of his tool? If he lets a women leave his bed unsatisfied? Things like that?' As she spoke, Armina rose and slowly, almost absent-mindedly, slid down the nylon zip at the side of her dress, treating Karen to an enflaming glimpse of a perfect breast, a supple bare waist and hip, a fragile thigh, and a tiny, svelte bottom cheek.

She stepped out of the puddle of velvet. Nude apart from her stilt-heeled shoes, she swayed across to where Karen sat. Standing in front of her, legs apart, she lifted her hands to her own breasts, her long lacquered nails lightly tracing over the nipples. They hardened, turning from pale to rose red, their tips on a level with Karen's mouth.

'I don't want intimate details about him,' Karen lied, resisting the frantic urge to tongue them. 'Just day to day things. For example, what's he like as a boss?'

She was becoming unbearably aroused. The combination of Armina's words, the nearness of that lovely flesh and the aroma wafting from the other woman's labia caused mayhem in her own wet and needy places.

It was incredible how someone so dainty could exude such unrestrained carnality. Karen could not tear her eyes away as Armina, obsessed with herself, cupped those tip-tilted breasts, lifted them, loved them and brushed her thumbs over the hard teats. Like a doll made by a master craftsman, her narrow shoulders dipped down to a handspan waist, concave belly and a pubis as naked as a prepubescent girl's.

'Why isn't it hairy?' Karen whispered, on the edge of the chair, drawn by the magical, alluring cleft stripped of its protective fuzz.

Armina was breathing deeply. 'I think my quim looks sexier bare. Men like it, too. It's a novelty. Sometimes I let it grow bushy when I feel like a change.' She became serious, tipping her pelvis forward so that her mons was even closer to Karen. As she moved her legs, opening them wider, the smell of her lovejuices became more pungent.

'Tell me about Lord Burnet,' Karen gasped, hovering on the brink, desperate to come.

'He's a bastard to work for, I should imagine, if his behaviour elsewhere is anything to go by,' Armina murmured dreamily, and now one of her hands crept down to her pubis. Her sex-lips pouted between her fingers, swollen and flushed, glistening with nectar. 'But there's nothing more exciting than an arrogant bastard, providing he looks like Mallory. He's hung like a stallion. His cock is a good nine inches long when he has a hard-on. Thick as a flag pole, and, boy, does he know how to use it!'

Karen was no longer listening, her mind spinning as she watched Armina playing with herself, ripples of lust coursing down her spine to centre on her pulsating clitoris. When Armina moaned, eyes half closed with longing, the urge to help her achieve orgasm was the most powerful thing Karen had ever experienced. Without realising what she was doing, she touched the velvet-smooth mound and inserted a finger alongside Armina's, deep within the hot, wet crease.

'Do you still have your maidenhair, Karen? Is it chestnut or a lighter shade. May I see?' Armina's voice rang with excitement.

'I've never – I'm no dyke. I like men,' Karen began, tripping over the words.

'That makes no difference.' The elfin eyes smiled encouragingly. 'If you've never tried, how can you tell? You may find you prefer women. Why restrict yourself? Enjoy the best of all possible worlds.'

'I'm not sure I want to.'

Armina moved away, scooped her dress from the floor and held out her hand. 'Let's continue this conversation upstairs. No one will disturb us. It's late, dark; we're quite alone. What happens between us can be forgotten or dismissed as a dream – or maybe remembered and repeated.'

With the scent of Armina on her fingers, Karen was unable to do other than trail after her, bewitched by the slender back and the perfect spheres of her buttocks, thighs elongated, calves clenched to keep her balance against the unnatural cant of high heels. Moonlight notched through the tiny panes of the first landing window, adding its blue-white frosting to the peachy glow of wall lamps.

There was deep-pile carpet underfoot, William Morris wallpaper on either side, lithographs of Edwardian subjects – sentimental, sensual – of an era when nudity was permissible as long as the subject was artistic and classical. An arched cedarwood door, and Karen stepped over the threshold of Armina's lair.

A sweet, spicy odour filled her nostrils, as of smouldering joss sticks. It took a moment for her eyes to adjust. Candles dipped and wavered as the breeze stirred the muslin curtains. A cool room – white carpet, white walls – a brass bedstead with misty lace cascading around it.

Armina leaned against an inner door, a tulip-shaped wine glass in her hand. 'I'm taking a bath. Will you join me?'

More candlelight, silver holders ringing the sunken black marble tub, the flames reflected in mirror tiles alternating with shocking pink. The incense mingled with other exotic odours – saffron and frangipani, carnation and attar of roses. Steam drifted over the dark water like mist on a bayou.

Karen's fingers shook as she unfastened her top. She had never been shy in exposing her breasts to male eyes, but now she wanted to fold her arms across them.

Armina stretched, ribs lifting, raising her tits high, then kicked off her mules and walked down the steps circling the bath. Her feet were immersed, then her legs and lower thighs. The perfumed, oily water, shining like onyx, cut across the lower point of her triangle, brushing the avenue dividing her pubis before diving impudently between her legs.

Karen was bemused by wine and a surfeit of beauty. 'You remind me of Leighton's *The Bath of Psyche.*'

Armina chuckled, patting her pudenda. 'Dirty old buggers, the Victorians.'

'I thought they were passionately obsessed with art.'

'Obsessed by their cocks, like all men.' After firing this volley Armina slipped into the tub, floating with her head supported on the rim, body and legs outstretched. Her skin shone like alabaster in contrast to the Stygian gloom, nipples crimson buds.

She sat up a shower of flashing droplets, reached out and grabbed Karen by the ankle. Her hand was wet, and warm trickles coursed between Karen's toes to puddle the shaggy black carpet. Slowy, luxuriously, her fingers walked up the wide trouser leg, a creeping heat radiating from them towards the fulcrum of Karen's pleasure.

Armina released her, sitting back, bright-eyed. 'Well?' she asked challengingly.

Karen gasped, flung open her arms, the heat growing as Armina's eyes roamed over her breasts. In one swift movement she dropped her pants and peeled down her briefs. 'There,' she cried defiantly. 'You wanted to see it.'

'Ah . . .' Armina's sigh was one of deep satisfaction. 'What a marvellous muff? It needs stroking, petting, bathing.'

Karen capitulated, sex the only imperative within her. Dreams were about to be realised –

soft hands rousing her clit, soft thighs entwined with hers, the feel of soft skin, the embrace of a lover who knew exactly where she wanted to be touched and why; a twin soul, another woman who shared the same requirements to bring her to sexual completion. She could feel her body tightening, the heavy drag of desire warming the base of her belly.

Caressed by the water as its sly fingers insinuated themselves into her love hole, Karen welcomed the feel of cool moisture on her heated skin. Armina's hands brushed through her hair, loosening it, spreading it across her shoulders.

Now there was music, swelling from concealed speakers. She recognised Debussy's *Prélude à L'Après-midi d'une Faune*. Mysterious, evocative. It was one of her favourite pieces. She had read how Vaslav Nijinsky – that tormented genius loved by the impresario Diaghilev – had choreographed the ballet. Against her closed eyelids, Karen experienced the sensual dreams cunningly provoked by the tone poem. A steamy, languorous afternoon in mythical Greece; the faun, half man, half beast, beautiful, passionate, lustful, a voyeur watching naked nymphs disporting themselves.

'I adore this piece,' she began, then gave a sharp, distressed cry as Armina's clever fingers dipped down, performing a measured dance over the wet brown floss of Karen's mons. The tiny sensitive hairs created electric shocks, spreading along her thighs, into her epicentre, tingling up to force her nipples erect.

'So do I, darling.' Armina lathered her hands with creamy soap heavily scented with ylang-

ylang. 'Did you know Nijinsky caused a scandal on the first night by wanking on stage during the finale?'

'Yes, I knew. It makes it all the more thrilling.'

'Music to jerk off to. Why d'you think I'm playing it?'

Karen shut her eyes and opened wide the doorway of her senses, imagined sunshine pouring on to her body and the smell of wild garlic, fresh grass, pines. The music soared higher, reaching a crescendo.

Armina gently massaged Karen's sex with soapy fingers, parting the fringed outer lips. Her finger was slickly wet over the furrow between, circling the vaginal opening, finding the mouth of her anus, dipping a finger in, then concentrating on the seat of power. The miniature foreskin was gently drawn back, the naked head of the clitoris bared in order to be thoroughly stimulated.

Karen's lids became heavy, the scent of the soap, the feel of those busy fingers on her bud lulling her into a trance-like state. She could feel the glorious glow of orgasm building up inside her. Then Armina's finger hovered, tapped the aching head lightly, stopped, was withdrawn.

She drew Karen close, nipples pressed to nipples, her mouth closing over hers, tongue tip darting between her lips. The kiss deepened, lengthened, and Karen was kissed as she had never been kissed before, every recess of her mouth explored.

Caught up in an anguished paroxysm of excitement, she lifted her hands, stroked Armina's shoulders, then moved down to touch those little breasts, marvelling at their firmness in her palm, enchanted by the tremor running through her lover's body. She gently disengaged herself from Armina's mouth and leaned forward, licking the tight teats, nipping them with her teeth, teasing them with her tongue. She slid down against the bath and gripped one of Armina's thighs between hers, hardly aware of what she was doing, beginning to rub her mound against it with a lithe movement of her hips. Her clitoris was erect and thrumming, overloaded with passion, ripe and ready to burst.

'Not quite yet. Lie back,' Armina whispered, smiling into her eyes, then taking the shower head in her hand.

This was bliss, the cool touch of the marble, the warm, stinging jets of the spray. It moved slowly, starting at her shoulders and then disappearing under the water, a miniature whirlpool betraying its presence, the feel of it swirling over her pubis, playing with her labia, toying with her clit. She moved her pelvis, thrust her shameless little organ towards that teasing fount.

With delicate precision, Armina lifted the shower to direct its humming stream to Karen's breasts, each nipple subjected to exquisite torture. Then she allowed the fanning tide to swirl over the swollen nether lips and wash the hard, greedy pearl so desperate for relief.

'Please,' Karen whimpered, gripping Armina's hand in an attempt to keep the force on her clit head, frustrated beyond belief.

'Only if you masturbate me after you've come.'

'I promise.' The idea roused her to even greater excitement. Let her only receive the bounty of orgasm and she'd willingly carry out Armina's every fantasy.

The jet died, and the women rested in the water while beneath Armina's skilled fingers Karen's roused clit bloomed. She began a soft circular motion around its sensitive hood. Karen heard a mewling sound and realised it was coming from her own throat. Armina's instinctive awareness of her body's needs was breathtaking. It was almost as if she was bringing herself to climax.

Tense, mad for release she worked herself against that artful digit, the water sloshing around them as Armina responded with a frenzied rubbing. Karen's need was basic – she didn't want gentleness now. Gasping, clinging to Armina's shoulders, she abandoned herself, coming in a thrashing, screaming frenzy, a surge of sharp, almost painful pleasure unlike anything she had ever known.

Armina's fingers plunged into the convulsing vagina, taking the tight spasms as wave after wave rolled over Karen. She did not withdraw them right away, allowing her time for them to subside – allowing her space to fall down from the stars.

With glowing eyes, she gently left her, rising from the bath, water streaming down her limbs. 'Come to bed,' she whispered, and as Karen joined her on the black carpet, she tenderly wrapped them both in an enveloping towel.

Karen felt like a virgin, shattered by the experience Armina had taken her through, anxious to please her. The satin bed sheets embraced them as they sank into the depths of the vast couch. Now Armina was the willing victim of pleasure, and Karen knew for the first time the delight of rousing a woman, every caress, each tender embrace she lavished on her echoed in her own secret parts.

Honeyed kisses, long and deep, the taste of scented flesh – smooth as silk, not hard and hairy like a man's, nipples that sprang alert at the merest brushing of fingers, satisfying nipples swelling against the tongue, the gasps of delight, the moans of want – an uninhibited creature writhing under her caresses, emotional, expressive, all soft, ensorcelled delight. And then the final exploration. Armina spread her legs, and Karen went down to enjoy the heart of her flower, labia like petals moist with honeydew. No stiff phallus with its hard ridges and aggressive thrusting- just delicate flesh with the bloom, scent and colour of a wild rose. Karen worshipped at the alter of Armina's sex, fingers adoring the clitoris enthroned at the top of the delicious avenue.

Armina moaned, rubbing her nipples in time to Karen's gentle friction on the treasured gem. 'Faster,' she begged. 'Don't hold back! Make me come! Bring me off!'

'I will. Oh, yes . . . I want you to come. I want to watch you do it. It's me giving it to you – and I love it!' Karen cried eagerly, forgetting any other lover she'd ever had, driven by this need to satisfy Armina.

She used a light, rhythmical stroke, feeling the clit stalk thickening, the head swelling even more, feeling the shivers gathering in Armina's limbs, smelling the fresh juices welling from the mouth of her vagina. It was heady stuff, making her own nub burn and quiver in response.

Armina bucked and yelled and forced herself up against Karen's finger, long shudders convulsing through her. Then she collapsed and lay prone, head to one side, eyes closed, at peace. Her breasts rose and fell with the quickness of her breathing, then gradually subsided.

After a while she stirred, opened her eyes, smiled at Karen and drew her into her arms. Cradled together the two women slept, the misty curtains enfolding them as in an enchanted arbour.

Dreams, half formed, fragmentary. Karen rose through layers of sleep into consciousness. Somewhere she could hear the thud of a horse's hooves. It was not important enough to awake her fully. She fell back into the velvet blackness of oblivion.

A door opened and closed. She felt the draught on her face. Then silence and darkness. There seemed to be a disturbance around her, the bed moving, no longer a bed but a raft floating on a spangled crimson sea. She heard Armina saying,

'I wasn't expecting you.'

A voice answering her, a deep, masculine voice threaded with amusement. 'So I see.'

Karen opened her eyes. Dawn was poking inquisitive fingers through the drapes, and she stared full into the face of the man leaning against the bedpost. Still part enmeshed in dreams, it was as if the portrait had climbed off the wall in the Long Gallery and walked to the Dower House.

He lounged there, legs crossed at the ankles, arms folded over his chest, audacious, beautiful, regarding her lazily through a masked expression, a coiled alertness in his indolent stance.

His stare shocked through her to the heartland of her being. In his eyes she read his awareness of her loving with Armina. His lips curled into a sardonic smile. His down-sweeping glance went over her nakedness, slowly, speculatively. It was like flame and frost, making her nipples rise and her sphincter clench. She pulled the sheet up to her chin.

'Who are you?' he asked.

'Karen Heyward.' She felt at a complete disadvantage, anger rising in a turbulent flood.

The bar of his black brows swooped down. 'I don't know you, do I?'

Karen swung her legs over the side of the bed, keeping her body covered. 'You know of me. I'm Tony Stroud's assistant.'

The silk was slippery, difficult to control. It slid away from her shoulders with consummate ease, its weight pulling it to the ground, leaving her nude. She grabbed at it, the fresh morning air invading her crease like a cold finger as she inadvertently raised her bottom. Her face flamed and she turned away from Lord Burnet, clutching the rebellious folds about her.

He moved, graceful as a panther, taking her place beside Armina, sprawling on the bed, relaxed and unconcerned. 'I remember. Tony told me about you. When did you arrive?'

'Yesterday,' she mumbled, cursing him, Tony, Armina and, most of all, herself. This was a lamentable start to her career. What must he think of her?

Armina smiled at him sleepily, secure in her position, one hand coming over to smooth the corded material covering the solid baton of his

518

cock resting along one thigh. Karen had never been more embarrassed in her life, bedevilled by odd thoughts and alien emotions that disturbed and infuriated her. Mallory was enough to unsettle the most self-confident of women. To her horror, she found she could not stop looking at him. He possessed that fatal combination of high-powered personality and aristocratic breeding well nigh impossible to resist.

He was too devastatingly handsome, a lock of night-black hair falling across his forehead. The glitter in his amber eyes caused a tremor of primitive fear and desire to bolt through her. The white linen shirt he wore fitted his arms and shoulders superbly; the tight buff riding breeches revealed the hard, muscular strength of his legs and the superb fullness of his genitals. Love-fluid eased from her vulva as Karen remembered Armina's assurance that his penis was formidable when aroused.

She watched as the long, thick rod in his breeches began to stir under Armina's ministrations. He lay supine as his mistress lipped his chest through the gap in the unbuttoned shirt, then opened it further. The skin was deeply tanned. Ebony hair grew in swirls around the nut-brown nipples, thinned out to a narrow line dipping to his navel, then vanished behind the silver buckle of his belt.

Karen knew he was observing her beneath lowered eyelids. She wanted to leave but her feet were rooted to the spot. Armina's deft fingers undid the belt and the top button of his breeches. Karen's throat was parched, her sex soaked, and Mallory's eyes were smoky, never leaving hers –

daring her, challenging her.

I won't yield! she vowed. *I won't become just another of his women!*

Armina coiled herself round him, then sat astride his thighs, her cleft spread wide, pink lips thickening, the round head of her clitoris bulging shamelessly. Her fingers nimbly unzipped him. His penis reared from the restricting jodhpurs. Karen shivered and ached to have that cock buried inside her. It was everything Armina had promised – long and thick, the mauve glans rising from the retracted foreskin. Pearly moisture bedewed the tip, and Karen longed to sip it with her lips, savour it with her tongue, take every last inch of him into her throat.

Armina looked up with an I-told-you-so expression.

Karen stood there like stone. No movement, no expression betrayed the torment she was enduring. Her whole body throbbed while she grappled with desire. Instead of going away, it got stronger. Arms held straight at her sides, fists clenched into white-knuckled balls, she refused to beg for release as she endured the frustration of seeing Armina pleasuring Mallory.

She watched her go down on him, taking that rock-hard phallus between her lips, teasing the cock tip, then absorbing it into her mouth, slowly, gingerly, as if unable to take it all in one swoop.

His eyes remained fixed on Karen's face, the bright, predatory eyes of a hawk. Up and down Armina went on the thick engorged bough of his phallus. His fingers were like talons in her hair, forcing her to go faster, thrusting mercilessly till his black pubic hair was against her lips. He gasped, eyes still spearing Karen's. She saw the sudden jerk of his body as he came, spurting his creamy load into Armina's throat. She coughed, spluttered, come streaming from her mouth.

Karen burned with frustration and fury. *He knows how much I want him, the arrogant devil!* she raged. *I'll teach him he isn't the only man worth fucking!* Deliberately she turned her back on him and stalked out of the door.

Chapter Five

'WHAT A JOB!' Karen exclaimed from her perch on the library steps. 'I shouldn't think anyone's been up here for a decade.' Hot, dusty, she had already spent three days at it but so far had only scratched the surface of the monumental task of correlating the vast amount of undocumented material.

'Take a break,' Tony advised, looking up at her legs, bared to the tops of her thighs by her cotton shorts. A divine vista from where he stood – the shaded area under her buttocks, the seam running between them drawn tight against the rounded swell of her closed sex-lips.

'You're too darn conscientious,' he continued, hands sunk deep in his pockets, the left one surreptitiously scratching his balls. 'There's no desperate rush. It's taken a couple of generations to get in this mess and you can't expect to put it right in five minutes.'

Karen climbed down carefully, a pile of books in her arms. Placing them on the only available corner of the table, she brushed the back of her hand over her sticky forehead. Her spine and calf muscles ached. She had hardly stopped since the day after she arrived, driven by a force far stronger than interest or ambition. Pride was the spur – the desire to show the high-handed individual who paid her wages that she was a competent, hard-headed historian, not one of his mistress's play-fellows who would fall over herself to provide him with an additional lay.

She had seen neither hide nor hair of him since that unfortunate introduction at the Dower House and told herself she was glad. The less contact they had with one another the better. Tony had carte blanche to catalogue the library as he saw fit, already putting his plans into operation. All Karen had to do was follow instructions, arrange the volumes by title, author and subject, and add fresh data to that already on file.

Dick Bedwell's masterpieces had been described and itemised before she came. Tony had not taken them out again, but she knew he was seeking an opportunity to do so. Lust stirred in her belly as she visualised looking at them. Work, however, came before pleasure, and she had much to do, not only in the library but also at Laurel Cottage.

She had spent time arranging the interior to her liking. More of her possessions had been delivered by carrier and it was beginning to look like home. A Volkswagen Golf had been placed at her disposal, and she'd driven down to Porthcombe to familiarise herself with the layout, and to stock up on provisions. Everything was to hand there – hypermarkets, hair stylists, several antique emporiums, a halfway decent record shop where she discovered a couple of CDs she had been seeking, even a cinema.

So far she had not met many members of staff, though they had returned when the master had arrived. *Far too many to cater for the wants of one man*, she thought scathingly. *It's armoral, almost obscene in this day and age.*

Seated on a bench on the terrace where luncheon was served, she leaned her head against sun-baked stone and raised her face to the cloudless cobalt sky. Her legs were tanned, arms bare as she soaked up the sunshine, radical views on the fair division of wealth fading. Gracious living was undeniably good. Servants to do the chores and bring trays of food, gardeners to keep the grounds in order. The staff were unobtrusive, going about their tasks with quiet efficiency.

'I could get used to this,' she confessed, running her hands down the length of her smooth brown thighs, stretching luxuriously as a cat will when taking its ease on a sunny windowsill.

Tony poured her a tumbler of iced orange juice. 'I already have.' Then he shot her a shrewd glance. 'You haven't told me much about your meeting with Lord Burnet.'

Her eyes darkened. 'I don't want to talk about it.'

'He talked to me about you. Seems he was impressed.'

'Really?'

'Oh, yes,' Tony said with a lopsided grin, and passed her the salad bowl. 'I think you're in with a chance there, girl.'

Karen took up the servers and helped herself. Each day they had eaten thus, every item beautifully prepared and presented. A cold collation with a continental touch. Lush beef tomatoes and wafer-thin slivers of onion saturated in tasty olive oil and spiced vinaigrette, to which had been added a whisper of garlic; a cheese board with Brie, Gruyere, Edam, Stilton and Leicestershire; a platter of sliced smoked sausage; a basket of crusty fresh rolls. The citron hue of lemon juice, the fiery blaze of orange, the purple velvet of grapes waited in cut-glass jugs, blended and iced and delicious, to be followed by dark coffee as bittersweet as love.

She lifted her fork and pushed the food about her plate, saying slowly, 'Let's get one thing straight. I don't much care what he thinks of me personally, as long as he's satisfied with my work.'

'Of course,' Tony replied solemnly.

'I'm not joking.'

He spread his hands wide and lifted his shoulders. 'Did I say you were? Perish the thought.'

'I mean it, Tony. Don't get any ideas. I've no intention of taking part in a cosy little threesome with him and Armina.'

His look was wide-eyed and innocent, but he reached out and ran a seeking finger along the low oval of the crop-top struggling to contain her full breasts. Her nipples immediately stiffened, two sharp points lifting the thin fabric. Tony tweaked them gently. She moved away, sliding along the bench, the action dragging her shorts across her secret lips. Like her nipples, they responded to the friction, perturbation starting in her core, juices welling to dampen her panties.

'Shall we make it a short lunch-time?' he murmured, and she could not fail to be aware of the high, taut line of his prick under the cotton trousers. 'I fancy working on the cartoons this afternoon. Don't you?'

The priest-hole was drenched in the somnolence of summer. The scent of newly mown grass drifted in through the arrow-slit window, along with the drowsy sound of bees hovering over heavy, pollen-coated stamens. A single ray of light, grainy with dust and circling flies, formed an aura round Mallory Burnet's head.

Lounging in a comfortable chair placed opposite the double mirror, he became alert as Tony and Karen entered the sanctum. Desire coursed through him. The archivist was carrying out his request.

Karen had the kind of looks that turned him on – tall without being gawky, graceful as a ballerina, slender but strong bodied, with hips wide enough to accommodate the largest of male members. Independent and fiesty, too. This added to her attraction. As he remembered her naked in Armina's bedroom, his penis stirred like an awakening serpent and he felt a heavy ache in the spunk-loaded balls loosely cushioned by his black jogging pants.

He saw Tony glance in the mirror, a half smile on his lips as he deliberately turned the unsuspecting Karen to face it. She leaned back languidly, wriggling her backside into the hardness of his groin. Tony kissed her neck, then freed himself and went to the cabinet, taking out the drawings. Karen followed him, moistening her lips with the tip of her tongue as she bent over to look at them. Tony draped an arm round her shoulders as he also scrutinised the drawings.

Mallory's excitement burgeoned as he watched the historian's hand wander down to cradle her left breast, thumb circling the pointed hidden nipple. Her face flushed as she responded to the pleasure and at the same time absorbed the rich sexual feast spread before her.

This was too much for Mallory's self-control, the ache in his cods needing relief. He loosened the cord of his pants, relaxed his thighs and slid a hand under the waistband. A shiver passed through him as his fingers made contact with the naked flesh of his belly, touched the wiry pubic hair and cupped the full globes resting between his legs under his sky-pointing penis.

Before him, framed in the mirror, was the disturbing sight of Tony removing Karen's top and then her shorts. He positioned her to give Mallory an uninterrupted view of her furry wedge, his fingers holding her sex lips open, the outer ones bordered with hair, the inner pink and smooth. Angled against him, her pubis was thrust forward as he began to massage her clitoris till it protruded like a miniature dick, hard and shiny, betraying its need for orgasm.

Ignorant of her audience, she watched in the mirror as Tony's fingers worked her bud, following the movement with her eyes. Mallory could almost feel the silken lips and smell the fragrance seeping from her, almost share Tony's excitement as he opened his fly, grasped her firmly by the hips and thrust his cock into her from the rear.

Slowly Mallory stroked the thick shaft of his phallus until it dribbled, aching for release. Karen's head rested back against Tony's shoulder, her long throat arched, hips gyrating sensuously against the double pleasure of a slick, wet prick driving into her and a finger frigging her love-button.

Mallory stifled a groan, the scalding heat of lust greater than he had ever known it, his cock-head slippery, his fingers curled round the trunk, plea-suring it with long, smooth strokes. It was as if he held Karen in his arms, thrusting his spear into her hot wet sheath, her tangled mane of hair flowed over them both, a perfumed curtain in which a man might hide himself and his fears. This mental image transcended the reality of the couple screwing in the sanctum and him mastur-bating as he watched them in a trick looking-glass.

Tony's movements were becoming frenzied and Karen ground her clit against his hand, eyes closed, an ecstatic expression on her face. Mallory drew his foreskin down over his glans then pushed it up, repeating the motion, sensation pouring through him as the frisson brought him painfully close to climax.

Karen's eyes were aflame, her skin flushed and glowing as Tony heaved and lunged, panting heavily. The fierce heat of Mallory's release thun-dered through his body, forcibly ejecting a spurt of liquid from his balls with such violence that it spattered the mirror with milky drops.

The phone was ringing as Karen opened the door of Laurel Cottage. She dropped her bag on the floor and reached for the receiver. 'Hello,' she said.

'Armina here,' a breathy voice answered. 'What're you doing tonight?'

'Not a lot. I'm about to take a shower—'

'Wish I was there—'

Crimson-tinted visions of spicy-scented female organs made a coil tighten in her womb, but Karen continued calmly, 'Then I'm going to cook myself something to eat and watch telly.'

'Come round to my place.' The mellifluous voice was temptation itself. 'The girls will be here.'

'The girls?'

'Celine and Patty and Jo. You've not met the rest of our happy band of pilgrims, have you? Mallory's tarts.'

OK, so the mistresses were turning up in full force. Karen could cope with that, but, 'Will he be there?' she asked tersely.

'No,' Armina replied and gave a silvery chuckle. 'This is strictly one for the girls. Nothing formal, just a few drinks and nibbles. A bitch session, if you like.'

It was one of those enchanted, balmy English summer evenings and Karen was restless. She could think of no plausible excuse to avoid accepting the invitation. In fact she was curious to see the ladies who had intimate knowledge of Mallory's body. Time to grasp the nettle, prepare herself for battle and meet the opposition.

She showered, deliberated, discarded one ensemble after another, then settled for a burnt-sienna skirt in cotton crepe, flowing, button fronted, semi transparent. It undulated about her legs, sometimes opaque, at other times displaying the misty outline of the gap between her thighs and the minute scrap of matching silk covering her full, rounded triangle of freshly washed pussy hair.

Good, she thought, turning this way and that before the mirror. *I'm not prepared to sacrifice my individuality. This looks unusual, very French Riviera, and cost a bomb, for all its throw-away chic.* The top was short, low necked, sleeveless and coffee beige, which showed off her tan. A chunky African necklace, big dangling earrings, an ivory and brass bangle of great width and thickness, gold strap sandals, and her outfit was complete.

Karen was never quite satisfied with her appearance, and had always regretted having curly hair, dreaming of locks as straight as pump water, but now those thick, scrunch-dried ringlets pleased her. They added to the image she was trying to project – of someone bold and fearless, who knew her own mind and followed her star, striding confidently through the world, disregarding the opinions of others.

She decided to walk, taking the woodland path towards the Dower House. And it was there she came upon Spike, leaning against a gleaming electric blue and chrome monster propped on its stand near the trunk of an oak tree.

He looked bigger than ever, loosened yellow curls brushing his shoulders, chest bare beneath a black leather waistcoat. His arms rippled with muscle; the skin was tanned a solid brown sprinkled with gold fur and ornamented with tattoos. A wolf snarled from his left bicep, a wild-haired Harpy from the right. Engraved bracelets of Celtic design coiled round his forearms. He was smoking a hand-rolled cigarette and registered no surprise on seeing her.

Karen stopped, acutely aware of her skirt lightly tangling between her bare thighs and skimming over her plump mound. Lingering rays of sunlight struck through the trees, lending the glade a copper tone. The arching branches met overhead, enclosing them in an Arcadian grove. A damp smell rose from the warm soil, redolent of growth and fertility, almost the smell of sex. And there stood that flaxen-haired young man, an Adonis in leather. The blood began to gather in her loins, thickening her labia, galvanising her sentinel clit into action. It never slept, always alert and hungry for sensations.

'Want to try out the hog?' he asked, and it was as if they were carrying on the conversation started in the pub.

'OK.'

He put on his helmet, dark visored, making him look sinister, blank faced, like Darth Vader. He could have been an alien or a knight errant – he was no longer quite human. Karen thrilled to this strangeness, every nerve sending urgent messages to her skin surface. He straddled the machine like a lover possessing the body of his mistress, his bulging tackle supported by the seat. He manoeuvred the bike's sleek bulk on to the footpath, his thigh muscles straining against his black leather trousers.

Taking its weight, one booted foot braced on

the earth, he kick-started the engine and let it idle as he handed Karen a helmet from his pannier. It felt foreign, heavy, hot. The visor darkened the forest, making it greenish, like being under water.

The action of spreading her legs astride the passenger seat sent a charge through Karen's cunt. This intimate contact with the Harley's leashed power quickened her desire. Legs clasped round the warm leather, knees open, skirt rucked up, her pudenda rested against smoothness underpinned with the edge of steel. Anus and pussy were pressed down into that surging force by her own weight, and she felt herself growing wetter, fragile panties soaking with the lubrication engendered by desire.

'You OK?' he glanced back to ask, a man with no face.

'Yes.' She nodded vigorously and slid her arms round his waist, clinging tightly as the bike roared into motion.

Bumping, skidding, it careered down the uneven path, then met the crossroad at the bottom and took the lanes at speed. Out in the open now, Spike let out the throttle. An arrow-straight Roman road lay before them, cutting a swathe through the countryside.

The wind tore at Karen's hair. It flowed from under her helmet, made her skirt stream back, the air stinging her legs, forcing itself between them, plundering her sex. Her inner lips were alternately exposed and covered, crushed by the leather seat, abruptly released. She inhaled the hot smell of tarmac and the scent of Spike's body, his broad shoulders bent under the shiny leather, broad hands gripping the handlebars. She clung to him frantically, maddened by the speed and her own lust, terrified yet exultant.

She was no longer Karen but a wild warrior woman, a Valkyrie riding the storm clouds to gather up the bodies of dead heroes from the battlefield and carry them to Valhalla on the back of her warhorse. And Spike was Siegfried, super hero, about to claim her as his bride. The majestic chords of Richard Wagner's *The Ring* thundered through her brain, and she found herself singing aloud.

Spike had absolute control over the brute: 1300 ccs it might be, but he was master. They purred along at seventy, accelerated to do a ton in a fierce rush of speed, then dropped back to a steady eighty. The miles flashed under the wheels. Karen was aware that he had slowed, turning back towards the woods, cruising now, seeking a place to pull over.

He killed the engine and free-wheeled to a stop. They sat there for an instant, Karen's face buried against his shoulder, her breasts crushed into his back, nipples erect with cold and excitement. He dismounted, kicked down the stand and supported her as she climbed off. Her knees felt like jelly. Her sex was on fire. He unfastened his helmet and took it off, his tawny hair matted with sweat. She removed hers and went straight into his arms.

They did not speak. Words were superfluous. He wedged her against the bike. His hands came up to hold her head steady and his mouth fastened on hers. This is how she wanted it, no tenderness, no pause, just sheer, unbridled animal lust. She felt intoxicated with it. Gasping with pleasure, she was desperate to feel him come inside her. Spike's tongue darted between her lips, exploring her mouth, and she savoured the taste of his saliva spiced with tobacco. She pushed open his waistcoat, running her hands over his crisp, light chest hair. Her questing fingertips encountered something else.

Each of his nipples was pierced by a small gold ring. This discovery roused her to fever pitch. Where else might he be pierced?

Spike's hands were under her top, pushing it up, exploring her breasts. Karen moaned; big though they were, they seemed lost in his enormous paws. They firmed to his touch, the tips taut. She could feel the hardness of metal at her back and the hardness of his stiff rod grinding against her front, twin pressure points of delight. Eyes half closed, she breathed in rhythm with Spike's finger kneading and rolling her nipples.

He lipped over her face and neck, his mouth finally closing on a rosy teat, sucking it with the avidity of an infant. One of his hands pushed up her skirt, fondling her buttocks, while the other made a beeline for her mound, fingering the damp cotton covering it, then working under one side, finding the margin of her swollen labia. Karen wriggled out of her knickers, the scrap of material abandoned on the earth between their feet, and slid her legs further apart to give him ease of access to her hot, hard centre. She could see his cock swollen behind its leather covering and yielded to the longing to undo his wide belt, lingering over the brass buckle.

He groaned, watching as she started to release him. His cock was big, long and uncut. It shot out, causing the zipper to descend on its own, not only delighting her with its size and stiffness but offering a surprise: a gold ring pierced the flesh, passing through the foreskin. Karen stared smiled, opened her legs wider.

Spike placed his hands under her backside, stretching the cheeks apart as he lifted her, supported her weight against the bike and lowered her on to his upright shaft. She was so wet that he entered her in one swift stroke. She gasped as she did her best to accommodate him, hanging on to him round the shoulders as he moved her up and down on that length of rigid slippery flesh, the blunt glans bumping against her cervix at every upward thrust, the ring a strange and pleasurable invasion.

She could feel him growing bigger, felt his cock twitch and knew he would come at any moment She held herself still, her fingers buried in his bush, pressing firmly at the base of his penis, preventing the spending of his abundant seed.

He got the message, pulled his prick from her and she sat sideways on the saddle, legs spread wide, holding her sex-lips apart, her pearl glistening between them, pouting and steeped in honeydew. Spike knelt before her, his phallus at a ninety-degree angle as he bent to kiss her clitoris, lapping greedily round the stem, taking it between his lips.

She shuddered, arched her pelvis to meet him as her body tensed, rushing her towards orgasm till she peaked, her vagina spasming again and again. Then Spike swept her high, her legs clasping him round the waist as he impaled her on his cock. His hips moved savagely, once, twice, thrice, then his convulsions matched hers as he poured out his load.

When he withdrew, he kept his arms round her, his wet cock cooling against her belly. 'You're OK,' he murmured, his face radiant.

'You're not so bad youself.' With a smile, Karen moved so that his softening prick slipped away from her. She bent and retrieved her panties, stepping into them and then smoothed down her creased skirt.

He tucked his penis away and zipped up. 'I'd like to see you again,' he said, with a disarming grin.

'I'm not looking for commitment,' she warned, pushed her fingers upwards through her hair, fluffing it out.

'And I'm not offering it.' He mounted the Harley. 'Can I give you a lift anywhere?'

'I was on my way to Dower House.' She got up behind him.

'One of Lord Burnet's women?'

She could not read his expression through the visor. 'No. I'm working in the Blackwood library.'

'Good.'

'D'you know him?' Karen fastened the chin strap of her helmet.

'Yep. My dad owns Cassey's Garage and we service his cars.'

'And the women? D'you know them, too?'

He nodded. No more talk; the bike was too noisy, the throbbing of its engine too enveloping. They reached the gates of the Dower House in a few seconds. Karen got off and gave him back the helmet. She felt a certain reluctance to leave, not that she intended to get involved, but she would have liked to have continued riding, experiencing the buzz of speed, the throb of power penetrating her core.

The front door was open but the house seemed deserted. After knocking, Karen waited for a moment, then walked round to the rear. Soon she heard the sound of voices, feminine laughter, the splashing of water, and inhaled the odour of smouldering charcoal, charred meat and fried onions.

She rounded a corner and came out on a patio paved with terracotta Spanish tiles surrounding a pool lined with blue and white mosaic. The shallow end had wide steps leading down into the water, and seated on the middle one were a pair of beautiful women, one black, one white, both superb.

Armina was by the barbeque, using tongs to turn the steaks and chicken portions browning on a grid above glowing red coals.

'Glad you made it,' she cried. 'Make youself at home. Meet Patty,' and she indicated the girl who was slicing baps on the pine table. She nodded at Karen and continued cutting. The women in the pool looked on curiously.

Karen felt overdressed. Everyone else was clad in next to nothing. Armina, water trickling down her body, had obviously been swimming. She was topless, her tiny breasts crowned with cold puckered nipples. Her silver Lurex G-string clung to her pussy like a wet stamp, and the straight line of her crease could easily be seen through the damp material.

Patty, a plump brunette, wore a pair of cutdown jeans with the legs hacked so high that only a thin strip of denim was left between them. She had nothing on underneath, and had pulled them up into the crotch so tightly that the two separate halves of her sexual fruit were openly on display, the seam only just visible as it emerged from between her lower lips. The fact that she had carefully removed every trace of pubic hair made it all the more intriguing.

'Meet Jo and Celine,' Armina said, slipping her arm round Karen's waist and leading her to the poolside. 'Girls, this is Tony Stroud's assistant.'

They smiled and stood up, women who gloried in their bodies and the power such beauty bestowed on them. Celine was tall and sleek, with broad shoulders and tight-muscled buttocks. Her jutting breasts were crowned with huge nipples. She stalked up the steps, her hips and lean legs moving rhythmically under the single layer of thigh-length chiffon shirt moulding itself wetly to every curve and hollow. Her chocolate-coloured skin, her pitch-black hair braided into a hundred tiny plaits tipped with gold wire and bright beads, gave her the aspect of an exotic tribal queen. Her abundant bush formed a thicket from her lower belly to the apex of her triangle, the fronds curling between her legs.

Jo was small by comparison, yet not as petite as Armina and of athletic build. She was honey-skinned from sunbathing, with ash-blonde hair falling to her waist in one long sweep. Her eyes were deep violet-blue with thick curling lashes, dark at the base and gold at the tips. Given to a certain eccentricity of dress, her narrow waist was made even tinier by a red satin basque trimmed with black lace. The half-cups pushed her breasts high, the nipples two pebbles standing out proud. The tightly laced garment ended at the hip bone, and her lower torso was bare, drawing the eye to a part-depilated quim. An individualist, she had left a narrow line of hair sprouting each side of her deep amber-coloured cleft

These, then, are Lord Mallory's concubines, Karen thought, fire coursing through her veins to settle and burn in her centre as she thought of him. She appreciated the freedom of this place where the women flaunted their nakedness with total unconcern. It was getting dark, but lights sprang on to illuminate the patio softly, underwater bulbs striking upwards from within the pool. All the scents of evening stole from the bushes and ornamental hanging baskets to seduce the senses.

'D'you want a drink, honey?' asked Celine, in a deep, husky American accent. She held out a champagne flute in her long, brown fingers. The filbert-shaped nails were painted strawberry pink.

Karen took it, and also accepted steak and salad, touched by how the ladies were taking care of her, each seeming concerned she should feel at ease.

'Did you have many lovers at university? Was there much talent?' Patty asked. 'I went for a while, studying sociology. Couldn't concentrate on work, though; too many distractions. I met my first husband there. He was a dork but I wanted to get away from my parents.'

'I'm a singer, between gigs at the moment,' Celine supplied.

'And I'm a model, darling,' added Jo, fingering the nipples that lifted above her boned corset, teasing them into even stiffer points.

'D'you live in the village?' The wine was going to Karen's head and she needed to sit.

'Celine stays here when she's down,' Armina replied.

'I have a penthouse in London and another in New York,' Celine informed her, and Karen could not keep her eyes off those up-thrusting brown breasts, longing to open her mouth over the big dark nipples surrounded by even darker areolas. Her experience with Armina needed to be repeated.

'Jo and I have a cottage along the lane,' Patty put in, seated on a low wall, the fold of her shorts deeply trapped between the lips of her labia. The denim was darkly stained from her quim juices. 'I like gardening, and it's great to be able to do what I want when I want without being bullied by a bossy husband.'

'How many have you had?' Karen warmed to the pretty, good-natured girl. Not too bright, perhaps, but of a friendly disposition.

Patty pulled a face. 'Three.'

'A glutton for punishment.' Armina laughed from her place on a wide padded lounger, bare legs elegantly posed, bare cleft exposed, the pink outer lips protruding. She patted the space beside her. 'Come and sit by me, Karen darling.'

'So, you're Lord Burnet's entertainment committee. He keeps you, does he? The ladies of his harem,' Karen said as she obeyed, her head spinning as the girls came closer, draping themselves on big, square tapestry-covered cushions circling the lounger.

They laughed, long throats stretched back,

wide red lips opening on perfect teeth, scents escaping from their skins, exotic products from French perfumeries – jasmine, verbena, musk – overlaid with spices. This mingled with their individual body odours, fragrant hair and strong vaginal emanations. They were women who were sexually active and aware, joyously embracing every apsect of bodily sensation.

'Not exactly. We're too independent. Each of us met him through the social scene, but we come and go as we like. Has he made a pass at you yet?' asked Jo, looking Karen over with the eye of an expert, then putting out a soft hand and gently touching her ankle.

Karen's skin tingled, goose-bumps stippling her limbs, yet her anger against Mallory remained. 'No, he hasn't, and I don't wish him to,' she snapped.

This provoked more laughter. 'That's what we all thought, in the beginning,' Jo said, with a shake of her long blonde hair. 'He can be a bastard, but he has much to offer. It's a buzz to be able to say that you sleep with a lord. Good for the image.'

'He's OK.' Celine flexed her limbs, reminding Karen of a tigress. 'He plays the hard guy, but I guess he got that way when his wife walked out on him.'

'He's been married? I didn't know.' This was a shock. Was there no end to the hidden depths of this man? Even as this occurred to Karen, she was very conscious of Armina stroking her upper arm, slowly, languorously, making her melt inside.

'Oh, yes, when he was twenty. Too young, of course. And she was a bitch by all accounts, after him for his title and money. Did well out of the divorce settlement, went back to the States and took their son with her.' Armina was watching her closely, a smile deepening the dimples each side of her mouth.

'A son?' Somehow Karen could not imagine him as a father.

'An heir, my dear. It's essential for someone in his position. The boy will go to an English public school when he's older. Mallory visits him. Has just come back from LA, as a matter of fact. He's always in a bad mood for a while after.'

'Understandably.' Celine seemed more sympathetic towards him than the others. 'He'd like the kid with him full time.'

'Would he?' Patty murmured. 'I'm not sure about that. It would put a stop to his parties. He'd have to behave more responsibly.'

'Have you been invited to the one he's planning for next weekend?' Jo's hand slid higher, stroking the inside of Karen's thigh under cover of the flowing cotton skirt.

'No. I've not spoken to him since that morning when he turned up here.' Karen managed to answer in a steady voce, though her clit was jumping in eager anticipation of Jo's further exploration.

'He'll ask you. It's up to you whether you accept or not,' Armina said slowly, the touch of her fingers on Karen's arm echoing those of Jo's on her thigh. 'But don't turn it down out of hand. You might find it entertaining. He's an exceptional man and has some interesting friends.' She stirred, swung her legs over the side of the lounger and rose to her feet in a graceful movement. 'It's getting chilly. Shall we go inside?'

Karen wanted to say it was time she was leaving, but her tongue seemed too big for her mouth and it was hard to speak. She wasn't sure how it happened but her glass always seemed to be brimming, no matter how often she drained it. They went through the French doors connecting the reception room with the terrace. It was a beautiful room filled with deep armchairs and couches, but this was not where Armina intended to spend the evening. After fetching further bottles, she led the way upstairs.

Karen followed, the stairs dipping and swaying, arms supporting her to the boudoir where she had been seduced by Armina and met Mallory. It was familiar yet strange tonight, wavering unsteadily. No more champagne, she thought, and tried to stand alone. She succeeded momentarily, leaning against the mullioned window embrasure. Behind her she could hear the girls laughing and Armina saying, 'Switch on the video, Celine. I want to see a porn movie.'

'Can't I watch *Salome*?' the American asked. 'You know I'm studying the role. It turns me on more than dirties.'

'It's too blood-thirsty,' Patty complained, plumping down on the four-poster, elbows resting on her humped knees.

'It's great!' Celine protested. 'John the Baptist spurns Salome. He's King Herod's prisoner, and she's the dirty old guy's step-daughter. He's got the hots for her. She does a striptease to give him a hard-on and demands John's severed head on a silver platter. Then she makes love to it.'

Karen turned to her, daylight dawning. 'I know

543

the opera. It is wonderful. You said you were a singer. I thought you meant pop.'

Celine's smile was wide and warm. 'No, honey. I sing opera. I know I'm black, but that doesn't matter. I can play Tosca and Carmen and certainly Salome. Other parts, too. With all these avant-garde directors no one minds about colour these days, just as long as there's a big voice. And mine's certainly big.'

'As big as your fanny,' put in Armina, smiling at her lovingly.

The screen lit up and Strauss's seductive, decadent music permeated the bedroom. Celine had fast-forwarded the tape to the *Dance of the Seven Veils*. The fine down rose on Karen's limbs. It was spine-chilling stuff. Savage, sweet – demonic, divine; expressive of yearning, of the longing for the unattainable that torments the human heart. With every musical phrase, each dynamic chord, the beautiful diva coiled and twisted in sensual dance, removing drape after diaphanous drape, slowly, lasciviously, until she was stark naked.

'Get her nerve!' Celine whispered, awe-struck. 'Showing her bush at Covent Garden Opera House!'

'She's marvellous!' Karen enthused, high on watching the singer portraying the obsessional madness of Salome, adoring the bloody head, kissing the dead lips, writhing on stage with it in her arms as if about to achieve orgasm.

Unified by their mutual love for this art form, Celine drew closer where they sat at the end of the bed, then slipped the T-shirt from Karen's shoulders, running her slender fingers over each bone and muscle. Karen drew in a sharp breath as Celine traced a line down between her breasts then, bending forward, opened her mouth to a nipple, not caressing it, simply warming it with her breath.

Karen braced herself, rejoicing in this intimacy, needing more, pushing upwards against that tormenting mouth, till Celine relented and closed her lips over the taut, needful teat, sucking it strongly. Karen straightened, gripped Celine and hugged her. Armina took an ornamental box from the bedside cabinet, opened the lid and lifted out several dildoes, handing them to Patty and Jo.

'D'you want one?' she asked Karen, and offered a selection.

'Not yet,' she whispered. 'I'm happy as I am.'

Excitement shivered through her as the opera reached its dramatic conclusion. Celine reached over to switch off the machine, then concentrated on Karen again. She felt those brown fingers brush over her upper thigh. Her legs opened involuntarily and Celine pushed down the little triangle of cotton concealing the feathery mons. Her finger slipped lower and slid effortlessly between the folds of the outer lips while her thumb flicked lightly across the eager clitoris.

'You're wet,' Celine murmured in that resonant voice, her face pressed in Karen's neck, lips moving against her soft flesh. 'It's almost as if you'd had sex recently. Have you?'

'Yes. On the way here,' Karen confessed, while those artful finger continued to rouse her bud. 'He's a biker called Spike.'

'Spike? He's a good lay, isn't he?'

'You know him?' Karen no longer cared who

had screwed who, when or how. All she wanted was for that smooth, perfectly timed caressing of her love-bud to continue till she erupted.

'We all know him, don't we, girls?' Celine looked up to say.

'We do,' they chorused.

Armina was seated on a chair, legs spread wide, running a huge black dildo across her slick-wet avenue, dallying to circle the head of her clit. It was a perfect model of a penis; veins running up its stem, knotted and realistic and a rounded, bulging cock-head. It hummed persistently, and she flicked a switch to make it move faster.

Patty, naked now, was kneeling over Jo who lay on her back on the bed. Patty's pussy was level with Jo's mouth and Jo's tongue was lapping at her juices and licking her bud. At the same time, Jo held a vibrator in her hand, pushing it between Patty's thighs and working it along her crack, touching her puckered nether hole and letting it idle over her plump button.

Armina squirmed and yelled, carried beyond the edge. She joined Celine and Karen on the bed and, as Celine slowly continued to move her fingers in a slow slick arc over Karen's aching bud, Armina inserted a thick pink rubber dildo into the singer's vagina, forcing a moan from her lips. When it was well moistened, Armina drew it out slowly and rubbed it over Celine's opened pussy, concentrating on her large red clitoris.

Karen lay there quietly, relishing every movement of Celine's fingertip – so wet now, slippery with that clear, fragrant juice seeping from Karen's aching vagina. Celine had settled down into a steady rubbing motion, the friction sending agonising need through Karen's entire body. It was gathering, centring, hot waves washing over her, the feelng tingling up from her toes, rushing down from her brain to explore in rainbow prisms of light and feeling.

While the ripples were still shuddering through her, she heard Jo and Patty cry out and felt Celine's spasm as she, too, climaxed.

Chapter Six

KAREN AND ARMINA cantered across the wide stretch of land joining the cliff tops. The wind was fresh, blowing from the sea, which rolled in remorselessly, pounding and crashing on the rocks far below. Huge clouds threw swiftly moving shadows over the mighty expanse of green water. Patches of sunlight broke through to cast a radiance on the curling white breakers.

It was Saturday, and Karen had escaped the stuffy library, accepting Armina's invitation to ride. She had brought equestrian kit with her, and Tayte Penwarden had fixed her up with a lively mare. Now she turned in the saddle and shouted to Armina, 'I'll race you.'

Armina grinned, leaning over to slap her impatient mount's finely arched neck gently. 'All right. Where's the finishing line?'

Karen pointed to a clump of stunted trees. 'Over there!' Her mare fidgeted restlessly, sensing a gallop.

They shot off, two speeding arrows, one piebald, the other grey. Karen loved being in the saddle again. She had ridden since she was a girl and understood horses, respecting their moods, their big hearts and courage. Now she rejoiced to feel the broad back between her legs, the skin-tight jodhpurs pressing hard against her cleft, stimulating her clitoris, but most of all she enjoyed the speed, the control, her mastery of the animal.

Armina was an expert, but Karen's pride insisted that she beat her. Head down, face flicked by the flowing mane, she dug her heels into the mare's sides, urging her to even greater effort. The animal stretched her graceful limbs in the air, touching the short springy turf only to leave it again with a single strike of her hooves. Armina was gaining, her wild, exultant shout carried on the wind. Her horse whinnied, his coat flecked with foam.

Karen felt her body lacked substance. She became one with the mare, wanting nothing but to fly like this for ever, the stormy sky, the fertile, spongy earth, the tumult of the sea mixing and melding with her own passionate being.

The trees were coming nearer. With one final burst of speed she reached them first. She slowed the mare to a walk, lovingly patting her streaming neck. Armina drew up alongside. She removed her hard hat, a gloved hand ruffling her springy curls.

'Well done, you.' There was genuine pleasure in her voice. 'You'd better join the hunt and enter the local gymkhanas. Ride for Blackwood Towers. Mallory's the champion at the moment, but we could do with a female challenger.'

Pink with exertion and Armina's praise, Karen

dismounted, petting the mare, who was recovering her wind. The animal's warm breath wafted over her skin; the big noble head nuzzled gently into her shoulder. Karen knew a moment of pure happiness. It was as if she had passed through an initiation rite and been accepted by the ancient manor and its environs.

Tayte was waiting for them in the stable and Karen, blood running hot from the exhilaration of the race, was sharply aware of him. As he helped her down his hand lingered for longer than was necessary, black eyes boring into hers. He was ruggedly handsome; ebony curls, a good body, long legs with a promising swelling in the fly area. She caught the strong, evocative smell of him, comprised of hay and horses, fresh sweat and the underlying odour of masculine genitals. Her pussy clenched and her clitoris rose.

They stood there for a heartbeat no more and then he jumped back at the clatter of hooves on cobbles and ran out to assist Mallory. Karen strolled after him, leaning against the lintel, her heart contracting despite herself in appreciation of the picture presented to her bedazzled eyes. It could have been in any century, any country – man, horse and dogs returning from the kill.

Mallory was easy in the saddle, seated like an emperor on a black beast of enormous height, power and magnificence, two hounds panting at its side. His head was bare, the sudden sunlight striking ebony stars from his hair. A thonged jerkin in a natural shade of leather covered his wide shoulders, the full sleeves of his white shirt ballooning to band round his strong wrists. On his left wrist perched a hooded hawk, bells jingling on the jesses bound to each of its legs, just as in the Long Gallery portrait.

Several carcasses dangled from the back of his saddle, grey fur streaked with crimson. As Tayte held the horse steady, Mallory swung down, the raptor still balanced on his gauntlet, the tired dogs panting at his heels.

His eyes met Karen's. An electrifying jolt darted straight down her spine into her root. He nodded coolly. 'Miss Heyward.'

'Good morning, sir.'

'Hello, Mallory.' Armina sauntered out, hands on her hips, a diminutive horsewoman in elasti-cated breeches that boldly emphasised her sex-lips and rump. 'Caught some bunnies?'

He gave a narrow smile, and his right hand caressed the bird's brown speckled feathers. 'Leila has done well. Haven't you, my beauty?'

Karen had never before heard that caressing, tender note in his voice, and the hawk responded to it, quiet under his sure touch. An entirely new and astonishing facet of his personality had been revealed. She felt her resolve weakening, moved by this show of affection to a dumb creature and bewitched by his extraordinary good looks and animal magnetism.

'She's lovely,' she ventured, putting out a hand to touch Leila in lieu of touching him. All she could think about was the reptile slumbering in the warmth of and darkness of his crotch.

He swung away.

'Don't even try,' he warned grimly. 'The hawk is a wild thing, not some domesticated canary. She'll peck you as soon as look at you. She's nervous, highly strung. Leila's a true peregrine

551

falcon. See her long sickle wings? If she wasn't hooded, I could show you her dark-brown eyes and the notch on either side of her beak.'

'I'd like that,' Karen answered, refusing to be intimidated. 'And I'd like to learn hawking.'

'I doubt you'd have the patience,' he said, with a scornful lift of his brow. 'Each bird is an individual, and all are difficult to train. They learn to obey one master and one only. I spent ten days and nights in the mews with Leila until she learned to accept me. We were alone the whole time.'

Karen's head spun as she visualised being alone with him in similar circumstances: the dimness of the mews, the soft rustle of feathers and the tinkle of jess bells, the isolation, with only this man beside her. Her sex ached, the lips swelling, the jodhpurs riding up her wet pussy, but she exerted her will power and did not betray this overwhelming longing, ice cool as she turned back into the stable.

'I'm sure I'd be able to do it,' she said levelly. 'I can do most things, if I set my mind to then. I've studied karate; that helps develop self-control.'

'Have you indeed?' He strode past her towards the adjoining mews.

'She's just beaten me in a race,' Armina called after him. 'I've said she ought to enter the horse trials.'

He paused, looked back over his shoulder, tall and lean and haughty. 'How d'you feel about that, Miss Heyward? Will you have time, or is there too much work for you to do in the library?'

Karen could feel her face flushing scarlet. 'Don't worry, sir. I won't neglect my duties,' she retorted, furious with him for suggesting she might be incompetent or lazy.

He smiled, that slow smile that never quite reached his eyes. 'I've no doubt you're a super-woman,' he said, his sarcasm cutting like a lash. 'We'll talk about it.'

'We won't!' she snarled, her breasts tingling, nipples aching for his mouth, brain refusing to admit it.

'I'm holding a dinner party tonight. You're invited.' He threw this casually over his shoulder as he disappeared into the shadowy mews.

'He approves of you,' Armina said, about to go after him. 'You'll have to excuse me. He likes me to give him head after he's been hunting. Catch you later.'

Damnation! Karen swore inwardly, disgruntled, disappointed and livid with herself for her reaction. *I won't go to his bloody dinner party!* But she knew she was lying. Curiosity would drive her there, if nothing else.

Her skin prickled as she became conscious of someone watching her. It was Tayte, leaning with his arms folded on the edge of a stall, his peaty, unsmiling eyes fixed on her breasts. Karen's breath shortened and her heart began to beat in slow, steady thumps. That uncomfortable feeling in her crotch refused to go away, the material chafing the moist, hair-fringed outer labia. She needed attention, needed it badly, and now, made desirous by the ride, the sudden appearance of Mallory and the strong emotions he provoked in her.

Tayte came round the stall and stood near her, not attempting to touch, simply looking, but his faded jeans were distorted by the erection stretching the denim. Karen wanted to free it, to see it spring out, to rub it until it paid her milky tribute.

'I've a room close by,' he said at last, and his calloused hand opened her riding jacket and rasped over the silk shirt she wore beneath, pausing when the nipple of one breast stiffened against his palm.

'Have you?' Her voice was unsteady, but she stood there rigid, only her wanton teat betraying the tumult raging inside her.

'Why don't I show you?' His thumb revolved on the excited tip, then he lowered his head and she felt his mouth fasten round it, the silk damp now, his tongue wetting it as he slowly teased the hard little peak.

'I'd like that,' she whispered.

Tayte kissed her fingers, clasped in his for guidance. The gloom was full of obstacles, old chains, saddles, tackle and empty crates. The building had once been a tower, one of a pair from which the manor had taken its name. Used for stabling cattle during sieges in the old days, it now formed the mews, housed horses and acted as a storeroom for harnesses and fodder.

Karen stumbled on the uneven treads of the stair and Tayte's arm steadied her. He had, it seemed, the entire loft at his disposal, not a single room but a well-appointed flat, with a kitchen, bathroom, living-room and bedroom, it was all lime-washed walls and knotty, blackened beams, with a wood-burning stove set back in the thickness of a brick fireplace. A perfect venue for an amorous bachelor. Soon they were standing on opposite sides of his big old-fashioned bed.

Karen was thinking of Mallory and Armina in the mews, imagining her taking his cock in her mouth and sucking it till he came. At the same time she remembered her nights in the Dower House when first Armina and then Celine had awakened her to the wonders of lesbian sex. She was burning, steamy, nectar escaping from her love-hole to make a wet patch on her breeches.

Tayte unbuttoned his check shirt while she watched, agitation rising at the sight of that gypsy-tinted flesh, his chest broad and hairless, the pectorals honed through breaking and training horses. His arms were coated with dark fuzz, his waist slim, clinched by the leather belt supporting his Levi's. He came round to her side of the bed, then reached for her, his wide mouth hovering about hers for an instant.

Karen reached up to meet his lips with a fire of her own, her tongue touching his. He held her firmly against the stirring mass of his cock, and her arms crept up round his sinewy neck. He explored her mouth deeply, his tongue working round her gums and teeth, tangling with her own tongue, sucking it between his lips. He released her and she helped him take off her jacket, then the silk shirt. It slithered to the floor, her breasts bared, round and firm, the nipples hard and rosy, arching upwards to be fondled.

Karen fell back on the bed, arms outstretched towards him. He left her momentarily, tugging at her boots and peeling down the riding breeches. She wore no panties, liking the feel of the rough fabric chafing her skin.

'I want to see your cock,' she demanded imperiously.

She sat up and worked at his fly buttons, taking his steel-hard rod into her hand while he stood there looking at her. It was large, red-capped, thrusting up from its crisp black bush. Karen ran a fingertip over the slit in its bulbous glans, then leaned closer, her tongue tasting the juice smearing it. Salty, sharp, its flavour stung but she took the shaft into her mouth, while Tayte arched his hips, pressing it in till the slippery head touched the back of her throat.

Spreading the opening of his breeches wide, she felt for his balls. The blood pulsed in those pendulous globes as she ran a finger over the ligament dividing them, weighing them, playing with the hardening pair in their velvet pouch. Tayte groaned and grasped her by the hair, pushing hard till she felt herself gagging. His creamy spunk ejected in a hot gush, filling her mouth, running from the corners of her lips to bedew her face.

He pulled away, his still erect prick covered in fluid. 'Don't worry, darling,' he gasped, 'there's plenty left for you.'

He lay on the bed and drew her on top of him. Karen, crazy for relief, moved upwards till her avid pussy was over his face. As his tongue met her engorged clitoris, she ground herself down and rubbed it over him frantically, coming in a welter of pleasure. Her spasms pouring through her, she felt Tayte slide her down till his stiff penis stabbed into her centre. Her legs started to tremble, the ridged sides of her vagina pulsing from her orgasm. It was as if it had a life of its own, grabbing and pulling on his cock, milking him of the rest of his juices.

It just kept coming, as if they were welded together. Karen almost fainted. Finally the convulsions subsided. His relaxed shaft slid from her and she lay across his chest, her face buried in his neck.

The loft righted itself and normal sounds penetrated the misty sex haze. She wriggled off Tayte and nestled beside him, her hand stroking his chest hair.

'God, you're great,' he said and kissed her temple. 'Armina told me you were a good screw, but I didn't realise just how good.'

'Armina?' It was disconcerting to realise they had been discussing her, but perversely exciting, too. No doubt they would now compare notes. 'Do you fuck Armina?'

'Everyone fucks Armina,' he chuckled. 'You'll see tonight, at the party.'

Karen raised her hands and pushed her hair back from her forehead, and the shower cascaded over her upturned face like a tropical rainstorm. She reduced the jets a little, allowing the water to penetrate every nook and cranny of her body, relaxing under its warm caress. It ran down her breasts in rivulets and trickled slowly over her bunched nipples, the gently friction stimulating those votaries of Eros.

She reached for the shower gel and squeezed a generous puddle into her cupped palm. Vanilla essence spiced the steamy air as she spread it over her shoulders and breasts – milky, viscous, reminding her of jism. Rendered languorous by memories of her session with Tayte earlier on, she smoothed the lather around her nipples, circling the pink peaks, flicking them, lightly pinching them, wondering if she could come by her tits alone. Certainly, everything that happened to her nipples went hot-line to her vagina. She could feel herself getting juicy, and ran her hands down her body to her pussy.

The luxurious feel of the scented lather mingling with the streaming water coursing over her belly and thighs awakened new depths of desire that even Tayte's energetic fucking had failed to satisfy.

Mallory's face appeared in her inner eye, and her fingers slid down towards the water-matted curls of her pubis. In an hour or two she would see him again. Slowly, she opened the pink wings of her labia and pushed back the tiny foreskin, shuddering as she made contact with her precious pearl.

Pictures of her lovers flickered against the screen of her brain: Kan and Jeremy, Tony and Spike and Tayte; most of all, the one who she had not yet had – the enigmatic Mallory. She circled her clit, teasing it, patting it, her finger poised above it without granting the frig it craved.

Which of those men would she like with her now, bringing her to the edge, filling her cunt with their cocks? Their faces faded. She was conscious only of her rapacious centre. The middle finger of her right hand descended on it with a deliberate force that made her squirm.

Of all physical pleasure, she enjoyed masturbation most, relishing the sensation of her fingertip unfurling the petals of desire, finding the bud within, enjoying the sensation of her own finger against her own clit. There was sorcery in the way she could manipulate it, dam the cataract, think of something else, read a book while caressing herself, always aware but playing a game. She could make it last for an hour sometimes, delay the leap into heaven, that high, tumultuous moment of release.

It was a duel between her finger and her trigger button, and now it seemed that rampant protagonist was winning. The first spasm began, and she looked down, legs apart, holding back the labia with her free hand, so excited by the sight of that pearly pleasure point poking from its cowl that other spasms followed, one tumbling over the next.

Karen moaned, wanted to delay it, couldn't, thrusting her pubis forward as a final huge surge swept through her carrying her to an orgasm so intense it left her shuddering and gasping. She put out a hand to steady herself as the convulsions died away, the ripe sexual lubricant mingling with the lathery water flowing down to her feet, washing round them, gurgling towards the outlet.

Refreshed and energised, she stepped from the shower and reached for a large fluffy white towel, draping it round her as she wandered into the bedroom. Dry now, she dropped her covering, staring at her naked body in the pier glass, running her hands down her sleek, damp sides, amazed as always because nothing showed in her face. No one looking at her would guess she had been indulging in a secret vice. She selected body lotion from among the bottles on the dressing table and massaged it into her skin. The pungent aroma of *Samsara* rose above the lingering odour of vanilla.

Dinner was set for eight. She had half an hour

to get ready. What to wear? It was a constant problem now, whereas at Oxford it had rarely bothered her. Undergarments or no? The weather was muggy, a storm threatening overhead. She thought no, but then again had not yet had the opportunity to try out the black satin underwired bra and matching girdle she had purchased on impulse in an Anne Summers shop.

The act of unwrapping the lingerie was thrilling in itself; such provocative, sexy scraps of nonsense. First she hooked the brassiere at the back. It was only just big enough, her tanned flesh rising above the half-cups, nipples peeking saucily over the black lace. Next came the girdle, a narrow, restrictive strip that gripped her waist and left her lower belly and mons exposed, drawing the eye to it. Seated on a stool, Karen rolled black stockings up her legs, so sheer they resembled pewter mist, and clipped the suspenders to the tops, thighs responding as her fingers brushed them.

Standing again, she thrust her feet into high-heeled sandals and pirouetted before the mirror, enthralled by the sight of herself. She looked like a hooker. The black satin bonded her breasts and waist, cutting into her flesh. Greyish black encased her legs in startling contrast to the pale area of her buttocks and furry pubic triangle with its fascinating furrow.

Eager for more, she stepped into a minuscule thong. It seemed a crime to cover that fragrant slit, so pink and hairy and mysterious; but it was the first time she had worn crotchless knickers. She could not resist pulling them tightly over her crack, enthralled to see the plump lips pouting through the lacy gap. Her nub jutted forth, and she gave it a quick stroke but resisted masturbating again, promising herself she would do it later.

Flinging open the door of the walk-in wardrobe, she scanned the rows of clothes. Which should it be? This was, after all, an important occasion. She pulled out a green crushed-velvet number from an exclusive fashion house, a wickedly expensive extravaganza, consisting of a long-sleeved bodice with a plunging cleavage. This fastened at the back with tiny ball buttons and had a slinky ankle-length skirt which opened to her stocking tops on one side.

Karen wriggled into it and surveyed herself critically. It was daring but suitable for a dinner party at a baronial hall – though from Tayte's hints, she gathered this bash was hardly likely to be a formal affair. She felt good in the dress, and the colour was just right for her.

After moisturising her face and adding a touch of blusher, she brushed her lashes with greenish mascara, added moss eye shadow, then carefully outlined her mouth with carmine. She switched on the hair drier and bent her head, letting her hair fall forward as she subjected it to the defuser's hot blast, scrunching and tousling, then tossing it back into an untamed mane of curls.

A string of emerald beads, swinging drop earrings and she was ready for anything, even the infuriating man whose very name made her feel unbearably randy – Lord Mallory Burnet.

In a mood of defiance she drove to the house, parked the Golf alongside several newly arrived vehicles and headed for the front door. The butler ushered her in after consulting the guest list and had a footman conduct her to His Lordship's apartment. Tony had offered to escort her, but on this occasion Karen had been determined to go it alone. Timidity had never been her way, and she certainly had no intention of starting now.

The red cord barring the entrance to the holy of holies had been removed. 'Just go down the corridor and turn right at the bottom, miss,' the young manservant said, his blue eyes twinkling, undisguised lust flickering across his pleasant features.

Karen had noticed him before on her daily visits to the library, had registered that he was stocky but well-built, had a thick mop of sandy hair and eyes that spoke volumes. She had already decided that maybe she would find out which pub he frequented and engineer a meeting.

'Thank you.' She gave him her most dazzling smile.

'You're welcome, miss.' His reply was prompt, his answering grin cheeky and too familiar. Karen left him with a spring in her step, fully aware he was sizing up her tush and probably wondering if she was wearing panties.

Long mirrors in gilded frames set at intervals along the panelled walls added to her confidence, throwing back reassuring reflections. Her gown was a perfect choice. She congratulated herself for being on the ball. Lord Burnet and his guests had better beware.

She reached the end of the corridor and stopped in her tracks. A pair of inlaid doors framed a glittering scene. The grandeur of the salon took her breath away. Her historian's eye noted the Carolean architecture and furnishings, carvings from the school of, if not actually executed by, Grinling Gibbons, Charles II's favourite interior designer, noted for his florid style.

Karen passed beneath the elaborate architrave featuring rams' heads and acanthus leaves, her feet encountering the plush pile of an Aubusson carpet, original and priceless, still perfect after maybe two hundred years of usage. Light radiated from three cut glass chandeliers positioned down the length of the ceiling between plaster swirls and medallions, interspersed with paintings depicting the travels of Odysseus.

Her ears pricked up. In the distance someone was playing the piano, a dreamy Chopin étude filling the night in perfect harmony with the setting and company. She did a double take. Mallory was giving as talented and polished a recital as any professional musician.

The men wore dinner jackets, the women evening gowns. There were a dozen couples, plus Patty, Jo and Celine. And Tony was there, his beard neatly trimmed, wearing a white shirt and black bow tie, bowing to convention except for his midnight-blue velvet coat. He saw her and waved.

'Karen!' Armina trilled, breaking away from a group near the marble fireplace. 'You must meet Sinclair.'

She floated over to Karen, a cross between a pantomime fairy and a debutante clad in an apricot silk-satin bustier and a full tulle crinoline skirt, satin court shoes, and carrying a satin and diamante bag. She wore no jewels except a pair of steel and gold earrings. Karen guessed the gown was probably by Kristensen and, added to the other pricy items, there couldn't have been much change out of £6000. Had Mallory footed the bill?

Armina linked arms with her and propelled her across to where a stranger leaned an elbow on the overmantel. He looked up as Armina cried, 'Here she is – the postgrad I've been telling you about, Karen Heyward. Karen, this is Sinclair, Mallory's brother.'

For a confused instant Karen thought it was Mallory, and then knew her mistake. He was the same height and build, had the same overpronounced good looks, but his hair was a shade lighter and his eyes were grey not golden sherrybrown. Like Mallory he possessed a powerful carnal attraction, but whereas his brother was aloof, stern, almost austere, Sinclair was a conquistador, an adventurer, with all the charisma of a man of that kind.

He bowed with a touch of irony, took her hand and raised it to his lips, hovering above it. 'Hello, Karen – if I may. So you're the one who has been dealing with those dusty tomes? Have you seen the Bedwell cartoons yet?'

He moved a shade closer, his sensual grey eyes questioning. Karen caught herself fantasising about how it would be to have him fuck her. She was certain it wouldn't be gentle; it would be more likely to contain elements of the jungle. A savage mating.

She struggled to keep her cool, realising she ought to say something, make polite, banal conversation. 'I have seen them, and think they're quite remarkable. Exquisitely drawn, not crude as such works often are.'

'Do you find them a turn on? Most people do, myself included,' he said, then boxed her in between an angle of the wall and his broad shoulders, lowering his voice and adding, 'I learned about sex through them. When I was a kid, I'd steal the keys, hide in the little room and wank my budding prick as I looked at them. My first come was over the one featuring the lady in the boudoir. I can even remember what it was called – *Morning Toilette*. I was frightened I'd stained it with spunk, but I'd managed to catch most of it in my handkerchief.'

Karen almost swayed towards him, tossed by a variety of emotions, uppermost of which was an intensity of attraction. Like Mallory? No. In reality they were as dissimilar as chalk and cheese. This man was unprincipled, not to be trusted, yet her body ached to have him penetrate it. She was wet between the thighs, mesmerised by his cynical smile and worldly eyes, that slim body under the tailored tuxedo, that narrow waist and a pelvis that seemed to throw into relief the solid bar of his cock beneath the narrow black barathea trousers.

Mallory rose from the piano when dinner was announced, resplendent in evening dress. 'You've not forgotten how to play,' Sinclair said. 'I suppose it's rather like riding a bike.'

Mallory's eyes switched from Sinclair's face to Karen's, then back to his brother. 'Why are you here?' he said, glacier cool. 'I don't recall inviting you.'

'Do I need an invitation to visit my old home?' Sinclair replied quietly, but with a sarcastic edge.

'I thought you were in Rio.'

'I flew into Heathrow today.'

'This has upset the seating arrangements.'

'Sorry, but my first thought was to drive down and see how you were getting on, old boy.'

What a smoothy, Karen concluded as she walked into the dining room with a Burnet brother on either side. And what a liar!

On the oval, lyre-legged Regency table, the light of a seven-branched candelabra was mirrored in Georgian silver and sparkled on Waterford crystal glasses. The Spode dinnerware was worth a fortune. Karen had been placed next to Tony, with a dapper, middle-aged stranger on her other hand, who seemed totally absorbed with his beautiful companion, a tall angular redhead in a fabulous Vivienne Westwood creation consisting of emerald-green satin stays and a bustle.

Further down Karen could see Armina next to Mallory, and Celine, looking like an exotic Brazilian orchid, draped in purple silk with a huge turban covering her locks. The unrepentant Sinclair was flirting outrageously with her, running a finger along the edge of her décolletage, causing the big nipples to stand out even more.

Amid light, inconsequential smalltalk, poker-faced footmen served one fabulous dish afer another, worthy of Le Manoir aux Quat' Saisons: wines of Bordeaux and Burgundy, both red and white, were poured with royal extravagance. Foreheads were beginning to flush, faces lighting up, eyes shining, reserve melting. And Mallory lounged at the head of the table, easy, gracious, regarding his guests from under hooded lids, though anger flashed in his eyes each time he glanced at Sinclair.

Karen leaned closer to Tony. 'Come on. Dish the dirt. What's the scandal scam? Why this vendetta?'

'Don't ask.' His lips twisted into a crooked smile. 'They've always resented each other, so the gossip goes. Sibling rivalry and all that. Then Caroline, that's Mallory ex, got the hots for Sinclair – before she was the ex, that is. It was almost a case of pistols at dawn.'

'But Mallory had other women,' Karen reminded him, while a strapping footman in formal gear leaned over her shoulder to remove her plate. He smelt good, a combination of fresh linen and aftershave on young skin.

'That's neither here nor there. Don't be so prissy, my dear.'

'I'm not being prissy. It's just that I've never been able to hack the "What's sauce for the goose isn't sauce for the gander" attitude.'

'Feminist!' Tony smiled and let his hand idle across her silk-stockinged knee under the cover of the damask tablecloth.

'I am, and proud of it.' She remained outwardly composed, though anticipation quivered along her nerves at that persuasive, expert touch and the whisper of his hand moving over silk.

It went higher, circling the top of her stocking and bare thigh, then plunging into the narrow gap between her legs, landing unerringly on the open crotch of her panties.

'Sinclair's jealous because he happened to be born twelve months after Mallory, missing out on

567

the inheritance. As for Caroline – well, I don't think Mallory was unfaithful until she started screwing around. Rumour has it that he was mad about her.' As he talked, Tony's finger insinuated itself between her secret lips, applying a delicious, warming friction to her rapidly engorging love-bud.

'Claret, sir?' the footman enquired blandly.

Tony nodded and Mouton Rothschild gleamed in a fresh glass.

Carefully Tony disentangled his hand from her wet avenue and, as he raised the wine to his lips, passed his fingers under his nose, inhaling her fragrance, murmuring, 'What bliss! The bouquet of a splendid vintage, and your glorious female perfume.'

Desserts were served as if by magic, magnificent concoctions to tempt the most finicky gourmet: sorbet, ice cream, gateaux fecund with juicy strawberries, dusky indigo grapes nestling seductively on beds of sugared vine leaves, luscious peaches, their downy skins flushed like a woman's breasts immediately after orgasm. This luxurious abundance was enhanced by the gleam of porcelain tipped with a green as light and delicate as sea foam, and the openwork of gilt-edged Sèvres dishes decorated with copies of Watteau landscapes.

Mallory made sure that his guests were properly stimulated, the butler ordered to produce the finest contents of the wine cellar. The voices grew thicker, louder. It was no longer possible to hear anything clearly, riotous laughter exploding like fireworks.

Champagne corks popped, and Karen knew

she was more than a little tipsy. Celine was singing, accompanied by Mallory, her vibrant voice and forceful personality assuring her of operatic stardom in the near future. The scene wavered, shifted. Karen shifted, too. Everyone was dancing; soul echoed from elongated speakers like miniature skyscrapers. Any sign of formality had vanished. So had Mallory.

The huge doors connecting the various rooms stood wide. A pornographic video was playing, erotic images appearing on the massive television scene, blown up and exaggerated. The size of the actors' penises was unbelievable, gargantuan appendages rearing from matted undergrowth above balls like hairy coconuts. The so-called actresses, were notable for their outsized tits, which they used vigorously, wrapping their lovers' cocks in them, rubbing them up and down. There were close-up shots of their pussies, looming larger than life – great dark caverns that might intimidate a nervous man.

'Look at her cunt!' Tony exclaimed in amazement, staring up at one particularly large lady. *Vagina dentata*. A toothed vagina. Bloody hell! That one looks as if it really might have teeth hidden inside to bite off a bloke's dick!'

The couples on screen were moaning, entering each others' bodies every which way, and Karen's bud was itching, hotly roused in spite of herself. She could feel juices wetting her vulva, and her nipples were painfully sensitive as they rubbed against the inside of her bodice.

The guests stopped dancing, staring at the brash, uninhibited display taking place on the video, inspired to follow suit. One man opened his trousers and brought out his cock, and his partner, ripping off her dress, took it in her mouth and started to suck it madly. Another stood behind the woman he was escorting, hauling up her skirt and sticking his cock into the deep division of her bottom while she played with her nipples. A third, hand raising his lady's gown, was stroking her pussy in a leisurely manner, while she reached round and grabbed his sturdy weapon.

The screen lovers were now showering each other with streams of golden rain. The guests whooped their approval, their activity frenzied. Each couch was occupied by couples straining in ecstasy. The lovely person who had sat near Karen during dinner began to remove her bustle dress. Her breasts were small, her waist slender, but as the gown slid lower, a small penis emerged from the folds. The transvestite stroked it fondly, spread its dew up his arse crack and bent over. The man who had been with him all evening whipped out his stumpy, broad-headed cock and thrust it into the pursed anus.

Tony put an arm round Karen and dipped a hand in her cleavage. White-hot desire snaked through her as he stroked a nipple with one finger. Where was Mallory? Her eyes sought him in the crowd, but she kept getting distracted, thinking, *I suppose this is an orgy. I've never been to an orgy before*.

'You want him? He's in the bedroom.' Tony was attuned to her desires.

They passed under a horseshoe-shaped Moorish arch, guarded on each side by two enormous statues of voluptuous naked slave girls. The

570

ambience of this retreat from reality was Oriental. Persian rugs were strewn on the floor, the fireplace decorated with Islamic tiles, and a narghile with a snakelike tube protruding from its squat brass side stood on an inlaid Damascus table. Subdued light glowed from Art Nouveau lamps with Tiffany shades, each moulded in sensuous flowing lines representing water, trailing vines or womens' tresses. The pungent, sickly sweet odour of joss-sticks played on Karen's already quivering senses.

It took her a moment to take in the whole scene, eyes adjusting to the dusk, then she saw movements in the dimness and a vast seigneurial bed – oak wreathed with carvings, elaborate tenting, heavy drapes. Mallory lay within, part covered by a brocade robe. Celine was poised over him, dreadlocks swinging forward, legs wound round his body, working her hips rapidly as she rode his cock, sliding it in and out of her generous, juicy opening.

Armina had shed her dress somewhere along the way. Patty and Jo were nude, writhing in sinuous dance to atonal Eastern music, the lilt of a sitar, the throb of drums, graceful houris for the master's entertainment, adjuncts to his lust – assistants in heightening his pleasure. They caressed one another as they danced, hands fondling breasts, nipples, fingers playing with rosebud nether regions and spreading scented oil and love-fluid over ripe labia and prominent clits.

Karen stared down at Mallory and his eyes opened, meeting hers, mockery in their golden depths. Celine worked harder, and his expression changed to the intense look of a man about to come. He gasped, reared against her pubis, gave a loud groan and spent himself inside her. On cue, the other girls entered the bed, wrapping their limbs round him till his body was buried in silken, aromatic flesh.

Still those magnetic eyes bored into Karen's, making her blood thicken with anger and thwarted desire. He hadn't suggested that she join him. What was wrong? Didn't he find her attractive? She was tormented with need, nipples and lips hot, a rising tide of tears threatening to overwhelm her.

She felt cool air on her legs as Tony pushed her skirt to one side. His erection was stirring against her thigh. She wanted to feel the long hard length of it plunged deep inside her, comforting, soothing her. In a moment she knew he would do it, and she didn't care – let Mallory watch – let him know his rejection meant nothing to her.

She opened her legs, and Tony's fingers penetrated her vagina, widening it, rousing it, his thumb coaxing her bud from its cowl. She reached out and clamped her hand round the stiff rod poking from the slit in his silk boxer shorts.

Suddenly, brutally and without warning, she was seized by the wrist and rushed across the room before she had time to draw breath or protest.

'Come with me, darling,' Sinclair said, smiling wickedly.

'Where?' She was half angry, half amused, totally intrigued.

'To my lair,' he countered dramatically as he steered her away from Mallory's apartment and paused in an angle of the stairs. 'You don't know the secrets of Blackwood Towers. There are passages – hidden rooms we can turn into jungles. The bower of Aphrodite, the cave of Dionysius, Olympus or Hades? Which shall it be? Dare you enter them with me?'

'Yes!' she cried, possessed of savage recklessness, her heart beating wildly.

Let the brother Mallory hated show her undreamed of depths of depravity. Let him use her while she used him – and just maybe Mallory would get to hear of it, and be hurt.

Chapter Seven

IT'S NOT EXACTLY fear I'm experiencing, Karen thought as she allowed Sinclair to guide her through a little door hidden in the shadow of the stairs. *Slight apprehension perhaps. No one can hurt me, Kan made sure of that. I'd react automatically. Even an assailant brandishing a knife would be floored in a couple of swift moves, with a broken arm.*

The blood was singing in her veins, alert for further sensations. The buzz was tremendous – lust, wounded pride, even the stirrings of an emotion as yet unnamed regarding Mallory. No, it wasn't he who led her along so subtly, hand touching her shoulder, fingers skimming across her bare arm, then alighting at the small of her back. But it was a man who resembled him yet possessed a magnetism of his own.

Karen's every nerve directed itself towards him. She could smell his expensive aftershave and tingled to the brief caressing of his fingers. She loosened, moistened. Something exciting loomed ahead. Whatever it was, she would never be quite the same again.

574

The way was narrow, twisting into the maw of the house, and the thin beam of Sinclair's pencil torch gave little illumination. The air was musty, and Karen's feet encountered steps that turned at a dangerous angle, ending in another, even dustier passage. Here the lighting was powered by electricity, but antiquated and dim – lamps with dingy glass shades, panelled walls black with age, stone flooring on which their footsteps resounded.

'It's a disused wing of the house,' Sinclair explained. 'I always stay here when I'm home. It's supposed to be haunted and no one bothers me, not even the servants.'

It was utterly deserted, a place of hollow, empty corridors and vast echoing galleries. There were reception rooms of sombre magnificence, rich with gilt, damask and drapes, and unsuspected mirrors throwing back at Karen sudden ghostly images of her passing face. In other rooms the furniture was shrouded in dust covers and there were empty spaces on the walls where once paintings had hung. The mirrors were fly spotted, the gilt tarnished, the brocaded chairs frayed, the couches sagging and threadbare. Repositories for unneeded items too valuable to be thrown away, these rooms had a sad atmosphere, keeping their secrets in dusky silence.

Sinclair, hand cupping her elbow, led her to another room, reached by a short flight of stairs. Lamps glowed on sumptuous velvets, on treasures he had siphoned off from other parts of Blackwood Towers or acquired on his travels. The figures on the tapestries appeared to dance, huntsmen and hounds, deer and harbourers –

shimmering, lifelike; foam-flecked horses, the fierce faces, the terrified eyes of prey with scarlet gouts of blood staining their hides.

The night was dense black outside, rain lashing the panes of unshuttered windows, adding to the chill that permeated the bones. The room reminded Karen of the interior of a church, with icons and statues and the swirling smoke of incense rising to the fan-vaulted rafters. In fact it was more like a temple. The black basalt figurine of a jackal-headed god stood on an ebony table supported by writhing serpents.

'This is your bedroom?' she asked, and shivered with desire and anticipation, skin prickling, that persistent, unsatisfied ache gnawing at the pit of her stomach, the unfamiliar feel of the open-crotched thong pressing against her sex lips.

'It is. D'you like it?' He watched her closely, eyes narrowed as he ran an impudent forefinger across the tips of her breasts. 'The bed belonged to the first marquis. Rumour has it that Queen Elizabeth slept in it, but isn't that what they all say?'

It was a truly spectacular couch, more like something from a Hollywood movie set, ornamented with beaten gold and hung with embossed velvet drapes, four bunches of plaster ostrich plumes decorating its foot and head posts.

'It's a monstrosity!' Karen said half in horror, half in grudging admiration, her hand coming to rest on top of his, pressing it closer, her nipples like iron. She revered old furniture, but this was beyond belief. It was the most ostentatious bed she had ever seen, wide enough for six people, a positive battleground for two combatants in the anguished, sweaty, passion-ridden field of sexual congress.

'You think so?' Sinclair grinned and led her towards it. 'It makes me feel like a monarch – omnipotent and horny, ready to spread my seed and service a hundred women.'

'You might find one would be enough,' she suggested breathlessly, her feet dragging unwillingly, her randy clitoris urging her on.

Senses raw, she looked at his dark curls, the elegant lines of his body, and imagined him naked, bending over her, his lips kissing her bud, visualised his cock, a solid bar filling her with its size. Would it be as big as his brother's? Did this characteristic run in families, like the structure of the nose or colour of the hair?

'I doubt I'd be satisfied with one woman, though it would rather depend on who she happened to be.' He stepped away, did not touch her as he spoke, his eyes like molten steel, full of questions. 'Are you Mallory's mistress? Armina says not, but I'd like to hear it from you.'

'Why d'you want to know?'

Keep talking, she told herself, *find out more about him. He's used to women capitulating. Make him wait.* But she was trembling with want, indecision crippling her will. She lusted for him, was certain he felt the same, was aware of that unspoken current flowing between them, a stream of mutual need, purely physical in content.

They stood looking at each other till the silence became awkward, then, 'I don't like being second-best to Mallory,' he growled, and his eyes were as bleak as the storm-racked sea battering the cliffs not more than a mile away.

'I'm sure that's not the case,' she prompted, holding his gaze with an effort.

The friction between the brothers heightened the tension. It was as if Mallory was in the room, standing on her other side with herself squashed between them. The heated passions of hatred, of revenge and flawed love seethed like a savage ocean. Sinclair's fists clenched and a muscle quivered by the side of his jaw.

'You don't know the first thing about it,' he snapped abrasively. 'But tell me he hasn't shafted you, and I'll believe it.'

'I don't care whether you believe it or not. I don't owe you anything.' Her anger was rising in time to the powerful throb in the secret depths of her loins. 'Take me back to the party.'

Sinclair's lips quirked, one eyebrow lifting. 'You don't really want me to do that.'

Taking her off guard, he hauled her against him, moulding her to his body, deliberately flaunting the length and hardness of his phallus. She didn't struggle, simply freed herself with an agile twist and fell into a forward stance, slit skirt opening on her long, shapely legs.

Her blow was blocked by his arm. A superb, seemingly effortless but technically correct deflection. *He's an expert!* The astonished thought pierced her like a spear.

'*Kiai!*' she shouted to concentrate her energies, the warrior within her accepting the challenge.

A crescent kick, a backfist strike, a lunging punch – all were blocked. Sinclair scarcely moved, yet fumed her every attack into one of defence, redirecting and parrying her blows.

Defeated, she stepped back and bowed with all the etiquette of the East.

'I underestimated you. I had no idea you knew the martial arts,' she panted.

'I'm rusty – out of training,' he replied with a smile and a formal resuming bow. 'I admire your *mawashi geri*, and I'd like to see you do it barefoot.' His grey eyes darkened to onyx and he added, 'You're used to being in control, aren't you, Karen?'

She threw back her tangled hair, scrutinising him, not quite trusting him, but kept seeing Kan's face superimposed over his. The warm blood of recollection made her almost sick with longing for the exotic hours spent in her sensed's apartment.

'I guess so. Why?'

Sinclair's voice was low, seductive. 'Haven't you ever wanted to hand your will over to someone else?'

Deep within Karen something awoke, a dark, forbidden seam of eroticism. To yield her will, to give herself into someone else's keeping to do with as he chose – the idea was powerfully attractive, obeying atavastic laws beyond civilisation and reason, directly opposed to her strongly held views on independence. *Yes, yes, yes!* her body screamed, but, 'That isn't the way of the warrior,' the coolly urbane woman answered. 'I like to be in control.'

He chuckled, wound his fingers in her mane, used it as a halter to bind her closely to him. Her face was pressed against his chest. She could smell the odour of *Jazz*, smell his own personal body scent, feel the smoothness of his dinner jacket under her cheek. Her bones seemed to crumble, the strength gone, overpowered by the heat laving her core, making her vagina spasm and send out a warm flood of elixir.

'So you can be, darling,' he murmured in a dusky drawl. 'I won't do anything you don't like. I promise.'

Before she realised his intention, he swung her up, one arm under her shoulders, the other beneath her buttocks. With lithe grace he stretched her on the bed. Karen protested, but he placed cool fingers over her lips, gazing down into her wide, angry eyes.

'No, Karen. Do as I say. Lie still – that's right.'

There was magic in the way his fingers stroked across her mouth, thumb caressing the full bottom lip in a way that made her unable to resist licking it, tasting the salty flavour of his skin.

With measured deliberation he rolled her over, undid the buttons at the back of her bodice, then slipped it down to her waist. She heard his quick intake of breath at the sight of her breasts barely contained by the black satin. She glanced down at them, seeing the astonishing surprise of the nipples protruding over the half-cups.

Still holding her arms spread wide, hands clamped round her wrists, Sinclair bent closer. Her nipples crimped as he breathed on them. She arched her back to raise those ardent teats to his lips, but he teasingly withdrew, wringing an exasperated groan from her.

'Poor darling,' he whispered and straddled her, pressing down to make her aware of the fullness and rock hardness of his cock swelling against the tight evening trousers. 'D'you want me to lick them so very badly? Tell me. Say it. Then maybe I will.'

'You bastard,' Karen hissed, ineffectively, attempting to tear herself from his grip. She half raised a knee, threatening to jab him in the crotch.

'Dear me, how unchivalrous!' he chided softly. 'Besides which, you'll lose out on a lot fun if you damage my goolies.'

Before she realised exactly what was happening, he had fastened a silk cord round each of her wrists and tethered her to the bed posts like a crucified prisoner.

His eyes were bright and animalistic, his sensual lips parted, the lower one rolled out. For an instant he hovered there, just above her breasts, then lowered his head. Karen cried out as his tongue flicked over the little peaks poking like ripe raspberries above the satin and lace brassiere. Pleasure saturated her body, pooling in her sex, the honeydew dripping, the hem of her G-string cutting into the ridge of her clitoris, almost, but not quite bringing her to climax.

Sinclair held off, barely grazing the aching points with the tip of his fleshy tongue, moving between them, but using the ball of his thumb to repeat the motion on the one his mouth had momentarily abandoned. Karen's legs trembled and her love bud quivered. She yearned to be sucked, nipples and clit, and squirmed to let him know her need.

With consummate artistry he drew a rosy teat between his lips, nipping playfully but almost painfully before relenting and mouthing it hard, Karen sighed, lay still, relished the sensation, as centred on that pleasure-filled spot as when focusing the force in her knuckles as she fought him. Pre-orgasm waves rippled down her spine, suffused her loins and coiled in her womb, but it was still not enough to bring her off.

She yelled with shock and frustration when Sinclair rose, leaving her hungry breasts. With a thin, triumphant smile he muttered, 'Not yet, darling – not for a long while yet.'

He pulled her dress down over her hips and cast it to one side. He stood by the bed watching her in a detached sort of way as a doctor might look at his half-naked patient. Karen was conscious of her bare flesh below her girdle, the tiny wedge of satin with pussy hair showing through the slit, the sight of her shapely black-stockinged legs. She raised one, admiring the curves: delicate ankle, rounded knee, calf muscles exaggerated by the high-heeled shoe. She wanted to run a hand down her leg, but was his captive. After what seemed like years, he took more cords and, nudging her legs wide apart, secured her ankles to the foot posts of the bed.

She was conscious of how ripe she looked, how exposed and vulnerable. A wave of pure excitement washed through her body. She was entirely at Sinclair's mercy. He started to massage her breasts, one in each hand, pinching the nipples between his finger and thumb. Karen gasped with delight, desperate to feel him inside her.

'Fuck me now,' she whispered. 'Please, I need it now.'

He laughed and replied, 'I know you do.'

As if she was of no consequence, a thing existing solely for his amusement, he unzipped his fly and exposed a swollen dick every bit as magnificent as his brother's. As she watched, he rubbed it slowly, caressing the thick dark-veined shaft and smearing the cap with the cock-tears oozing from its single eye. Leaving it supported by its own stiffness, he shrugged his shoulders out of his jacket, waistcoat and shirt, the smooth bronzed skin contrasting with the pristine whiteness of linen.

Now he was naked to below the waist, his trousers sliding down, that impressive phallus swinging from side to side as he moved, jutting above the twin jewels of his impressive balls encased in their hairy sac. Karen's tongue came out to wet her dry lips and her clit spasmed as she imagined taking that mighty weapon in her mouth, milking him till he yielded his seminal libation.

Kneeling over her, Sinclair wielded it expertly, rubbing the tip up and down the division in the thong, making contact with her erect nub till it was slippery with fragrant juices. Shifting up, he circled the creased pit of her navel, then went higher, each nipple in turn caressed and wetted by his cock-head.

'Ah . . . ahhh!' Karen whimpered, but knew by now that it was useless to beg for the beneficence of its hardness plunging into her vagina. Resting his weighty penis against her, Sinclair's mouth found hers, his tongue diving between her lips, sucking as he had sucked her nipples, probing, darting, sipping the honey-sweet dew of her saliva while she made mewling noises deep in her throat.

He rolled away from her to free himself of his trousers, and she drank in the sight of his strong, muscular body, marked here and there with the scars of old wounds. But beautiful though it was, her eyes kept returning to the dense dark plume spreading over his lower belly and the powerful prong rising from it: the source of pleasure by which her hunger could be appeased. Her fingers itched to touch it, but she was helplessly dependent on his will.

Now Sinclair flourished a strip of black velvet. His cock leapt and grew even bigger as he said, 'I'm going to blindfold you. Are you ready for this?'

She gulped, nodded, hoped that if she was obedient he would insert his generous spike into her yearning cunt. 'I've never done it before.'

'That's good. One should experiment with every aspect of sex play.'

His hands were gentle on her face and the velvet shut out everything as he tied the mask round her eyes. Now her other senses sharpened as sight was denied her. She became a creature of hearing, taste, smell and, above all, touch.

For a moment she lay there disoriented, lost in black silence. Then she heard him moving about, felt the mattress sag as he rejoined her. She waited in breathless anticipation, knew a thrilling stab of fear. Supposing he was unbalanced? Just supposing he was a perverted maniac? He might leave her there to starve. He might even kill her!

She could smell the sharp odour of his sweat above the spicy deodorant and caught a whiff of his cock-juice. Then his fingers touched her right nipple, the pleasure heightened as her senses funnelled into one huge bundle of sexual hunger.

He withdrew, and it was as if she was alone. Her skin was cooling. She was aware of a draught. The smell of incense penetrated her nostrils. Had he left her? Fear rose to a cutting edge. She heard a rustling sound, then felt a touch. Not his fingers – something soft was being smoothed over her belly. She struggled to remember where she had felt it before. It wasn't leather. It had a rough nap. Suede! That was it. She'd once owned a suede skirt, supple, sensual, sinfully impractical and expensive.

The feeling was rapturous, heightening as the suede cruised down, rasping over the insides of her thighs, skating across the satin triangle covering her mound, tangling with the fur fringing her nether lips. Oh, to have it titillating her exposed clit! Karen moaned and twisted, seeking that ultimate contact. The suede was removed.

Fingers tweaked her nipples, rubbing each one with a vigour that made her gasp. The fingers were replaced by lips, sucking, nibbling, tormenting when she needed them on her wildly agitated love-bud. Her torturer refused to touch it. Spread-eagled, wrists and ankles trapped, she could do nothing to relieve her frustration. Anger and irritation with this game that had gone on a smidgen too long were now mingled with something deeper, darker, more intense.

'You want me to untie you?' Sinclair asked, a thread of mockery running through that bland voice. Karen picked up on the inference: *if you do, you'll have lost. Come on, warrior. Take everything I can hand out.*

'No!' she muttered through gritted teeth.

'Good girl.' His voice warmed with admiration. But her whole body convulsed in an instinctive reaction when the cold bite of steel touched her pubis. She felt the knife's icy kiss slither between her skin and the tie at her right hip bone. A jerk, a chill as the thong fell away. The blade inched lovingly across to the other fragile strap. A slight scratch, a nick not deep enough to draw blood, a tension as the material surrendered. Then slowly, tenderly, the knife tip trailed up her body, heated by her skin, making contact with each nipple in turn. Would it caress or cut?

Hovering between terror and desire, she felt an ache in her bladder, pressure building up unbearably.

'I need to pee,' she said.

'Then do it,' Sinclair murmured.

'I can't – not here. The bed?—

'Is protected. Go on, darling, piss for me.'

My God, she thought, eyelids fluttering against the blackness of the blindfold. *How many other women have lain here like this? What sort of a man is he?* Yet the excitement was acute, the fear sending adrenaline roaring through her veins, the need to pass water increasingly urgent. Now she began to have a glimmer of the true meaning of relinquishing her will.

Karen clenched her muscles. There was no way she was going to obey Sinclair's last command. He was touching her again, a soft textured touch this time – the touch of velvet. Starting with her feet, he allowed the fabric to whisper round each toe, over her instep, glide past her knee, caress her inner thigh. He moved it slowly, tauntingly, the strokes delicate, lascivious, as he gently parted her warm, moist lips, moving the plush pile over her swollen crack, allowing it to flirt with her clitoris, which stood proud and erect starving for attention.

Her breath shortened, her skin flushed. Climax was so near, her clit ached for a firmer touch, ready to explode into pleasure. With a sudden change of pace Sinclair replaced the velvet with a hard object – inhuman, rubbery, infinitely strange yet deliriously pleasant. He teased her by running the tip of the dildo around her vulva, then slid the whole thing deep inside her. Karen could feel her body expanding to take it, slippery wet, the end butting her cervix. Her bladder throbbed demandingly, its need accentuated by the size and force of the alien object. She wanted desperately to let go but was too inhibited.

Slowly, Sinclair withdrew the penis substitute almost completely, then equally slowly pushed it right back in again, twisting it slightly on the return stroke. He eased it out to let it fondle her perineum and slip between her buttocks, nudging against her rectum. More pressure, and the artificial glans was penetrating her anus, inch by slow inch. Karen moaned. With his free hand, Sinclair deftly stimulated her nipples, moving back and forth between them, the vibrator returned to her silken haven, bumping her G-spot.

'More,' she wailed, thrashing against her bonds, longing to feel him ploughing through her female parts. 'Give me more! I want your cock!'

'Tut, tut, such impatience,' he chided, and she felt him shift down, his hair brushing her thighs, his breath warming her labia.

She wriggled, lifted her pubis in supplication, and he removed the remnants of her thong, grasping the gusset in his fingers, pulling it aside and exposing her full, pouting lips. He pressed hard on the engorged button swelling shamelessly from its hood. Karen waited with bated breath as he lapped at her juices and placed his mouth against her thickened lower lips, nuzzling in, finding the head of her clitoris and starting to suck and tongue it. The surge of orgasm soared through her, a shuddering, earth-shattering climax.

She screamed, and felt her bladder relax – a few powerful jets and then a longer trickle as her bladder emptied, the relief coupled with the thrill of orgasm making her forget that her urine was running into Sinclair's mouth and over his face.

'Gorgeous,' he muttered harshly. 'The ultimate turn on.'

The control he had shown so far vanished. With rough impatience he covered her body with his, and she felt his penis plunging like tempered steel between her soaking pussy lips. The scarf was snatched from her eyes, and she saw him above her, weight supported on knees and elbows. Looked down to see that mighty cock as it pistoned her, working in and out, faster and faster, till it finally exploded. He slumped on her, face buried in her hair, ripping over her neck and ear lobe.

'Now Mallory can't say he was the first of us to have you,' he whispered, and moved over to the other side of the bed, taking her with him and settling her down so she lay with her head pillowed on his shoulder.

'Does that mean so much?' She was sleepy, sated and utterly relaxed. Having someone else control your will was not so bad, not if it was a man like Sinclair.

'Hmmm, maybe. I get a kick out of putting one over on him.'

'Like when you screwed his wife?'

She felt him stiffen. 'Who told you that?'

'Never mind. It's true, isn't it? You are a bastard, aren't you?'

'The Honourable Lady Burnet was game for anything. I've never met such a horny bitch. She'd have anyone, given half the chance. Mallory took it badly, played the outraged husband to perfection. I enjoyed riling him.'

'What makes you think you've done so now? He's given no indication of the slightest interest in me.' She nestled against him, one of his large brown hands cupping her breast while she toyed with his chest hair and the small dark nimbus of his nipples. *He's totally unscrupulous and amoral, but I could grow to like this*, she thought hazily.

She could feel laughter rumbling in his chest. 'Don't be deceived by his standoffishness. He's interested all right. I know him, Karen, probably better than anyone alive. My brother wants you, and what Mallory wants he usually gets. I try to spoil it for him, that's all.'

The eastern sky was tawny red banded with grey, then came an expanse of lemon-yellow light, and above it pure clarity with here and there a small cloud tipped with gold floating like an island in a fairy sea. Mist hung at the base of the heavily wooded hills, curving in and out of the gullies, presaging another fine day, and bird calls fluted from the tree tops as Karen walked out into the garden.

The storm had passed: the fecund earth was washed clean and the crystal air felt like chilled wine. Karen stood for a moment, breathing deeply, absorbing the sounds and scents, taking the dawn into herself. The grass beneath the trees sparkled with diamond dew, wetting her bare feet. She curled her toes downwards, rejoicing in this contact with the chthonian realms beneath that green carpet. The grasses were coarse and she could almost feel the tremor of their fibres.

She closed her eyes, cleared her mind, raised her arms and began the slow, meditative moves of *T'ai Chi* by which she could draw out the essence of earth power, making it a part of herself. Dressed in her pure white *gi*, her body swayed like a graceful sapling, the ritualistic hand and leg movements bringing her ever closer to tranquility. Her spirit soared to the tops of the trees towering above her, sensing their urge towards growth. Carried higher, she drifted far from Blackmoor Towers to ethereal planes where physical sensations no longer existed.

Gradually she came back to herself, aware of the stirrings in the great root systems sucking up gallons of water, breathing out vapour through their leaves to ensure the survival of the planet. She was conscious once more of the beauty surrounding her, the verdant lawns and flowers seeming to possess an extra brilliance, the brooding ivy-hung walls of the manor standing foursquare like age-old rocks. Ecstasy saturated every corner of her being, the joy of being young and alive and ready to take up any challenges life offered.

Slowly she retraced her steps, heading through

the silent corridors towards the gymnasium. There Sinclair had said she would find a *makiwara* board fixed to the floor, a padded pole which she could use in the absence of a sparring partner. It was necessary to train if she was to enter the contests to be held in London next year. So far she hadn't found a local *dojo*. Sinclair thought the nearest was in Exeter and had offered to help her start one by hiring a hall in the village one or two nights a week and taking advertising space in the *Porthcombe Times*.

Karen ruminated on the complexity of Sinclair's personality, sometimes bordering on cruelty, at others the acme of gentle understanding. Last night had been a first in one respect: never before had she met a man who celebrated the tender act of urination. Bodily juices and secretions enriched lovemaking, but it had been a complete surprise to find that the sight of her coming and peeing had proved a massive turn-on for him.

All in all, her time with him had been well spent. Not only had she discovered hidden depths to herself, but she had found another martial arts enthusiast into the bargain. And, perhaps more important than either of these, she had learned a little more about Mallory. *Not that I'm interested*, she told herself firmly as she approached the door of the gym. *Interest suggests caring, and the last person on this globe I care about is my irritating, arrogant boss.*

The house was quiet as the grave, but now sounds from behind the door shattered the silence – the hard, bright ring of steel meeting steel. She frowned, paused, then stepped inside.

Two men were fighting, instantly recognisable,

though wearing white padded fencing jackets, their faces hidden by protective masks. Tall men, equally matched in height, vigour and skill, they were wielding rapiers. Their feet pounded the cork matting as if strictly choreographed – lunge, parry, riposte: backward and forwards. They were so intent that they ignored Karen, were probably not even aware of her presence.

Sinclair seemed indolently relaxed in style yet gave Mallory no opportunity to pierce his guard, unhurriedly retreating before his slashing attacks, parrying easily, almost lazily. The air whistled and rang with the clash of expertly handled steel. It hummed with fierce antagonism that communicated itself to Karen. Her reaction to the fighting men was visceral. She felt it in her blood, guts and vagina, was overwhelmed with molten desire, her descent from a higher plane rapid and absolute.

A gasp escaped her lips, and Sinclair glanced across, momentarily off guard. Mallory's blade slipped like a serpent under his guard. For an instant the rapiers locked, the duellists close as lovers. Then with a flick of his wrist, Mallory hooked his quillon under his brother's, and the sword was jerked from Sinclair's hand to sail across the room in a flashing arc, hitting the floor with a clunk.

'Fuck!' Sinclair exploded.

Mallory bowed ironically. 'You always did lose concentration when pussy appeared,' he chided acidly, pulling off his gauntlets then removing his mask. Sweat drenched his face and ran in rivulets from his matted black hair.

'It was bloody bad luck. I slipped,' Sinclair lied,

tugging at his helmet and tossing it aside. He looked furious enough to hurl himself on Mallory and garrotte him.

With haughty unconcern, Mallory stripped off his padded jacket, torso bare as he towelled over his chest and armpits. Karen's vaginal muscles clenched, her sex dampened and her nipples rose as the coarse linen of her *gi* chafed them. He possessed such a perfect physique, iron-muscled arms, wide shoulders tapering to a narrow waist, and below it the tell-tale line of his cock pressed against the close fit of his jeans.

Sinclair watched her with a wry, cynical smile. He, too, was part naked and had Mallory not been there her lust would have been directed towards him.

'I'm going to take a shower,' Sinclair announced. 'Are you coming, Karen? I could do with a handmaiden in more ways than one.'

In a few well-chosen words he had indicated to Mallory that he was on intimate terms with her. Karen was angry yet satisfied. Mallory might have beaten him in sword play but Sinclair had shafted her last night: screwed and pleasured her while Mallory fucked his bevy of mistresses. Somehow this adjusted the balance in her book.

'Sorry to spoil your fun, but I need Miss Heyward in the library,' Mallory said with a wolfish smile. 'You'll have to shower alone, Sinclair, and take yourself in hand, if that's what's on your mind.'

He turned to Karen, the towel draped round his neck. She could smell the musky odour of his sweat, see his wet hair clinging to his brow, and her hand almost lifted to the zipper of his Levi's, almost caressed the heavy bulge between his thighs. Almost, but not quite.

'I'll change first,' she replied, distrusting this trembling, knee-weakening emotion that shook her.

He cast a supercilious glance at her *gi*. 'Ah, the very nearly black belt,' he said sarcastically. 'Have you been training this morning, Miss Heyward?'

'No, sir. I did *T'ai Chi*. I came here to practise, but it doesn't matter.'

'Too right it doesn't,' he rapped out smartly. 'I've important things to discuss with you. Are you fit?'

'Yes, sir.'

The library was dim, a warm, dawn-pink dimness. The perfume of roses mingled with the spice of leather – Persian, Russian, Moroccan calf – and with the pungency of old parchment and old print on ancient pages. The air was filled with the breath of ages, the room enfolding them in dusty, spangled intimate silence.

Karen wondered why Tony had not been summoned but was glad that she and Mallory were alone, and impatient with herself for that gladness. It was the first time. Would it be the last? What was it he wanted of her?

He was so tall. Her head did not quite reach the pit of his throat, yet she stubbornly held her ground. 'There was no need to be so rude. I would have been more comfortable in ordinary clothes.'

'You can skip off and change in a minute,' he replied, a new expression creeping into the amber eyes that were regarding her thoughtfully, hypnotic eyes under black brows that soared like wings. A hint of regret, a glimmer of interest, the beginning of respect?

'Why the urgency? What's wrong? And where's Tony?' She held herself erect, hands loosely at her sides, her head thrown back, awaiting his next move.

'Wrong, Miss Heyward? Should anything be wrong? As for Tony, I imagine he's still in bed with a congenial companion or nursing a hangover. Did you enjoy the party?'

She was fascinated by the cadences of his voice, a deep, rich baritone, soft, steeped in honey now, whereas before it had been crisp, authoritative, even scathing. Pulling herself together, she said, 'It was unusual, to say the least. But why this early morning meeting?'

'I want to check on the Bedwell cartoons. Irwin Dwyer is arriving in under a week.'

'The American? Tony told me about him. I'm sorry you're selling the drawings. It's a shame when they've been in the family for so long.'

' "Needs must when the devil drives",' he quoted coolly, staring at her with those forceful eyes, his look seeming to penetrate her very soul. 'Anyway, what's it to you? You're merely working for me, and can't possibly understand what it's like to be the owner of Blackwood. It's not just a house. It carries massive responsibilties and needs a mint to keep it going. I have my son's future to consider and don't want to hand it over to the National Trust. Irwin Dwyer did offer an alternative. Everything would remain as it has always been, and he would advise me how to increase the estate's income.'

'I'm so glad,' she countered, swallowing hard, aware that she had been staring at him. 'This is more than a job to me. I love the house and want to see it preserved.'

'You do?' He raised a sceptical eyebrow. 'Most people are out for what they can get these days. The old feudal loyalty is a thing of the past.' His voice hardened, his eyes too. It was as if he had forgotten Karen as he continued in a voice charged with bitterness. 'My wife was a prime example of this, a greedy, mercenary woman. She didn't care about Blackwood.'

He was restless, unsure, taking a few irate strides, then whirling round and coming back to her, driving his fist into his palm. 'I can't trust anyone. Even my own brother has betrayed me.' She felt his unhappiness like a bleeding wound in her own heart, and touched his shoulder impulsively. Fire leapt through her fingers to her womb at the contact with his bare skin. She realised that her panties were soaking wet beneath the *gi*, his very presence rousing her to melting, lubricious excitement.

'You can trust me,' she whispered.

'Can I?' Their eyes held, and she could feel herself drowning in those golden depths, wanting it, needing it, willing to lose herself in him for ever.

He moved towards the door leading to the inner sanctum and she followed, mesmerised, her mind lighting up, her body shaking as if racked by fever. All sound in the little room was muffled, sunshine pouring in at the diamond-paned windows. Mallory did not open the cabinet as she had expected. Instead he went over to the fireplace and pressed a Tudor rose decorating the mantel. There was a click and a panel opened, revealing an aperture. He lifted out a canvas.

'I wanted to show you this,' he said, propping it up against the far wall and whipping away the covering.

Karen moved closer, feeling herself growing hotter. The power flowing from this man augmented by the power of the painting caused a maelstrom of arousal within her that dissolved her will.

'Is it Dick Bedwell's work?' she managed to croak.

Mallory shook his head, adoring the picture with his eyes. 'No, it's a Giovanni, but based on one of the cartoons. He paints like Goya.'

'The girls on the swings.' She recognised it, though it shone as never before, luscious, vibrant with colour. It was almost possible to hear the girls giggling as they displayed their pink, wet and wonderful lower lips to their beaux.

Flower-wreathed, breathing out a corrupted innocence, the wanton girls were tempting, the skill of the artist portraying every nuance. Their young breasts, their nubile flesh, the subtle hues, the detailed sketchwork combined to produce a work of art both pleasing in an aesthetic sense and torrid in the extreme. Involuntarily Karen's hand dipped down to the apex of her thighs. Through the linen she could feel the warmth of her pubic hair. She felt strangely hazy, breasts tingling, her clitoris beginning to stir.

'Giovanni was a master. He's captured the spirit of the scene to perfection. Look at the colouring and detail,' Mallory said, giving her a slanting glance.

'Why hide it away? Wouldn't it be better to show it?' Karen was inching towards him, unable to prevent her feet from moving in his direction.

'It pleases me to keep it for myself or share it with a very close friend. No one has seen it except me since Caroline left.'

'Your wife?'

'My wife.'

A close friend? He can't mean me, can he? The idea made Karen's head reel. 'Then why me?' she faltered.

He shrugged. 'Call it an impulse. You'll not tell anyone where it is, will you? Particularly Sinclair. Even Tony doesn't know about it.'

'And Irwin Dwyer? Is he to be informed?'

'I never want to sell this one.'

Our secret, she thought, burning, aching, close to tears, close to joy. He was near her, his arm brushing her shoulder as they looked at the painting. The proof of his arousal was visible, as clear to her as if he was naked, that long protuberance swelling under the thin covering of denim. Karen stood beside him with a soaking gusset and the triple ache of nipples and clitoris demanding relief, and he made no attempt to touch her.

Minutes passed and then he walked to the door, saying over his shoulder, 'Make sure the cartoons are in order and the contents of the library catalogued as far as possible in the time left before Dwyer arrives. I'm relying on you, Miss Heyward.'

Karen sank against the table when he had gone, unable to believe that he could leave her, just like that. For her part, she was shaken and exhausted, disordered and confused. The hot waves of sensation that had swept her were still there. She sank into a chair, opened her legs wide and inserted a hand into her *gi*, letting her fingers walk down over her belly, brush through the crisp hair and dip into her cleft.

Her clitoris was thrumming. Karen wetted a finger in her love-hole and smoothed it over the hot little head, gently easing back the cowl. Her left hand found her breasts, skimming from one aching nipple to the other, teasing, pinching, their need echoed in her nub. She was not in the mood for delay, and frigged herself vigorously, bringing on a sharp, frenzied climax.

In the priest-hole, Mallory watched her masturbating, his eyes serious, mouth too. He held his erect phallus in one hand, rubbing it, pulling back the foreskin, anointing it with the pearly drops oozing from the slit.

Like Karen, he could not restrain himself and poured out a hot stream of abundant seed within seconds. Even as he watched her playing with herself and reaching climax, he was wondering how it would have been if he had yielded to the impulse to make love to her, which was the main reason he had asked her to go to the library.

But it was better this way. If he didn't tempt fate then he couldn't be hurt again. Better to watch her, better to pretend that it was her hand on his cock instead of his own – better anything than the raw pain he had suffered when Caroline left him.

Chapter Eight

'WELL, WHAT D'YOU think of her?'

Sinclair started at the sound of Armina's voice and looked up, appreciating her beauty as she walked across the conservatory – a blonde, curly-headed sylph wearing a sleeveless, backless, button-through cotton dress, deceptively simple, but from a top Italian fashion house.

He knew all about her extravagant tastes, having paid for the ball gown she had worn to the dinner party. A bribe, of course, but then Armina was always open to bribes, out for herself and pledging loyalty to none. He accepted this and liked her no less for it. Besides which, she was one of the sexiest ladies around, with a penchant for the bizarre that matched his own. His spine tingled and the blood thickened his phallus as his eyes caressed her tiny, upward tilting breasts and the shadow where her skirt pressed between her thighs.

'Would you like a cup of coffee?' he asked, speculating on what might have brought her there.

From the depths of a deeply cushioned wicker armchair, she smiled to herself, noting the swelling in his beige linen slacks and then lifting those innocent seeming blue eyes to his.

'I'd love some, darling. I've only just got up. What a night! I had a most amusing time. How about you? Did you manage to seduce our lovely academic?'

'I did.' He found it impossible not to sound smug.

'Tell me about it,' she demanded eagerly with that flush and sparkle he recognised as sex oriented.

He concentrated on the cups and coffee-pot set out on the round rattan table. The conversatory was humid, the afternoon sun striking through the glass roof, every rare and exotic plant giving forth steamy tropical aromas. He and Armina were old friends, or rather associates, each wary of the other, withholding information they suspected could be used against them at a later date. Yet at times collaboration was essential for their mutual advantage.

He placed a cup, the sugar bowl and cream jug before her.

'Black, no sugar,' she said.

After pouring, he flicked his lighter, little flames, jets of amber, reflected in his inky pupils as he held it to the end of her cigarette. Armina inhaled luxuriously and crossed one slim leg over the other, a delicately arched foot swinging in a fragile gold leather sandal, toenails lacquered to match. Sinclair caught the smell of *Joy* emanating from between her breasts and the wonderful seaweed perfume of her secret parts.

He wanted to take her there and then on the Spanish ceramic tiles, to release his burgeoning cock and guide it into that lithe, lascivious body. His mouth filled with spittle, tormented by the killing need to taste her, to dabble his fingers in her fluids, to suck and flick and rouse her rosebud teats – to pinch and hurt her as she liked to be hurt.

Her eyes darkened from blue to violet, slightly out of focus as she stared at him from beneath black-tipped lashes. She uncoiled her legs, opened them, slipped a hand down to cradle her nest, her every movement suggestive, even lewd. This was her charm, this dichotomy between the upper-class girl from finishing school and the rapacious vampire, ready to drain her victims dry, physically, mentally and materially.

'Let's make love, Armina,' he murmured, his chair creaking as he edged it closer.

'You haven't told me what happened between you and Karen,' she pouted, stroking her breasts, pulling at the nipples through the cotton, teasing him by remaining in her seat.

'Everything happened,' he grunted, sitting back, legs apart, making her fully aware of the slant of his penis lifting the lightweight fabric of his trousers. 'I tied her up, frigged her, sucked her, made her come. She loved it. Couldn't get enough.'

'I told you she was a natural, didn't I?' Armina said unsteadily.

Talking about it ignited her fire and made her wet. Still fondling her breasts, she rested her foot on the table bracing the other leg against the floor so that her thighs were spread wide. Her skirt fell back. She wore no panties, her depilated mons shiny pink, the lips opening like a sea anemone in search of prey.

Sinclair dropped to his hunkers between her knees, his eyes level with that honey-sweet furrow. He didn't touch, simply admired, a connoisseur of female genitalia. Hers were perhaps the most perfect he had seen. Firm, full, glossy, surmounted by a prominent clitoris. He drank in the sight of her pearly organ, then stroked its head with a dry fingertip. Armina squealed and pushed her pubis upwards.

Sinclair denied her, rising to lean an arm on either side of her chair. He smiled down into her face. 'Of course, there's more she can learn. I thought a visit to Mistress Raquel might be in order.'

'When?' Armina's fingers were busy, taking over where he had left off. Her hips pumped slowly, the rhythm deep and steady.

'When you've finished wanking,' he replied, remaining where he was, lighting up a cigarette and watching her.

The Lamborghini purred like a sleek panther as it ate up the miles. Karen nestled her bottom into the voluptuous leather of the passenger seat beside Sinclair, who mastered this feral beast. Armina and Jo were crammed into the back, for this was a sports model, not some run around people carrier designed for transporting families to supermarkets. The speed was ferocious, the monster roaring belligerently when given its head, Sinclair handling it with the aplomb of a contestant in the Monte Carlo Rally.

It was a sultry evening, the sky flaming crimson. Framed against the distant luminous background, the branches and foliage looked black. Above hung a single large star like the earring of a giantess gazing dreamily across the cosmos.

The car shot through a couple of sleepy hamlets and careered along a succession of side roads, eventually braking at a pair of imposing gates flanked by a lodge house. A man in shirt-sleeves came out. His head was shaved, his neck bull-like, and he had a broken nose and cauliflower ears.

Sinclair leaned from the car window and stated his business. The man nodded, grunted, returned to the lodge and within seconds the gates opened. 'He's one of Raquel's mincers,' Armina said, leaning over the back of the seat, her breath tickling Karen's ear, followed by her tongue tracing the rim gently, then darting inside, mimicking a more intimate penetration.

The fine down rose on Karen's skin, her blood warming, breasts swelling, longing for the touch of lips, teeth, hands. Although she had reached orgasm alone in the library, her interview with Mallory had left her burning and unsatisfied.

What was this place? she wondered as Sinclair drove up a long beech avenue. And who was Raquel? He hadn't told her, merely called at Laurel Cottage and asked if she'd care to visit a friend. Karen had been working all day, rushing to get everything in order for Irwin Dwyer, and had thankfully accepted the respite.

The trees parted, framing a fine example of Palladian architecture, a simple but elegant building with a central block connected by white colonnades to wings on either side. Nothing could have been more gracious than this splendid mansion surrounded by lawns and gardens.

As the car rolled towards it, another vehicle appeared from round the side of the house. It resembled a Roman chariot, carved and gilded and supported on iron-bound wooden wheels.

The rays of the sinking sun glittered on the charioteer, on metal rings and straps, on scarlet leather and naked flesh. She held the reins in one black-gloved hand, whip in the other fist landing with a resounding crack on the steed tethered between the shafts.

'Oh – ooh – thank you – thank you,' he moaned through the bit in his teeth.

'What else?' his tormentor demanded, adding emphasis by hauling on the reins and lashing his bare shoulders. 'What else, you miserable slave?'

'*Mistress*! Thank you, mistress!'

The chariot jolted to a standstill below the ornamented entrance reached by two flights of stone steps.

'Hello, Raquel,' Sinclair shouted, stopping the car alongside.

The big woman remained in a spread-legged stance, giving him a haughty stare. Coarse black hair flowed across her wide shoulders. Her body was encased in a red leather basque, her opulent breasts spilling over the cups, white, fleshy, with brown pebbly nipples. Her bare buttocks swelled out from under the tight leather. Crimson suspenders crossed her naked belly, connecting with the tops of black fishnet stockings. Her pubis was fully exposed, a wiry thatch with salmon-pink labia. Thigh-length black PVC boots with six-inch heels added to her formidable stature.

Goddess. Witch. Artemis. Astarte. Kali. Earth mother. Whore priestess. Bringer of destruction, ecstasy and release. This was Mistress Raquel.

'Good evening, Sinclair,' she said, her theatrical accent ringing across the grass. Her steed shifted between the shafts and the darting tip of the whip seared his buttocks. 'Don't dare move till I give permission!' she thundered.

He cringed and shook, no wimp but a big, deep-cheated man, his muscles slack, belly hanging over his tumescent penis. He was naked, apart from leather accoutrements, a spiked dog collar with chains indenting his skin as they strained down to the rings piercing his nipples, a studded belt attached to the harness binding him to the chariot. It was a replica of that worn by carriage horses, with highly polished brass buckles, a tribute to the lorimers' art.

At the back a leather thong was craftily fashioned to pass from his waist into the deep umber crease of his behind, down between his legs to loop round balls the size of goose eggs, pushing them forward, his upright dick held high. The strap was tight, but his mistress could make it tighter, creating the pain for which her slave hungered and paid handsomely to endure.

Raquel leapt down, striding round to stand in front of him, legs apart, arms akimbo. He quivered, gazing at her adoringly. She propped one foot on the first tread of the stone steps, the dark wilderness of her female parts exposed.

'Suck my cunt!' she commanded.

The slave groaned, bending with difficulty, his

bonds excruciating, but an expression of ecstatic delight lit his heavily jowled face as his big, fat tongue came out to lap at her. Raquel showed no emotion, though her slit glistened with juice. She arched her hips, rubbing the moisture over his lips and cheeks, then suddenly changed position, grabbing hold of his erection and massaging his balls.

'I'll bet you'd like to let go of this spunk, wouldn't you, slave?' she sneered. 'But you can't. Masturbation is forbidden till I say you can do it. Take the chariot back to the stable and clean it thoroughly. I order you to lick the mud off the wheels with your tongue. D'you hear me? Put some effort into it. You're pathetic, lazy and disgusting.'

'Yes, mistress. Thank you, mistress. You're so good to me,' he whined.

'Too good, I agree,' she snarled, and caught him a hard slap on his dimpled arse that made drops of pre-come juice dribble from his cock. 'Go away! Get out of my sight, you useless, ugly object.'

'Humiliation. Lesson number one in being a dominatrix,' Armina murmured to Karen. 'Would you like to try? Does it appeal? I'll admit it floats my boat. Men are such bastards, it's fun to torment them, even though one knows they're enjoying it.'

Sinclair introduced Karen to Raquel. Armina and Jo were already acquainted with her. Had they taken part in these SM games? Karen wondered. Her clit twitched and a skein of something dark and vengeful tightened in the heartland of her being.

'Welcome to my home,' Raquel said, beaming at

her. 'Come inside. We'll have a drink and then I'll give you a conducted tour of the torture chambers.' She laughed loudly. 'Don't look so horrified! They love it and pay vast sums of money for the privilege of being ill-treated. The slave pulling my chariot is a high-court judge and can't get enough of trotting barefoot along the cinder path my other slaves have constructed. The more his feet bleed, the happier he is, and the bigger my fee!' She gestured towards the magnificent façade. 'This place was given to me by a satisfied customer. He wanted somewhere safe where he could put on his mother's dresses and have me whip him till he came. Oh, yes, we cater for all sorts here.'

They followed her to where several more chariots with willing steeds commanded by war-like Amazons.

One of the stables had been converted into a double fronted garage housing a collection of gleaming cars. Karen's head snapped up as she saw a tattooed man with windblown blond hair sitting side-saddle on a blue and chrome Harley. He glanced towards her, his expression one of total unconcern. He looked more gorgeous and sexy than ever.

Raquel clocked her interest, a smile curving her red lips. 'That's Spike. He services my cars, and me, too, when I'm in the mood for cock, which isn't often. My job's equivalent to working in a chocolate factory.'

'Karen already knows him, don't you, darling?' purred Armina, her arm linked with the willowy Jo's, both women presenting their bodies as near naked as public appearance allowed, in miniskirts and cropped tops.

Spike just sat there without speaking, his booted legs crossed in front of him, his neat tush parked on the seat of his mean machine. He wore faded, ragged, obscenely short cutoffs. Only a skimpy vest covered his upper body, and his muscles bulged, matching the impressive lump in his crutch. His pectorals were crowned by erect nipples on an almost hairless chest turned golden brown by the sun.

Then Raquel said, 'Let's go inside. I've a client waiting, and he likes an audience.'

She started off in the direction of the terrace. Gardeners were working on the herbaceous borders and there was the distant purr of a lawn-mower. Raquel strode among them, cracking her whip.

'Faster!' she cried, prodding one wearing a sequinned evening gown and stiletto heels. 'Haven't you finished weeding that patch yet? I've never met such a worthless bunch. No treats for you tonight!'

'I'm sorry, mistress,' he bleated. 'I keep break-ing my nails.'

Raquel let out a harsh, barking laugh and landed a well-aimed kick on his rear. 'Tough! I'll see you break more than that if you don't get on with it.'

The others stood watching with hangdog expressions, longing for her to reprimand them. She cast a scathing glance over her slaves and swished the whip, making them yelp at the touch of its fiery kiss. With a final disdainful glance, she abandoned them, leading her guests into the house.

Sinclair slipped a hand under Karen's elbow,

managing at the same time to caress the side of her breast. 'I expect you're finding this weird,' he said quietly. 'Look at it this way. Raquel and women like her provide a harmless outlet for the cravings of certain men. In real life they're probably solid, stable, respectable chaps who love their wives, their children and the world they've carved out for themselves. They're usually men who wield power in their daily lives and who like to relax by being controlled and manipulated by someone else.'

The reception room was huge, with a large fireplace at each end and a row of tall, graceful windows facing the garden. It was superbly elegant yet comfortable, with chesterfields and wing chairs grouped in cosy conversation areas on the parquet floor. Oversized Limoges bowls filled with aromatic potpourri stood on Louis XIV buhl tables. Flowers were arranged in ornate jardinieres to give the effect of a tumbling, natural profusion. Eggshell-blue paintwork picked out in white decorated the walls between pilasters of fluted marble. The high ceiling was a riot of exquisite plaster ornamentation.

'It looks sedate enough to invite the vicar for tea,' Karen commented.

Sinclair grinned. 'I believe she has had one or two vicars, as patrons though, not shepherds of their flock.'

Raquel swaggered across the room, crying, 'Sit down! Sit down! Don't stand on ceremony!'

She spoke in the bossy manner with which she addressed her slaves. After tugging imperiously at the embroidered worsted bell-pull near one of the fireplaces, she dropped on to a cushioned day bed, accepted the cigarette Sinclair offered, inserted it into a long jade holder and held it to her red slash of a mouth.

A servant answered her call, wearing the pert outfit of a French maid: a short black skirt over taffeta petticoats, a brief bodice, black stockings and court shoes, a frilly apron. The maid was skinny but fairly convincing till one noticed the military moustache on the upper lip and the clipped iron-grey hair beneath the white cap with flying streamers.

'Madame?' he asked, his voice gruff though years of bawling across barrack squares.

'Bring drinks, Fifi, and look sharp about it! And some canapes, I hope you've been hard at work making them, for if you haven't I shall be extremely displeased, and you know what that means, my girl!'

Karen sat quietly observing this Mad Hatter's cocktail party, where nothing was as it seemed. Fifi returned, staggering under the burden of heavily loaded trays. People wandered in, some dressed as schoolboys, some in furry dog suits, others in women's clothes. One man was wrapped in clingfilm, limbs, body, every part of him, with the exception of his face and the penis rearing out of a gash in the plastic.

A stern-faced nanny in a severe grey uniform led in a giant infant wearing a pink frilled frock over a nappy and plastic pants, a matinée jacket, a bib, ankle socks, white bootees and a woolly bonnet.

Raquel chucked the child under one of its several chins. 'And how is Baby Debbie today?' she cooed.

'She's been a very naughty girl,' answered

Nanny, standing stiffly to attention. 'She spat her dinner everywhere and nearly fell out of the high-chair. I had to pull down her nappy and smack her little botty. And then she wet herself all over the nursery floor.'

'Did she indeed? Well, Baby Debbie, we can't have this, can we? I'll have to get out my cane, won't I?' Raquel scolded.

Baby Debbie started to blubber loudly, the dummy drooping from between jutting, masculine lips. After a thorough shake and a hard slap, Nanny marched her charge away.

'*Chacun à son goût.*' murmured Sinclair. 'Becoming a baby's not my bag but it turns a lot of men on.'

Karen found herself in a sumptuous, candle-lit apartment, the curtains pulled across the windows. A man was bending over the bed, arse in the air, a large white towel spread beneath him. He was forty-something, well-preserved and handsome, and wore a taffeta frock tucked up to his waist, his buttocks and thighs naked, hairy balls dangling between them, the incongruous sight of socks and desert boots sticking out below.

'D'you want to assist?' Raquel asked Karen.

'Why not?' she answered with a shrug, willing by now to try anything once, the scene excitingly reminiscent of one of the Bedwell cartoons.

'Change into these. Over there, behind that screen.'

Raquel gave her a bundle of clothes, and Karen found Armina and Jo already stripping and donning the costumes supplied. They were giggling, roused at the prospect of the next act.

Armina wore a skin-tight body suit in black plastic. Jo was dressed in a gymslip over a white blouse with bare thighs, navy-blue knickers, grey knee socks and her hair in two pigtails.

Karen shook out her own costume. It consisted of a short white tutu with a boned bodice and slender straps – no panties – and flat ballet pumps crisscrossed with ribbon round the ankles. A birch lay to hand.

Raquel, all powerful, approached the man, asking, 'And have you been a good boy today?'

'Yes, Mistress, I have,' he whispered, and looked across at Spike, adding, 'I want to see his prick.'

'I don't know if you can. I'll have to ask him. Spike, can this gentleman look at your plonker?'

Undaunted, Spike unsnapped his shorts and his semi-hard cock bounded out, the ring glinting in the foreskin. Sinclair smiled salaciously at Armina, and Karen, who had been positioned at the man's head, birch at the ready, became impatient with this perverted game, wanting Spike to herself somewhere private.

'Let me touch it,' begged the man, fingertips pressed together as if in prayer.

'You can't. Now be a good boy or Mistress will beat you,' Raquel commanded, flexing a whip-like cane in her hands.

'Oh, no! Don't do that,' he whispered in reply.

'Why not? You're a dreadful sinner, very, very wicked, and Mistress shall punish you,' Raquel continued, signalling to Jo who leaned forward and jiggled the man's half-erect prick. He grabbed her bare knee and slid a hand under her gymslip, moaning as he fondled her sex through her knickers.

With a rushing swish the rod contacted his bare rump. He howled, jerked. The rod rose, gathered momentum and fell again. This time Karen was motioned to feel his cock. It was stiffer, getting bigger still as he reached sideways, diving under her gauze skirt and fingering her cleft.

He laid his head against the bedpost and grasped it with both hands as the birch rose and fell, his buttocks reddening, bright weals appearing on the pasty white skin. His whispering sobs and infantile protests carried no weight with his strict mistress.

'Let me play with his willie,' breathed Armina, unzipping the catsuit, her breasts, belly and smooth mound showing through the opening. She took his weapon in her hand and rubbed it vigorously while the cane thwacked his writhing backside. Armina gave his prick a few more firm strokes, handed it over to Jo who did the same and then passed it on to Karen. She made a fist, slid the foreskin up and down over its bulbous tip. He sobbed his pleasure and spurted out a shower of semen, covering her fingers with creamy jism and spattering the towel beneath him. He cried out in the tumult of release and fell across the bed, quiet and appeased.

Spike gave Karen no time to change back into her own clothes, rushing her down the backstairs to the garage. Hazy, drugged by the wine they had drunk, probably laced with an aphrodisiac, every person who had taken part in the flagellation had been roused to uncontrollable lust. Sinclair had fallen into bed with Armina, while Raquel and Jo had pleasured one another.

Once they reached the garage, Spike crushed Karen to him, grinding his penis into her belly, his mouth against hers, plundering the lush cave with his tongue, drinking her spittle, crushing her lips with his. He was harsh, brutal, worked into a frenzy of desire by the atmosphere created by Raquel. He pressed Karen back and back till she could go no further, meeting the barrier of the hard, shiny surface of a midnight-blue Mercedes.

Hands beneath her buttocks he lifted her, spread her over the bonnet, spread her legs wide open, pressed up against her, shorts undone, hips thrust out, that thick hard rod pumping into her slick, wet opening. The surface of the car was slippery, his cock ramming against the muscles of her womb. She wasn't comfortable, but he was heedless of this, driving into her savagely, and a part of her revelled in this harsh way of taking.

Her breasts swelled from the low bodice, and his mouth seized a nipple, sucking, pulling at it, till she was ready to explode with frustration. Her clit wanted the same treatment. Wildly she brought up her legs and wound them round his waist, thrusting her pubis against him, grinding the stem of her hungry bud on the base of his penis, attempting to capture that elusive pressure. His deepening strokes missed it, even though she enjoyed the friction of his pubic hair against hers, the rap of his hardening testicles bumping that sensitive area between vulva and rectum.

'I want more,' she gasped, pulling out from under him. 'I can t come like this.'

'Sorry, babe,' he whispered, suddenly humble, and drew back, cradling her mound in his hand. 'I didn't realise . . .'

He found her core, pinching the aching clitoris, and she sighed and sighed, knowing he wasn't going to disappoint her. It took so little to tip her over the edge, but it had to be done in the right way. Clumsy, selfish lovers were no use to her, no matter how handsome and macho they might be.

Cooling his own passions, Spike worked his fingers round the stalk of her love-bud, wetting it, stroking it, parting the lips and sliding across one side then the other before returning to the centre point. His other hand plucked at her nipples, toying, rubbing, matching his movements to those rousing her clit. Up he went to the miniature hood, easing it back, making her jewel stand out, bending to admire it, lick it, coax it to climax.

The dark-blue lacquer beneath her warmed. She was no longer conscious of discomfort, focused on the pulse beating at her epicentre, arms coming up to clasp him, body moving into his. She started to convulse, felt the spasms shaking her, swept up in the mindless, glorious eruption of orgasm. Swiftly he poised over her entrance, and she reached down a hand and guided his huge member into her, her muscles gripping it as he groaned and shot into her with furious driving force.

'Spike, Spike,' she whispered, sinking down, the aftershocks of her climax still roaring through her. 'Take me back to the cottage. Stay with me tonight.'

'Anything for you, love,' he murmured into her neck.

Normally, she liked to sleep alone, but not this time. They rode back on the Harley, stumbled up the stairs, played music on the CD, drank coffee, talked and made love again. It was comforting to have him there, sharing her bed, having him fold himself against her, spoon fashion, his penis swelling again, moving against her backside, slipping between her legs to rest against her nether lips, the ring piercing its head nudging her clitoris. His attention made her feel so alive, so female, so happy with herself. It dispelled the loneliness she dreaded. That time between sleep and daydreaming, the soul's midnight, when she might lie thinking about a pair of piercing amber eyes and sensual lips, a haughty look, power, a sense of mystery, a promise of magic. And a name that slipped like liquid honey over her tongue, one she could not forget no matter how many men she fucked.

'Oh, God, my back aches,' Karen complained, arching her spine and stretching, the operator's chair swivelling towards Tony.

'You've been at that computer for hours,' he said, pushing the horn-rimmed spectacles up to his forehead. 'Bloody Dwyer and this damn rush!'

'It's OK. It's got us motivated. We might have dawdled for ever if he hadn't been expected. Too fussy, too particular, that's our trouble. Now we've just had to get a move on.'

'Hard at it for almost a week! And the weather's glorious, and every other bugger is having fun,' he groused, glaring out of the library window at the sun-drenched garden.

Karen chuckled and picked up her bag. 'Let's have a change. Lunch at my place. OK?'

'You're on.'

They stopped off in the village and picked up fish and chips, the hot little shop reeking of frying fat, mushy peas and fast-food treats.

'How decadently unhealthy. Oozing cholesterol,' Karen said as she unwrapped the steaming parcels on the kitchen table, offering plates and cutlery.

'I'll put that on my fret list,' Tony grinned and waved them away. 'No thanks, I'd rather eat it with my fingers. Pity it doesn't come in newspaper any longer, it loses a certain *je ne sais quoi* without the flavour of printer's ink. Pass the salt and vinegar – oh, and the tomato ketchup.'

'You're a slob,' she remarked, scalding her mouth on a sizzling chip.

'I am. Haven't you white sliced? Put the kettle on. Nothing goes better with fish-shop chips than buttered bread and hot strong tea. A meal fit for a king.'

'How common!' she taunted.

'As muck,' he agreed.

They idled at the table, mugs in their hands, then, by mutual consent, wandered up to her bedroom. Heat breathed in at the dormer window, spiced with the scent of warm grass and roses. The stillness of noon held the countryside in thrall.

'Let's go skinny-dipping before we get back to the treadmill,' Tony suggested as they undressed. 'When we've done this, of course. I haven't had a fuck since the night of the party.'

'You're slipping,' she mocked, smiling as she stood naked by the bed.

He reached up to hold her breasts in his hands. 'And you're not? How many men have you bonked since the last time I shafted you?'

'None of your business.'

The cool sheet warmed quickly, heated by their bodies. Karen lay on her side, facing away from him but with her back pressed against his stomach and chest. Reaching round he fondled her nipples. She ground her naked buttocks against his erection, wriggling as it pushed between her nether cheeks. He lifted her thigh and spread it over his, half turning her as his cock slipped into her wet love channel from the rear. She was partly on top of him and his tongue dipped into her ear, slurping, licking, sending little shocks right through her.

Now he was embedded deeply inside her, one hand plucking at her upthrusting nipples, the other gliding over her belly to her mound. She stretched her thigh to open her silky avenue wider. Tony's finger worked her clitoris as he pumped his prick into her, faster and faster till she climaxed, her inner muscles pulsating round his cock as she felt him reach his own *petit mort*.

Driving back to the house, Tony looked at her sideways and said, 'There's something different about you, darling. It's puzzling me. Could it be to do with Lord Burnet?'

The car was open topped, and she lifted her chin, letting the wind cool her face and tug at her hair. 'Why should it be?' she answered casually.

He grinned, shrugged and watched the white road unwinding ahead. 'No reason. Just a hunch.'

'Hunches aren't always right,' she snapped, and remained silent till they swung round to the back of the house, parked the car and headed for the pool, a shining blue oval surrounded by stone tubs massed with brilliantly coloured flowers.

They had it to themselves and stripped naked before plunging in. Karen swam several lengths, arms cleaving effortlessly through the sun-warmed water, and then lay back, resting against the rim and closing her eyes, her body floating as she drifted and dreamed.

'I've been looking for you.' A crisp voice roused her and she bobbed down, hiding her body. Mallory was standing on the tiled edge of the pool just above her.

'It's our lunch-time,' answered Tony levelly, seated on the steps, his hair and beard spiked and wet.

'I've just had a phone call. Irwin Dwyer's in London, staying at the Dorchester. He's arriving here tomorrow.'

It was impossible to fathom Mallory's expression behind his dark glasses, but he sounded impatient, even harassed. He wore a white T-shirt and white Armani jeans, so tight that it was obvious he wore nothing beneath them. Karen could see no line denoting boxer-shorts or even a jock-strap, but was achingly aware of the shape of his cock. The sunlight glittered on his blue-black hair and touched sparks from the gold Seiko banding his wrist.

'Everything's under control,' Tony said calmly, the water cascading from his limbs as he climbed from the pool.

'Are the print-outs ready?'

'More than a dozen copies. He'll have everything he wants to know.' Tony stood on the side unconcernedly, shaking himself before reaching for his trousers.

Karen wanted to get out too but was embarrassed to be naked in front of Mallory. She told herself sternly not to be such an idiot. After all, he had seen her nude before. Had it been anyone else, she'd not have given it a second thought.

He was obviously waiting for her to make a move. *He's only worried about his library and the American*, she thought angrily. *Any other man might get a hard-on watching me. Not him! For some reason he's denying the chemistry sparking between us.* She had no idea why or how it had happened, but a huge wave of sadness overpowered her.

She tossed up her head, her tangled mane dark with water, swam to the steps and hauled herself out, ignoring Mallory. She struggled into her briefs, the material sticking awkwardly to her damp skin, and shrugged her arms into her cotton shirtwaister, never looking once in his direction.

Behind her, she heard him say to Tony, 'Will you meet him at Exeter Station tomorrow? I gather he's bringing his aide along.'

'No problem,' Tony replied calmly. 'Don't worry, sir. It's sorted.'

'I hope so,' Mallory answered gloomily. 'There's a lot at stake.'

Karen kept her face hidden behind the fall of her wet hair, fighting the temptation to look in his direction. Every nerve alive, she knew the instant he had gone inside the house. Suddenly it seemed as if a cloud had passed across the sun, a chill running through her.

'Back to work, girl.' Tony touched her arm, put a finger under her chin and lifted her face to his. 'Let's show him what a team we are, eh?'

Chapter Nine

'*I OWE YOU* an apology, Miss Heyward.'

Karen, about to close and lock the library door, could hardly believe her own ears. 'I beg your pardon?' she said, looking up at him, stunned.

'I've been unfair. Can we start again?'

This was incredible. Mallory, the lordly and arrogant, was actually expressing regret for something he had done, and to a woman, too!

The corridor was filled with the somnolence of a summer afternoon, a time when the servants had absented themselves from that part of the house, idling in their quarters or quietly undertaking some task that was not too taxing.

Sinclair had gone to London that morning, roaring off in the Lamborghini, taking Celine and Jo with him. He had spoken airily of business in town. The singer was working with her *répétiteur* in preparation for the starring role in *Carmen* due to open in Vienna in October. Jo had the opportunity to glide the catwalk for a leading fashion designer. Armina was absent, presumably humping Tayte or getting her kicks at Raquel's establishment. Patty was busy in the greenhouse, interested not only in the horticulture but in the well-endowed young gardeners.

Karen, the work completed as far as she and Tony were able to take it before Dwyer's arrival, had made certain that all was in order for the important visitor and had decided to head for home. The last person she had expected to see was Mallory.

'You don't have to apologise to me, sir,' she replied tartly. 'I'm just doing a job. That's all.'

'It's not all,' he insisted, leaning a shoulder against the panelling, the angle of his body preventing her from passing him without being downright rude. 'You told me you loved the house, and I think that is true.'

He was heart-stoppingly sexy – lean, masculine, casually chic, his sleek hips, long thighs and divine arse displayed in an unbroken line from waist to knee, riding breeches fitting without a wrinkle. The ridge of his penis drew Karen's eyes like a magnet.

'It is,' She was trembling, wanting, the hot lava of desire soaking the gusset of her panties.

'And I've treated you badly.' He held out a hand, his frank smile making him look even more devastatingly handsome. 'Let's shake on it and be friends. What d'you say?'

What *could* she say? What could any red-blooded woman say in the circumstances? An electric charge shot through her as his warm, dry hand closed over hers. She felt the hardness of his palm, accustomed to riding and hawking, the strength of his fingers practised in coaxing beautiful music from piano strings, the touch she had seen encountering Armina's body, and Celine's. Her need was appalling, her nipples contracting, womb yearning, clitoris avid.

Karen returned his smile, felt the hesitant release of her hand, felt hope striking cautious roots. Till now his mind had been opaque, his body in denial. She had an intense desire to open up both shuttered, enigmatic areas.

'I'm fascinated by the history of the house,' she managed to say through the lump in her throat. 'There's absolutely no need for you to worry about the library. Tony and I are dedicated to it. He can't wait to show it to Mr Dwyer.'

'Ah, yes – our millionaire. He's gone to fetch him. I suggested he drive the Rolls. Americans are usually most impressed by that symbol of English gentility. Irwin asked me how he could get his hands on a title.' Humour flashed in his eyes, an unsuspected quality.

Karen suddenly realised Mallory might be fun, with maybe a keener sense of humour than the satirical wit favoured by his brother. It was possible they could laugh together once her stabbing, dragging, obsessional passion had been slaked.

'They're sometimes sold, aren't they?' she responded conversationally, attempting nonchalance to hide the raging lust urging her to dive a hand between the unbuttoned front of his blue cotton shirt, caress the sepia chest hair and tweak the dark nipples.

'I believe so. Unfortunately some of our oldest families are forced to sell up, can no longer afford to be choosy. Acres of English soil are being sold off to foreigners.' His voice was cutting again, all humour leaving his face, replaced by that sombre expression lurking there at all times.

Karen wanted to draw his head down to her breasts, to hold him like a child and kiss away the pain. *Don't be a hypocrite*, she lectured herself. *It's common or garden lust you feel, nothing more. You want him close to your tits so he can suck them, draw the nipples between his even white teeth, driving you mad with longing. And then – ah, then – down to your clit. You'd open to him like a flower opening to the sun and, once ripened, would absorb him into the depths of your rampant, lecherous cunt.*

Her eyes misted as she cartwheeled back in time to when she had first seen his erect phallus, recalling the length and girth disappearing into Armina's mouth:

'Are you all right?' His concerned voice recalled her.

'Oh, yes. I was just thinking – the cartoons, you know. Mr Dwyer is bound to be over the moon about them,' she spluttered, the heat receding from her belly and cleft, leaving a dull ache.

'They are splendid, aren't they?' He sounded amused, a trifle puzzled, his amber eyes boring into hers.

'I must go,' she said, longing to escape, to rush back to the seclusion of Laurel Cottage and there gloat over this meeting while relieving herself with the vibrator Celine had insisted she accept as a present.

'Must you?' There was a hint of regret in his voice. 'I'd rather hoped you might have time to ride with me. I'm taking Leila out. Have you ever seen a hawk strike?'

She wasn't to be dismissed! Her heart fluttered like that of an infatuated girl or a tripping groupie backstage at a rock concert, but she despised her weakness. He was, after all, only a man, not a god to be worshipped.

'I'd like to watch you put her through her paces.' She consulted her wristwatch in a businesslike fashion. 'I am rather busy, but I can spare an hour or so. I'm hardly dressed for it,' she added with a gesture towards her linen shorts, thin blouse and espadrilles.

'It will do. We won't go far. You look lovely,' he said, heaving his shoulders from the wall.

If I were a Victorian maiden I'd probably swoon at his feet right now, she thought.

A golden glow covered the earth, the sun high in a cloudless heaven, skylarks soaring into the azure depths, their song vibrating on the thermals. Ringdoves gave vent to their doleful, amorous calls from the dark bank of woods the riders left behind as they rose to the open ground beyond – the wide sweep of moor that bordered the sea.

Heat on her cheeks, wind in her hair, tumult in her sex, Karen rode beside Mallory like a comrade from far-off times. It felt right, as if she had entered an existence long remembered, secretly missed and desired, beyond recollection or comprehension.

There are some moments so magical that nothing thereafter ever quite measures up to them, she mused. *This afternoon is one of them*. The conviction grew as they paused near a great outcrop of granite which a mysterious people had raised into a barrow thousands of years before.

'It's reputed to be the haunt of hobgoblins,' Mallory said, looking at her gravely. 'Are you afraid, Miss Heyward?'

Not of spirits, she wanted to retort, *only of you, or rather my erratic emotions concerning you. I don't fancy becoming your doormat, my Lord Marquis of Ainsworth.*

Then she forgot everything, completely captivated by Leila's performance. The falcon was a diva of the skies – powerful, heavy and perfectly mannered, but temperamental nevertheless.

'Don't stare at her,' Mallory warned as he removed the hawk's hood. 'She'll get upset if you look directly into her eyes.'

I'm jealous, Karen decided, watching the tender way in which he handled the bird, whispering endearments as he prepared to cast her off from his wrist. *And Leila's jealous of me. She loves him and doesn't wany any other female around. Possessive bitch of a thing! I'll bet she'd peck me if she could, go for the throat – no, the eyes! And, hell! I don't blame her.*

'Watch this,' Mallory commanded and tossed up his arm. Leila, who had started to bate restlessly, shot upwards at speed. 'See her go! The most exciting part is the stoop from perhaps one thousand feet. She drives down on her quarry at a hundred miles an hour and strikes with her foot closed like a fist, killing it stone dead. Let's follow her.'

The dash across the moor in pursuit was mindblowing, hounds and horses going full tilt. Once Leila struck she had to be coaxed away from the kill, and Mallory did this on foot, whirling a long rope with feathers tied to it round and round above his head while whistling her special call.

Leila obeyed, descending on the lure, which Mallory dropped to the ground. Then he made after her, taking her on to his glove, rewarding her with a titbit. The strike was repeated, and Karen and the dogs were given the job of locating the dead rabbit, hare or grouse and bringing it back to him, Karen's only lure being the promise of that wide, sensual mouth, his fiery eyes and the firm bough of his penis temptingly displayed by his form-hugging breeches.

They jogged home through the twilight, and Karen wished Blackwood Towers would remain for ever in the distance, a mirage seen but never attained. When they cropped into the yard, Tayte came forward to assist but, to her amazement, Mallory handed the hooded falcon to him, swung down and appeared by her side before she had time to slide a foot out of the stirrup.

She felt his hands at her waist, the strength of him as he lifted her effortlessly to the ground, remaining there holding her lightly, looking down into her face. 'Thank you, Karen,' he murmured. 'I've enjoyed this afternoon. Will you come to dinner? I'll be entertaining the American and his assistant. I could use your support.'

'Will Tony be there?' She could hardly speak. He had used her first name, but even now she did not quite dare to return the intimacy. Her thighs ached from riding, the inner sides sweaty from contact with leather, slippery with love-juice through contact with him.

'Oh, yes. You'll come?'

'I will.'

Armina had said he liked fellatio after hunting. Would he want it now? She could feel the grip of the flimsy triangle cupping her mons, feel how wet it was, how taut against her clit.

'Shall I take the horses, sir?' a guttural voice enquired.

'Yes, and tell the kitchen staff to make sure the game is hung.'

Karen was plummeted from Disneyland to the reality of the darkening stables and Tayte grinning knowingly at her, a reminder of sexual congress in the loft, of the big pink serpent he kept in his jeans and his willingness to share it.

Wantonly, she lusted to see it again, to compare it with Sinclair's. Maybe tonight after dinner, if Mallory didn't come up with a more alluring proposition. The thought that he might, plus the heat of his hand imprinted on her waist, made her even more conscious of her breasts and nipples unfettered by a brassiere under the light, almost transparent covering of her Indian cheesecloth shirt.

'We're back,' Tony's voice carolled cheerfully down the mobile phone. 'Mission accomplished.'

'What's he like?' Karen, naked, her hair tied up in a towel, balanced the headset between her ear and raised shoulder and lit a cigarette.

'The tycoon? Seems an OK sort of guy. Down-to-earth — easy to get on with. Crazy about England.'

'And the aide?' She sat on the side of the bath tub and blew smoke rings.

'Earnest, eager to learn, very much an all-American girl. Not bad looking but repressed.

629

Wears specs. Terrible dress sense. She's got the hots for her boss. Typical secretary type.'

'Oh, I somehow thought it would be a man.'

Tony's disembodied chuckle rippled through the ether between his cottage and hers. 'Sorry to disappoint you, love. Isn't there enough cock at Blackwood Towers?'

'Don't be crude.' She smiled and tapped her cigarette into a shell-shaped ashtray.

'Me? Crude? You sure you're talking about the right bloke? Anyway, Mallory tells me he's invited us to dinner. Is that right? He also said you two had been riding this afternoon. What's been going on during my absence? I can't trust you, can I? As soon as my back's turned you're off dicking it. I thought you hated his guts.'

'I wanted to see Leila at work. There was absolutely no sex involved,' Karen lied coolly. She didn't intend to have Tony prying and teasing and generally making her feel foolish.

'Ah, I understand. You rode with His Lordship in the interests of falconry,' he said sceptically.

'You know I like to find out about things.'

'Of course, ducky – I quite understand. Now then, about tonight. Dinner first, followed by a grand viewing of the library and Dirty Dick's porn.'

Nervousness clawed at her vitals as she realised just how heavy a responsibility she and Tony had taken on. It *must* go well. She had worked without let, giving herself no spare time. While managing to maintain the daily ritual of *T'ai Chi*, plans for the *dojo* had been temporarily shelved.

'Who else will be there?'

'Armina and Patty. Irwin likes quim, so get on

630

your best bib and tucker and forget your drawers.'

Karen could feel her hackles rising. 'Fuck off, Tony!' she shouted down the phone. 'I'm not turning tricks, if that's what Lord Burnet expects.'

'Chill out. No one's asking you to. You'll like Irwin, anyway. All we've got to do is make him feel welcome. If there's any shagging to be done I'm sure Armina will oblige. Shall I pick you up, or d'you want to play Miss Independent?'

'I'll drive the Golf, then I can leave when I've had enough.'

She laid the mobile by the bath, within reach should it ring while she was immersed. Everything was to hand and she was looking forward to preparing herself. She had brought up a bottle of white wine, slightly overchilled. It felt good on her tongue, the cold snapping her into a greater awareness. She relaxed in the luxury of the warm, jasmine-scented water, eyes closed as she listened to the music swelling from her portable CD player.

Celine's interest in *Salome* had reawakened her own love of that high-camp opera, and she had bought the latest recording. The thrilling soprano voice plucked every ounce of feeling from Strauss's music as the unhinged princess, victim of a dysfunctional family, sang. Dark, brooding, desperate, her plaintive elegy for the prophet who had been slain so she might kiss his lips made the hair stand up at the back of Karen's neck.

She lay in the bath languorously fondling her nipples and seeing Mallory's sherry-gold eyes with her inner vision. The music welled to a crescendo as Salome took Jochanaan's severed head in her hands and placed her lips over the dead ones. It flowed over Karen's body, culminating between her legs. Jochanaan. Mallory. Her fingers found her wet pubic hair, parting it, seeking the tiny, hard, essential kernel.

She shared Salome's anguish. Tears pricked behind her closed eyelids, ran from the corners to fall across her cheeks. She could taste them, salty on her tongue. The princess knew that killing Jochanaan had given her no peace. Kissing him wasn't enough. She wanted his body and this was now impossible. She had destroyed the thing she loved.

Karen circled her clitoris, played with it, stimulated it and, as the final, dissonant chords reverberated through the air, she surrendered herself to the violence of an explosive orgasm.

Salome died, crushed by the shields of Herod's soldiers. The compact disc finished. Karen came out of her sensual trance. She left the tub, towelled her hair, went through the routine of preparing for an important evening, the same as on other occasions, yet with a major difference: in her heart she knew why she was taking extra care, and it wasn't on the American's account.

Her bedroom became a sacred place, consecrated to the worship of her womanhood. Pouring a puddle of lotion in her palm she worked it into her skin till her flesh felt as soft and tender as a rose petal. Every toe was massaged, the nails manicured, painted the colour of sand. Armpits were shaved of every trace of hair, her pubis left in its natural state, covered in short, feathery, reddish curls, several shades lighter than the ringlets corkscrewing across her bare shoulders.

Last summer her parents had visited Turkey and brought her back a present. There had never seemed an appropriate moment to wear it, until now. The jellaba was long, dyed in the vibrant hues of the desert at sunrise. Made of hand-spun wild silk, it was bordered with gold embroidery and seed pearls. The wide, loose sleeves were ornamented, and the deep slash between her breasts fastened with loops over buttons covered in gilt thread.

She twisted a rope of variegated semi-precious stones about her neck, and hooked a pair of dangling beaded earrings into her lobes. Beautifully crafted jewelled sandals had come with the outfit, a copy of those found in a pharaoh's tomb, flat soled, supported by a thong between the big toe and its neighbour, the kind of footwear in which she was most at ease.

Beneath this exotic creation Karen wore absolutely nothing, the silk caressing her skin like a lover's lips. Such attire called for equally colourful make-up and she didn't hesitate, eyes accentuated by kohl, slanting at the outer corners, cheekbones dusted with gold blusher, mouth shaded a deep, warm apricot. She sprayed on *Shalimar*, a sensual perfume, the very name conjuring up images of the mystic East.

Cigarettes and lighter went into a drawstring pouch, with her keys and some loose change. Her pulse was beating rapidly, her root chakra throbbing with molten fire. Tonight she'd share Mallory's ancestral couch. She was ready. For anything? Almost anything.

*

'It's great to meet you, Karen. Lord Burnet has told me so much about you,' said Irwin Dwyer, clasping her fingers in a firm handshake with that innate politeness of the educated, well-heeled American male.

'How d'you do, Mr Dwyer. I'm sure he's been exaggerating,' Karen answered, pleased and confused, even a little shy.

Before her she saw a genial, smiling man, but guessed at hardness beneath the marshmallow exterior. He was handsome, wearing a hand-tailored tuxedo. Clever plastic surgery made him look closer to fifty than sixty, his jaw tight, eyes unlined. He was a bulky bull of a man, flab kept at bay by rigorous work-outs, thinning dark blond hair streaked by the sun. His eyes were a twinkling blue, his face broad, his skin deeply tanned. He had a narrow mouth that could have looked mean but for the lips. These were full, sensual, the lips of a successful tycoon who enjoyed every aspect of sex, was able to buy it, to win it, to woo women into loving him.

'Hey, call me Irwin. Exaggerating? I think he sure played it down. He certainly didn't tell me you were cute as well as clever.' There was no doubt that he charmed on a grand scale.

Power emanated from him, a potent aphrodisiac. It would set women's hearts racing and make them cream their knickers. It had that effect on Karen, her nipples puckering as she wondered how it would be to have him kiss them and if sleeping with a great man performed a kind of magic: was one able to absorb his success along with his spunk?

They had gathered in the salon, so full of

634

antiquities it resembled a museum, but with a lived-in look. Tony was already there, and Patty, wearing an oyster satin dress with off-the-shoulder puffed sleeves and a boned bodice that accentuated her breasts, an ingénue with a single white camellia in her dark curls in contrast to the gamine, racy Armina.

She had arrived late, her slinky silver lame gown clinging to every curve, naked under the glittering fabric, displaying the hint of a nipple, the tautness of her buttocks, the shaded valley between them opening and closing intriguingly as she walked. Tiny, waiflike, she was sin incarnate. Surrounded by gorgeous woman, Irwin appeared to be in seventh heaven, but he paid Karen the most attention, making her feel special.

Mallory's dark head bent towards Martha Reiner, Irwin's secretary, a thin woman wearing a shade of heliotrope that did nothing for her sallow complexion. Her brown hair had been scraped into an upswept style, and she peered at him through the lenses of her expensively framed glasses while trying to catch what Irwin was saying to the other women. It was obvious she was cock struck and hero-worshipped her employer, her notebook and ballpoint poised, attempting to cushion him from life's vicissitudes when he was more than capable of coping alone.

'D'you think he screws her when there's nothing else on offer?' Tony whispered to Karen, debonair with his rakish beard, dark-blue velvet bow tie and cummerbund.

'Probably,' she replied, sipping a Margarita, savouring the salt rimming the glass.

'Poor dear,' he continued, swirling his whisky,

the shaved ice tinkling. 'Maybe I should step in. Give her a rogering.'

'Maybe you should.' Karen was hardly listening, watching Mallory without appearing to do so.

Dinner was superbly cooked, the hors d'oeuvre delectable fruits of the sea, followed by a traditional saddle of beef, crispy roast potatoes, plump Yorkshire puddings and verdant home-grown vegetables swimming in butter. Then the exotic surprise of peach and meringue pudding, covered with cream and served with hot brandy sauce. Coffee was brought out to the terrace.

Mallory leaned against the stone balustrade, wearing his dinner jacket with as much ease as his riding clothes. He held one of Irwin's cigars between his fingers, its tip glowing, sometimes near his lips, sometimes a red beacon emphasising a point as he gestured.

'I thought a series of mazes to intrigue the punters when we go public,' he said, his eyes cutting to Karen. 'There used to be a maze. Have you seen it on the old plans of the grounds?'

'It was situated beyond the lawn near the lake.' She was feeling full of food and wine, slightly light-headed. It seemed incredible that he was actually asking her opinion, his voice caressing her ears, vibrating down her spine, a melting sensation pooling in her groin.

'But a maze will take a long time to grow, won't it?' Irwin put in sensibly.

He was seated on a Regency bergère chair, opulent with gilt fantasies – chimera heads, animal legs, stars and Egyptian winged sun motifs. Armina and Patty were close at hand, determined not to lose sight of this important visitor, acting on Mallory's behalf but also on their own: Irwin would be generous.

'Not if we construct one of roses, or buy semi-mature box hedging. I'm even considering a Zen garden, with pebbled paths, bamboo screens and unexpected views of water and bonsai trees.'

'I've a Japanese friend who could advise you,' Karen said, transported back to Kan's flat at the mention of dwarf trees and thinking of the lovers she'd enjoyed – and the as yet untested one.

'I think different mazes are a great idea,' Irwin enthused, beaming at Armina who coiled nearer, arranging her legs in such a way that her skirt slipped open affording a brief glimpse of her hairless mons. 'We'll get a landscape gardener working on designs. Make a note of that, Martha.'

'Yes, Mr Dwyer.' Her face was flushed, and she fumbled with her notebook, obviously affected by the wine and the majesty of her surroundings.

Karen sympathised, guessing that this romantic setting must be playing havoc with her libido. The terrace was softly illuminated, the garden clear and dramatic in the radiance of the full moon sailing serenely across the sky attended by her retinue of stars.

'Have you ever been to the States, Karen?' Irwin asked, and something in his tone made her think of a world hyped with promise and excitement.

'No, but my parents are there at the moment.'

'You must visit. Come to LA as my guest.' He gave an expansive gesture, a great cuddly cat at play, claws sheathed momentarily. 'You must all come.'

'I'd love to.' Armina leaned over to rest her hand on his knee, sliding it higher, flirting with

637

the substantial bulge of the mature tackle cradled between his legs.

'So would I,' breathed Patty, angled so that he could look down at the curve of both breasts and the tips of rosy areolae.

'That's settled. Come back with me at the end of the month. You too, Karen. I fly Concorde and have my private jet meet me the other end.'

Martha's face was blotched, a flush spreading up from her neck. Tears sparkled behind her lenses. Tony, lounging on a cane-backed settee of Art Deco vintage, looked on with his Pan-like smile. Karen noticed Mallory had vanished.

Piano music sounded from the distance. She drifted towards the door, lured by the cascading arpeggios. She found him in the salon, thundering out dark, stormy cadences as if to relieve some torment deep in his soul, face carved in hard lines of concentration. She walked across the space separating them like someone under a hypnotic spell, gravid with desire.

Beneath the raw-silk jellaba she could feel drops of perspiration trickling down her spine. Her labia were unfolding, moistening, her clitoris aching like a nipple waiting to be sucked. He ignored her and she inched closer, till her arms rested on the polished black lid of the Steinway.

It's not true that a pianist's hands should be slender and delicate. The thought fired her mind. *His are strong, positive, each sequence of notes attacked mercilessly yet with rapier-like precision. He plays as he fences, knowing when to attack. Like everything else he attempts, he'll want to be the best there is.*

The softness of the silk was an irritation now, her nipples erect, almost painfully sensitive. She opened the front of her robe, spreading it wide till her breasts were bare, then circling the dark rings, pinching them into peaks. There was something profoundly erotic in arousing herself while he sat there interpreting a Beethoven sonata as if nothing else existed.

Mallory raised his eyes but kept playing, the most delicious, searing heat radiating through her as he watched her pinching her nipples harder, rolling them between her fingers. As he fed on her hands, so she continued to gaze at his. She could see the sinews, the dark down on the backs, the way they bunched to attack a chord or spread wide to coax a melody. 'I want them to touch me,' she gasped, no longer simply wet between the legs, now flooding in a hot tide.

As the final, climactic notes resounded, he sat back, hands on his knees, still looking at her. Something seemed to come from his eyes into hers, just as light fills a cloud at sunset. She dropped her hands, let him see her swollen, aching breasts, the tips red with arousal. He reached up and touched one. A shiver of delight raced through her.

'Music is the greatest art form,' he said, and she pushed against his hand. 'Emotions can only be expressed through music.'

She reeled under the impact of his touch, nerve endings quivering as he rose and stood behind her, hands sliding under her armpits to reach her breasts again. She strained back against him, felt his breath whispering over her skin, felt one hand trailing down over her belly. Through the silk she felt his pressure on her clitoris, could feel the juices soaking it, dampening his fingers. His hardened phallus moved, restricted by his trousers and her robe, but even so she felt its hot strength as she parted her thighs, lifting her backside to rub over it.

Now his seeking fingers became impatient, undoing the jellaba, seeking the texture beneath. Karen sighed, shuddering at the ecstasy of his touch, turning her head to meet his searching lips.

'Ah, there you are, Mallory,' said Armina, gliding into the room. 'I wondered what had happened to you. Irwin wants to see the cartoons.'

He froze, stood back, released Karen. Her body was suddenly chilled, bereft of his warmth, the sensations that had been surging through her slackening with cruel abruptness.

'Hope we haven't interrupted anything,' Irwin grinned, appearing in the doorway, his entourage in tow. 'Thought we'd get down to business first, then concentrate on having a ball.'

Mallory became the perfect host, conducting Irwin through the house to the library. Tony unlocked the door and stood back for them to precede him.

'Wow! Will you look at that?' Irwin gasped, 'Gee, I'd like it in my ranch house!'

Several thousand books stood behind the fronts of tall bookcases in this baroque room designed especially for study. Karen and Tony exchanged a congratulatory glance. They had produced order out of chaos. Irwin almost tiptoed, his voice hushed as if he was in church.

'It's all so *old*,' whispered Martha, taking her cue from him.

'Fantastic!' He was craning his neck, staring up at the richness of the ceiling, then pummelling

Mallory on the shoulder. 'You're sitting on a gold mine. No need to open it to the public. We'll advertise it in trade magazines. Shoot a video. Turn part of the place into an exclusive guesthouse. Seminars, business conferences, literary conventions. What a venue!'

He swung round to his goggle-eyed secretary. 'Make a note of this, Martha.'

'Yes, Mr Dwyer.'

Irwin was launched, cash registers ringing in his ears. He looked directly at Karen. The pussy cat had gone back to sleep, a tiger taking its place. 'D'you have a fax machine?'

'We're on the Net.'

He rubbed his hands gleefully. 'Great. You get on to it first thing tomorrow, Martha.'

'You've not yet seen the *pièce de résistance*,' Mallory interjected quietly. 'Follow me.'

He had a key for the sanctum and, grinning like a child about to be presented with a new toy, Irwin was at his heels. Karen's hands clenched into fists. This was the moment of truth. The little room was bathed in soft light, glowing, intimate. Mallory crossed to the cabinet, then stopped. 'What's this?' he said sharply. 'It's open.'

'It can't be,' Karen exclaimed. 'Everything was secure when I left this morning.'

But he was right. She could see the catch had been forced. Mallory dragged the drawer open. It was empty. The Bedwell cartoons had gone. He turned on her, the rage in his eyes paralysing.

'Where are they? What have you done with them? My God, if I find out you've stolen them I'll see you go down for years!'

Chapter Ten

BLACKWOOD TOWERS SWARMED with uniformed police and a dash of plain-clothes officers disguised in jeans, Reeboks and anoraks.

'But you can tell a copper a mile off, can't you?' Armina said, so aroused it was all she could do to keep her hands off her crotch.

'Daddy was in the army,' Patty confided, sitting close to her in the salon, where suspects had been herded. 'I just adore men in uniform. I hope I get interrogated by one.'

'Kinky,' Armina responded, eyes bright as they wandered over every constable, male or female. 'I thought you were keen on Neanderthal studs dripping testosterone. I'll settle for the inspector. He can grill me any time.'

Mallory had reported the robbery to Porthcombe substation and Exeter had been alerted. Panda cars had come screaming up the drive and disgorged a stalwart band led by Detective Inspector Callard. He wasn't in uniform, just an ordinary suit, but his authoritative aura had almost brought Patty to climax.

Everyone was ordered to remain in the house for questioning while the boys from forensic dusted powder all over the library and took fingerprints.

Mallory, in the blackest mood on record, accused Karen, the newest recruit to staff and the least known. Even Tony was suspect in his eyes, for she was his protégée.

'I think they may be in partnership,' he said, alone with Callard and a constable in the study, which had been commandeered as an interview room. 'They know the value of the drawings.'

'But the window was tampered with, sir, and the alarm system disconnected,' Callard reminded him patiently, used to dealing with all sorts and having insurance fraud in mind.

Mallory bit his lip, face pale under the tan. 'I know, but don't you think that could be a blind?'

'I'll question everyone,' Callard said, drumming on the desk top with his fingers. 'Can you provide me with a list of people who've visited recently and photographs of the missing articles?'

Mallory had prints and was able to show Callard one of the Giovanni painting, though reluctantly as no one knew of its existence, with the exception of Karen. He now regretted bitterly his impulse. His life and plans had been disrupted, and he blamed her for it. Irwin might still be interested in the development scheme, but without an injection of American dollars Mallory would be hard put to manage.

'Works of art are ordered by rich collectors,' Callard continued, watching Mallory's reaction. 'Thieves are given a shopping list of requirements and where to find them. This won't be an open-market job. It's unlikely that whoever took the drawings will be touting them round. Still, we must explore every avenue.'

'But that's ridiculous!' Mallory exploded, hardly able to remain in his chair. 'That means if a dishonest collector's got them they can never go on show – they'd be kept hidden away in a vault.'

'Have you had them on show, sir?' Callard fixed him with a stern eye.

'No, but I was about to. Mr Dwyer and I planned to exhibit them.'

Mallory fetched a folder, and Callard examined the prints, then said, 'We'll make some copies.'

'Don't worry, honey,' Irwin said soothingly.

He and Karen were sitting in the conversatory where they had been permitted to have breakfast though they were still under surveillance. It was a scrappy meal as the servants were in a ferment – toast and marmalade, a pot of strong coffee, another of Earl Grey tea.

'Of course I'm worried,' she cried, hand shaking as she refilled her cup. 'He's accusing me!'

'That's crazy. I'll talk to him.'

'You don't believe I stole them?'

'No way, babe. I judge character pretty good, and you're no thief, but my gut reaction says it was an inside job.'

She frowned. 'One of the staff?'

Could it have been Tayte? she wondered. He was always short of money. Or maybe Spike? It seemed unlikely, though he did have expensive taste in fast bikes. Maybe they were in league. Armina? Possibly. Patty? Not really; she was too straightforward. The horrible thought struck her that Tony might have been tempted. It was too preposterous to contemplate yet lingered on the periphery of her mind.

Karen drooped in her chair, and Irwin patted her shoulder kindly, his touch far from avuncular. 'You like your boss? Did you have something going with him?'

She shook her head, tousled russet curls glinting. 'Our relationship never really got off the starting blocks.'

'And you're sad about that?'

'Not really. It's best to keep work and pleasure separate.

'I'd like to have you work for me. Does this mean what I think it means? No fooling around?'

His voice was as seductive as silk and he leaned forward, raised her hand and just grazed his lips over the back of it.

Karen came out in goose-pimples. She was surprised how attractive she found him, even in the harsh morning light when his clothing was crumpled and he needed a shave. Something warm flowed from his fingers, tingling through her nerves into her core. Mallory had wounded her deeply, being so quick to name her as the culprit. She wanted to retreat like a sick animal, to hide away till she had healed. Irwin could help that healing process.

She rose. So did he. She slipped her arms round his neck and placed her lips on his, leaning her body into his. She took command, tasting coffee on his tongue, winding her own into the cavern of his mouth, feeling his broad back under her hands, the long solid stalk of his phallus pressing against her belly.

He licked her lips, tasted and savoured them, then said in a husky undertone, 'Where can we go?'

'My cottage. If the police will let us.'

'Leave it to me.'

She waited for his return. He was not gone long. 'What did Callard say?' she asked, as he strode across and picked up her wrap, placing it across her shoulders.

'It's OK. But we mustn't leave the estate.'

Karen drove to Laurel Cottage through the early-morning freshness, dazed by lack of sleep, trying not to remember the mood in which she had left it last evening. Hopeful? Anticipatory? She battened down the hatches on her emotions. No commitment, no entanglement. Carnal pleasure would do nicely from now on, just as it had in the past.

While she took orange juice from the fridge and carried it upstairs, Irwin showered, coming to her bed squeaky clean. The full, thick, arching length of his cock was completely exposed, all the swellings and veins standing out, and the hard, red naked head. Luxuriant folds of hairy skin joined the base of his shaft to the heavy balls pulsating and moving in their energy and excitement. Karen slithered out of the jellaba and lay back, taking comfort from the admiration in his eyes.

'Oh, baby, you're beautiful,' he whispered, a catch in his voice. 'I've wanted you since the moment you walked in the door last night.'

He stood looking down at her, massive, powerful, overwhelming her with a superabundance of sexual fire. His hand came to rest on her breasts as he stretched out beside her, firm experienced fingers playing with the teats. She gasped, twisted in his embrace, rubbed her face against his coarse chest hair smelling of her shower gel, his skill, gentleness and controlled passion obliterating the memory of any other man. He knew what he was doing, his caresses following a pathway down her torso, around her navel and hovering over her bush.

Karen's hands wandered his fine body. He was past middle age but firm muscled, such heaviness as there was adding to her sense of well-being and security. Here was the father she had wanted but never had, to adore her, admire her, fulfil her.

Irwin's fingers parted her cleft, dipped down into the fluid running from her vulva. He spread some of it lightly over her engorged lips, teased and petted the erect crown of her clitoris. She moaned her pleasure as he rubbed it, and could hear by his ragged breathing that he desired her as much as she wanted him. Then he dived down to her furrow, drinking in her juices. She felt the sensual warmth of his tongue. Pleasure shattered her. White-hot waves roared and rippled, bearing her to a swamping orgasm.

Still convulsing she shifted her thighs up and apart, offering him entrance. She wrapped her arms and legs around him, leaving love bites on his neck. He drove into her, a sword thrust reaching her womb. Karen looked down, watching that great weapon pulling out, lingering, then sliding back, the tense sac of his scrotum tapping against her anus.

'Oh, honey,' he groaned, and his movements quickened.

Now he was almost hurting her with his size. All she could do was take it, hanging on to him as she coasted towards climax, the final shuddering dilation of his cock-tip telling her that he had arrived.

Martha cried when she came. Tony was glad. A satisfied woman was the best of allies, an unsatisfied one the worst of enemies. He thought the famous quotation should have been changed to, 'Hell hath no fury like a woman cheated of her orgasm.' Men would do well to remember that when they humped and grunted their way to climax with scant regard for their frustrated partner.

'I shouldn't have done that,' she murmured smugly. 'You'll think I'm an easy lay.'

'Not at all,' he said gallantly. 'It was just one of those things. Too strong for both of us.' *What a load of bullshit!* he thought.

She disposed of the condom, washed his dick and wiped it on a pink hand towel. It was pleasant, rather like being attended by a maiden aunt or one's mother.

'How old are you, Martha?' he asked, tucking the sheet around him and fumbling for his cigarettes and lighter.

'That's not the sort of question to ask a lady,' she simpered, flapping her hand at the smoke and adding, 'I do wish you wouldn't do that, honey. It's so bad for you. Anyhow, you're not exactly a spring chicken.'

Whoops! A teensy bit sharp there. Could she turn into a nag? Yet he found even this sweet: he was genuinely fond of her and glad to bring a little sunshine into her life.

He had barrelled up to her room on the pretext of delivering a message from Irwin and found her in tears. She had seen her beloved boss go off with Karen.

He knew Karen and he were in a spot, the finger of suspicion well and truly pointing at them. They needed friends in high places. Karen was sensibly screwing Irwin. Tony could do nothing less. He had never seen a woman so much in need of a thorough shafting as Martha.

'I've been unfaithful to Mr Dwyer,' she continued, snuggling down beside him. She had put on her dressing gown, but he slid his free hand in the front and found one of her ample, nicely shaped breasts. The nipple immediately hardened.

'Does he hump you?' Tony asked, rubbing his thumb over the appreciative teat.

'Not exactly,' she confessed, looking younger, prettier with her hair falling in thick brown waves over her shoulders. 'He likes me to give him a blow job when he's tense. Says it relaxes him.'

'And he doesn't return the favour?'

She blushed. 'No, he's never – I mean no one has ever . . .'

'Sucked you off? Dear me, we'll have to do something about that, won't we?' And Tony disappeared under the bedclothes.

He found her lush thicket, spread the wings of her cleft and fastened on her well-developed clitoris with all the aptitude at his command. She came almost at once, crying again.

How lucky I am to enjoy my work, Tony thought, smiling to himself as he subjected her to a series of mini-climaxes that reduced her to putty in his hands. *She'll do her utmost to see that I'm not picked on. Mallory'll have a hard time dismissing me, and Irwin will defend Karen. We're home and dry, or rather home and wet.*

The press gathered at the gates like a conclave of vultures. TV cameras were in evidence. Mallory gave an interview. Facsimiles of the rollicking Bedwell cartoons flashed across screens throughout the nation well before the watershed. No doubt letters of complaint would appear in the *Radio Times*.

The police made discreet enquiries in Porthcombe and the surrounding district. Nothing came to light. Patty, by now rampant with desire for anything in uniform, got into her car and drove to the station, her sights set on Sergeant Harvey, briefly glimpsed when he came to Blackwood with the inspector.

She parked outside the police station, now closed for the night, and knocked on the door of the adjoining house. Harvey answered, in his shirtsleeves and in the middle of his supper.

'What you doing here, miss?' he asked, frowning. 'Aren't you supposed to stay put? No one's allowed out till Inspector Callard says.'

'I know,' Patty confessed, artless in a brief skirt and figure-hugging jumper, nipples pointing directly at him. 'But I had to see you.'

His interest was roused, both by the nipples and the hope of information. 'Is it in connection with the burglary?' It would do his career a power of good if he could put one over on the big boys from Exeter.

'Can we go to the station? I'd rather talk there.'

He put on his regulation jacket with the three stripes, fastened the polished buttons and lifted his peaked cap from the hall stand. The whole of Patty's pelvic floor was aflame, the fire leaping upwards to her breasts. She regretted not wearing panties to soak up the essence bedewing the inside tops of her legs.

The station was empty. He led her through the reception area to his office. It was plain, functional, ideal for the scenario she planned.

'Please sit down, miss,' he said, indicating a chair facing the desk.

'I'd rather stand.'

Harvey's rugged face became stern. 'Look here, miss. What's all this about? You've interrupted my supper, and if I find you're wasting my time . . .'

'What will you do, sergeant?' she breathed, leaning languorously against the wall. 'Will you punish me?'

'Punish you, miss? I don't know what you mean.'

Harvey was out of his depth, a bachelor whose only experience had been with a barmaid at the Ainsworth Arms. He recognised Patty, knew all about the goings on at Blackwood Towers. She was one of His Lordship's girlfriends, a scarlet woman according to the desiccated hags who ran the Women's Institute.

Patty arched her back and lifted her ribs, tits pointing to Jesus. Harvey started as her breasts brushed the front of his coat. He retreated, tightening the grip on his cap, held under one elbow.

'I have been naughty, haven't I? Coming here under false pretences,' she whispered, cushiony red lips pouting.

'Why did you come?' He realised as soon as he said it that the word had another connotation. A flush reddened his weather-browned cheeks.

'I wanted to see the inside of a police station.' Marlene Dietrich as *Mata Hari* could not have been more seductive. 'Is it true that you carry handcuffs and a truncheon?'

He fumbled at his belt and produced a leather pouch from which he took a pair of manacles. 'Here you are, and here's my truncheon.' That too was in a special pocket, about the same size as the solid rod she could see lying thick and inflated under his dark-blue trousers.

'I've always wondered what it would be like to be handcuffed,' she murmured, the tip of her pink tongue wetting her lips. 'Could I try?'

Sweat broke out on Harvey's brow beneath the short haircut. His control snapped. 'Arms behind your back!' he ordered in that terse, clipped tone he used when apprehending malcontents.

She obeyed, turning around. 'But, Sergeant, I shan't be able to reach my love button. Supposing I want to frig myself? Will you do it for me?'

'Stop that dirty talk!'

She heard the snap of steel meeting steel, felt cold metal banding her wrists. 'Are you cross with me?' she asked, so wet she could smell her juices wafting from beneath her mini-skirt.

'I bloody well am! Dragging me away from my supper.' He was breathing heavily, the upward arc of his cock distorting the shape of his pants.

'Go on! Tell me off!' she begged, edging closer.

'And sergeant, please put your hat on. It makes you look so sexy!'

Harvey did as she asked, then pressed up against her, her locked hands contacting the emulsion-painted wall. He ravished her lips, forceful tongue plunging and plundering, aping the motion of coition.

Patty kept her eyes open, wanting to see the black and white band of his hat, reduced to jelly at the feel of coarse serge as his collar brushed her throat and the discomfort of buttons marking her flesh.

'You're a tart!' he shouted. 'A filthy little whore. I should give you a good seeing-to.'

He jerked at the buttons of his jacket. Disappointment mingled with Patty's rampaging desire. 'Don't take it off!' she cried.

'I'm not. Just want to get at my old man easier. That's what you want, isn't it?'

His flies gaped open. His lively member sprang out, the purple glans rising from the wrinkled foreskin. Patty gasped as he rucked up her skirt, cock hopping at the sight of her bare belly and fluffy pubes. He gripped her brutally, lifting her with a palm under each bum cheek. She opened her legs and felt the blunt tip of his tool nudging her opening. He pushed upwards, spearing her, filling and stretching her till it was buried deep inside.

Keeping her positioned, her back supported by the wall, one of his hands worked under her sweater, raising it above her breasts where it lay like a crimson band.

'God, you've got nice titties!' he muttered, pinching the tips till she screamed. 'I'm going to suck 'em raw, bitch!'

He slid out of her, and her feet touched the floor. He freed her hands and propelled her across to the desk, stiff phallus sticking out from his flies. Patty sprawled across the surface, scattering papers and files, gazing up at a framed photograph of the queen on the wall above her head. Her Majesty was shaking hands with officers-in-chief (all uniformed) on an official visit to her guardians of law and order.

Harvey pounced on Patty's naked breasts, gnawing her nipples. Jolted between pleasure and pain, her hand found his phallus. She ran her nail across its weeping eye, relishing the feel of the smooth shaft between her fingers.

'Make a fist,' he commanded. 'Rub it hard. That's right. Oh – yes – yes!'

Now her own odours were joined by his – the gamey smell of cock-fluid, sweat, Old Spice aftershave, fabric in need of dry-cleaning. It was a potent brew and she was crazy for orgasm, jerking her hips in an effort to contact something, anything, on which to masturbate her clit. She grabbed at the shape hanging from his loosened belt, tugged at it impatiently, pulled out the wooden truncheon.

A libidinous smile on her wide mouth, she stroked its smooth end up her slippery cleft. Harvey watched her, his prick growing larger, dribbling its need. She guided the makeshift dildo into her love-hole, just the end to begin with, then pressing in further. Its brown, polished length almost disappeared.

The sensation in her vagina was making her clit envious. It stirred, demanding a share of the action. Slowly she slid her new plaything out of her cunt, across her streaming avenue and touched the head against the very tip of her love button. It electrified the glowing bud, sharp waves of delight shooting through her as she came in a blinding rush.

Harvey thrust his prick between the swollen lips of her sex. He rammed against her ferociously and she heard herself cry out, the tight muscles of her sheath clenching over his width as he pounded his way to completion.

Later, over a cup of hot, sweet tea in the police house, he said, 'What was it you were going to tell me, miss?'

She smiled at him, catlike and content. 'It doesn't matter. I got what I came for,' and she was thinking, *This will be something to tell the girls when I get home.*

'What the hell's going on, Mallory?' Sinclair asked as he entered the Red Drawing-Room two days later. 'Police ringing me up at dead of night.'

'It couldn't have been.' Mallory fixed him with a jaundiced eye. 'They contacted you hours after the event.'

'Oh, Christ, picky as ever!' Sinclair helped himself to a brandy from the tantalus on the chiffonier. 'So? Have they got whoever stole the damn things?'

'Not yet. I'm sure it was Karen or Tony, or both of them,' Mallory gloomed from the depths of a crimson-upholstered armchair.

'Really? Could it be you made an error of judgement when you employed her? I remember thinking she was a little too clever, a tad too keen,' Sinclair mused, nursing the goblet between his palms.

'And how was your alibi?' Mallory barked. 'Perfect, I suppose?'

'Well, I did have to embarrass a married lady by asking her to confess I'd spent the afternoon in question at her pied-a-terre in Knightsbridge.'

'And had you?'

'Too right I had. What a screw! Frustrated, poor cow. Wife of a Tory MP.'

Mallory stared at him through slitted eyes. 'Celine and Jo?'

'Both working their rocks off. Lots of witnesses. Which leaves us precisely nowhere. Looks like you've lost your drawings, brother.'

Inspector Callard had withdrawn but police presence was still felt. The press had simmered down, having wrung every last ounce out of Mallory's habit of living like an Eastern potentate with his harem of beauties. They hadn't dropped the story entirely, but had rushed off to cover a more salacious news item concerning a member of the royal family.

Karen, incarcerated in Laurel Cottage by choice, was avoiding contact with anyone except Tony and Irwin, trying to calm her jangled nerves through meditation and failing miserably. It was horrible to feel like a criminal when she had done nothing. She hadn't been charged but was obviously the prime suspect. The case was bound to be dropped through lack of evidence but mud stuck and she doubted she'd be able to find a similar post elsewhere.

It was a shock when Sinclair turned up on her doorstep, insouciant in Calvin Klein sunglasses and a camel double-breasted suit, beige cotton shirt, herringbone tie and plaited leather belt all by Giorgio Armani. He looked relaxed and fit and carefree. Too full of himself, in fact.

Karen wondered, not for the first time, what he knew about the theft. He had been absent, it was true, but could easily have had an accomplice. She clearly recalled checking on the cartoons before she went hawking with Mallory. Every one had been in place.

'Sorry to hear you're in trouble,' he began, stepping inside without being invited. 'Is there anything I can do?'

'Thank you, but no.' Karen was aware of looking scruffy, in a sweatshirt and peg-top trousers.

He, on the other hand, was bandbox fresh, his bold glance sliding over her impudently. 'You look great, Karen. Is the prisoner on parole? Can I take you out to dinner?'

She grinned wryly; he had the power to charm and amuse her, even now, when she distrusted him. She had little to go on, but it would be in character for him to sit back and let someone else take the rap. She told herself it was immaterial to her whether Mallory recovered his precious cartoons or not. All she was concerned about was clearing her name.

Sinclair wined and dined her in an exclusive restaurant between Porthcombe and Exeter, but she drank little, offering to drive back through the moonlight. It was no longer a full moon but lying on its side like a drunken woman with a mottled face.

'I can't wait to get away from here and never come back,' she said grittily.

'That's a pity.' Sinclair's voice was slurred, his

body sunk low in the passenger seat. He gazed at her owlishly, wagged a finger and added, 'Did you take the drawings?'

'No!'

'Course you didn't. Mallory's a fool to pin it on you. You know you didn't steal them, and I know you didn't steal them.'

'How do you know?' Karen slowed going through the woods, on the lookout for deer but also to listen carefully to his words and their subtext.

Sinclair tapped the side of his nose with drunken solemnity. 'Ah, that would be telling. Come back to my place and we'll talk some more.'

His bedroom in the disused wing was every bit as bizarre as she remembered, but this time there was a difference: she was in absolute command of herself.

'D'you want a drink?' he asked, shrugging his arms out of his coat and slinging it over a throne-like chair upholstered in leather.

'No, I've other pleasures in mind,' she murmured, sidling up to him and slipping her arms around his body. Despite herself, her pulse was racing, his very presence making her nipples harden and juices flow. He was a rogue, but then weren't the bad boys always the most exciting?

His response was immediate, and she unzipped his trousers and lifted out his massive prick until it was vertical against his taut belly. He groaned, sobering by the minute, hands delving under the long floral muslin skirt till he touched bare flesh and the hem of her panties trapped between her buttocks. She flinched at the surprise of his finger edging past the damp, flimsy fabric and finding her tight nether hole. Desire was lashing through her, making it difficult to carry out her intentions.

'We make a fine pair, Karen,' he whispered, mouth close to hers. 'You don't really love Mallory, do you?'

'What gave you that idea?' She raised one leg and hooked it round his hips, pressed the other against his thigh, gyrating her pelvis to bring the much needed friction to her clitoris.

'Because the bastard always gets everything I want.' His hands grabbed at her breasts through the sheer cotton, manipulating the nipples till she was ready to yell with frustration.

'And you want to punish him?' Her brain was still functioning clearly, even though under assault from her senses. 'You like to dominate people, don't you? Remember how you did it to me?'

'Ummm . . . yes. D'you want some more?' He was backing her towards the four-poster, almost carrying her.

'How about if I do it to you?' The visit to Mistress Raquel had taught her a salutary lesson: even the most powerful of men liked to reverse roles. 'Mutual sub-dom – you first, then me.'

He collapsed across the bed, grinning up at her, amused by her keenness to explore sexual deviations. 'OK. I get off on being tied up. You'll have to do everything – even undress me.'

'It will be a pleasure.'

Soon he was spread-eagled on the black silk sheet, multi-hued Hermes scarves tethering his wrists and ankles to the posts. Karen surveyed him, possessed of a primitive satisfaction at seeing him naked and helpless like a victim about to be sacrificed to the Great Earth Mother.

His skin was sheened with sweat, phallus jutting aggressively from the tangled mass of pubic hair, balls cushioned on the sheet between his splayed legs. Karen smiled to herself as she shed her dress and knickers, seeing Sinclair's weapon thicken at the sight of her naked breasts, slim thighs and wet pussy.

It was time to begin the ordeal. She wheeled over two floor-standing pier glasses and angled them so he could see her from several viewpoints and also himself wriggling uselessly like a landed fish. Excitement bit deep, her loins red hot, love-bud straining from its enfolding cowl. She felt powerful, omnipotent, woman incarnate, with the male roped out before her in all his weakness and vulnerability.

He was her creature to pleasure or abuse as fancy dictated. Standing, legs spread, Karen stroked her breasts, playing with the stiff nipples, then walked her hand down to her mound, almost idly fingering herself, wetting a digit in her juices and leaning over to trail it across his lips.

Sinclair, nostrils flaring as he inhaled the spicy odour, shot out his tongue to lick it. Smiling she withdrew her hand, tormenting this horny man who was unable to do anything about it. She straddled him, lowering herself on his chest while his cock strained to reach her pink and parted avenue. She inched up to make this impossible.

'Karen, for God's sake!' he rasped. 'Get on it! Ride me!'

'Impatient,' she chided, sliding higher, a trail of

silvery fluid glittering on his chest hair. She reached her goal, stopping with knees spread wide over his face.

His head lifted, tongue darted out to caress her labia and clit. She sighed, sank down, let him fill his mouth with her fragrant essences, feeling the heaviness in her loins, the surging waves predicting orgasm. This was not to be permitted – not yet – and the pleasure of denying herself, and him, was exquisite. She moved, lithe as a cobra, coiling down to examine his genitals. It was fun to lift and weigh the bulky testicles, tense in their downy pouch, to run light fingers up his shaft, hearing him moan, seeing the pearly fluid poised on the tip of his glans. She rubbed his erection, but not enough to relieve him.

Her control was slipping, almost yielding to the burning desire to feel him inside her. Should she indulge? How close could she bring herself without tipping over the edge? Well aware that intercourse had never given her orgasm, she permitted that ardent cock head to brush against her pudenda. Sinclair was a wily protagonist in the torrid sexual duel. With a sudden lift of his hips he thrust upwards and in, but Karen was on guard, rising to her knees to deny him full access.

'Damn you!' he muttered, furious.

There were adult toys on the bedside cabinet, curious objects to heighten sensation – oriental duo balls, penis rings, a vibro vagina, a choice of dildoes. She selected a huge black one. It felt and looked like the real thing. A flick of the switch and it hummed busily. Moving away from Sinclair, but well within sight, she rubbed it over her clitoris, neck arched, eyes closed, moaning at the intense pleasure it evoked.

Don't give in, she told herself. Moving position, she sat in a chair close by, her legs open so that he could see the vibrator protruding from her pussy. She ignored it, lit a cigarette and picked up a magazine, flicking the pages. One foot lifted, straying across the bed, toes rubbing absently at his bulge.

He moved against that impertinent caress, and she wondered if this might be enough to bring him to climax, waiting to see a fountain of spunk shoot upwards before creaming his belly and chest. This would have been entertaining, and she might have lapped his tool to make it stand again. Keeping the vibrator aimed at her clit, she could have impaled herself on his cock, lunging furiously till the heat shattered within, exploding into orgasm.

Don't even think about it, she warned herself. *This isn't your mission.* She slowly eased her foot away.

'All right. What is it you want?' he panted, penis hard as a rock, so near and yet so far from ejaculation.

'Want? *Moi*?' She did a Miss Piggy impersonation, tossing her head.

'Stop winding me up. Are you going to fuck me?'

She removed the vibrator, leaned over him, put the buzzing rubber against his lips, let him lick her fluid from it. 'Are you going to tell the truth?' she countered.

'Concerning what?' The smell and taste of her was sweet agony.

'Concerning the cartoons.' She ran the pseudo penis over his blunt male nipples. Then she switched it off and laid it down.

'Jesus, you demand blood, don't you?'

'No, only the facts. I don't like being called a thief.'

Her free hand encountered that erogenous area between his balls and his arsehole, ticking and caressing before moving away. 'The Inquisition should have employed you,' he groaned, sweating. 'For God's sake, Karen, fuck me!'

There was a phone near the bed. She picked it up and held it above him. 'I'm going to ring your brother. I want you to speak to him. Tell him the truth. Will you do that?'

'Blasted female,' he raged. 'It was a joke, that's all. I wanted to rattle him.'

'And make a small fortune into the bargain.'

He grinned suddenly, totally unashamed, and Karen's lips twitched. Bastard he might be, but an irresistible one. 'Will you shag me blind if I do?'

'Perhaps.' She connected with Mallory. His voice crackled down the line. 'I've Sinclair here, sir,' she said. 'He was something to tell you.'

'Put him on,' the deep voice breathed in her ear, and she visualised, hated, wanted him, despised herself for that wanting.

She held the receiver so Sinclair could speak into it. 'Mallory? Look here – it was a hoax. Yes, I took the damn things. Where are they? Quite safe, old boy – hidden in the west wing. I say, there's no need to speak to me like that! All right, I'll come and see you – and bring them with me. Calm down. You'll burst a blood vessel.'

The phone went dead. Karen took it away. Sinclair looked at her with hot eyes. She placed herself on his face so that he could dip into her spicy nest. He found her clit, his tongue slick smooth, working over it while she added her own frantic movements, spasm after spasm rolling and rolling in the pit of her belly, till climax roared through her like a hurricane and she collapsed on his chest.

An instant later she was riding his prick, rising and falling, lunging and pumping, rewarding him for his confession with a wild trip to the highest peaks of sensation.

Chapter Eleven

KAREN TOOK THE path winding down to the beach, the uneven surface jabbing through the soles of her sandals. She had come to say goodbye to a spot she had grown to love during the hectic days following Sinclair's confession.

Though now vindicated, she was still angry and hurt, seeking solace in the cave-pitted cliffs and miles of beach washed by an ever-changing sea. Let Mallory sort out his own problems.

A statement had been issued to the press: Lord Sinclair Burnet had perpetrated a hoax, not expecting it to be taken seriously. He expressed regret for any upset caused. Mallory dropped charges and made an official apology to the police, but only the timely intervention of an influential uncle at Scotland Yard had prevented Sinclair from landing in serious trouble. He had taken himself off to South America till the dust settled.

Tony was prepared to forgive and forget. Karen wasn't. That morning a hand-delivered letter had arrived at Laurel Cottage formally reinstating her.

Suppressing her first impulse to trash it, she had told the messenger to wait, sat down and dashed off her resignation.

There was one option open to her. Irwin wanted her as his secretary now Martha had elected to stay on at Blackwood Towers and organise the exhibition of Bedwell cartoons and the manor's emergence as a conference centre. Tony would still be head librarian, and it was obvious they were now an item.

Irwin had offered not only a job: he wanted her to become his mistress, possibly something more in the fullness of time. But he already paid alimony to five wives and supported numerous offspring. There must be a major flaw in his character with that amount of failed forays into matrimony. Karen had no ambition to find out.

It was a backward step, but there seemed to be no alternative to living with her parents while she looked for work. Her indignation blazed. She wanted to slap Mallory, scratch him, thump and kick him into admitting he had treated her unjustly. No chance of that. He was avoiding her as if she had the plague.

Her toes sank into dry sand as she reached the huge rocky amphitheatre. Noisy gulls wheeled overhead or picked over the dead fish, stranded crabs and other flotsam drifting in the shallows. A deep rock pool glinted at the base of a tumbled mound of boulders. Karen quickly untied her bikini bra, wriggled out of her shorts and removed the matching G-string. The tangy breeze played over her, stippling her nipples, her body losing tension under the sun's warm caress.

Her spirits rose as she waded in. It was icy; the

tide only just receding. Cool fingers crept up her thighs and dipped into the secret places concealed by her curling pubic hair. The water was transparent, light touching the molluscs clinging to the rocks. She ran a hand under the surface, seeing how the droplets sparkled on her tanned skin, her worries dissolving.

'I want to talk to you, Karen.' Mallory's sudden, unexpected voice sent fiery arrows darting through her.

'Leave me alone,' she stammered, crossing her arms over her breasts and thinking, *Christ! How clichéd! I'm behaving like a maiden in a melodrama. In a moment I'll be saying, Unhand me, villain!*

'No.' He loomed above her, barefoot, bare chested, legs astride in stonewashed jeans. Gone was the austere expression. His amber eyes were as mild as the ocean, deep pits of pain and rage. 'You can't resign. I won't let you.'

'Get real!' she stormed. He couldn't have chosen a worse tack if he'd tried. Hadn't he learnt anything? 'No one tells me what to do.'

His eyes snapped. 'You're the most bloody-minded female I've ever met!' he snarled. 'Get out of that damn pool. We've got to talk about this.'

She held out her hand. He clasped it and she deliberately pulled him off balance. He landed beside her, a tidal wave swamping them.

'Bitch! You did that on purpose!' he bellowed, drenched and furious.

'Now will you leave me alone?' She scrambled to her feet, and lust blossomed in her as his eyes fastened on the globes of her breasts.

Get out of this, my girl, she scolded herself, heading for the towel that lay on a rock with her clothes. *You don't want anything to do with him. You're your own woman again and it's great!*

Mallory leapt out. He reached the towel first, planted a sandy foot on it. The soaking denim emphasised his penis, so clearly that she could see the bump of his foreskin. That huge weapon menaced and frightened her, yet filled her with a scalding flood of desire.

'You're going to listen to me, Karen.' He seized her by the upper arms, shook her till her breasts bounced, then dragged her closer, his mouth on her throat, kissing, sucking, leaving the imprints of his teeth.

She groaned in unwilling response as his lips fastened on a naked nipple, dragging on it till she was nearly mindless with need. 'Don't, Mallory – please.' She barely knew what she was saying, her hard-won resolve disappearing.

Making one last desperate bid for freedom, she resorted to a karate chop and pelted towards the sea. He was after her, she knew, hearing his panting breath carried by the wind. Her mind was in turmoil – she abhorred the idea of surrender but felt she would die if she didn't.

The water was ice cold, clutching at her thighs, freezing her vitals to aching numbness. She waded further in till the sea was waist high, the swirling current threatening to sweep her feet from under her.

'Let go, Karen,' Mallory shouted above the noise of crashing waves. 'Don't fight it any more. You want me in the same way that I want you.'

'What are you saying? I don't understand,' she yelled back.

His hair was dripping, spume milling round his

crotch. He clutched at her, caught her, pulled her towards him, crying, 'I was afraid of how I felt about you. I tried to ignore you, but it was no use. Then, when I'd weakened, the drawings disappeared. I thought I'd been made a fool of again, and that you'd betrayed me – like Caroline.'

'Oh, no, it wasn't like that,' she gasped, shivering with cold and passion.

'I know that now.'

He kissed her, his lips tasting of brine, and she warmed in his arms, heated by his hard muscles and the stiff promise of his cock. She struggled with his buttons, released the mighty, uncoiling python, supporting it in her hands, while he opened her honeypot to the lecherous wave tongues lapping and licking at her.

Locked together, they stumbled to the shore, a tepid bath warmed by hot sand and sun. Tiny wavelets bubbled over their bodies as they lay there oblivious to everything. Karen lifted her breasts to his hands, the nipples steel-hard with cold and arousal. This was what she had dreamed of, yearned for, yet all the while a part of her – the reasoning, sensible part – told her it was only a dream.

His mouth was on her labia, sucking in seawater and her juices. Riven by exquisite pleasure, she felt his tongue probe and explore that most sensitive portion of her body. Her groping fingers fondled his wet black hair as she urged him to go on, the blood drumming in her ears, the incandescence growing, the sea rippling round her thighs and penetrating her vagina. The sky started to spin, forming a brilliant kaleidoscope, as she twisted her head from side to side in her extremity.

The most acute pleasure carried her to the peak, then tumbled her down to reality, and she felt him rise to his knees between her relaxed thighs and drive his penis into her. She thrust against it with every vestige of strength, her muscles expanding to take him – big, bigger, a final surge distending it even more as he surrendered to his own passion. She felt him convulse, heard him give a husky cry of satisfaction as he poured out his tribute.

She had him! He was hers. With her fingertips she explored his face, the soft, silky brows, the aquiline nose, the sensual lips. She could tell that he was smiling as she moulded her body round his lean hardness in the balmy wash of the sea.

Then, just as she was preparing to sink herself into him, to subjugate her will, her ambitions, her very soul, words spoken to her long ago by her wise mentor, Tony, drifted into her mind: 'Be very careful what you ask for – the gods might be listening and give it to you.'

Karen lay sunning herself on a lounger near the swimming pool. It was early September but still hot; her tan was deep and golden after the continual exposure of summer. Armina was with her, lithe, supple, nude – no longer the tenant of the Dower House, having banished herself to Raquel's mansion. She sometimes visited the girl who had succeeded her, but without the slightest trace of rancour. Sinclair, with an odd spark of chivalry, had not implicated Armina, but Mallory had guessed that she had been his partner and had told her she was no longer welcome.

'C'est la vie!' she remarked, rising up on one

elbow and reaching for a Martini in the shade of the umbrella. 'It was time to move on.'

'I don't imagine you mind fending for yourself.' Karen sat up and applied another layer of coconut oil to her body, adding to its bronze lustre.

'I'm hardly doing that, darling.' Armina gave her a shrewd stare through her dark shades as she sipped her drink. 'Money's never been a problem, and Raquel runs a funhouse. It'll amuse me for a while, and that, after all, is what life's about – being amused. You should try it sometime.'

Karen smiled across at her. 'I have. You've introduced me to a number of amusing things.'

Armina moved her lounger a little closer and pointed to the sun oil. 'Would you like me to do your back?' she offered, rising gracefully to her naked feet.

Karen rolled on her stomach and gave herself over to Armina's skilled ministrations, a sigh escaping her lips as she felt those soft hands working over her shoulder muscles, down her spine, around her buttocks, slipping between, delicate fingertips massaging the sweet-scented lotion into her cleft. Her thighs and calves received attention till she felt she was melting into the padded cushions beneath her, languorous, pleasure-loving, under the guidance of her hedonistic friend.

It was quiet, peaceful, idyllic. Sappho's island of Lesbos must have had the same atmosphere, she thought dreamily. Women sunning themselves, pleasuring one another – gentle, understanding beings whose sensuality was so much more advanced than men's.

'Does he satisfy you?' Armina murmured, and her hand returned to Karen's twin entrances. She opened her legs a little to make its passage easier.

'Mallory? Oh, yes. He's good, but you should know that, Armina.'

'He has a big cock, I'll grant you. A little too big, maybe. And he is terribly handsome. I hope you haven't fallen in love with him.'

Her finger had found Karen's love-bud and was massaging the oiled head softly, bringing her closer and closer to climax. The tiny nub of erectile tissue transmitted waves of sensation to every part of Karen's body, gathering, concentrating, pulling all her energies into itself.

'I think I may have loved him, or been on the verge of it,' she gasped, moving her hips in appreciation of the experienced finger. 'But I've never felt quite the same about him since he accused me—'

'Or since you actually had him? Sometimes the fantasy is better than the reality,' Armina murmured, pausing, fingertip hovering over Karen's throbbing clit, prolonging the build-up to orgasm. 'He seems smitten with you. You're the only mistress now – Celine's launched on her career, Jo's face is on the cover of every fashion magazine.'

'And Patty's fucking most of Devon's constabulary,' Karen added, wriggling to indicate her eagerness for Armina to continue masturbating her. 'Mallory wants me to marry him. He has sentimental ideas of having his son live with us.'

'So that you can play Mummy?' Armina crouched by the sunbed, knees apart, her bare, rosy pubis nicely aligned with Karen's eyes, the subtle perfume of her damp avenue blending with that of coconut oil.

'Exactly,' Karen was finding it hard to concentrate on anything except the waves of desire coursing through her groin.

'Have you said yes?' Faster, that finger now, working busily up and down on the swollen nub.

'Oh – oh! Ah – yes! Do it! Go on! Bring me off!' Karen cried piteously, suddenly swept to the top of a beautiful, exquisitely orchestrated climax. Limp and saturated with pleasure she collapsed, heated by passion, heated by the sun. What more could she ask?

She smiled into Armina's eyes and spread herself out on her back, her friend returning to her couch, smoothing her wet finger over her own moist clit. 'You haven't answered me,' she said. 'Are you going to marry him? I think the title of marchioness would suit you.'

'I haven't made up my mind.' Karen stretched her arms above her head, resting them on the plump pillow. 'And the more I prevaricate, the keener he gets.'

'Good,' Armina said, with a grin. 'Keep him insecure. I know him, and he'd soon lose interest if he was sure of you. Play him at his own game.'

The phone trilled and Karen reached for the handset, pulling a face at Armina as Mallory's voice caressed her ear.

'Hello, darling. Thought I'd give you a ring.'

'That's sweet of you. How's the London meeting going?'

'Fine, fine. We're off to have lunch at Irwin's hotel. The plans for Blackwood are in the bag.' He sounded jubilant.

'I'm pleased. So you'll be able to start alterations? Hold the first conference very soon?'

'So Irwin says. I'll be back tomorrow. What are you doing right now?'

Karen smiled and watched Armina playing with herself. Supposing she were to tell him the truth, say that orgasmic spasms were still rippling in her sex? She decided against it. 'Me? I've been working in the library. You still employ me, you know.'

'Don't do too much. There's no point in getting overtired. I want you fresh for my return.'

'Worry not, my love. I'm lazing in the sun.'

'And tonight?' He sounded vaguely uneasy and Karen liked that.

'Oh, don't really know. I've been invited to a gay party and may go along. They can be fun, as long as one isn't looking for a fuck.'

'What d'you mean? Are you looking for a fuck?'

'I didn't say that,' Karen answered sweetly and winked across at Armina who held up one hand, thumb and forefinger pressed together in a gesture of success. 'Anyway, I thought you weren't sexually jealous.'

'I'm not,' he replied, a shade too quickly.

'Then it's no problem. I may stay in, of course, or go for a drink with Tony.'

'And Martha, I hope. They're a couple, aren't they?'

'I believe so.'

'That's good. Darling, when can we plan our wedding?'

'I'm not sure. We'll be so busy for the next few months.'

'That shouldn't stop us.' He was getting

agitated, and London was a long way off. It wasn't her intention to discourage him too much.

She murmured sweet, soothing nothings in his ear and when he had hung up, turned to Armina, saying, 'He's promised to ring me again, and he will, maybe several times. I'll leave on the answerphone whether I'm in or not, just to keep him on tenterhooks.'

'That's my girl,' Armina said approvingly. 'It's the best way. And what exactly have you planned for tonight?'

Karen flopped back on the cushions, almost purring with contentment. Only that day a card had arrived from Jeremy bearing a Greek stamp and a 'wish you were here' message that sounded sincere, though she wouldn't hold her breath. Also a letter had come from Kan, reminding her to keep in training for the May event. Sinclair had rung her, suggesting she might like to visit Rio. Irwin had not given up, and then there was Mallory himself, her gorgeous, sexy, mean and moody aristocrat with the biggest cock she'd ever sucked.

'I thought we might spend it together,' she answered, reaching across the space between the loungers and linking her fingers with those of her female paramour.

'There's always Tayte, should we fancy playing with a dick,' Armina suggested.

Eyes closed, the two women lay on the terrace, the sun burning down on their naked bodies, lazy, dreaming, content. Then from the distance came a sound – the throbbing, blood-stirring, throaty roar of a powerful machine.

'It's the Harley,' Karen murmured sleepily. 'What say we invite Spike along, too?'

'That's a brilliant idea!' Armina agreed. 'Oh, and remind me to show you the secret passages sometime. They could prove useful, especially if you do become the lady of the manor and want to play away from home. A girl has to look after herself, you know.'

'And you'll be my ally?'

'Bet your sweet life I will. I helped Sinclair, didn't I?'

Karen listened and agreed, though knew she could never entirely trust Armina. But she'd look out for herself, all right, marry Mallory and work at the relationship one hundred per cent. But should it not prove to be an alliance made in heaven, then there were other roads open to her, and she wouldn't hesitate to take them.